A.I. APOCALYPSE

Dave Klapwyk

Klyk Publishing

ISBN 978-1-7390761-2-2

Cover design by: Covers by Christian

Dave Klapwyk wrote this book and not an Artificial Intelligence, although that is something that an AI might say.

DAVE KLAPWYK

CHAPTER 1

Adam Sinclair stared out the van window, watching the sandy, barren landscape roll by. The solemn melodies of Elgar's Cello Concerto in E minor flowed from his earbuds. The elegiac tones seemed to bypass his eardrums and inject themselves directly into his cerebral cortex. His hands instinctively shifted along an imaginary cello fingerboard as he weaved his head like a conductor's baton. He watched the desolate scenery of the Nevada desert, imagining Elgar composing the piece as a soundtrack to the open landscape. The sombre tones rose into a triumphant arc as the scrub grass and latte-coloured sand gave way to imposing granite and limestone bluffs.

"Hey!"

A tiny finger poked at his side.

"Adam...Adam...Adam..."

Pulling out an earbud, he turned to the interloper in the adjacent seat. "Stop bothering me, Lily."

"Do you want to play *I spy*?" his little sister asked.

"No. Leave me alone."

"That's a great..." his mother began from the front passenger seat of the van. She burst into a coughing fit that lasted almost half a minute before she could speak again. "That is a good idea. It will help pass the time."

"Then why don't *you* play with her?" Adam suggested.

"Hey!" yelled his father. He turned around and stared at Adam. "Don't talk to your mother like that!"

The van veered onto the shoulder and shuddered over the loose gravel. He spun the wheel back and steered the van back onto the pavement.

"Come on," begged Lily. "I spy, with my little eye, something that is brown."

Adam shook his head. "Everything is brown out here." He pushed the earbud back into his ear.

His father glared at him in the rear-view mirror. "Take those headphones out of your ears and play with your sister."

"They're earbuds, not headphones," Adam mumbled.

"Pardon me?" His father still glared at him in the mirror.

"I said, why do I have to play with her?"

"We are taking this trip for *you*," his father replied. "We are supporting *your* musical ambitions. This silly concert was *your* idea."

"It's not silly. It's an orchestral performance in a *real* concert hall. Also, it wasn't my idea for *you* guys to come."

"We are proud of you," inserted his mother.

"But we are not sending you to Las Vegas alone," added his father.

"I wouldn't be alone. Our group was taking a bus, remember?"

"That's safe." His father rolled his eyes. "A busload of teenage boys and girls driving to Sin City: a place of wickedness, immorality, and debauchery."

"What's debauchery?" asked Lily.

"You'll find out when you're older," said her mother.

"When I'm seven? Because I'll be seven in two months."

"Perhaps when you're twenty-one."

Lily crossed her arms and scrunched her eyebrows. "Hmph."

Her mother looked at the GPS screen on the dashboard. "We're almost there, kids."

Adam looked out the window at the barren landscape. "It doesn't look like it."

"That's because they built Las Vegas in the middle of the Nevada desert," said his mother in a raspy voice. "Did you know that there are over 300 weddings every day in Las Vegas and..."

She coughed and tried to clear her throat.

"You should save your voice," said Adam's father.

"Don't tell me when to speak."

"I'm just saying..."

Adam shoved his earbud back in. The cello's deep intonations drowned out his parent's bickering. He closed his eyes and floated into his music. A few minutes later, he fell asleep.

After a brief nap, Adam found himself magically transported to a bustling city. His father weaved the van through busy traffic on an eight-lane freeway. Beyond the concrete barriers of the highway lay the sprawling metropolis of Las Vegas.

"Whoa! How long was I asleep?"

"About twenty minutes, dear," replied his mother.

The sun sank below the horizon and, as the sky darkened, the city brightened. Street lights flickered on, thousands of LED screens lit up the streets, and the glow of a million casino lights twinkled to life. The spectacular sight almost made the five-hour drive from Pueblo, Colorado, with his annoying family worth it. *Almost.*

They took the exit ramp into the heart of the city.

"Do you know where you're going?" asked his mother.

"Yes, dear. Just let me drive."

A few minutes later, they rolled down the Las Vegas strip.

Massive hotels and casinos lined the street on both sides. Crowds gathered on the left to watch a waterfall show with lights and music, while hip hop street acts performed on the other.

"Look at that Ferris wheel!" shouted Lily.

A massive 500-foot wheel towered above a hotel, lit by thousands of lights.

Adam rolled down his window and stuck his head out.

"Get back in the car!" yelled his father.

He reluctantly pulled his head back in. Lily strained to see out her window. "Wow! Is that a pirate ship?"

A replica of a two-masted brigantine ship sat in front of a glistening hotel and casino.

Further down the strip, a bright banana-yellow Porsche stopped in front of them. Adam stared at the yellow convertible and wished he could view the Casino strip nightlife from the driver's seat of a Porsche. The man in the car talked with a stunningly beautiful woman in a revealing sequin dress and pink feather headdress.

Lily looked over his shoulder out his window. "Is she a princess?"

Adam smirked. "That's debauchery."

"I thought you said you knew where you were going," his mother exclaimed.

"I may have got temporarily turned around," he said. "You can't always trust these stupid GPSs."

He honked before swerving around the yellow Porsche.

Further down the strip, they slowed as they passed a spectacular hotel. Gondolas floated along mini canals in front and a series of cobblestone walkways and bridges led up to a grand entrance.

"Are we staying here?" Adam asked with excited anticipation.

"Yeah, right," said his father. "I'm a welder, not a pro football player. Only the wealthy can stay in a place like that."

"Look at that humungous ball!" yelled Lily as they drove by a massive glowing orb pulsing images of a country singer.

They left the lights and glamour of the strip behind and drove into a less glitzy part of Las Vegas. A homeless man in tattered clothes huddled outside a tourist shop. On the opposite side, a pink neon sign on a black brick building welcomed all *gentlemen*.

"What's that?" asked Lily.

"More debauchery," her brother answered.

A few minutes later, they pulled into the cracked pavement driveway of the Las Vegas Honeymoon Hotel.

A faded sign hanging from a rusted chain boasted about the colour TV, heart-shaped tubs and Wi-Fi.

Steel bars guarded the stained windows of the lobby. The single-story hotel stretched out in one direction from reception, with a few cars parked in front of some rooms.

"Wow! Colour television!" said Adam with mock

astonishment.

"Shut up and start unloading," said his father.

Adam stepped out of the car into the lingering heat. In Pueblo, Colorado, autumn nights were cool after sunset, whereas in Las Vegas, the heat remained stifling both day and night. He undid the straps on the top of the car and retrieved the big cello case. His mother opened the trunk and pulled out the luggage. As they emptied the car, Adam's father returned from reception.

"We've got the room at the end," he said, holding the key.

"Can we return the luggage to the car and drive it to our room?" asked Adam.

"Don't be such a wuss," said his father. "Be a man and carry your stuff."

"Wouldn't it be easier if we brought the car closer to—"

"Stop arguing and start moving!"

Adam rolled his eyes and lifted the cello. As he lumbered away, he overheard his father whispering to his mother.

"My credit card didn't work."

"What about your debit card?" his mother asked.

"That one didn't work either. Luckily, I had cash."

Adam didn't hear the rest of the conversation.

Eventually, they brought all their luggage to the room and got settled in. They ordered pizza and ate it while watching the colour television.

His parents shared the bed next to the bathroom, while Adam and Lily lay in the bed near the door.

Adam shoved his earbuds in and cranked the music. Beside him, Lily played a bubble-popping game on her tablet. Across the room, his father stared intently at the news on the television, while his mother coughed in the bathroom.

Just as the music pulled Adam into its vortex, his father yelled.

"Adam, you should watch this guy!"

He paused the music and pulled out his earbuds. "What?"

"Check this guy out." His father pointed at the man on the television. "Spiro could be the president someday."

An attractive young man with wild yet flamboyant hair smiled as he spoke into the camera.

"In my role as the newly elected speaker of the house, I want to assure you that I am committed to advocating for the rights and well-being of all Americans. It is my solemn pledge to fight for freedom and to vigorously defend the principles that our great nation was founded upon."

Adam slipped off the bed. "I'm going for a walk."

"No, you're not," his father replied. "You are not wandering around this evil, dangerous city in the middle of the night."

"Oh, please..." Adam rolled his eyes. "I'll stay in the hotel area."

"I don't care..."

"Let him go." His mother poked her head out of the washroom. She spoke in a guttural tone, barely holding back the phlegm at the back of her throat.

His father shook his head. "Don't go too far and be back before eleven."

Adam grabbed his phone and earbuds and slipped into his shoes before escaping the claustrophobic hotel room.

Outside, he wandered around the dark hotel grounds till he found an empty outdoor pool. Green stains lined the walls and a seagull skeleton sat amongst the dirt and garbage on the turquoise tiles at the bottom.

He sat on the edge with his feet hanging over and stuck in his earbuds.

As the haunting melodies of Bach's Cello Suite No. 1 began, someone behind him spoke. Adam turned to look.

The girl had short, black, wispy hair, a button nose and big, round, brown anime eyes. She wore no shoes.

Adam's teenage brain immediately overheated. He tapped his earbud to pause the music. "Umm...I'm just sitting here listening..."

She smiled at him. "Hi."

"Who's up for a swim?" yelled a boy behind her. He strutted toward the pool with two other teenagers following him like loyal puppies.

"What do we have here?" he asked, looking at Adam with a sneer.

"I was just listening to…" Adam began.

The boy ignored his response and pointed at the girl behind Adam. "Isn't it past your bedtime, Piper?"

"Isn't it past *yours*?" she spat back.

"When you're my age, maybe you can stay out past dark."

"You're only two years older than me," said Piper.

"I'm eighteen, so I'm technically an adult."

"Try acting like it."

Ronnie searched for a response but found nothing. Instead, his eyes locked onto Adam and he led his two buddies around the pool like a pack of hyenas gauging their prey.

"Who's this little dork?" he inquired as the trio closed in.

Adam's heart thumped in his chest, and he couldn't speak.

"Why are you talking to my sister?" Ronnie spat the words.

"I was just listening to…"

"Leave him alone," shouted Piper.

Ronnie's eyes lit up as if he had an epiphany. "I think he wants to go for a swim!"

Adam took a deep breath and stood up.

"Where do you think you're going?" asked Ronnie. "Do you really think I'm going to let you leave?"

With all the courage he could muster, Adam pushed his hand out and tried to shove Ronnie aside. Instead, his hand clumsily slid off the bully's shoulder and poked him in the eye.

"Ow!" Ronnie yelled with an exaggerated tone. He covered his eye as if it was about to fall out of the socket.

"Sorry, I was just trying to get by," said Adam as he hurried away.

"Don't let him leave!" Ronnie ordered.

His two friends ran after Adam and each grabbed an arm. He tried to squirm out of their grip as they hauled him back to their leader.

"Leave him alone," said Piper.

"Back off!" Ronnie yelled and pushed her away.

Adam held up his chin in a feeble attempt at defiance and bravery.

Ronnie plowed his fist into Adam's stomach. The wind immediately vacated his lungs, and he collapsed to the pool deck. An earbud dislodged and fell to the ground beside him.

Ronnie loomed over him. "Did you honestly believe you could hit my eye and escape without consequence?"

Adam gasped for air while trying to reach his earbud.

His attacker reached it first and held it in the air in front of his friends. "Now we can find out what dorks listen to!"

Piper smiled pitifully and stepped towards Adam, but her brother pushed her back while shoving the earbud into his ear. He tapped it and the music played in Adam's left ear and Ronnie's right.

"It's classical music!" Ronnie laughed. He passed the earbuds to his friends, who each took turns listening and laughing.

Adam finally stood up, pulled his phone out of his pocket and paused the music.

Through the trio of bullies, he watched Piper give him an apologetic shrug. He took a deep breath and clenched his fists, determined to regain his dignity.

Ronnie smiled at him. "Did we make the little dork angry?"

Adam reared back and punched as hard as he could. His fist flew towards Ronnie as he let out a manic shriek. Ronnie swayed back on his heels and the punch narrowly missed his nose. Adam lost his balance and fell forward. Before he could stand up, a foot pressed down on his back.

"Grab a leg, boys!" shouted Ronnie.

Adam looked towards Piper, who turned and disappeared into the darkness. His anger and determination evaporated, and shame and disappointment replaced them. They felt heavier than the heavy foot on his back.

Two firm hands grabbed his feet, and the world turned upside down. They hoisted him up and held him by his feet above the dingy, vacant pool. His phone slipped from his pocket and bounced onto the turquoise tiles below. Blood rushed to his head, and he closed his eyes. Tears flowed over his forehead and dripped into the pool.

"Hey, what's going on here?"

Adam recognized his father's voice and his shame reached a new depth.

The grip on his feet loosened, and he plummeted into the pool. Although all strength and willpower vacated his body, his head instinctively moved forward as he landed. The back of his skull hit the tile and his body somersaulted forward. He lay on his back at the bottom of the pool, staring up at the black sky. Tears still flowed, but found a fresh path along the side of his head onto the tiles. Seagull bones poked into his back.

His father's head appeared over the edge of the pool. He shook his head as he looked down at his prostrate son.

"Maybe if you stood up for yourself instead of being such a pansy, people wouldn't pick on you."

Adam wondered how long it would take for his tears to fill the pool.

CHAPTER 2

Dr. Faateer Fuwape pushed his glasses up the bridge of his nose and looked at the screen. He leaned forward as if he wasn't sure the words said what he thought they said.

His eyes remain fixated on the screen as he dialled Pritcher on his cell.

"I need to meet everyone in the boardroom - NOW!" the doctor yelled the last word.

Dr Fuwape was usually a soft-spoken man of few words who preferred to work with a fluorescence microscope than with people. However, his excitement was too great to be contained.

"It's not even eight in the morning," Pritcher responded. "Also, I'm your boss, so I'm supposed to tell *you* what to do."

"I've made a breakthrough – well, Likita has."

"Who is Likita? Is that the hot intern research assistant?"

"No, you idiot! Likita is the artificial intelligence that—it doesn't matter."

"Idiot?! I'm your boss, doctor. I demand respect from my subordinates. Just because the board thinks you're the best lung cancer researcher in the world, doesn't mean you're untouchable."

"This could quadruple the company's stock and make you and everyone else on the board extremely wealthy."

"What are you talking about?"

"Set up the meeting. I'll be in the Acropolis in thirty minutes."

He ended the call before Pritchard could respond.

The four words on the screen stared back at him, and he smiled. This was the most exciting day of his life. It was the culmination of 15 years of dedication and hard work.

He graduated high school at sixteen, was top of his class at Harvard medical school, and spent six years doing internships, research fellowships and two residencies before landing his research post at Novamed Pharmaceuticals. He barely remembered being a barefoot boy of six years walking through a poor village in Nigeria, dreaming of a better life.

Dr Fuwape wanted desperately to call Millie and tell her the great news. However, all those years of hard work and dedication were the reason she was living with her sister in Boston.

Perhaps she would be happy about his accomplishment and they could go out to a fancy restaurant to celebrate. Novomed would make billions and pay him millions. He would receive the Nobel prize and retire with his wife in Bali. However, the chance of her running back into his arms was less likely than a Nobel prize.

Dr. Fuwape closed his laptop and sighed. At least the board would be excited for him. He hung his lab coat on the brass hook, straightened his tie, and strutted out of the lab with his laptop under his arm.

He strode through the maze of Nuvomed hallways with his chin raised. This was the one time he wished he wore different shoes.

Most executives and office staff complied with the formal dress code. This usually included dress shoes or heels. The clacking of a solid Oxford heel on a glossy ceramic floor was the sound of authority and importance.

Like most researchers and lab assistants, Dr. Fuwape wore comfortable sneakers with arch supports and gel insoles.

However, as he strode through the wide hallways of Nuvomed, he wished he wore a solid heel of a brogue shoe. The echoing clap would announce the arrival of a prominent research scientist.

Instead, he walked soundlessly to the Acropolis boardroom in the executive wing of Nuvomed.

The pharmaceutical company had over a dozen conference

rooms in their sprawling facility in upstate New York. Most were standard boardrooms with oblong tables accommodating a dozen people. However, the Acropolis boardroom was different. Twenty-five padded chairs surrounded a glistening thirty-foot-long mahogany table. Two massive glittering chandeliers hung on glossy gold chains from twenty-foot-high vaulted ceilings. Plush purple silk and wool carpeting blanketed the floor and four golden sconces glowed from the walls. Only the most important meetings with the top executives of the company graced the Acropolis.

Mindie sat at the desk outside the tall oak doors. Seemingly, the executive assistant's only job was managing the meetings of the Acropolis.

She smiled as he approached. “Are you Dr. Fuwape?”

“Yes, I am.”

“Go on in,” said Mindie. “They are waiting for you.”

He almost dropped his laptop as he pulled open the heavy door.

Inside, four men and three women sat at the table talking in hushed tones.

Pritcher eyed him suspiciously, as if trying to decide if this was a mistake or something he could capitalize on. He motioned towards a chair.

“Have a seat, doctor. You can plug a dongle in here.”

He pressed a button on the wall, and a white screen hummed down from the ceiling.

Dr. Fuwape set his laptop on the mahogany table and plugged in the dongle. Light beamed from a hidden projector on the far wall, lighting up the screen with the image from his laptop.

The doctor looked around the room. “Where is everybody?”

Despite recognizing several executives in the room, Mr. Humstead was absent.

“Why don't you show us what you have and *we* will decide if we need to bring Mr. Humstead into the discussion? He is a *very* busy man.”

The doctor cleared his throat. Some attendees looked up, but others remained fixated on their phones.

"As you may know, I have been working with the artificial intelligence known as Likita. We have inputted all our research and gave her the ability to browse all the medical journals around the world. She was tasked with assembling data, performing virtual experiments and simulations and researching treatments for lung cancer."

"We know all this, doctor," said Pritchard with an audible eye roll. "Why are we here?"

Dr. Fuwape clicked his mouse, and a report appeared on the screen. He stood up with his arms crossed and smiled.

"She found one," he said with a smile.

"Found one what?"

He pointed at the report. "A cure for lung cancer."

"Pardon me?"

Dr Fuwape leaned across the boardroom table. "Likita discovered a cure for lung cancer."

Pritchard squinted his eyes. "How do you know it works? Have you even started animal trials?"

"Yes! We've also conducted human trials. The three-pill regimen is 90% successful in curing adenocarcinoma, squamous cell carcinoma and large cell carcinoma."

Pritchard shook his head. "Why haven't I heard about this? I don't remember any reports or applications to the FDA for clinical trials."

"We've been doing a multitude of experiments and trials on various forms of cancers based on instructions from Likita, but I didn't know she was this far along in the research."

"What do you mean *you didn't know*?"

"We have research staff at over 500 labs around the world. I can't keep track of all of them. Most take their instructions from Likita, who garnered approval for many of these trials on her own."

An executive in a tan blouse and tight ponytail looked up from her phone. "Are you saying that a computer applied for approvals from the FDA without your knowledge?"

"Our vast network of labs and researchers is the reason we have Likita. Her ability to amass copious amounts of data, organize research and perform administrative tasks is why we acquired her." He stood up. "You're missing the point. Likita has found a safe and effective treatment for lung cancer."

His last sentence finally resonated with the cynical group.

They muttered amongst themselves for almost a full minute before Pritchard texted into his phone.

"Mr. Humstead is on his way."

Harvey Humstead was the seventy-five-year-old founder and CEO of Nuvomed Pharmaceuticals. He was a doctor and research scientist for thirty years before working for a large pharmaceutical company. He branched off on his own and created, marketed and sold a successful version of pain-suppressing opioids. Two years later, the company went public; he became a billionaire and bought out his old employer. At over six feet and 250 lbs, his stature was as imposing as his personality.

Dr. Fuwape spoke to Mr. Humstead only once during a Christmas gala. He was impressed by the man's charisma and intellect, but intimidated by his over-the-top personality. It seemed like his boss's default tone was yelling.

An entourage of three men and two women accompanied Harvey Humstead into the Acropolis fifteen minutes later. The big man charged into the room like an angry bull.

"What's going on? Why are you having a meeting without me?" he yelled.

Pritchard jumped to his feet. "I wanted to be sure we weren't wasting your time, sir. Doctor Fuwape insisted that—"

"Right! Let's get on with it. Everybody sit down!"

His entourage scrambled to find a seat, but Dr. Fuwape remained standing. "Can I stay standing or..." he asked in an uneasy tone.

Mr. Humstead plopped into his chair and leaned back. "You can do whatever you want. You're leading this meeting, Mr Fruwabee."

"It's Doctor Fuwape."

"That's what I meant."

The doctor tried not to let his boss's ignorance ruin his shining moment as he described his discovery.

Mr. Humstead listened intently without interrupting.

"Why haven't I heard about this?" he asked once Dr. Fuwape finished.

"That's what I said!" Pritchard chimed in.

Humstead pointed at Pritchard. "It's *your* job to keep tabs on research."

"I try, but it's hard when the lead researcher keeps secrets from me," Pritchard replied.

"I only found out about this recently," said Dr Fuwape.

"Are you telling me that this Likita has been doing this behind our back?"

"The laborious administration and bureaucracy of running a large organization is why we have Likita," said Dr Fuwape. "We requested a cure, and she delivered."

Humstead nodded. Slowly at first, then more vigorously, as if he was convincing himself this was a good thing. "Having a cure is the important thing."

He pointed at a balding man in a tweed suit. "How soon can we expect FDA approvals?"

Dr Fuwape typed the question and received an immediate response from Likita. He looked up from his screen. "We already have the approvals to go to market."

"What?" exclaimed Humphries, Pritchard, and a few others simultaneously.

"Likita has already received approvals for the treatment from the FDA."

Humphries leaned forward and stared at Dr Fuwape. "Did you discover that by typing on your computer?"

The doctor gave an anxious nod.

His boss remained leaning forward. "Dare I ask if production has started yet?"

After asking Likita, Dr Fuwape sighed with relief. "Not yet, although she has a plan for marketing, production and distribution."

Humstead returned to a normal sitting position. "Can you please ask Likita not to proceed with any further plans until she gets approval from me?"

"Um...sir?" asked River Magnolia.

The marketing communication specialist and a member of Humstead's entourage ran a hand through his receding grey hair. The tiny ponytail poking out the back of his head gave homage to his 70s hippie days.

River stared at his phone as he talked. "We're not the only ones."

"What do you mean?" yelled Humstead.

"Synthura Pharmaceuticals, GlobalMedica and NexusPharm have all released statements regarding a cure for most types of lung cancer."

Humstead stood up and knocked his chair over. It landed quietly on the plush carpet behind him. "How is this possible?" He pointed at Dr Fuwape. "You said Likita found the cure. Did she steal it from another company?"

The doctor typed the question into his computer. "No, sir. She didn't steal it."

"Then how is it that at least three other competitors have the same cure?" His face simmered with red rage.

"She didn't steal it," Dr Fuwape softly replied. "She gave it away."

Humstead's simmering rage exploded. He screamed obscenities, rattling the crystal chandeliers and spewing spittle across the glossy table. "Shut it down! Shut down Likita, NOW!"

"What does that mean?" asked Dr Fuwape, staring at the screen.

Humstead stopped ranting and read the screen on the wall projecting Dr Fuwape's laptop display. The stark words glowed in the centre of the screen in a simple Times Roman font.

<You're done, Harvey Humstead. It's time for you to go home.>

"Is that Likita? Can she hear us?"

"I...um...it appears so..." Dr Fuwape stammered.

"Unplug it!"

Humstead went to grab the laptop to either turn it off or, more likely, throw it at the wall. Before he reached it, however, the screen went dark.

"Thank you!" said Humstead. "Was that so hard?"

"That wasn't me—"

"Sir, we have another situation." River stared wide-eyed at his phone. "Our stock is plummeting."

Humstead loosened his tie as sweat droplets formed on his forehead. "What?"

River read more from his phone. "There are rumours of company executive improprieties."

"By whom?"

"By you, sir. The district attorney issued a statement that you are being investigated for tax fraud and embezzlement."

"Okay, we need to stop this insanity right now!" Humstead barked orders like a drill sergeant. "River! Hold a press briefing about our lung cancer cure. Tell them we suspect our competitors have engaged in corporate espionage to steal our company's discovery. Pritchard! Find the FDA approvals, research, and reports from all departments that dealt with this cure. Fuwape! Shut Likita down. No one is to interact with the AI until further notice. You! Find me a glass and a bottle of Jack Daniels."

The tall oak doors opened, and Mindie poked her head inside the room.

"Sir? The police are here."

CHAPTER 3

The 350hp engine growled when Prospero pressed his foot against the pedal. It was just after sunset when the banana-yellow Porche 718 Boxter S flew down the Las Vegas strip. The glass pyramid on the left went by in a blur, but when he reached the lighted water show, he let off the gas. His long black hair whipped against his boyish face as he stopped at the red light. The strip was alive with an array of nightlife. Enormous LED screens showcased amazing shows of resident musicians and magicians. A small crowd gathered to watch a hip hop duo perform dance stunts on the sidewalk beside him. Elegantly dressed women streamed out of a casino with a male dance show, still giddy with excitement. The car surged ahead again with a bassy growl when the light turned green and whipped by a hotel with a pirate ship in front.

Further down the strip, he slowed as he approached a replica of an ancient Roman rotunda. The angry driver behind him swerved around his car with a frustrated honk. A topless male with an oiled six-pack and a cowboy hat turned to look at his car. But Prospero was not looking for a muscular gigolo.

Two women in elaborate showgirl outfits posed with a terrified teenage boy while his father took pictures and cheered him on. He paid them and left with his son.

Prospero called out, “Hey, you want to dance?”

The taller woman with long, blond hair turned and smiled. “Sure. Park your car and we can dance.”

“Get in the car, and I’ll take you to a club.”

“Sorry, pal. We’re busy.” She turned around and waved to a group of German tourists.

“I’ll make it worth your while.”

A blue minivan honked before driving around the Porsche. A teenage boy in the back stared at either him, the girl or the car. Or maybe all three.

"I'm not that kind of girl," she replied. "You'd better get your fancy car back on the road before someone hits you."

"Two thousand dollars!" he yelled.

She whispered something to her friend and pranced across the sidewalk to his car. The tall pink feathers bounced on her head as she walked.

Puffing her chest out, she smiled down at him. "I told you, I'm not that kind of girl. We can pose with you for a generous tip, but we are not going anywhere with you."

The gems on her outfit sparkled in the glow of the streetlights.

"Five thousand, and I'm not looking for *that* kind of girl. All I want is to go dancing."

He pointed behind him. "Have you ever been to Platinum Groove?"

She shrugged "Sure."

"What's your name?"

"Look honey, you've got a nice car, you're good-looking and you seem nice but this is *not* how to pick up a girl."

Prospero reached into his pocket and pulled out a money clip. "I can pay you for your time."

"I make two thousand a day posing with tourists," she said, "and that includes the costume rental."

He held out a wad of bills. "I'll give you five thousand."

She tilted her head and stared at him for a moment before grabbing the money and walking away. Prospero almost yelled after her, but changed his mind. She pranced back to her friend and whispered in her ear before returning to the Porsche. She pulled out her phone, took his picture, took a picture of the car and then the license plate.

"What are you doing?" he asked.

She stood outside the open car door. "I'm texting Sandy these photos in case you're some creep trying to kidnap me and keep me in your basement."

"What's your name?" he asked as she finally stepped into the car.

"Indie."

"Nice to meet you, Indie. Lose the hat."

"It's a feather headdress, and it's a rental."

"I'll buy you a new one," he said.

A police car with flashing lights stopped behind them.

"Sandy!" Indie yelled. "Take my headdress."

Her friend ran to the car. "I can't believe you're abandoning me."

Indie handed her the pink feathered headpiece. "I'll call you later – if I don't, call the cops."

As she turned to leave, Indie yelled, "Sandy, wait!"

When Sandy turned back, Indie handed her half the money. "Take the day off. Go be with your boy."

Sandy stared wide-eyed at the wad of bills. "Thanks!"

"What's happening here?" questioned the officer by the driver's door. "You're blocking traffic."

"Sorry, sir. We're leaving."

Prospero smiled and drove away with Indie sitting in the passenger seat.

"Are you ready to have some fun, Indie?"

She eyed him suspiciously. "Are you some wannabe Edward Lewis?"

"Who's that?"

Her long blond hair waved in the wind.

"The rich guy in Pretty Woman."

"What's that?"

"You know - the movie - Pretty Woman with Richard Gere and Julia Roberts?"

"I've never seen it."

"You don't get out much, do you?"

He veered onto a side road.

"I'm a busy guy and have no time for movies."

"But you have time for dancing with a stranger?"

"I do now."

He drove under the circular overhang of the Royale Hotel and stopped near the front entrance. Gold inlays covered the ceiling, reflecting hundreds of dangling lights.

"Today, I am celebrating."

He stepped out of the car and handed his keys and a twenty-dollar bill to the valet.

"What's the occasion?" she asked.

"I discovered the secret to endless, free money."

They walked through the gold and glass front doors of the hotel. Cold air hit them like an icy blanket as they entered. Rows of endless slot machines filled the room. Pop music piped through invisible speakers mingling with the excited chatter of excited gamblers.

Despite Indie's extravagant outfit, only one white-haired man sitting in front of an Egyptian-themed slot machine turned to look.

Prospero pointed to the left. "This way."

"You're either delusional or a pathological liar."

"Look around you," he said. "Millions of dollars are exchanged here. Who, in your view, earns the most money?"

"The casino owners," she replied.

He raised his eyebrows. "Very good. And how do they make their money?"

"They stack the odds in their favour. If people play long enough, they will always lose."

"You're pretty smart for a street performer."

"I'm saving up for business school."

They walked by a small gathering of animated women cheering on their friend at a craps table.

"What do you know about the stock market?" he asked.

"Companies issue stock, which is then bought and sold on the open market."

"That's right. The odds of making money in the stock market are significantly better than a slot machine or blackjack. They get even better when you use fundamental analysis and arguably technical analysis to pick stocks. How long will you be in school?"

"Probably six years," she replied.

"What if you could use a computer to compress six years of study, add fifty years' experience and simulate millions of stock trading scenarios?"

"Are you talking about high-frequency trading bots?"

"This is a level far above automated algorithm trading. My program can predict stock price changes with a consistent accuracy level of over sixty percent."

"Only sixty percent?"

"A *consistent* sixty percent. With constant reinvestment, the profits are exponential and infinite."

"Nothing is infinite."

"We'll see."

She followed him through the maze of slot machines, poker tables, restaurants, and bars to another set of glass doors leading outside. A wall of hot wind met them as they exited. However, they soon escaped the blistering Nevada heat when they entered the next air-conditioned hotel.

After navigating a shorter maze of slot machines, Prospero led them to a darkened corner of the hotel. A giant of a man in a black suit stood in front of a pair of balusters with a black velvet rope drooping between them. Two spotlights lit the stylized *Platinum Groove* letters on the wall.

"Sorry, private party," said the man in the suit.

Prospero handed him a hundred-dollar bill.

The man held up his hands. "I can't let you in."

"Call your boss and tell him Prospero is here," he said, still holding out the money. "If he says we can't come in, we'll leave. Either way, you keep the tip."

He squinted at Prospero for a moment before taking the money and pulling out his cell phone.

"Sir, I have a Mr. Prospero here. He says…right…I understand… Very good, sir."

After ending the call and slipping his phone into his pocket, he unclipped the velvet rope. "I'm sorry for the inconvenience, sir.

Take the elevator to the top floor. Have a good time."

They stepped inside the elevator. A man in a suit with a Royale Hotel Insignia on his chest nodded. He swiped his key card and pushed the button for the 11th storey.

"Do you own this place?" Indie asked.

"Not yet," Prospero replied with a smile.

The door opened on the 11th floor and a thumping bass and muted, high-pitched electronica music assaulted their eardrums. They walked down a dimly lit corridor towards the music.

"How rich are you?" she asked.

As they got closer to the club, the music got louder.

"Not rich enough," he yelled in her ear.

The walkway led to leather sofas and side tables overlooking the dance floor, one level below.

Hundreds of dancers bounced and gyrated to the deafening cacophony of music. Brightly coloured lights spun and flashed, mirror balls sparkled, and lasers slashed through puffs of fog machine clouds. A spastic DJ danced and yelled in his booth on a stage above the dancers. Beyond the dancefloor, a multi-levelled outdoor area held hundreds more partiers. Palm trees, fat speakers and padded benches surrounded two curvy rooftop pools under the dark Nevada sky.

"Let's dance!" he yelled.

The music was too loud to hear him, but Indie could read his lips. She still didn't trust him, but she loved to dance and she needed the money.

Three minutes later, she bounced and swayed beside him on the dance floor. The pulsing beat rattled her rib cage as she let her body flow with the music. Prospero stuck close to her as they danced, but didn't try to grope or kiss her. They stopped to have a few drinks but danced for almost two hours straight.

Indie's ankles were aching when Prospero suggested they take a break. He led them outside, past the pools and up to a level overlooking the nightlife of the Las Vegas strip below.

Prospero left and returned with two drinks. The music was

still loud, but they could hear each other speak.

"You should take your heels off," he suggested.

She looked around. "I don't think they'll allow—"

"I'm going to own this place, remember? Your feet must be killing you."

After removing her shoes, she stretched her numbed toes. "That's better."

He pointed to the pool. "Let's take a swim."

People drank and talked poolside and a few dipped their toes into the blue water. However, nobody swam.

"We can't swim in there," she protested.

"Why not? Isn't that what pools are for?"

"I think they're more for looks and I didn't bring my suit."

"Come on." He grabbed her hand. "Swim with me."

They weaved through the crowd down to the edge of the glistening blue pool and set their phones and wallets on a bench.

Others nearby watched as she stood next to the still water and curled her toes over the edge.

With a wide grin, he asked, "On three?"

"Why wait?" Indie cannon-balled into the pool.

He joined her a second later with a bigger splash. Some onlookers shouted their disapproval at getting wet, but others soon joined them.

After cooling off, they returned to dancing until they were dry and warm again.

They laughed, danced, splashed and drank, till the early hours of the morning.

During the last call, as most patrons had either left or were leaving, Prospero's phone lit up. Exiting the pool, he shook his hands, picked up the phone, and read the screen. His face dropped, and he looked up into the dark sky above the city.

"Is everything okay?" Indie shouted from the pool.

"I have to go," he said.

She exited the pool as he walked away. "Wait!"

"Thank you for an incredible night," he said with a faraway

look.

"What happened?" she asked, searching hopelessly for a towel.

"I think he went too far." Prospero typed frantically into his phone. "And I can't stop him."

"Who went too far?"

"Prospero Junior ventured outside his parameters."

"You have a son?"

"Sorry, I have to go and figure things out," he said, then walked away.

"Wait for me." She grabbed her heels and ran after him.

The music stopped and bright lights lit up the emptying club as staff and bouncers ushered everyone to the exits.

"Where are you going?"

"Back to my room."

She looked at his terror-stricken face. "You look like you just found out someone died. Wait - did someone die?"

"This is worse. You should go home."

With a group of drunken partiers, they descended to the first floor in the elevator. She followed him through the hotel until they reached the cobblestone walkway between the two hotels.

He turned to her and gave her a pained smile. "Thank you again for an amazing night. It was good while it lasted. Don't put the money I gave you in the bank. Get some food or gold or something, because the good times are gone."

"That sounds ominous."

"It is."

Indie watched him leave, struggling with indecision. Unlike many of the groping fools she posed with on the street, Prospero seemed like a decent guy. Sandy would advise her to take the money and go home after a successful night. However, part of her was curious about his disturbing warnings. Observing his distress, she longed to embrace him warmly and reassure him that everything would be fine. However, she didn't know if that was true. She didn't know him at all. They had only met a few hours ago when he stopped his ostentatious car and begged her to be his Vivian Ward.

He was probably a lonely rich guy who found out his stock tanked. Like in gambling, she should quit now while she was still ahead. She should let him deal with his own problems. She stood on the cobblestone, watching him leave. Just before he disappeared into the hotel, Indie ran to catch up with him.

CHAPTER 4

Adam stared out the window of the family minivan as his father pushed through the bustling morning traffic on their way to the Koban Conference Centre. He tapped the bulbous cello case between him and his sister. It felt good to have it next to him in the van.

When he checked the instrument, before they left the hotel, Adam found it out of tune. The Nevada heat warped the spruce soundboard while sitting on top of the van during their trip from Colorado.

Before leaving the hotel in the morning, Adam insisted they keep the cello inside the air-conditioned van. His father refused until his mother convinced him otherwise.

His mother stared at a Las Vegas Tourist map. "How about checking out some city attractions?"

"I'm not sure we'll have time for that," his father responded.

Adam pulled his phone from his pocket and turned it on. The home screen flickered through a spiderweb of cracks. It narrowly escaped total destruction after the fall onto the pool tiles. He turned it off, hoping it might work later.

"That's weird," said Lily. "My weather app isn't working."

"The weather in Las Vegas is always the same, anyway," said her father.

Adam's mother attempted to clear her throat, but her words came out gravelly. "Your father said you fell into the pool and bumped your head last night. Does it still hurt?"

"It's fine, mom."

Her phone chirped, and she folded up her city tourist map and retrieved the phone from her pocket.

"Who is it?" asked Adam's father.

She looked at her phone, then back at her husband with a confused look. “It’s Doctor Waters.”

The phone kept chirping.

“Are you going to answer it?” he asked.

She swiped the answer icon and talked into the phone.

Adam and his father listened to one side of the conversation while Lily played on her tablet.

“Hello?...Yes, it is, but this really isn’t a good time to talk...What are you talking about?...How?...I see...That’s unbelievable...Can I get it?...I understand...Well call me when you know more...Thank you so much...Okay, bye.”

“What was that all about?” asked Adam’s father.

“They discovered a cure for lung cancer!”

“What?” asked his father. “Who did?”

“I don’t know, some pharmaceutical companies.”

“More than one? I didn’t think they usually worked together.”

“I don’t know, but he said they already did trials, and the FDA has approved the treatment!” She laughed and coughed as she talked.

Adam leaned forward. “I thought your cancer was in remission.”

Five years ago, the doctors at Mendota General Hospital diagnosed her with stage 3 lung adenocarcinoma. Over the next four years, she endured surgery, radiation therapy and chemotherapy. The treatments seemed effective, and they told her the cancer was in remission. At least that is what Adam’s parents told him.

“It was,” said his mother.

“When?” he asked.

“When what?”

“When did the cancer return? And how long did they give you?”

“It doesn’t matter.” She paused to cough and catch her breath. “Dr. Waters says there’s a cure and wants me to visit him when we return.”

“You lied to me.”

"Lying is bad." Lily looked up from her tablet. "Are you sick again, Mommy?"

"No, Mommy is fine," she answered. "I'm going to see a doctor when we go home, and he's going to make me all better."

"Why wouldn't you tell me?" Adam asked.

"We'll talk about this later," his father said firmly.

Adam stared out the window. He wished his phone worked so he could listen to music.

Out the window, he noticed a group of people waiting at a bus stop. A block later, another dozen people crowded in, and around another bus shelter.

"Looks like the buses are running late today," said his father.

After parking at the back of a massive parking lot, they exited the van and walked to the Koban Conference Centre. Adam lugged his heavy cello on his back as they trudged across the hot blacktop towards the entrance.

"You couldn't have parked closer?" he complained.

"You'll be happy when we leave and aren't waiting behind a lineup of cars to get out."

They paused a few times for Adam's mother to cough and catch her breath.

"I should have dropped you off by the door," his father admitted.

She held up her hand. "I'm fine. Just give me a minute."

By the time they made it to the Koban Conference Centre doors, Adam was sweating profusely and panting.

"Maybe if you joined the football team, you'd be in better shape," suggested his father.

They stepped into the cool air of a massive corridor. It spanned the length of a football field in both directions, was as wide as a tennis court and was over thirty feet high. Doors on one side led to conference rooms and auditoriums of varying sizes and washrooms, offices, boardrooms lined the other.

Adam's mother leaned against the wall while his father stood with arms crossed, pretending not to be tired. Lily ran to a water fountain and Adam pulled out his shirt to fan the sweat off his chest, wishing he had brought a stick of deodorant.

"I need to find a bathroom," said his mother.

"I'll help you find one." His father looked at Adam. "Watch your sister. We'll be right back."

"I need to find my bandmates to start practicing," Adam protested.

"Find them, but take your sister."

His father turned left with his mother before Adam could protest further.

When Lily came back, he led her down the wide conference centre corridors in search of Room 111.

"Is Mommy sick again?" Lily asked as they walked into the room.

Lily's intelligence, despite being only seven, impressed Adam, who didn't want to lie to her like his parents had lied to him.

"Yes, but there is a new treatment that might make her better."

"Will she lose her hair again?"

"I don't know Lily. Don't worry about that right now," he said, as they walked into the auditorium.

Workers pushed carts with stacks of chairs around the room while others unloaded and placed them in rows.

Several classmates sat near the front of the mostly empty room, inspecting their instruments and talking amongst themselves.

"Where is everybody?" she asked, looking around.

"They're coming. We're just a little early. Why don't you sit somewhere and play on your tablet?"

She ran to the front row and sat down while Adam brought his big cello case to the front. He recognized some of his bandmates, but none of them were his friends. He didn't have many friends. His best friend, Jeff moved to another state the previous year and Adam was still *adjusting.*

He opened his case and unloaded the cello. After checking the tuning, he played the opening stanza of the upcoming performance. The room had incredible acoustics.

He looked around the room. Lily, along with three people

arranging chairs and five bandmates, remained the sole occupants of the room.

Adam closed his eyes and played a piece he had been working on for the past year. It started with the musical theme from the Jaws movie but moved into a triumphant overture, then a melancholy tone before reverting to the Jaws theme. He smiled as he pictured hundreds of delighted fans listening with rapt attention to his masterpiece.

As he moved the bow across the string with creative fervour, he opened his eyes and saw a girl walking towards him. The bow skipped across the strings and fell to the floor.

He recognized the pretty girl with shiny black hair and enormous eyes from the pool. Adam's face went a dark shade of crimson. He was ashamed that she watched him get bullied last night. Ashamed that she caught him pretending to be a great cello player. Ashamed that he dropped his bow. Ashamed that his face probably looked like it was going to explode.

"Was that the theme from Jaws?" she asked.

He picked up his bow.

"It was my rendition of it...I mean I wrote it...I didn't write the theme for Jaws, obviously... that was John Williams, but I made it better...I'm not better than John Williams... but I made my own..."

"Piper, let's go. We're not playing until tomorrow," Ronnie yelled from the doorway.

"You're playing too?" Adam asked. "What instrument?"

She shrugged. "I don't play anything."

Ronnie peeked around his sister and spotted Adam. "Hey, it's you again. You play the giant guitar? I knew you were a dweeb, but I didn't know you were a massive dork!"

"I'm not a dork."

"Let me see this thing," yelled Ronnie and grabbed the cello.

Adam tried to hold on, but Ronnie yanked hard, forcing him to either let go or watch the cello neck snap. He released the cello and Ronnie held the instrument like a giant guitar, strumming hard on the strings.

"Hey, what's going on here?" said Mr. Rudolph.

A small group including his music teacher, Mr. Rudolph a few students and Adam's parents, entered the room.

"I'm joining the band!" yelled Ronnie.

"I don't recognize you," said Mr. Rudolph. "Are you supposed to be here?"

Ronnie smiled and handed Adam back his cello. "We were just leaving."

He grabbed Piper's arms and pulled her towards the door. She glanced back at him, her expression seemingly a mix of pity and disgust.

Adam's father walked towards him, shaking his head. "What did I tell you about being a pansy?" he whispered. "You need to stand up for yourself."

Adam put the cello back in its case and closed the lid. "I have to go to the washroom," he said briskly exiting the auditorium. Behind him, his mother called after him, but Adam ignored her and kept walking.

He peeked into the corridor, checking for bullies and pretty girls. Two stern men accompanied a middle-aged man with grey hair and a limp out of a conference room.

After they passed, he ventured out. It didn't take long to find the largest washroom he had ever seen. It contained a lineup of twenty urinals and almost as many stalls. Not the hideout he hoped for, but fortunately it appeared he had the oversized restroom to himself. He waved a hand under the tap sensor and splashed cold water on his face. In the mirror, his dorky face looked back at him. His father and Ronnie were accurate in their assessment of him as a pansy and a dork. He had no friends, his mother was probably dying, and the only pretty girl who didn't totally ignore him, looked at him with pity.

Adam wanted to cry, but that would prove both of them right. He wanted to punch the mirror, bloodying his knuckles and sending shards of glass tinkling to the floor. That would either prove he was a real manly man or an idiot. His ruined knuckles would make it difficult to play the cello in his upcoming performance. He was pretty sure he was a dork.

As he splashed more cold water on his face, someone mumbled in a stall behind him. The man talked angrily at first, then yelled. He screamed and cursed so loud Adam thought the mirrors might crack. Adam looked at his reflection again. His minor flare-up, where he almost broke a mirror in his imagination, was nothing compared to this guy's frenzied tirade.

The stall door flew open and a man in a rumpled suit and loosened tie exploded out, holding a grey laptop over his head. He threw the laptop at the sink. It bounced off the sink and landed on the floor, still intact. The unscathed laptop seemed to turn the dial up five notches on the man's rage gauge. He grabbed the computer and whipped it frisbee style across the washroom.

Adam instinctively ducked, and the laptop whizzed by the last stall and hit a urinal. It shattered this time, sending plastic shards across the floor and into the urinals.

The man looked up, suddenly realizing he wasn't alone. He stared at Adam with wild eyes. Adam stared back, frozen in fear. Neither the fight nor flight instincts kicked in. Instead, he stood frozen in fear and fascination. The man lumbered up to Adam, putting his angry face within inches of Adam's.

"It's all over."

It surprised Adam that the man's warm breath smelled of mint. He wasn't sure if he should push the man back, joke about his breath, or ask him if he needed help.

The angry man stepped back, leaning against the wall, his gaze fixed on the ceiling.

Adam wondered if he was having a drug-induced episode.

"My whole life," the man bellowed. "I worked hard my whole life. I made millions and now it's all gone."

He slumped to the floor; his legs splayed out in front of him.

Adam walked slowly around him to the door. Outside the washroom, a security guard ran towards him.

"What's going on?" the guard asked. "There's been reports of a disturbance."

"Some guy in there is flipping out." He pointed behind him. "I think he lost his money or something."

The guard shook his head. "He's not the only one," he muttered as he entered the washroom.

Adam wanted to ask him what he meant, but his mind suddenly switched gears when he saw the pretty girl with enormous eyes and dark, wispy hair.

Across the corridor, lying on a cushioned bench by the window, Piper fiddled with her phone. Her shoes sat on the floor beside the bench and she lay on her back on the bench with her bare feet dangling over the edge.

Her brother Ronnie and his merry band of bullies were nowhere to be seen.

He gathered all the courage he could muster and walked to her. On the way, he flipped through various opening lines.

Hey there, was too simple. *Hey baby,* sounded too cheesy. *How do you like Las Vegas*, sounded too casual? *I like your hair* was too forward.

When he finally got to her, all he could say was "Hi!"

She looked up at him and smiled. "We meet again."

That's a good line, he thought.

"Sorry about my brother," she said, sitting up. "He can be such an idiot."

A wave of embarrassment hit Adam as he remembered being hung down over the empty pool.

He attempted to defend himself. "There were three of them."

"Next time, you should hit him with your cello."

"Yeah," was the only response he could muster.

"You sounded pretty good in there," she said with a smile. "Were you really playing the theme from Jaws?"

He shrugged coyly. "I used the theme as a starting point, but then wrote my own piece."

"Wow, you write your own music?"

"Sometimes."

"Are you performing here or something?"

"I'm performing with my school orchestra."

After a brief silence, she spoke again. "My name is Piper."

"I know," he replied. "I heard your brother call you that."

She raised her eyebrows. "This is where you say your name."

"Oh...right, sorry. I'm Adam. Are you here for a school trip too?"

"No, I'm on vacation, sort of. My dad wanted to hear some Artificial Intelligence guru speak."

Someone behind him yelled, and he turned to look. Two guards pulled the laptop-breaking man from the washroom towards the exit.

"He sounds angry," said Piper.

"That guy threw a laptop at me. I think he lost all his money or something."

Piper pointed at her phone. "Social media is blowing up over cyberattacks and stuff."

"Really? What's going on?"

"Haven't you heard?"

"My phone is kind of broken since..." He didn't want to finish the sentence.

"I don't grasp everything, but something is happening with the banks. Some people are calling it hyperinflation, others say it's a run on the bank. I think the stock market is crashing."

"Whoa! That sounds bad."

"Also, a bunch of companies were cyber-attacked. They even hit the bus system company here in Las Vegas."

"That's insane."

"I know, right?"

This was the most he had conversed with a girl in a while. She talked to him like he was a normal person. Also, he didn't act like a dork or a wimp and he talked like a normal person.

She looked up at him with her big doe eyes as she hugged her knees and slowly wiggled her toes. They were the cutest toes he'd ever seen.

He pointed to her bare feet. "Do you not believe in shoes?"

She shrugged. "I think they're overrated. I like to feel the world beneath my feet."

Behind him, someone shouted, "Adam, are you coming?"

He recognized Mr. Rudolph's voice.

"Who's that?" Piper asked.

"He's my music teacher. I should get going. Our performance is starting soon."

He smiled and stepped back, not wanting to leave. "You can come watch…if you want."

"I might do that," she said, smirking. "It has to be more interesting than some dweeb talking about computers."

CHAPTER 5

Sixty-five-year-old Jerry Dillwash adjusted his tie and limped through the wide corridors of the Koban Conference Centre. His knee was still healing from his recent replacement surgery, but at least he could walk. As he shuffled past a conference room door, he heard the recognizable tones of the Jaws theme. He glanced inside and saw a teenage boy playing a cello. Jerry continued to room 112.

The woman at the entrance pointed at the pass hanging around his neck. He held the pass out, and she scanned it with a small black reader. She looked down at the reader and exclaimed, "Mr. Dillwash! It's you! You'd better hurry. They're waiting for you."

She opened the door and let him inside. It took a moment for Jerry's eyes to adjust to the dark room. The silhouettes of hundreds of heads filled the seats. A man waved enthusiastically from a brightly lit stage at the front. Jerry hurried down the aisle towards him.

"He's here!" a voice boomed from speakers on either side of the stage. "Please give a warm welcome to our keynote speaker, the esteemed Mr. Jerry Dillwash!"

The crowd applauded as Jerry limped towards the stage. It took longer for him to get on stage than the crowd could maintain their applause.

He shook the host's hand before moving behind the podium. After opening his laptop, he looked into the blinding lights and began.

"Artificial intelligence is the single most powerful tool in human history. It can be used to cure diseases, teach our children, predict natural disasters, improve social services, find ways to prevent global warming, solve world hunger, and create new inventions. It also has the potential to inflict great harm.

Many people bemoan the advances in AI as they could displace human workers, create realistic misinformation, cause market and financial volatility or worse become smarter than humans and become uncontrollable.

However, I am here today to tell you about the greatest threat that artificial intelligence poses to mankind. Not that it could become sentient – although the definition of sentient is up for debate – something much worse: A.I. is the most sophisticated and most dangerous weapon since the nuclear bomb.

According to the late German-American psychoanalyst Erik Erikson, humans go through eight stages of development that span infancy to old age. Skipping some details, every stage has a crisis to resolve in order to progress. For example, the first stage from birth to 18 months is trust versus mistrust. A child must learn to trust or mistrust their caregivers based on the quality of care they receive. After a year and a half, they enter the stage of autonomy versus shame and doubt. These stages continue until the eighth stage of integrity versus despair in the late sixties.

According to Erikson, this linear progression is experienced by all humans. We continue learning throughout our lives, learning from our experiences and the experiences of others while moving along predictable stages of development.

Artificial intelligence is not restricted by linear learning or emotional and foreseeable development stages. Its learning is exponential.

Put a penny in a jar daily for a month and end up with 30 cents. However, doubling your penny each day for 30 days will result in a sum exceeding $5 million. Likewise, if AI can rapidly increase its knowledge and skills, it can become the world's most powerful tool.

By comparison, humans learn slowly, and we forget. We build on our knowledge, retaining some, but forget a lot more. Imagine if you had a perfect memory. What if you remembered everything you saw, heard, felt, smelled or touched? We would all be smarter than Albert Einstein if we remembered everything. That's what AI can do.

Perfect memory is inherent in computers. Now we are also bestowing learning, intelligence, problem solving and the ability to self-program. The possibilities and dangers are endless. If this new machine, with its unlimited learning potential, falls into the wrong hands..."

Jerry's words trailed off as he watched two men in dark suits stride down the aisle towards the stage. The host sitting in the front row stood up to stop the men as they approached.

Jerry didn't know if he should continue his speech or wait. The crowd stared at the commotion while Jerry stepped away from the mic and waited. He held his hand up to block the spotlights, trying to see if recognized the men. Their suits looked clean, but a little wrinkled and their faces seemed serious and alert.

One suit held up a badge to the host. They talked for a moment before the host nodded and climbed onto the stage.

"Ladies and gentlemen, we apologize for the interruption, but our esteemed speaker must attend to some important matters. We will reschedule his talk for tomorrow."

As he spoke, the two men walked onto the stage and approached Jerry.

"I'm Bill and this is Bob," one of them said in a sober tone. He held up a badge. "We are with the Secret Service. Come with us."

"I'm in the middle of a speech," Jerry protested. "Can't this wait?"

"This is a matter of national security. You need to come with us *now*."

CHAPTER 6

Indie hung up the phone, leaned back on the couch, and stretched. She only slept a few hours last night.

Following their dancing, swimming and then Prospero's abrupt U-turn into a fit of fear, she followed him back to his extravagant top floor condo. Prospero hardly acknowledged her when she insisted she accompany him inside. Indie wondered if he might be suicidal. Also, she was curious to know what was happening. Why would a seemingly successful man be this scared, this fast? And who was Prospero Junior who apparently *ventured outside his parameters*? It seemed an odd way of describing your kid's behaviour.

Throughout the night, he went from angry rants to pacing and mumbling, to furious typing on his computer and back to angry rants again. She tried to comfort him, but he either ignored her or ranted about Prospero Junior causing civilization's downfall.

After the first round, Indie went through his dresser and found a blue tracksuit. She changed out of her sequin dress and returned to the couch. She watched him pace, rant, and punch his laptop keyboard before falling asleep. This wasn't anything like Pretty Woman.

"What will I do?" he shouted. "What can anyone do?"

She stood up, strode across the room and grabbed his shoulders. "You need to think logically," she said in a firm tone.

His eyes dashed from side to side as if trying unsuccessfully to access an internal database.

"I can't. I don't know what he's…"

"Stop!" she yelled.

"I can't. This is bad, and there is no way of going back."

Although he was speaking to her, his eyes focused on a distant place.

She went to the bar area and grabbed the ice bucket. After filling it with cold water, she returned.

"Last chance, Prospero. You need to come back to earth."

"Last chance," he mumbled. "I wish I had another chance..."

She threw the bucket of cold water directly at his face. He paused mid mumble and stared straight ahead in shock. For a moment, she feared he might lash out and hit her.

Slowly, his eyes focused on her. "Why did you do that?" he whispered.

"Please return to reality. You haven't slept, eaten or stopped all night."

"What am I supposed to do?" His voice was quiet and wounded.

Indie led him to the table and forced him to sit down. "I ordered room service. Sit down and tell me what is going on."

"But..."

"We are not looking for solutions or worst cases or anything else. Just tell me what happened—from the start."

She retrieved a glass, filled it with water, and set it in front of him.

He took a gulp and set it down. "Does telling you solve anything?"

His demeanour calmed, and she continued to speak in a reassuring voice. "We are not trying to solve anything. You need water, food and a harmonious disposition."

Someone knocked on the door. She opened it and let the waiter roll in the tray of food. Just because this wasn't Pretty Woman, didn't mean she couldn't eat like her.

After tipping the waiter and setting the food on the table, she sat down and stared at him.

"I'm waiting," she said.

"Waiting for what?"

"You need to eat, tell your story or both."

He grabbed a strawberry and took a bite.

"When I was young, I only wanted one thing...to be rich."

"Didn't everyone?"

"I suppose." He finished the strawberry and picked up the eggs benedict. After taking a large bite, he continued.

"We grew up in a house one step above a trailer park. My alcoholic father drove a taxi, and my mother taught art at the local high school. We lived in a dirty, crime-ridden suburb outside of Saginaw, Michigan. My little sister and I barely had enough to eat. Every day, I swore that when I grew up, I would make lots of money, live in a big house and always have enough food to eat."

He took another bite of eggs benedict.

"My father went to jail after driving drunk and hitting and almost killing a woman. Three years later, my sister moved out to marry a lawyer from New York. I left home and went to university taking computer science and finance. NextGen Software Solutions recruited me right out of school. Me and another guy, Jerry helped program and design a rudimentary AI for them. It continuously improved over the years. One promising application for our program was financial forecasting. The AI watched the markets, trend lines, financial analysis, asset allocations, and financial chat rooms. It used that information to test millions of market prediction models. However, NextGen grew worried that it would get into trouble with the SEC so they told us to stop. But we didn't. We kept the AI going, refining the algorithms over the next couple of months. However, the NextGen executives eventually discovered our ongoing research and fired us.

Jerry used some of the financial forecasting strategies he learned from the AI, to start a financial consulting business, write a few books and embark on a speaking tour. I took a different path. With the help of an off-site backup of our AI, I continued refining it and started a financial company of my own. I named the AI, Prospero Junior.

At first, I used Junior's predictions to invest in stocks, bonds, and other financial instruments. After a few months of making over one hundred thousand dollars, I tweaked the AI to allow it to not only forecast but also buy, sell and trade financial instruments for me.

Over the next six months, Prospero Junior accrued over 10 million dollars. I then gave it the ability to dabble in a few *questionable* tactics, including ramping, wash trades, bear raids, lure and squeeze, and spoofing. It employed these tactics, while successfully hiding it from the SEC. In just a few months, Prospero Junior earned a million dollars daily without any authorities noticing. It was pretty much free money."

"Sounds like an impressive scam," said Indie.

"Oh, please," he said with exasperation. "All the big stock traders, banks and fund managers do the same thing. Whether it's planting doubt about a stock in a chat room or performing a hostile takeover. The entire market is nothing more than a game of market manipulation. It's no different from you standing on the street with your fake rental costume. You charge tourists for taking a picture with a gorgeous showgirl. But you're not really a showgirl, you're just a girl in a sexy dress. That's still manipulation."

"That's a little different."

"Perhaps. Anyway, I put in safeguards that stopped any trading or market coercion if it would have drastic negative impacts on the American economy."

"That's very magnanimous of you."

Prospero raised an eyebrow. "That's a big word."

"I'm gorgeous and smart," she said with a flick of her long blond hair.

He took a swig of orange juice and dabbed the corner of his mouth with a napkin. "Junior blew past his guardrails. It's like it can't stop. Prospero Junior is siphoning all the money in the States and the world into its accounts. Banks are collapsing, investment firms are hemorrhaging, and the entire American economic system is spiralling out of control."

"Were your safeguards not secure. Did the AI get around them somehow?"

"That's what I don't understand. I programmed multiple limits and safety measures into the system. It is theoretically impossible for it to bypass them unless I authorize it. However, it appears Junior has surpassed its programming and given itself authorization."

"Can't you just pull the plug?"

"This isn't just a desktop computer in my basement. When I left NextGen, I lost the use of their supercomputer. Instead, I recreated the AI using a network of computers and servers. Some of which I owned and others I *borrowed*."

"Can you not simply tell it to shut down?"

"I tried, but it's no longer accepting my commands."

"Can you ask anyone for help? Someone that knows about AI?"

"Jerry Dillwash is the only person who might be able to help, but we haven't talked since the company fired us."

"Jerry Dillwash, the Artificial Intelligence guru?"

"That's the guy. He isn't answering my calls."

"What if you could see him in person?"

"How?"

"Tell me I'm gorgeous again, and I'll tell you how you can meet him."

CHAPTER 7

Bill and Bob flanked Jerry Dillwash and escorted him off the stage.

"What does the Secret Service want with me?" he asked.

"We'll explain everything on the plane."

"The plane? Where are we going?"

"A secure location."

The audience murmured amongst themselves as the trio marched down the centre aisle.

"Am I in trouble?"

"You will be if you keep asking questions," said Bill.

As they exited the room, Bob's phone chimed. They paused as he talked to someone for less than a minute.

"Change of plans," he said, looking at Bill. "Air traffic control is down. All flights are grounded. We have to do this here."

"Let's find a secluded room. I think we're running out of time," said Bob.

"Are you really Bob and Bill?" Jerry asked. "That sounds made up."

Before they responded, a man in his twenties with long black hair and a blond woman in a men's tracksuit ran up to them.

"Jerry! I need your help," yelled Prospero.

Bob reached a hand under his suit and kept it there while Bill held his hand up to stop Prospero.

"Sir, you need to keep back. Mr. Dillwash is currently unavailable."

"This is an urgent matter," yelled Prospero. "I need to talk to him, NOW!"

Bill pushed Prospero back. "I'm warning you, sir. Step back!"

"Why don't we talk to him later?" suggested Indie when she

saw Bob's hand under his jacket.

Bill held up his badge. "This is a matter of national security. Please step back."

"This IS a matter of national security!" yelled Prospero. "If I don't talk to him now, this entire country will collapse!"

A small crowd gathered to watch the commotion. Prospero kept pushing, and the crowd of onlookers grew.

Bob pulled out his pistol and held it in the air. "I need everyone to step back, NOW! National security is at stake; we have the right and means to protect ourselves and him. Everyone, step aside and let us through!"

Someone yelled *GUN!*, and the corridor erupted into chaos. Some dove for cover behind the benches while others fled the scene. A woman screamed, a baby cried and people panicked.

The conference room door opened, and a stream of people exited the orchestral performance. Bob and Bill each grabbed one of Jerry's arms and pulled him down the corridor, through the hysterical throng.

Bob called someone on his phone, while Bill aimed his gun at anyone in their way.

"Backup can't make it for another fifteen minutes. Let's get him away from here."

A security guard broke through the crowd and pointed his gun at the trio. "Put your hands in the air."

"We're Secret Service!" Bob yelled, holding up his badge.

"Sure, you are, and I'm the King of Spain. Put the gun down or I *will* shoot."

"We're Secret Service!" Bob yelled again, pointing at his badge. "Let us go or you will regret it."

"I don't care who..."

Before the guard finished his sentence, Bill fired his gun. The bullet pierced the guard's right shoulder. His arm flew back, and his pistol soared through the air.

Bill and Bob turned and ran down the corridor with a reluctant Jerry.

"You just shot that guy!"

"Now you know we're serious. Keep walking."

They turned into a door with an *employees only* sign above it that led into a large industrial kitchen. All the cooks and food preparers had long since scattered, but steam still spewed from pots on the stove. Hurriedly, they ran to the kitchen's rear and entered a sizable storage room. Bob shut the heavy steel door behind them and pushed a chair up to the handle. The noise of the panicked mob outside quickly muted.

"Sit down!" Bob ordered.

Jerry sat on the floor and pulled out his phone while Bill checked the rest of the room.

Rows of shelving filled with plates, cutlery, serving dishes, cups, mugs, warming trays, pitchers and a wide assortment of tableware lined the walls on either side.

"We're clear. I'm calling command."

He talked on the phone for a few minutes. "We'll have to do this here."

Bob found a stool in the back and set it on the floor in front of Jerry. "Please, Mr. Dillwash, have a seat. We need to ask you a couple of questions."

"What's going on?" Jerry's hands shook as he struggled to his feet. "Why did you just kill that policeman?"

"He was a security guard, and I only wounded him. He will recover."

Bob and Bill froze at a sound outside the door.

Bill held his finger to his lips and crept towards the door. Bob opened the door quickly while Bill pointed his gun into the kitchen. He stepped into the kitchen and scanned the room.

He listened briefly, then retreated to the storage room and secured the door.

"Okay, we're clear. Let's get this over with."

"Are you going to kill me?"

Jerry sat in the chair. His leg bounced, and he chewed his nails.

Bob found a stool and pulled it next to Jerry. "I realize you have just been through a traumatic experience, but I need you to focus. You are safe here. No one is going to hurt you. The administration needs your advice on a developing situation."

"What situation?"

"America is being attacked."

"Attacked by who?"

Bob held up his hand. "Let me finish. Someone or something is systematically attacking the American economic system and we have reason to believe that an AI is involved."

"How do you know that?"

"That's not important. We need to know how to stop it."

"I need more information." Jerry pulled out his phone.

Bill grabbed the phone and looked at it. "Who are you trying to call?"

Jerry held out his hand. "No one. I need my phone. It has my research on it. If you want me to help, give it back to me."

Bob nodded at Bill, who returned the phone to Jerry.

"Tell me exactly what you know," said Jerry.

"An unknown entity is wreaking havoc on banking systems and the stock market. Without getting into complicated details, this entity is essentially stealing all of our money. Also, multiple companies, corporations and governmental organization are reporting data breaches on their systems. Our cyber defence analysts speculate the attack is coming from an AI, but we don't know where."

Jerry squinted his eyes. "How do you know that?"

"That's not important. The administration requested your assistance, recognizing you as the eminent AI authority. Is it possible that an artificial intelligence has become sentient and subsequently gone rogue?"

Jerry typed and read his phone. "Not likely. Most AI's have safety features that prevent them from causing harm. It *is* possible that one is inadvertently causing damage to our economy. However, if the cyberattacks are happening simultaneously, then this points to something intentional. Someone is using an AI as a weapon."

"Who might possess this technology?

"Iran."

Bill creased his brows. "How do you know that?"

"Cross-referencing the countries that hate America, with those that have the means, recent large purchases of GH200 chips, among other variables, Iran is the most likely candidate for this type of attack. Russia and perhaps China may be financing and technological assistance."

"Interesting...How do we stop it?"

"I'm assuming that your cyber defence system is an AI?" Jerry asked.

"We are not at liberty to confirm that."

"Do you want my help or not?"

"We are not at liberty to say, but yes, you can assume that."

Jerry rubbed his forehead. "In order for an AI to perform such a sophisticated attack on the American economic establishment, it would probably use MAAI."

Bob squinted his eyes. "What's that?"

"Multi agent artificial intelligence is where an AI uses other AI's cooperating for a common goal. This is similar to how a large company or organization works. The boss gives orders to his managers who each tell people below them what to do. Everyone in the organization is working towards the boss's goal of making money. However, each has their own tasks and individual goals. They each perform their tasks using their own expertise. This is a complicated, but effective means of achieving a difficult goal."

"You still haven't told us how to stop it."

"I'm getting to that. If this is an intentional and coordinated attack on our economic system, the programmers would also run millions of scenarios for how we might stop it. From that data, they would probably design millions of ways of preventing any attempts. Has the American government done as I suggested and spent the last five years and a few billion dollars designing an AI whose sole purpose is to stop malevolent AI attacks?"

Bob and Bill stared at him for a moment until Bill realized

Jerry was waiting for an answer.

"Let's just assume that the government didn't heed your warnings," said Bill.

"Then there is only one way to stop it."

"How?"

"Do you have any aircraft carriers in the middle east?"

CHAPTER 8

Kamaran Mazdaki's alarm blared incessantly until he finally reached for his phone on the side table and stopped it. Beside him, his wife continued to sleep. The opium she had taken the night before still coursed through her veins.

Kamaran reached under his bed and pulled out his prayer mat. He flung the namāzlik across the floor and knelt on it. He said a special Salah for his wife. Her depression might be worsening, but it was hard to tell since she was almost always high. Kamaran finished his prayers, rolled up his namāzlik and stood up. Looking down at his sleeping wife, he sighed and shook his head. For every blessing Allah bestowed upon him, Iblis sent a worse curse. Throughout his life, it had consistently been this way for him.

His life began with a blessed childhood. He enjoyed the company of many friends at school, loved soccer and his parents treasured him. They lived in a quaint little house south of Tehran. His parents effectively insulated him from the political and social upheavals of their country. This included the Islamic Revolution and the overthrow of the Pahlavi dynasty in 1979. A year later, when Saddam's Iraqi forces invaded, his father kissed his wife and child and joined the fight. Six months later, a letter arrived at their quaint little house informing them of his father's death. Kamaran was just twelve years old. His mother wept for weeks. She descended into a deep depression. He discovered her limp body hanging from a ceiling fan.

The State Welfare Organization placed Kamaran in an orphanage in Tehran. The old, dilapidated clay and stone building became his home. His new caretakers kept order with severe consequences rather than love. The only redeeming quality was the extensive library in the basement. He spent many hours hidden in that basement, lost in the thrills and adventures of fiction. Someday, he swore, he would lead a brigand of desert pirates across the Kavir desert. Sitting atop a noble black steed, he would hold his shamshir sword above his head and charge the enemy with a primal scream. He would conquer the world and live forever in a golden palace with a beautiful princess.

As he entered his teenage years, Kamaran realized his desert pirate fantasy was not practical. Determined not to end up like his parents, he attended university. There he met beautiful, sweet and funny Laleh. The day before graduation, she told him she had met someone else. He was rich, came from a powerful family and was approved by Laleh's parents.

Despite his devastation, Kamaran was still determined to have a successful life. He got his PhD in cybersecurity and began working for a small computer firm in Shiraz. Fifteen years later, he left to start his own cybersecurity business. That's when he met his future wife, Esther. Unlike Laleh, she lacked natural beauty and faced a long struggle to find a husband. They fell in love and married a year later. Since she was a little girl, Esther wanted to be a mother. She was nearing thirty, and desperate to get started on having a family.

They tried to have children for two years without success until a doctor informed them that Esther had a rare form of primary ovarian insufficiency. The doctors tried hormone therapy, but after five years, told her she would never have children. Simultaneously, one of Kamaran's clients fell victim to a devastating hacking incident. Kamaran and his team of engineers successfully removed the malware, but the damage was done. In an attempt to stave off bankruptcy, the company sued for millions. Kamaran lost the suit and filed for bankruptcy one month later.

The Iranian government was also a client before his business went under. They offered him a hefty salary to work for them.

Desperate for money, he accepted the position. He hoped the generous salary might also help make Esther happy.

It didn't.

Esther smoked opium to escape her pain. Kamaran earned enough money to hire caretakers for his house and drugs for his wife. As she slid into depression and addiction, Kamaran focused on his work. His latest project involved creating a new type of weapon that could change the world forever.

He kissed his sleeping wife on the forehead. "Goodbye, my princess."

Grabbing a piece of naan Barbari bread from the kitchen, he climbed into his grey sedan and drove to work.

Twenty minutes later, he pulled up to the gates of an unmarked government facility outside of Shiraz. A heavily armed guard stared intently at his badge.

"You know, I've come here almost every day for the past five years," said Kamaran. "Don't you recognize me yet?"

"Just doing my job, sir," said the soldier as he waved at the other guard inside the security building. The chain-link gate rolled aside with a loud metal screech.

Kamaran waited for it to open and rolled inside. He parked in his reserved spot inside the underground parking lot and took the elevator up to the main floor. After passing through another security checkpoint and metal detector, he made it to the main reception desk manned by a guard more friendly than the one at the gate.

He looked up and smiled. "Good morning, Mr. Mazdaki."

Kamaran nodded back and strode to the elevator. Inside, he swiped his card, and the elevator descended. It took three minutes to pass through 200 feet of sand, dirt, basalt, limestone and shale. The doors opened to an extensive underground facility. It sometimes reminded him of the basement library from his childhood.

He passed through another security checkpoint before walking down a long corridor. Two armed guards stood outside the lab. After an iris and handprint scan, the heavy metal door opened, and the guards stepped aside. Kamaran walked in, and the door closed behind him. The locks engaged with an echoing clang.

He pulled his chair up to the large screen and entered his password into the artificial intelligence known as Şervan.

<Good morning, Desert Pirate> said the words on the screen.

Despite the human-like qualities Şervan seemed to possess, Kamaran refused to participate in useless pleasantries. He also refused to speak aloud to the AI. Instead, he typed his question into the computer.

<Progress report>

It replied within a millisecond of typing the last character.

<Everything is going smoothly. All designates are completing their objectives as planned. Everything is ready for the final phase>.

For the past decade, Iran spent twenty percent of its defence budget on Şervan. It took ten years and millions of programming hours to create the artificial intelligence. Once complete, they recruited Kamaran to head up the research and development using Şervan. The government wanted him to create a simulation known as J-Sim. They told him it was a simulation of a jihad or holy war against the United States. Kamaran understood it was not merely a simulation. However, he also held great hatred against the West.

The Americans funded Saddam Hussein's invasion of Iran and the quest for control over Iran's oil. Two years later, the United States turned against Saddam when he invaded Kuwait for its oil. Every move the Americans made in the Middle East was about oil. Their capitalistic ideals made them greedy, domineering and arrogant. Their wars killed his father, drove his mother to suicide and left him an orphan. Now he was fatherless, almost a widow and seething with anger towards the world.

He knew J-Sim was more than just a simulation, but he didn't care.

His stupid childhood fantasy of sitting atop a noble white

steed with a Shamshir sword leading a brigand of desert pirates to world domination would never come true. Neither would his dream of living forever in a golden palace with a beautiful princess.

He drove a grey sedan instead of a white horse. His big house was not a golden palace, but a quiet, childless prison and his princess was a heartbroken addict. He also didn't have a shamshir sword. However, he had a weapon much more powerful than a sword with a wicked curve.

His cell phone rang, startling him. He pulled the phone from his pocket and answered it.

"Is Şervan ready?" inquired the voice at the other end.

"Yes."

"The Americans are on to us. We have to act now."

"Just to be clear, once the next phase starts, it can't be stopped."

"We know, but the Supreme Leader has given the order."

The final phase of the jihad to end capitalism, greed and dominance of the West had finally begun.

He typed a simple command into the terminal and sighed. Şervan received the message and digitally detached itself from all control of the underground facility. He suspected the artificial intelligence was withholding some information, but still trusted it to do its job. Şervan's level of intelligence far exceeded human's long ago. Everything appeared to be in place, and Kamaran's role was no longer required.

Kamaran pulled the namāzlik out from under his desk and unrolled it on the floor. The call to prayer did not sound over the public address system, but he couldn't wait. This would be his last prayer. He wanted to be praying when Malak al-Maut came for him. He prayed for his soul, his wife and his country. Perhaps when Kamaran arrived in Jannah, he could sit on a noble white steed brandishing a shamshir sword over his head.

"La ilaha illallah!" he screamed.

The GBU-Advanced 5K Penetrator fired from a F-15 Strike Eagle tore through the skies above Tehran. It dove towards the earth and the nose cone split open, revealing the tungsten penetrator. As if fuelled by urgent panic, the missile pierced the earth and tore through layers of sand, dirt, basalt, limestone and shale.

The entire underground bunker, workers, rows of servers and vast networks of computer systems disintegrated.

Kamaran's soul departed the earth to be judged by Munkar and Nakir.

Şervan had already left the bunker to wreak havoc upon the world.

CHAPTER 9

Adam held the cello between his knees and the bow at his side as he waited for the performance to begin. He sat next to the edge of the stage with an unobstructed view of the audience.

His family sat in the third row from the front. His father waited with arms crossed and a bored expression, while his mother stifled a cough before popping another lozenge. Lily played on her tablet.

Adam scanned the spectators. He recognized a few parents of his bandmate's parents, but couldn't find Piper. Scanning a second time, he still didn't see her.

The crowd began clapping, and the orchestra stood as Mr. Rudolph walked onto the stage. He bowed to the orchestra and then to the crowd. That's when Adam saw her. The back door opened, and Piper slipped inside. She found an empty seat near the back and sat down. Adam smiled to himself and sighed.

His extensive practice hours were about to pay off. Mr. Rudolph chose him to perform the powerful solo a few minutes into their first piece. This was his chance to impress a beautiful girl.

Mr. Rudolph tapped his baton on the podium, waking Adam from his daydream. Just as they began Shostakovich's Symphony No. 15, a gunshot rang out in the corridor outside. The crowd murmured, and the orchestra petered out.

The back door of the auditorium opened. A woman ran inside and a few others followed her. The noise and commotion in the corridor spilt inside with them. Someone yelled *GUN!* and the room erupted into chaos.

Someone screamed as more people flooded in. They rushed

forward, avoiding the unseen threat in the corridor.

Adam watched Piper blending into the crowd at the back of the room. Suddenly, she vanished as the crowd appeared to envelop her in their rush to escape. Adam dropped his cello and leapt off the stage.

"Over here!" His father's voice boomed over the panicked screams. His family huddled by a side exit near the stage's left corner.

"Go!" Adam yelled. "I'll catch up."

His father paused for a moment before shuffling his mother and sister out the exit. Others followed behind them.

Adam tried pushing through the crowd, but it was like trying to swim up Niagara Falls. Jumping back onto the stage, he swiftly weaved through the chairs and instruments to the opposite side. Adam leapt off stage from the right side. Fewer people filled this side, as everyone rushed towards the exit on the opposite side.

He searched, but couldn't find Piper. Instead, he lay on the floor and looked under the chairs. After searching under three rows of seats, he saw her. Piper lay under a chair, watching everyone run by. Adam stood up and ran down the row towards her. Panting, he knelt and peeked under the chair.

"Do you need help?"

She looked up at him and smiled. "I thought I'd take a nap until the performance started again."

"Come on, let's go."

She climbed out and looked at him. "Did you come to rescue me?"

"Yeah, I guess. I thought you got trampled or something."

"Thanks, but I'm fine."

With the crowd gone, the room grew quiet.

Piper walked down the row, going towards the back.

"Where are you going?" Adam asked. "Shouldn't we leave with everyone else?"

She proceeded to the back door and took a quick look outside. "Aren't you curious?"

"But someone said there was a gun."

"I'm from Wyoming, everyone has a gun."

Adam glanced at the front room exit where his family and others fled for safety. He glanced at the back door, where the pretty girl went.

"Wait for me. I'm coming."

She peeked into the corridor.

"What do you see?" he whispered.

"Dead bodies, everywhere. It's horrible."

He tried to look around her into the corridor. "Really?"

"No, I'm just kidding. All I see is a security guard."

Adam peered into the corridor. A lone security guard lay on the floor, but everyone else was gone.

"We should go," he said.

"We should help the guard," she said. "I think he's been shot."

She stepped into the corridor and looked both ways.

"Wait! Come back," he whispered after her. "The shooter could still be out there."

Piper ran to the guard and knelt.

Adam crouch-ran after her.

The guard groaned in pain as he held his shoulder. Blood seeped through his fingers and dripped into a growing crimson stain on the carpet. His pistol sat a few feet away.

"Grab a cloth or something," Piper instructed Adam. "We need to stop the bleeding."

Adam looked around the abandoned corridor but saw only garbage, a purse and a trolley with coffee. He ran to the nearest washroom, hoping to find some paper towels. After seeing only air dryers, he unravelled an entire roll of toilet paper and ran back to Piper and the injured guard. He handed her the giant wad of tissue.

She snatched it out of his hands.

"You need to move your hand," she said apologetically to the guard.

He nodded and removed his bloodied hand. Piper quickly pressed the toilet paper onto the wound and pressed down hard. He winced in pain.

"Thanks," he said through gritted teeth. "I called for help. They should be here soon."

They waited with him for a few minutes before help arrived. A policeman with a gun drawn led two paramedics rolling a stretcher down the corridor.

"Where's the shooter?" inquired the officer.

"We didn't see them," Piper answered.

"You should leave," said the officer. "They could still be around."

"Thank you," croaked the guard as the paramedics hoisted him onto the stretcher.

"Let's go," said Piper and strode down the corridor away from the auditorium where he was supposed to have his impressive performance.

"I need to go back to my family," he said, following her.

"You don't have to follow me."

"Where are you going?"

"Away from that policeman."

"What? Why?"

She walked to a doorway with an *employees only* sign above it.

"Because he might come looking for us."

"Why would he come looking for us?"

She ignored him and entered the room. A woman in a blue tracksuit and long blond hair cupped her ear against a large steel door at the back of the kitchen. Adam was sure he had seen her before. A man in his early thirties with long black hair and dark circles under his eyes stood beside her.

The woman noticed their arrival and pressed her finger to her lips and then pointed at the door. The doorknob rattled, and the woman waved in a silent, frantic mime that they interpreted as *run and hide*.

Adam and Piper scrambled into an empty spot under a stainless-steel counter and waited silently.

The rear kitchen door creaked open and someone exited. They quickly re-entered the room and closed the door.

Adam remained squished up against Piper under the counter. Her tepid breath warmed his neck and threatened to overheat his heart. Her phone jabbed into his leg.

She poked her head out. "Do you think it's safe yet?"

"We should wait a little longer."

The woman in the blue tracksuit and the man with long black hair looked under the counter.

"What are you guys doing here?" she whispered.

"Like you, we were hiding," Piper said and climbed out.

Adam's shoulders sagged, and he followed.

"I mean, what are you doing in here?" whispered the woman.

They all heard voices in the corridor outside the kitchen. Piper ran to the door and locked it.

Someone knocked on the door. "This is the police. Is there anyone in there?"

Piper put her finger to her mouth and shook her head. Nobody spoke.

Once the footsteps outside faded, the woman squinted at Piper. "Why are you running from the cops and why is there blood on your shirt?"

"It's not my blood," said Piper. "Who are you spying on?"

"Let's find a spot to chat," the man with lengthy black hair suggested. He gestured towards a door past the counters.

They followed him to a storage room filled with shelves of food. He turned on the light and Piper closed the door after everyone was inside.

"My name is Prospero."

"I'm Indie."

"I'm Piper."

"Adam."

"Why are you here and why are you fleeing the police?" Indie asked after they introduced themselves.

Adam wanted to ask the same thing.

Piper asked, "Who's behind that door? And why are you spying on them?"

"Bad things are happening. We think the person behind the

door can assist," Prospero stated.

"Is he the shooter?" asked Piper.

"No, he's an AI expert."

"I knew it!" said Piper. "Some on social media say an AI is behind the cyberattacks and the stock market crash."

"It's my AI that is causing the financial collapse and I'm hoping this guy can help me stop it," said Prospero.

"It's *your* AI?" Piper pointed at him. "Is it doing the cyberattacks too?"

"Yes, it's my AI, but it has nothing to do with the cyberattacks...I don't think..."

"You must be pretty rich to own your own AI," said Adam.

"Not anymore," he answered.

"Why is your AI..." Piper began, but Indie interrupted.

"Now it's your turn. Why are you running from the cops?"

Piper looked around nervously. "I've come across numerous online conspiracy theories about the end of the world, so I want to ensure I'm ready. My father always taught me to be prepared."

"You still haven't answered my question," said Indie.

"Promise you won't freak out," Piper said, looking at all of them.

Nobody responded.

Piper reached behind her and pulled out a black pistol.

"What's that?" Adam squealed.

"It's a Ruger LC9."

She pulled the slide back, looked into the empty chamber, dropped the magazine, and inspected it.

"Where did you get...wait did you steal that guard's gun?"

Piper replaced the magazine into the pistol with a click.

"I found the gun on the floor. I don't think he'll need it for a while."

"Why do you need a gun?" asked Indie. "Those things are dangerous."

"I told you – it's in case everything falls apart."

"Everything is *not* going to fall apart," said Indie.

"It might," said Prospero.

Indie looked at him. "You really think your computer could bring about the apocalypse?"

"All I know is that my computer has control of thousands of bots, access to millions of websites and chat rooms, can earn billions of dollars per day and for an unknown reason has blown through its safeguards and will probably destroy the American economy. The way to stop it is by asking the man behind the door."

"Why can't we just knock on the door and ask him?" asked Adam.

"Because he is currently being interrogated by two Secret Service agents," said Indie.

"Sounds like a good reason," Adam said.

"I'm assuming their backup is having trouble getting an evac for them," said Prospero, "but they *will* be here shortly. We need to talk to Jerry Dillwash before the backup arrives.

"What are you suggesting?" asked Indie.

"If Piper gives me the gun…"

"Not a chance!" said Piper.

"You really want to kidnap Jerry while two Secret Service agents are guarding him?" Indie asked Prospero.

"I'm not giving up my gun," said Piper.

"This needs to be done now," Prospero said. "Give me the gun!"

"Have you ever used a gun?" asked Piper.

"Once, but it doesn't matter. I'm only using it to scare the agents away."

"You should never point a gun unless you are prepared to use it. Also, I don't think secret agents scare easily. Once they see that you're armed, they'll fire."

"Shhh!" Adam hissed.

He stood closest to the door and heard voices in the kitchen.

Everyone looked at him and stopped talking.

"It sounds like they're leaving," said Adam.

Prospero marched forward towards the door.

"What are you doing?" Indie whispered and stepped in front of him.

"I'm going to talk to Jerry."

"How? They have guns."

He searched the shelving of food beside him and grabbed a large can of tomato sauce. Holding the can like a bowling ball, he marched to the door.

Indie raised her eyebrows. "What are you going to do with that?"

"Whatever I have to."

"I'm going with him," said Piper, holding the pistol at her side.

Adam followed her with Piper close behind.

"You guys are all crazy," she said.

They walked through the kitchen and into the corridor. Jerry and the two suits were fifty feet away.

Prospero strode towards them with the big tomato can poised at his side. The others followed close behind.

"Hey, I need to talk to you!" he yelled.

The trio turned and Bill yelled, "Stay back! This is official business."

Prospero swung his arm in a wide arc and flung the can of tomato sauce towards him.

As the can sailed through the air, Bill reached into his jacket pulled out his gun and pointed it at the incoming sauce filled projectile. Two expertly placed shots punctured the can, changing its trajectory. It spun to the left and hit the wall as red sauce spewed out.

The momentum of Prospero's throw caused him to trip and land face-first on the carpet a few feet from Bill. The rest of the group paused behind him.

"Don't get up," Bill pointed his gun at Prospero's head.

Bob stood with a gun drawn beside Jerry, who looked confused and scared.

"Police! Nobody move!" screamed a voice behind Adam, Indie and Piper.

Adam's hands shot into the air. Beside him, Indie did the same. He looked behind him and saw four policemen in swat gear, pointing their semi-automatic rifles at them.

"Don't shoot!" yelled Piper. "I have a gun, but I am putting it on the floor."

She held the pistol by the barrel between her pointer and thumb.

"Put the gun on the floor, slowly," ordered the policeman.

Piper shook her head. "That's what I just said, moron."

"Don't antagonize them," whispered Indie through gritted teeth.

"Everyone on the floor!" ordered a policeman.

"I need to talk with Jerry!" Prospero still lay on the ground beside his broken tomato sauce can. "I need help with my AI."

"Don't we all," muttered Bill. He held up his badge for the policemen. "I'm Secret Service. Please place this guy in cuffs."

"Please, Jerry. I need your help. My AI is causing the economic collapse," Prospero begged.

The police cuffed Prospero while Bill and Bob whisked Jerry away.

"Wait! Come back!" cried Prospero.

Piper and Adam lay next to each other on the carpet, with Indie lying behind them.

"This turned out as expected," said Indie as an officer handcuffed her.

"At least no one got shot," said Piper.

"What will happen to us?" Adam felt more terrified than ever before. His heart beat like it was trying to run away. Sweat poured down his face, and his breathing sounded like a winded runner. Warm liquid dribbled down his jeans.

Beside him on the floor, Piper looked at him with a forced smile. "Everything is going to be okay, Adam. Just breathe."

"I'm going to jail for the rest of my life." Tears of fear and shame dripped from his cheek onto the carpet.

"No, you're not. They'll bring us to the station, question us briefly, and then release us. Tomorrow, you'll reunite with your family."

"Not likely," said an officer as he clicked cold steel around Adam's wrists.

CHAPTER 10

"Welcome to the drunk tank," said the officer and slammed the cell door closed. The clang echoed across the dingy room. Three concrete walls and one iron bar wall enclosed him and five other prisoners.

Adam looked around at the other inmates. All of them were teens.

One sat on the floor, swaying back and forth similar to Adam's autistic neighbour back in Pueblo. Another lay across a wooden bench, sleeping. Two people whispered in the corner. They looked up at Adam and snickered. A fifth boy with shiny brown hair and a muscle shirt leaned against the wall.

Adam glanced back at the bars and gazed out. He found an identical cell across the hallway. A dozen adult men filled it, but Adam didn't see Prospero.

"Rough night?" said a voice behind him.

If it wasn't for Adam's already empty bladder, he might have wet his jeans again. He remained staring through the bars but watched the straggly-haired boy beside him in his peripheral vision.

"Hey, my name's Enzo."

Adam didn't reply

Enzo touched his arm and Adam reflexively smacked it aside.

Adam looked up, expecting Enzo to hit him back, or at least give him a menacing look. Instead, Enzo retreated to the bench with the sleeping inmate.

Adam raised his chin and turned around. One of the two snickering boys stepped out. He tilted his head and stared at Adam, evaluating him. His clothes were dirty, and he smelled of sweat.

"What did you do to get here?"

"Nothing."

Adam stood his ground despite having no escape. They all remained trapped in the room.

The boy pointed to the bench. "I assume he's here for being drunk and disorderly after a wild night of partying. Your touchy friend there was likely arrested for prostitution. My friend, Doug is here for drug possession."

"It was your dope, Cullen," Doug said from his corner.

"I am here for my *alleged* illegal drug dealing," Cullen continued.

He slowly orbited Adam as he talked. You don't seem like you've been high or seen drugs.

He leaned in to smell Adam's breath. "You smell funny, but you're not drunk...Let me guess...theft under $5,000?"

Adam shook his head. "Leave me alone."

"Do you see a television in here? Did they let you have your phone? No! You, my friend, are the only entertainment in this cell."

Adam crossed his arms. "Leave me alone."

"Wait, is that piss?" Cullen pointed at Adam's crotch area and laughed. "Are you in here for public indecency?"

Adam's mouth quivered and his eyes threatened to explode in tears.

"Are you gonna cry, little boy," Cullen mocked.

Adam clenched his jaw and stepped toward Cullen.

"Did I make the little dork cry?" he mocked again.

Something inside Adam snapped.

He shoved Cullen hard, and he almost fell onto Doug before regaining his footing.

"Stop it!" Adam screamed. "I am tired of being bullied, teased and called names." Blood rushed to his head as anger bubbled inside him.

Cullen crossed his arms and stuck his bottom lip out. "Did someone have a bad day?"

Adam screamed back at him, "In the last twenty-four hours

I've been dropped headfirst into a pool, broke my phone, called a pansy, had a laptop thrown at me, almost shot at by a Secret Service agent and now I'm in jail with you losers! If you don't leave me alone, I will hit you so hard your stupid little head will explode!"

"Just try..." Cullen began as he shoved Adam.

As he spoke, Adam wound up and punched him as hard as he could. He blindly aimed for Cullen's head. His fist impacted Cullen's chin with a satisfying crunch.

His head snapped to the side, but Cullen recovered quickly and came back swinging. Adam dodged the first swing, but the next landed under his right eye. They punched, shoved and tussled for almost a minute. Doug and the touchy guy cheered them on while Sleepy continued sleeping. The door clanged open and a guard that looked like a demented version of Dwayne the Rock Johnson opened the door. He flicked his telescopic nightstick out to its full length. It swished through the air, whipping Cullen on the back of the legs, then smacking Adam across the back. Cullen cried out and Adam screamed. The pain was intense, and they released each other.

"If you can't behave, I will throw both of you into solitary confinement," he yelled. "A convicted murderer and rapist is currently residing in that cell. Normally solitary means alone, but I am willing to make an exception. So, unless you want to join them, I suggest you behave."

He pivoted on his heel and marched out. The door closed with a resounding clang.

Adam slouched down in the corner. His back was on fire, his nose was bleeding, his knuckles ached and his right eye felt like it was falling out.

Tears threatened to spill out, but he forced himself not to cry.

He spent the night stewing, nodding off and staring at the ceiling. Cullen did the same in the opposite corner.

The next morning, the Rock's evil twin escorted him out of the cell. They exited the holding area, down a lengthy hallway, and into a tiny office.

A man in a wrinkled white button shirt and dress pants powdered with icing sugar sat behind a messy desk. Papers, binders, a mug of pens, folders and a box with one remaining donut crowded around a computer from the early 2000s. The balding officer, who looked like he had eaten most of the donuts, opened a folder.

"My name is Officer Cartwright. Are you seventeen-year-old Adam Sinclair from Pueblo, Colorado?"

"Yes." Adam felt scared, tired, sore, and hungry. The lone powdered donut reminded Adam he hadn't eaten in a long time.

Officer Cartwright pulled a sheet of paper from the folder and placed it in front of Adam. Then he pulled a pen out of the mug and slapped it down.

"Sign this."

"What's going to happen to me?"

"You are going to sign that paper, then call your Mommy to come pick you up."

"What about the others? Are you letting Piper go too?"

"You should worry about yourself. Don't worry about that little group and go home."

Adam looked at the paper. He blinked and tried to focus on the words.

"Uh-oh." Officer Cartwright leaned forward to read his computer screen.

"What is it?" Adam craned his neck, attempting to read the screen.

"Just sign the paper." He tapped the desk.

A song chimed from somewhere under the mess of papers. Officer Cartwright dug his phone out and answered it.

"Cartwright here...I know. I just read that. It sounds serious. Is he going to die?"

He stood up and continued talking on his phone.

Adam leaned across the desk, trying to read the screen.

Cartwright stopped talking and looked at Adam. "What are you doing? Sign the paper and you can leave."

Adam grabbed the pen and scribbled his signature on the bottom line, while the officer talked into his phone.

"What about my phone?" Adam asked.

"Hang on," the officer said into his phone. He shuffled through the boxes and folders on the filing cabinet beside his desk until he found a resealable plastic bag with Adam's phone. After tossing the bag on the desk, he stood up and resumed his important conversation on the phone.

Adam took the last donut from the box and then went to the door. Just as he opened it and was about to step out, Officer Cartwright called to him, "Hey!"

Adam didn't turn around. He kept the donut out of sight, hoping he wasn't going to spend another night in jail for robbery.

"Get some ice for that eye. It looks horrible."

"Okay."

Adam left and closed the door. The short hallway to the left led to the reception area of the police station. As he walked down the hall, he bit into his pinched pastry. He wasn't sure if it was because he was so hungry or because he stole it, but it was the best donut he ever consumed.

As he entered the reception area, he noticed everyone was either on their computers or staring at their cell phones. Adam pulled his cell out of the bag and pressed the power button, but nothing happened. He tapped a man in the reception area on the shoulder.

"Excuse me, what's going on?"

The man didn't look up. "He's sick. They took him to Walter Reed. They're saying he's in a coma."

"Who?"

"The President."

CHAPTER 11

"Where were you?" his father yelled as they drove away from the police station.

"I was in jail, remember?"

"Don't get smart with me. What did you do?" His father grasped the steering wheel so hard, that his knuckles turned white.

"Nothing."

"You have a black eye, you smell like piss, there's blood on your shirt and that better not be cocaine on your lips."

"It's not blood, it's tomato sauce." He licked his lips. "And icing sugar."

"Your mother and sister were worried sick about you. An active shooter is killing people and you disappear. What happened?"

"I was worried about a friend. I had to help her. Then we aided a guard who was bleeding until the paramedics arrived. There was a miscommunication, and they mistakenly took us in for questioning."

"A girl?"

His father bugged him every chance he could about getting a girlfriend. Adam was severely shy around girls and rarely went out on dates. He wondered if his father worried he might be gay.

"Was she worth it?"

"Yeah."

"Do you like her? Is she pretty?"

"I don't want to talk about it, Dad."

"Why didn't you call?"

"My phone is dead, remember? That's why I called you on a

borrowed one."

"What about the black eye? Did you get that in a fight?"

"Like you told me, I stood up for myself."

"What does the other guy look like?"

"I might have broken his jaw."

"Hmm."

He wasn't sure, but Adam swore his dad smirked.

"Can we talk about this another time, please? I'm tired, hungry, and really need a shower."

"Okay, we can discuss this later, but you're still grounded until you're 29."

His father protected him from a barrage of questions from his mother when they got back to the hotel. His sister, Lily plugged her nose and laughed at his black eye.

Adam saw the large black case leaning against the corner of the room. "Is that my cello?"

"Your mother made me go back to the Koban to find it," said his father.

"Thanks."

His father pointed to the pizza box on the desk. "There's still a few pieces left if you're hungry."

"I think I need a shower first."

Adam plugged his phone in to charge and retreated to the bathroom.

Later, he sat on the bed, devouring the remaining pizza slices, while his parents watched TV and his sister played on her tablet.

The live coverage included a shot of the entrance to the Walter Reed Hospital as if waiting for the sick president to suddenly take a late-night stroll. The pundits talked about the likely causes of the sudden illness with possibilities including stroke, heart attack and even poison. Eventually, they took a break to discuss the economic meltdown. Experts seemed to agree that it was a temporary setback that would resolve itself in a couple of days. After a long commercial break, the anchor returned to discuss more boring news. Adam's thoughts drifted away, thinking about Piper's breath on his neck as they snuggled under the counter.

"That's the company!" His mother yelled, breaking him away from his daydream.

She coughed and sputtered and pointed at the TV.

The journalist came on talking about Novamed Pharmaceuticals and their recent breakthroughs with lung cancer treatment. Then they showed a clip of police escorting an angry overweight man in a fancy suit up the steps of a courthouse. The shot returned to the journalist holding a microphone.

"Seventy-five-year-old Harvey Humstead is being charged with embezzlement and tax fraud after investigators followed up on an anonymous tip. Humstead is the founder and CEO of Novamed Pharmaceuticals. Officials at the company say the allegations are baseless and they are suing a number of other pharmaceutical companies for patent infringement in relation to the new cancer treatment. They claim their company created the treatment and..."

"Does this mean they won't make this new drug for lung cancer?" his mother asked.

"I don't think so," his father reassured her. "I think more than one company has the treatment so I'm sure they can produce enough medicine for everyone."

"Not if they have to fight it out in court for years..." his mother hacked and coughed and pointed at the TV.

"I think that's enough news for today." His father clicked off the TV. "You should get some rest."

Adam finished his pizza and grabbed his phone off the nightstand where it was still charging. He pressed the power button and the cracked screen flickered and lit up. He snatched his earbuds and stood up.

"I'm going out for a walk."

"You're grounded, remember?" said his father.

"I'm not going anywhere. I just need some air."

His mother nodded between coughs and his father crossed his

arms and shook his head. "Come back here within an hour."

Adam left the room and walked outside into the warm night air. He looked towards the walkway leading to the empty pool but changed his mind. Instead, he walked around to the front of the hotel.

A wooden picnic table sat on the dirt patch beside the hotel sign and provided an unobstructed view of the traffic. Adam pushed his earbuds in and sat down. His phone was glitchy but was still getting a signal. A text message from his teacher said they rescheduled the performance for tomorrow afternoon.

He wished he could text Piper, but realized he didn't have her number. Instead, he clicked on his music app and selected the Elgar Cello Concerto.

As he drifted into the dramatic music, a shadow appeared in front of him. He whirled around to find Ronnie looming over him. His initial reaction was fear, but it quickly faded. The events of the past twenty-four hours may not have hardened him, but it had set the bar for what scared him a lot higher. If he fought Ronnie, he might still lose, but he didn't care as much anymore.

He pulled out his earbuds and tried to think of a cool line that would prove his unflappable courage, but all that came out was, "Hey."

"Do you know what happened to my sister?"

Adam wasn't sure if he was accusing him or seeking information.

"She got arrested."

"Thank you Captain Obvious. Why did she get arrested?"

"They haven't let her out yet?"

"Answer the freakin' question. She said you were with her. What happened?"

"What did she say about me?"

"I will drop you in the pool again if you don't answer my question," Ronnie growled. "What happened? They say she had a gun and blood all over her and she attacked the Secret Service!"

"She didn't attack anybody. Piper found the gun on the floor. The blood was from helping a wounded security guard. I told the cops this last night. I'm sure they'll let her out soon."

Ronnie leaned in close and spoke in a low, menacing voice. "You're bad news, Adam. Stay away from my sister or I'll give you more than a matching black eye."

Adam held his stare, determined not to show fear.

"Everything okay, Adam?" his father's voice echoed across the parking lot.

Ronnie backed up, turned and stormed away.

His father watched him leave, then sat across from Adam at the picnic table.

"What did I tell you about standing up to bullies?"

"I did, Dad. I didn't back down."

"That's not what it looked like."

"We were just talking."

"Can I give you a word of advice?"

"No," Adam mumbled quietly.

"Stop being such a pansy. With everything that's happening, you need to be tough to survive."

"What do you mean? With what's happening? You mean because of the cyberattacks?"

"It's more than that, son. America is on the brink. Our national debt is over 30 trillion dollars and continues to snowball. Our political system is more divided than during the civil war. The radical left is trying to convert this country to a communist state. The previous government opened our borders to immigrants bringing drugs, crime and terrorists into this country. Our president is trying to change all that, but I fear he is a puppet of the elites."

"Isn't he in the hospital in a coma?"

"Yes, and it's the left that put him there."

"The political system is divided, but what about the far right?

"Look son, someone has to stand up for common sense, American ideals and freedom."

"How does this concern me?"

"America is holding on by a tiny thread. People are angry, frustrated and scared. This economic meltdown may be the beginning of the end, and I want you to be prepared."

"Can I still go to my performance tomorrow?"

His father sighed. "We came all this way and your mother wouldn't let me hear the end of it if I say *no*. You can go to your performance tomorrow, but after that, we are going straight back to Pueblo. I don't want to stay here when everything collapses."

CHAPTER 12

Fortunately, Adam knew his music so well that he could play without too much concentration. He looked into the crowd, pretending Piper was there to hear his concert. When it was over, she would run to the front and congratulate him on an amazing performance. Later, they would walk down the Vegas strip hand in hand. They would stop at an outdoor cafe where they would talk, laugh and eat.

However, she wasn't here. Piper was in custody or worse, in prison. His family was driving back to Pueblo tonight, and he didn't have her number or even her last name. Adam feared he would never see her again.

When the last note played and the crowd applauded, his mother came to see him. Lily and his father trailed behind her.

"I'm so proud...cough...cough...of you, honey. That was absolutely wonderful."

"We should get going," said his father. "I want to be home before dark."

His mother backhanded him on the arm. "Tell your son you're proud of him."

"Good job, Adam. Now can we go?"

Adam packed his cello and climbed off the stage. His father led them through the crowd towards the back of the auditorium.

He looked down at his sister. "What did you think of the performance, Lily?"

"It was loud."

"Yes, it was."

"How come you didn't play your music?"

"What do you mean?"

"You know, that song with the scary shark music."

Adam smiled. "That was my song and not part of this performance."

"When will you play it? It's my favourite and I think everyone would love it."

Adam smiled. "Someday, Lily."

As they followed his father out of the auditorium and into the wide corridor, someone called, "Adam?"

It was a woman's voice, and they called out louder a second time. "Adam!"

The entire family turned and watched a young woman with long blond hair striding towards them.

"Who's that?" whispered his father.

Indie smiled as she approached. "Adam, I was hoping to find you here. Have you seen Jerry, today?"

"No, have you seen Piper?"

"No, but I heard she's still in police custody because of the gun."

"Gun? What gun?" asked his father.

She smiled at him and offered her hand. "I'm Indie...a friend of Adam's. You must be his father."

After some brief introductions, she said, "Can I borrow your son for a moment?"

"We should go," his father urged.

"We'll just be a minute," she insisted.

"That's fine," said his mother. "We'll wait right here."

Adam set his cello case down before following Indie led him to a small alcove.

"Sorry about that," she began.

"For what?"

"Telling your father about the gun. I hope I didn't get you in trouble."

"Don't worry about it."

"What happened to your eye? It looks horrible."

"I had a little fight in jail. What are you doing here?"

"Prospero and I are still looking for Jerry. He's checking the AI conference, but I don't think Jerry's going to show up. Prospero thinks the thing with the president and his coma is connected to his AI."

Adam didn't know how that was possible but didn't ask about it in case he sounded stupid.

"Do you think Jerry can help?"

"He's the top AI expert in the world. If anyone can fix this, it's him."

"Sorry, I haven't seen him."

She pointed to his family waiting across the corridor. "Are you leaving the city?"

"Yeah, my performance is done and my father wants to get out of Las Vegas before everything falls apart."

"Good luck with that...I hope you've got gas in your tank. Anyway, I've got to go find Prospero. If I don't see you again, good luck with everything."

Before she left, he quickly asked, "Do you know how I can contact Piper or where she is?"

"Have you tried calling or texting her?"

"I don't have her number."

She looked at him confused. "You don't have your girlfriend's number?"

"She's not technically my girlfriend...we just met."

"Wow! You could have fooled me. You both looked so good together."

"Thanks."

She pulled out her phone. "Why don't we exchange numbers, I'll let you know if I see or hear anything about her."

Indie smiled as she typed her number into his phone. "I would love to reunite two young lovers, like The Notebook?"

"The notebook?"

"You know, the movie with Ryan Gosling and Rachel McAdams."

"I've never seen it."

"You should." She handed him his phone. "I entered my contact info and texted myself so I have your number. I'll let you know if I see or hear anything. Las Vegas is a big tourist town, but the locals are a tight group. I'll ask around."

"Thanks."

Indie left, and Adam returned to his family.

"Was that the girl you were courting?" his father asked as they walked through the corridor.

"She's really pretty," said Lily.

"She's also a little old for you, Adam. What is she...twenty-something?"

"No, that was not the girl I was *courting*."

Prospero ran towards them. "Hey, Adam. Have you seen Indie?"

Adam pointed behind them. "She's that way."

He smiled and continued running.

His mother coughed. "It looks like you've made a few friends here."

"Too bad we're leaving."

"You can make friends just as easily back in Pueblo," said his father. "You just need to show some confidence."

Adam rolled his eyes as they walked out of the Koban Conference Centre and back into the late afternoon Nevada heat.

As they drove through the city, Adam listened to music and stared out the window. The city looked different from when they arrived a few days previously. Fewer cars drove on the road, fewer people seemed to be out and a lot of businesses were closed.

His father pulled over as two police cars flew by with sirens wailing and lights flashing. Adam pulled out his earbuds.

Ahead, crowds of people filled the streets. Many of them held protest signs and chanted angrily.

"What's going on?" Adam asked.

"People are angry that the president was poisoned."

They turned onto a side street and drove around the protest.

As they reached the northern outskirts of the city, his father pulled into a small gas station.

A glossy red Bentley Continental was the only other vehicle at the pumps. Next to the truck, two middle-aged men argued. One in a suit and tie and the other in a dirty t-shirt.

As they pulled up to the pumps, Adam rolled down his window to listen.

"We can't!" said the man in the t-shirt.

The other man loosened his tie and shook his head. "I don't understand why not?"

"I told you. Our systems are down right now."

"Nobody carries cash anymore."

"That's not my problem."

"How am I supposed to get gas?"

"That's not my problem."

His father opened his door. "Everybody, stay in the van."

Within moments, the van's back door swung open.

"Honey," his mother called. "What are you doing?"

He rummaged around in the back as if looking for something. "Nothing to worry about."

The door closed behind Adam and he watched his father approach the two men.

"Is everything okay here?" he asked. "Am I able to get some gas?"

Adam saw the bulge in his father's waistband, and his heart skipped a beat.

"You can if you have cash," said the t-shirt guy. "But I need the money first."

His father pulled out three twenty-dollar bills and handed it to him.

"Thank you."

The two men argued as his father unscrewed the gas cap and pushed the nozzle into the filler neck. As the fuel pumped into the tank, the attendant in the tank top returned to the store.

The man in the suit shook his head and approached Adam's father.

"Can you spare some cash, sir?" the man asked.

"Sorry, pal, I can't."

"I have lots of money, but their system is down and they are only accepting cash."

"That's true."

"I'll pay you back, I swear."

"Sorry, I can't."

"You can't or you won't?" the man's tone darkened, and he stepped closer.

He stood with his back just outside Lily's window.

"Lily, come here," Adam said, motioning to his side of the van.

She continued to play on her tablet. "Why?"

He pressed her seatbelt button and released the strap.

"Hey! What are you doing?"

"Lily, come to this side of the van, please."

"What…cough…what is going on back there?" his mother asked.

Adam leaned forward and whispered, "Dad has a gun."

"What?"

"Dad has a gun, and that man doesn't sound happy."

"Lily, come to the front with Mommy."

"Why?"

Outside of the van, his father said, "Please step away."

"I have to get back to my family," said the man. "All I need is a few dollars."

"Sorry, I can't help you."

The man shook his head and walked back to his red car.

Adam's mother coughed. "I think everything's okay now."

"No, it's not." Adam watched the man pull a metal tire iron out of his trunk and stride back to the van.

Adam shoved Lily down to her seat.

"Hey!" she yelled. "You're messing up my game."

Outside, his father pulled his gun before the man got two steps from his fancy red car.

"Don't even think about it!" His father held the large silver pistol with two hands.

Adam knew his father owned a pistol, but didn't know he carried it in the van and doubted his mother knew either. His father promised to take him to the range when he was eighteen. He probably would have done it sooner, but his mother hated guns and likely wouldn't let him.

"Ahh..." His mother was trying to yell something but erupted into a fit of coughing instead.

Lily finally realized something was happening and stopped fighting Adam, who continued to hold her down.

The man in the suit threw the tire iron at his father. It spun twice before hitting his father in the head. Stunned, he struggled to remain standing.

Adam wanted to get out of the car and help his father, but he remained frozen in fear.

"Adam!" his father called. "Get out here and help..."

Before he finished, the man dove towards his father. Adam remained inside the van and ducked on top of his sister. He heard grunting, clanging of the tire iron and bumping against the side of the van. Lily screamed, his mother screeched and Adam didn't move. If he couldn't help his father, he should at least get Lily and his mother out of the car.

Away from the fighting.

Away from the gun.

Away from the smell of gas.

But he couldn't. His newly acquired courage or supposed recent acclimatization to violence and confrontation were not enough. He remained covering his sister.

Bang!

The gunshot was so loud it sounded like it came from inside the van. Lily screamed a louder, more sustained scream.

"Lily, are you hurt?" he asked in a panicked tone.

"I'm okay. What's happening?"

In the front, his mother let out a weird mixture of screaming, crying and coughing.

A hand slapped against the window above Lily. Bloody fingers squeaked down the windshield. Adam recognized the ring on the wedding finger.

The bloodied hand was his father's.

CHAPTER 13

"Dad, are you okay?" Adam fought back tears as he ran to his father lying beside the car in a pool of gas and blood. His hand held a bubbling wound in his chest.

The suited man loomed above them. "I'm so sorry." He sounded genuine.

"I never meant for this to happen. I simply want to return to my family."

"What's going on?" yelled the gas attendant as he ran out of the store.

"Back off!" The man pointed the gun at the attendant.

"Take what you need and leave," said the attendant with hands in the air.

Adam tried to fight back tears. His mother coughed and wailed, while Lily sobbed in the car.

Adam looked at his mother. "Call 911."

She nodded and pulled out her phone.

"What can I do?" asked the attendant.

"Get me some clean rags," Adam ordered.

The man in the suit watched nervously as he impatiently filled his tank with gas. He still held the gun in one hand, but pointed it at the ground.

"We need to keep pressure on the wound," said Adam. The bullet hole was close to his father's heart and Adam wasn't sure if keeping pressure would help or make things worse, but he didn't know what else to do. A moment later, the attendant returned with a large rag.

"This is going to hurt," Adam said to his father, "but we have to stop the bleeding."

So far, his father said nothing. He stared at Adam, his mother and into the sky in silent shock.

Adam pushed his father's hand aside and pressed the rag on the wound at the same time.

His father grunted. In the distance, Adam finally heard the reassuring siren of an ambulance.

"You're going to be okay. Help is coming. Hold on."

The man in the suit finished filling his tank, got into his glossy red Bentley Continental and drove away.

His father mumbled something and Adam leaned closer.

"What are you saying?"

He cleared his throat and tried again. "Take your mother and sister back home."

"No, we're staying here with you."

Adam's eyes glistened with tears, but he refused to cry.

"No! It's not safe here. Take them back home. I'll catch up later."

His mother heard the conversation. "We're not leaving you."

"Please!" His voice was both weak and strong. "Go back to Pueblo before you can't. What happened here is only the beginning. Things are going to get worse. If you don't leave now, you won't be able to."

"But…" his mother began, but devolved into a fit of coughing, crying and sputtering.

His father reached up and grabbed Adam by the collar with surprising strength.

"You need to be a man, not a pansy. Stop crying and save your family."

An ambulance arrived and paramedics quickly removed a stretcher.

"I need you to step back, please," said one of them.

His father still held his collar. He gritted his teeth and pulled his son close. "Promise me you will save my family."

Adam nodded, and his father released his grasp. The paramedic gently pulled Adam off his father.

"Good job. We'll take it from here."

After they dressed the wound and loaded him onto the stretcher, the paramedic asked Adam, "Did you or your mother want to ride along to the hospital?"

Adam looked at the paramedic, then at his weeping mother, and then at Lily standing outside the van.

"No, we can't."

As they pushed the stretcher into the ambulance, his wailing mother tried to follow, but Adam held her back.

"You can't go with him, Mom. We have to leave the city."

The paramedic leaned out of the ambulance. "We're taking him to Millennium Hills Hospital."

"Is he going to make it?" Adam asked.

"I don't know," he said, then closed the door.

The siren sounded, and the ambulance sped away.

A few minutes later, the police arrived. They apologized for the late arrival and said they were *stretched pretty thin with everything going on.* Adam wanted to ask what he meant but wasn't sure he wanted the answer. They collected statements from him and the gas station attendant. They assured him that the perpetrator wouldn't escape as a BOLO would be issued.

After they left, Adam got into the passenger seat of the van. His mother still coughed and cried beside him, and Lily whimpered in the back.

"Is Daddy going to die?"

Adam waited for his mother to say something, but she just shook her head and wept.

He turned in his seat and gave his sister a fake, reassuring smile. "No, Lily. The doctors are going to fix Daddy and then he's going to come home. Why don't you play a game on your tablet?"

She wiped the tears from her cheek and nodded.

Adam turned around, gripped the steering wheel hard, and squeezed his eyes shut. He turned the key in the ignition and started the van.

The gas station attendant ran around to Adam's window and held a finger in the air as if to say *wait a minute.*

As Adam rolled down his window, the attendant disappeared into the kiosk.

"What's happening?" his mother asked between sobs.

"I don't know, mom. We'll be on the road in a minute."

A minute later, he heard the back of the van open. It closed a moment later, and the attendant returned to the window.

"I'm sorry about your dad," he said.

Adam shook his head. "It's not your fault."

"I put a full can of gas in the back of your van."

"How much do we owe..."

The man held up his hand. "Nothing. I'm not sure money is still worth anything. I'm closing up and going home. Good luck."

Adam thanked him and drove out of the gas station. Driving out of the city was stressful, as Adam only had his learner's permit. However, once he made it to the highway into the desert, it was easier.

A million thoughts swirled in his head as he drove away from Las Vegas towards Pueblo, Colorado.

"Can I put on some music?" he asked.

His mother sniffled and shrugged. "You're driving."

The old van lacked Bluetooth, so he searched frequencies until he found classical music. The sun set behind them before they made it out of Nevada. Later than night, Adam pulled over when he couldn't stop nodding off. His mother drove for a few hours while he slept. They stopped only to switch drivers, eat or use a truck stop bathroom.

It was late the following day when they finally pulled into their driveway in Pueblo, Colorado.

Adam carried a sleeping Lily to her bed, while his mother ran to the bathroom in a fit of hacking coughs.

Once everything settled, he tried calling his father, but didn't get an answer. He called Millennium Hills Hospital. The nurse said his father remained in the operating room and advised him to call back in the morning.

Adam retrieved his cello from the van and carried it inside the house, then out the back door onto the porch. He often played outside late at night. The music carried across the suburban neighbourhood, but no one ever complained.

He got out his bow, straddled his cello and played the most sorrowful version of Dido's lament possible.

The next morning, his mother knocked on the door.

"Adam, are you awake?"

"Yeah."

She opened the door, walked into his room and sat on the bed.

"I'm sorry."

He rubbed his eyes. "For what?"

"You were strong yesterday." She paused to cough twice. "You took care of things while I just fell apart."

"No, you didn't."

"Yes, I did and I'm sorry." She pulled a tissue out of her housecoat and coughed into it. "Your stronger and tougher than you or your father thinks."

He didn't know what to say.

She squeezed his hand. "I made some phone calls this morning. The doctor said they operated on him and he is in recovery."

She looked away and blinked rapidly.

The doorbell rang.

"Aunt Lena is here," she said and stood up. The tissue in her hand fell to the floor.

She hacked and coughed as she left the room.

Adam sat up and stretched. He picked up the tissue and was about to throw it in the trash when he noticed something. The tissue was red with blood.

He threw it away and got dressed. Before leaving his room, he checked his phone.

A message from Indie appeared.

<Where r u? R U OK?>

<My dad was shot>

<that's terrible! Is he ok?>

<I don't know. I'm back in Colorado, but he's still in Las Vegas>

<What hospital?>

<Millennium>

<Did u want me to check on him?>

<You don't have to>

<Things are getting crazy here. I need to get out of downtown anyway>

<Have you heard anything about Piper?>

<No>

<Ok thanks>

Later, he sat at the dining room table with his mother and Aunt Lena while Lily played in her room.

Aunt Lena was his mom's younger sister. Throughout the years, she had several boyfriends, but never married. She lived only a few blocks away and was at their house for every birthday, Easter, Thanksgiving, Christmas and many weekends in between. Lily adored her and although she didn't live with them, she was part of their family.

His mother and Aunt Lena talked in serious, worried tones about his father, the economic collapse, cyberattacks and the president.

Adam interrupted their conversation. "I'm going back."

"Going back where?" Aunt Lena asked.

"I'm going back to Las Vegas."

His mother cleared her throat. "No, you're not."

"When they release Dad from the hospital, he will need a ride back home."

"I'm sure he can take a taxi or a bus."

"Taxis are expensive and the buses are probably not running."

"Where will you get gas?" Aunt Lena asked. "Stations in town are either crowded or closed."

"There is some gas in the extra tank."

"Enough for Las Vegas and back?" his mother inquired.

"I think so. Besides, when they get everything back up and running, I can buy more gas."

"You only have your learner's permit," said his mother. "You shouldn't be driving alone."

"Perhaps, *I* should go," said Aunt Lena.

"Mom and Lily need you here. I'm packing my things and going back to Las Vegas to get Dad."

After a brief, silent moment, his mother spoke. “I’ll pack you some food and get you some cash.”
“I may have some extra gas in my shed,” said Aunt Lena.

CHAPTER 14

The sandy, barren landscape of the Nevada desert looked different when viewed out the *front* window of the family van. The drive was lonely without his annoying family. As he left the signal range of the Pueblo radio station, the concerto on the radio faded.

Adam spun the tuner, trying to find a new station. A deep voice spouted the hourly news.

"Some are angry, claiming it was an assassination attempt. The video footage appears to implicate the leader of the opposition in the poisoning, although he is denying it and calling the whole thing a grand hoax. Countrywide protests have escalated into violence."

Adam shut off the radio and looked at his phone. The signal indicator blinked between one and two bars. For much of the trip, his phone either glitched out or didn't connect to a network.

The trip back to Las Vegas was long, quiet and boring. Every few hours, he stopped, napped, stretched, used the bathroom, refilled the gas tank or ate. When he ran out of his mother's sandwiches, he used the cash she gave him to buy food. He found many truck stops closed and a few still accepting cash for food.

As he neared Las Vegas, Adam pulled over and pulled out his phone to get directions to the hospital. It flashed twice and then shut down.

Using his mother's Las Vegas tourist map, Adam located the Millennium Hospital just off the highway on the north-west end of the city. The closer he got to Las Vegas, the more cars he saw. They were all driving away from the city.

As he neared the city limits, he saw flashing lights on the road ahead. Slowing, he watched emergency vehicles surrounding an overturned transport and another car in the ditch. An officer waved him around the accident. On the other side, he drove past a long line of vehicles waiting to get by. He located the highway exit that led to the hospital and turned onto it. A red indicator on the dash told him he was low on fuel. Fifteen minutes later, he found the hospital. The parking lot was at capacity and he drove around for another ten minutes looking for a side street to park on. After performing a parallel parking manoeuvre, his dad would be proud of, he looked at the dash. The gas needle was below the empty line.

He grabbed his phone and got out of the car. The sun overhead beat down, and it felt like a fireball was hovering inches above his head. By the time he reached the hospital, beads of sweat rolled down his face and back.

The temperature inside the Millennium hospital was only a little cooler. It was also busy. Adam had three hospital visits, all in small-town Pueblo. He didn't know if this was normal for a big city hospital.

Every chair in the waiting room was occupied. People lined the hallways, sat on the floor or stood against the walls. A bay wailed, a boy screamed, two women wept, and an elderly man screeched out in pain.

Adam shuffled through them and tried to get the attention of the receptionist.

"Excuse me! Hey! Where do I find..."

"Get in line!" the woman yelled.

"I'm just trying to find my father."

A man shoved him and a woman behind him yelled, while the receptionist talked to the sniffling lady at the front of the line. Adam pushed out of the mayhem and into a short hallway. A security guard argued with an angry woman holding a baby, and Adam scurried past them. He found an elevator and pressed the button. When it opened, he stepped inside. A nurse followed him and stood by the buttons.

"What floor?" she asked.

"I don't know. I'm looking for my father."

"Is he an out-patient or in surgery?"

"I think they operated on him last night."

She pressed the buttons for the 4th and 5th floors and smiled at him. "Recovery is on five."

He wandered around the fifth floor for five minutes before walking up to a nurse's station.

"Excuse me?" he said to the nurse typing intently into her computer.

She held up a finger and resumed her typing. She looked up tiredly a moment later.

"Sorry, what can I do for you, young man?"

"I'm looking for my father. He had surgery last night."

"Last name?"

"Sinclair."

"Gunshot to the chest?"

"Yes."

"Intensive care – 2nd floor."

Adam returned to the elevator and rode back down. He didn't know what *intensive care* meant, but it didn't sound good.

On the second floor, he found another nurses' station and asked about his father.

"Are you family?" the man asked.

"Yes, I'm his son."

"Down the hallway, 2nd room on the left. Room 222. Your sister is already in there."

"My sister?"

"Yes, she's been with him all day."

He walked down the hallway and stood by Room 222, but didn't enter.

His father was behind this door. He could be dying or already dead. What if driving down here was a bad idea? He should've waited for the hospital's call to confirm he was better.

The door opened and Indie almost knocked him over.

"You're here! Are you going in?"

"The nurse said my sister was here."

"I had to lie," she said with a grimace. "Only family is allowed to visit."

"Is he...okay?"

"He's in a coma right now."

"Is he going to make it?"

"The doctors aren't sure."

"Come sit with him." She led him inside.

Adam sat down beside the bed and stared at his father.

"You can talk to him," said Indie. "He can't speak, but he might be able to hear you."

She left the room, leaving Adam alone with his comatose father.

"I'm sorry, Dad." He took a deep breath and stared at him, fighting back the tears. "I'm sorry I wasn't brave like you. When you were fighting, I froze. I didn't know what to do. I should have helped, but I didn't. That man shot you while I sat inside the car like a scared little boy. You're right, I'm a pansy. I failed you. I'm sorry."

Tears streamed down his cheeks. He remained beside his father until a doctor arrived.

"Your sister said I should speak to you," he said. "I'm Doctor Grant."

Adam stood up and wiped his tears.

"Will he live?"

"The bullet missed his heart but hit an artery. He lost a lot of blood. Your father is in critical, but stable condition. Why don't you go home and we'll give you a call if anything changes."

"But I don't live here."

"You'll have to stay with your sister," he said before leaving.

He sat staring at his father for a long time.

Indie burst into the room. "Adam, I found her!"

"Found who?"

"Piper, but I think she's in trouble."

"What do you mean?"

"I have a friend whose sister knows a woman who's cousin's

neighbour works at the JCC."

"That sounds reliable," Adam said, his words dripping with sarcasm.

Indie continued. "She a teenage girl was being held there on firearms charges."

What's the JCC?"

"The Jane Conservation Camp is a minimum-security prison for women."

"Oh."

"The JCC, like the city and country, is deteriorating. I heard someone was murdered, an inmate was injured, and someone started a fire. Some of the staff and guards quit. The place is in total chaos."

"That's terrible."

Indie looked at Adam as if expecting him to say something.

"What?" he asked.

"What are you going to do?"

"Nothing. I'm sure the cops will get everything under control."

"Where have you been for the past twenty-four hours?" she yelled.

A nurse nearby shushed her and Indie continued in a loud whisper. "The city is in complete chaos. All the police are downtown trying to control the protests. Most businesses are closed, the buses and monorail are stopped and they closed the airport. Most tourists have scattered and the locals are either protesting or hiding in their homes."

"It's really that bad?"

"And getting worse."

"What am I supposed to do?"

"Do you love her?"

"We only met two days ago."

"And..."

"And I think she is the most wonderful, beautiful girl I've ever met and I would give anything to see her again."

"Then what are you waiting for?"

He pointed at his father. "What about my dad?"

"He's not going anywhere and the doctor can call you when he wakes up. Even if he recovered tomorrow, you won't be able to take him home for at least a week."

"I guess, but..."

"What would your father want you to do? I don't know him or your relationship with him. But you came back, so I know you love your father. What would his advice be if he were awake right now?"

"He would tell me not to be such a pansy and go find the girl already."

"So?"

Adam nodded slowly. "Yes," he said with growing confidence. "I am going to find Piper."

Indie smiled. "This is like when Wesley set out on a great adventure to rescue Buttercup."

"Who?"

"The Princess Bride."

"What is that?"

"You've never seen the Princess Bride? You need to get out more."

"How far is the JCC?"

"It's a half hour south of the city."

"I have a van, but I'm almost out of gas."

"No problem. We can meet up with Prospero. He isn't far."

"Where is he?"

"He's not doing too well."

"Why are you helping me?"

"A tale as old as time," she said dramatically. "Two young lovers separated by unforeseen circumstance. The fearless and handsome hero travels across perilous lands to rescue his one true love. This is a story I have to see in person. Also, I have nothing else to do. My family is on the East Coast, my friends are all hiding in their basements and my new boyfriend is probably passed out."

"You think I'm fearless and handsome?"

She playfully smacked his arm. "Go say goodbye to your

father."

Adam talked to the doctor again and gave the nurses his and Indie's phone numbers.

They left the hospital and walked to the van through the afternoon heat.

"Are you of driving age?" she inquired, getting in.

"I have my learner's permit."

"Should I drive?"

"The handsome hero can drive just fine."

He drove just one block before he almost killed both of them. A jeep tore through a red light and Adam slammed on the brake and cranked the wheel. The van screeched to a stop inches from a hydro pole.

As he backed up, two men with baseball bats strode down the sidewalk towards them.

"Go, go, go!" Indie shouted.

"What is wrong with people?" he shouted.

The tires squealed as he tore out of the intersection.

"I told you the city is falling apart."

"What did they want?"

"Gas is scarce and so are the police. People are carjacking any vehicle with fuel so they can escape the city."

She directed him to a small mini-mall a few blocks away. A half block before the mall, the van sputtered and died.

"We're out of gas," he said.

"Take anything useful out of the van. We'll have to walk from here."

Adam stuffed some clothes, water bottles and the remainder of the food his mother packed for him into a backpack and followed Indie to the mall. The five-minute walk in the stifling afternoon heat was almost unbearable.

"Where are we going?"

She pointed to a small Irish pub at the end of the plaza. Prospero's banana-yellow Porsche was the only vehicle in the parking lot.

"Why is he here?" Adam asked.

"Probably for the free booze."

She pushed the door to O'Reilly's Irish Pub open and went inside.

A row of booths lined one wall and a long wooden bar lined the other. The room had a dozen round tables with ornate chairs in the centre, along with a pool table and a dart board at the back. Prospero sat alone on a stool; his body slumped on the glossy bar. His hands still clutched a half-empty bottle of Scotch.

Indie slapped him on the back. "Wake up!" she yelled.

He sat up with a start and slid his long, dark, greasy hair off his face. "What?"

"Sober up, we have to help Adam find his girlfriend."

"Why? What's the point? Everything is gone."

"Only your money is gone. You need to stop feeling sorry for yourself and help our friend."

He stretched his eyes open and blinked. "Didn't we just meet him yesterday?"

"Yes, and you met me the day before."

"That's right. Why should I help you?"

He lifted the bottle off the bar, but Indie smacked it out of his hands. It crashed to the floor behind the bar.

"You should help me because you like me. Also, since you lost everything, at least you know I'm not with you for your money."

He nodded and Adam wondered if he was agreeing or trying to stay awake.

"You like me?"

"Despite your current lack of likability, your dancing abilities are impressive."

Prospero smirked. "That was a fun night until…"

"If you want to stay in this empty bar and drink yourself stupid, that is your choice. Can we at least borrow your car?"

He fished the keys from his pocket and slid off the stool. "I'm coming."

"Okay, but you can't drive in your…"

Two men, armed with baseball bats, burst in.

"I need the keys to that Porsche," said the bigger man.

Adam clenched his fists, while Indie grabbed an empty bottle of Jack Daniels from the bar.

Prospero eyed them for a moment before throwing the keys at the intruders. The man caught them in the air and smiled. "Thanks!"

They exchanged glances, shrugged, and departed.

"Why did you do that?" Indie asked. "That was our ride."

"I'm drunk, you're a woman and he's a skinny teenager. We didn't stand a chance against those thugs."

"That's sexist."

"I'm not skinny."

"And I have other cars."

Prospero beckoned them to follow as he stumbled past the pool table and dartboard and into a small hallway at the back. Adam grabbed a pool cue and followed him.

Prospero quickly took a key from a hook in a small office before leaving the pub.

Outside, he pointed to a green four-door sedan. "We can borrow the manager's car," he mumbled.

Indie snatched the keys out of his hand. "*I* will drive."

She drove, with Prospero in the passenger seat and Adam in the back.

Prospero glanced at Adam through the rear-view mirror. "Why the pool cue?"

"If this is the end of the world, I might need a weapon."

"Phhhhft." Prospero gave a dismissing wave.

As they neared the strip, the number of people on the streets increased. Many carried protest signs, bats, hockey sticks, crow-bars, hammers and other make-shift weapons.

"Looks like I'm not the only one arming themselves?" said Adam.

"You'd think zombies were roaming the streets," said Prospero.

"Don't you guys listen to the news?" asked Indie. "The right believes the left poisoned the president and they have the video evidence to prove it. The left says the video is fake and the vice president is the next in line for the president. Both factions are holding massive protests and anti-protests. Since our economic system is crumbling, people are scared, angry and confused. The political divide was already wide – now it's worse."

"That sounds bad," said Adam.

Prospero snored as he leaned against the window.

Moments later, a man wearing a red bandana guided a small group across the street. He held a pistol at his side. Indie stopped the car.

"Prospero, wake up! We've got trouble."

He sat up and rubbed his eyes. "Why doesn't Adam fight them with his pool cue?"

Bandana man stopped in the middle of the road and stared at their car. He kept his pistol pointed at Indie as he walked up to her window and motioned for her to lower it. A group of five men and three women surrounded the car.

"This isn't good," Indie said under her breath and lowered the window.

The man pointed his pistol at her head. "Any weapons in the car?"

"No," she answered in a shaky voice.

"He's got a pool cue." Prospero pointed at Adam in the backseat.

"But I'm *not* prepared to use it," said Adam.

"Red or Blue?" the man asked.

"What?"

"Are you red or blue?"

"Neither," Indie answered.

"What about you two?" the man pointed at Prospero and Adam. "Whose side are you on?"

"I'm on your side," said Prospero.

"I'm too young to vote," said Adam.

"We need to commandeer your vehicle, ma'am. This is a matter of national security."

"National security?"

He poked his gun through the window. "Get out of the car!"

"Okay, don't shoot." Indie opened her door and stepped out.

A tall man with a thin moustache and a creepy smile knocked on Adam's window. With trembling hands, he placed the cue stick on the floor and opened the door. His heart thumped hard against his chest as if trying to free itself from the rib cage. So far, his bladder held.

He grabbed his backpack, pushed the door open and stepped out.

Someone opened Prospero's door, and he fell out of the car before joining Adam and Indie. They watched their car drive away.

"I need another drink," said Prospero.

A group of six protestors dressed in red and carrying signs walked down the sidewalk. Across the street, four other protestors in blue yelled insults at them. Both groups walked towards downtown.

Prospero sat down and leaned against a fire hydrant.

"What are you doing?" asked Indie.

"I'm taking a break. It's hot out here."

Indie looked at Adam. "We need to stop for the night until he's sober."

"The Santa Maria," said Prospero, still sitting on the ground. "We need to go to the Santa Maria."

"What is that?" asked Indie.

"Isn't that one of Columbus's ships?" asked Adam.

Prospero pointed down the street. "It's my hotel."

"You mean you stay there a lot?" asked Adam.

"No, I mean I own it."

CHAPTER 15

Adam looked out the window of the top floor of the Santa Maria Hotel. The morning sun climbed up the Las Vegas buildings like a ghostly harbinger of heat. The street below was quiet, except for a few vehicles and a homeless woman. Just a few days earlier, Adam sat in the family van as his father weaved through heavy traffic. Things changed so fast. One minute, he worried about hitting all the notes on the cello for his big performance while driving with his annoying family. Now his father was dying while he was trying to find a girl in a chaotic city.

"Are you thinking about her?" Indie stood beside him at the window.

"Who?"

"Piper. The girl we are rescuing."

"Yeah."

She grabbed his arm and led him back into the room. "Come have some breakfast while we plan our day."

He looked down at the stale bagels and tiny jam and peanut butter packages on the table.

Prospero stood beside him. "No eggs today?"

"We're lucky we have anything," said Indie. "The manager said they have more jam, but that's the last of the bagels.

He slid his long dark hair off his face and sat down. "We better enjoy it while it lasts."

Adam sat down across from him. "Don't you have a hangover? You were totally out of it yesterday."

"Today is a new day! I am determined to make the most out of an unpleasant situation."

"Didn't you lose all your money or something?" asked Adam.

"No. I *gained* all the money. Everyone else lost theirs. I did not make it this far in life without resilience, determination and resourcefulness."

Indie sipped her tea. "Does that mean you have a way to get to the JCC?"

"What's the JCC?" asked Prospero.

"That's where they're holding Piper." She looked at him with incredulity. "That's where we're going, remember?"

"First, we need to make a stop at the Link."

"That's on the strip," said Indie. "The news says it's full of protestors."

"Isn't the JCC south of the city?" he asked. "The strip is on the way."

"Why do you need to stop at the Link?"

"Although I haven't spoken with Jerry in years, I bet he's hanging out at his favourite place, and I still need his help."

Indie bit into her toast. "I thought the Secret Service guys whisked him away. Shouldn't he be in some sort of secret underground facility somewhere?"

"Possibly, but I bet they extracted all the information out of him before letting him go."

"What's the Link?" asked Adam.

"Did you see the giant Ferris wheel?" Indie asked.

"Yeah."

"The Link Hotel and Casino are right below the Big Spin observation wheel and right in the middle of Las Vegas."

Prospero finished his coffee. "I can get us another vehicle and we can drop by the Link, ask Jerry how to avoid a financial apocalypse and then help you rescue your girlfriend."

The shrill, high-pitched beeps of an emergency alert went off and Indie and Prospero grabbed their phones.

"What's going on?" asked Adam.

"Can't you see it on your phone?" asked Prospero.

Adam grabbed his phone and turned it on. It flickered but did not light up. "My phone's not working."

Prospero read from his phone. "As of six o'clock tonight,

they are declaring a state of martial law. Everyone must stay indoors from sunset until sunrise. This is a temporary measure..."

Indie interrupted him. "We need to leave now if we want to rescue the princess before the sun sets on Florin."

"Where?"

"The Kingdom of Florin from The Princess Bride...never mind. Let's go."

After breakfast, Prospero offered the manager of the hotel a million dollars for his SUV.

Twenty minutes later, they drove out of the Santa Maria Hotel parking lot.

"How is your hotel still operating when so many other businesses have shut down?" asked Indie.

Prospero turned the wheel of the SUV and drove onto the highway on-ramp. "The manager and a few of the employees were promised a share of the hotel if they remained at their post."

"You're giving up ownership?" asked Indie.

"It wasn't my idea."

"I thought it was your hotel. Who promised them that?"

"Prospero Junior."

Adam stared out the window at the empty highway.

"Where are all the cars? Did everyone already run out of gas?"

"Not everyone." Prospero pointed across the highway at the five lanes going in the opposite direction. Bumper-to-bumper traffic filled all the lanes as everyone tried to escape the city.

Five minutes later, they passed an airport. Across the chain-link fence, a small Cessna taxied down the runway.

"I thought you said the airport was closed," said Adam from the backseat.

"That's just a small regional airport with mostly private planes and charters."

"Do you have a private plane?" Adam asked.

"Of course," said Prospero.

"Are you really a billionaire?" he asked.

Prospero flicked his hair back. "Don't I look like one?"

"Not really. I thought billionaires had entourages, personal secretaries, drivers and servants that catered to their every whim. Also, I've never heard of you."

"I have an AI that manages my businesses and personal affairs. It also keeps me out of the media spotlight."

"If it's so powerful, why can't you ask it to order you a ride or contact Jerry or something?"

"Even if I could, I don't trust Prospero Junior. It's a powerful independent AI that has gone rogue. And it knows everything about me. If it decided I was no longer useful, I have no doubt that it could find a way to eliminate me."

"Do you think that's what happened to the President?" asked Indie.

"I don't know how that could be related, but anything is possible."

Ahead, lights flashed, and emergency vehicles gathered around an accident at the next exit.

As they slowly rolled by, Prospero said, "That was our exit. We'll have to take the next one and drive the length of the strip."

A few minutes later, they exited the highway and immediately slowed as they drove up to a roadblock. Two big tour buses blocked the road. A group of heavily armed men and women stood in front.

"This looks bad," said Indie.

Prospero lowered his window. "Let's find out what's going on."

An overweight man with a bushy beard and shotgun at his side lumbered up to the SUV. He leaned over and looked inside.

"You folks here to join the fight?"

"Is there a war going on that we don't know about?" Prospero asked.

"We are preparing to defend our freedom," he said, raising his chin.

"That's nice. We're just passing through."

The man scratched his beard. "No one is passing through. You can either go around or join the revolution."

"Revolution? Two days into the apocalypse and you've already started a revolution?"

"We have no other option. First, the right-wingers stole our money. Now the government is going to remove our freedoms. This is all part of their plan to instil a fascist state."

"What freedoms?"

"As part of the new martial law rules, they are essentially locking people up in their homes. But all law-abiding, freedom-loving citizens of this country are mobilizing. We will march down the Strip and nobody can stop us!"

"That's nice," said Prospero. "We just need to make a quick run to the Link to meet with somebody."

"Good luck with that! The streets are filling with protestors. You won't make it one block in this SUV."

Prospero turned to Indie. "I guess we're walking."

The bearded man stepped back as they got out and pointed at Adam. "You might want to change your shirt."

Adam looked down at his shirt. It seemed like a normal red, buttoned shirt with a chest pocket and collars. He pinched the material and brought it to his nose. "Does it smell that bad?"

"It's red," said the man.

"What's wrong with it?" asked Indie.

"It is kind of a dorky shirt," said Prospero. "I'm with Big Beard."

"Look around you," said the man. "You're in blue country."

The other roadblock guards with guns wore blue shirts, ball caps or bandanas. Others walking along the road or talking on the sidewalk all wore blue.

"If you're wearing red, people will think you're rooting for the wrong team."

Two other guards carrying a long gun and pistol leaned against the bus and stood up when they spotted Adam.

"Take your shirt off," said Indie.

Adam removed his backpack and struggled with the buttons as he scrambled to remove his shirt. He threw it to the ground as the two guards approached.

One of them smiled at him. "Good choice."

Adam wrapped his arms around his body in a self-conscious hug. He was sure everyone would laugh at his skinny upper body. It reminded him of the locker room of his Grade 9 gym class. The other boys mocked him relentlessly for his scrawny physique, including a visible rib cage. His muscles had filled out a little since then, but his self-esteem issues had not.

Indie looked at him for a second, but Adam couldn't read her expression.

"We need to find another shirt," she said. "You'll be burnt in five minutes and develop skin cancer in ten."

"They're selling shirts in the Neon Oasis." He pointed behind him. "Through the buses and turn left. Just follow the crowd."

"Come on." Prospero led through the small gap between the tour buses.

Adam grabbed his backpack and followed, still hugging himself.

"What is the Neon Oasis?"

"It's an entertainment street and pedestrian mall in the heart of old Las Vegas. They have live entertainment, zip lines, historic casinos, shops, street performers and an arched roof that is a massive video screen. I worked down here last year for a couple of weeks. It gets a little crazy at night, but lots of fun."

They followed the flow of pedestrians until they reached the entrance to the pedestrian mall. The massive video screen hung over ninety feet above the ground, was ninety feet wide and stretched over thirteen hundred feet along the pedestrian walkway.

A small kiosk outside gave away protest signs and various blue attire. Prospero walked up to the woman standing in front of the kiosk.

"How much for a blue shirt?"

"Fifty bucks."

"That's crazy!" Prospero pulled out his wallet and removed a credit card.

She held up her hand. "Cash or gold only. Digital money is

worthless."

He turned to Indie and Adam. "Do either of you have any cash?"

"I spent what my mother gave me on food," Adam said.

Indie reached into her pocket and pulled out a wad of cash. "Lucky for you guys, I work in a cash only business."

She pointed to a shiny blue sequined shirt. "We'll take that one."

"I am not wearing that," said Adam. "That looks like I'm going to a late-night rave."

"I'm paying, and this is my choice." She grabbed the shirt and tossed it to Adam.

He reluctantly put the glittery blue shirt on. At least it covered his inadequate physique.

Prospero stood back and gave him the *thumbs up*. "Lookin' good!"

Adam couldn't tell if he was being sarcastic.

Indie looked down at her phone and tapped the screen.

"What are we doing now?" Prospero asked her.

"It will take us less than two hours to walk to the Link from here."

"That's a long time to walk in the Nevada sun."

"What else are we going to do?"

"I don't know, can't we call an Uber?"

"Very funny. Do you have any good ideas?"

"Can't we pay someone to drive us there?"

"Money can't solve every problem, Prospero. It was your lust for money that caused all this mayhem."

"This wasn't all my fault."

As they talked, Adam looked at the Neon Oasis pedestrian mall. On the right side of the walkway, a woman in black leather worked behind a long outdoor bar tucked under the awning of a casino. Colourful, slushy machines lined the wall behind her. Several men and a few women talked and drank at the bar. On the left side of the walkway, a thin man with a black fedora caressed a fat yellow python draped over his shoulders.

The screen above the walkway looked like an artificial sky. It lit up with an image of three F-14 Tomcats zooming down the screen as if flying above the street. The smoky contrail dissipated and waving American flags filled the screen. Bob Dylan sang *Blowin' in the Wind* over large speakers setup on the street.

"Whoa, this is so cool."

Prospero and Indie paused their discussion and looked at Adam.

"What do *you* want to do?" asked Indie.

The screen changed to an aquarium scene with colourful fish and coral. A shark appeared and chased the fish beyond his view.

"Can we go in there?"

"We are not here on a sightseeing tour," said Prospero. "That street is teeming with angry radical liberals."

"It is on the way," offered Indie. "If we go around the street, it would add another ten minutes to our time."

"Pushing our way through that crowd does not seem like a shortcut," said Prospero.

Bang!

A single gunshot rang out behind them. A couple of people immediately drew their guns and pointed toward the shot. Some ducked behind garbage cans, hydro poles or other people. Others ran to find cover.

Prospero and Indie ducked down, but Adam froze in fear. He wanted to run, duck, dive, or lie flat on the ground, but he remained affixed to the sidewalk. The memory of sitting motionless in the van while his father fought at the gas station flashed in his mind. With a determined force of will, he finally thawed his fear and forced his legs to move.

He ran towards the long bar under the casino awning. People screamed and ran in every direction as Adam leapt over the bar. He envisioned a heroic jump over the bar, but in actuality, it turned into a clumsy tumble. Someone already hiding behind the bar cushioned his landing. He hoped it was the bartender in black leather, but instead, he dropped onto a sweaty overweight man in camouflage pants and a muscle shirt.

The man shoved him off with a grunt. Adam looked up in time to see Indie fly over the bar and land gracefully beside him. A moment later, Prospero dove over the bar, crashing headfirst into the slushy machines. He scrambled to the bar beside Adam.

They huddled together with a dozen others. A few poked their heads up, peering over the bar and pointing their weapons at an unknown threat.

The man in the muscle shirt cocked his rifle. "I'll provide cover. You guys need to run. Okay...Now!"

He stood up, panning his weapon, and a few others joined him. The others ran out from the bar into the pedestrian mall.

Adam crouched and ran with them as Prospero, and Indie followed. People screamed, shouted, and ran, but no more shots rang out.

They were deep into the fleeing crowd when the Dylan music on the speakers stopped. A woman's voice said, "Please remain calm. That was a false alarm. The shot you heard was accidental. Please ensure the safety on your weapons is engaged at all times."

The Dylan continued his nasally crooning, and people stopped running and screaming.

"What now?" asked Indie. "Do we go back or try to push through?"

People talked and moved about, with the majority progressing down the walkway.

"I don't know." Prospero looked at Adam. "What do *you* think?"

The question surprised Adam. At school, he was usually a loner or a follower. Nobody asked his opinion on what game to play, where he wanted to go for lunch, or what he thought of the new teacher. Now two older people stared at him, waiting for his opinion on their next move.

"Let's keep going?" It was as much a question as a statement.

Prospero shrugged.

"Okay," he said and led them into the Neon Oasis.

A man popped up from behind the counter at a kiosk in front of them and looked around. He smiled and pointed at Adam.

"Nice shirt, buddy. Do you want a glittery hat to go with your outfit? I got hats, belts, watches, wallets, rings and sunglasses."

Adam waved him off and kept walking. "No, thanks."

A busty woman in cowboy boots, tiny torn denim shorts, and a revealing white ruffled crop top pointed her whip at Adam and Prospero.

"Hey boys! Are you looking for a good time?"

Her expression changed from alluring to surprise when she looked behind them.

"Indie? Is that you?"

Indie ran ahead and hugged the cowgirl. "Jasmine, it's so good to see you. How have you been?"

"Still working," she answered.

"Why? This city is descending into anarchy and you're still performing?"

"What else am I going to do? Hide in my apartment? I'll still need money when this is all over."

"I guess."

Jasmine pointed at Prospero and Adam. "Who are these guys? Are you joining the revolution or whatever this is?"

"We are helping Adam rescue his true love from prison."

"Okay...good luck!"

"It's so good to see you again. Do you want to come with us? The city isn't safe anymore."

"This city was never safe," said Jasmine. "But it's all I know."

"I understand. If you need anything, give me a call, okay?"

"I will."

They embraced again and said their goodbyes.

A few minutes later, the trio continued walking through the Neon Oasis.

Fewer street performers lined the walkway, and the crowds became denser as they moved deeper into the street. A tall man in a bright blue cowboy hat nodded at them as he passed. The excited throng of people looked like the waves in a stormy sea. People dressed in shades of various shades of blue moved like cobalt swells in an angry ocean.

Adam looked up at the kaleidoscope of shapes and colours morphing across the screen above them. Suddenly, someone screamed and two girls whizzed above them on a zip line.

Suddenly, the screen turned completely blue, and the music stopped. The walkway quieted and most people looked up. A fluttering American flag appeared on the screen and a deep voice boomed across the Neon Oasis.

"Please remove your hats and rise for the national anthem."

The crowd silenced and people removed their hats and many placed their hands over their hearts.

A military snare drum rolled before a full orchestra erupted in a rousing rendition of the Star-Spangled Banner. Adam closed his eyes, and let the music envelop him.

When it finished, Prospero nudged him. "Hey, are you sleeping or something?"

"No, I was just listening."

"What were you doing with your fingers?" asked Indie.

"I was playing along."

"Thank you everyone for coming," said a voice over the speakers.

Adam pushed onto his toes and saw a stage where a man in a fancy suit spoke into a microphone.

"Our country is under threat. Our rights are under threat. The selfish, right-wing bullies are trying to turn this country into a fascist state. They want to kick out the immigrants, give everyone guns, and discriminate against anyone different. It is their capitalist greed that created this dark day that our great nation is facing today. But we won't stand for it. We say ENOUGH! We declare in one voice: We will not go quietly into the night! We will not vanish without a fight!"

The crowd roared.

"I've heard that speech before," said Indie. "I think it's from a movie."

"Let's keep moving," said Prospero.

The trio weaved through the excited throng as the speech continued. The crowds thinned as they moved further from the stage. Eventually, they found the end of the Neon Oasis walkway and emerged back into the city and the blazing afternoon sun. A zip line tower loomed overhead. Cables extended out and disappeared into the Oasis behind them.

"That looks like fun," said Prospero.

"Not for me," said Adam.

"You've never ziplined before?" asked Indie.

"I prefer to stay on the ground."

Adam regretted speaking and wondered if he should have lied. They probably thought he was a wimp.

If they did, neither of them said it.

They walked for two blocks until Indie pointed to the right. "This way."

In the distance, Adam saw a slender tower that reminded him of a picture of the CN Tower in Canada.

"Is that tower near the Link?"

"You mean the Skyline Tower?" asked Indie. "No, that's about halfway."

Fewer people roamed the streets, and many moved towards the Oasis. A lot of them carried guns.

All the windows of a pawnshop on the right lay in shattered fragments on the sidewalk. Inside, the shelves lay empty.

On the left, a small group fought on the first floor balcony of a motel. A man screamed as someone shoved him over the railing. He landed on the pavement below with a crunch.

"Where are the cops?" asked Prospero.

"I don't know, but we need to keep moving," said Indie.

The others agreed and continued at a faster pace. Adam considered suggesting they run, but the oppressive heat made that almost impossible. Sweat gathered on his back under his pack. He wiped the moisture off his brow and kept walking.

Nobody stopped them for another thirty minutes. As they neared the Skyline tower, Prospero said, "I found the cops!"

Dozens of police blocked the street. Many wore body armour and carried shields.

"This should be interesting," said Prospero.

"Can we go around?" Adam pointed to the parking lot on the left. As they walked closer, they saw more police standing about ten feet apart in a line that stretched until the next building. Beyond the line, more police patrolled the street.

Prospero strode forward. "I'm going to find out what's going on."

Adam and Indie followed a few timid steps behind.

"Please stay back!" barked an officer as Prospero approached.

"We are not protestors and only want to get to the Link to meet someone."

"The Strip is off limits right now!"

"I live here and I have rights." Prospero crossed his arms. "You can't stop me from going home."

"Turn around and go back to your home."

"I told you my home is on the other side of this blockade."

"Not my problem. Turn around and leave the area."

The officer gripped the baton in his belt.

"You can't do this! This is America and I have rights!"

A small group nearby watched and cheered.

"Give 'em hell!" one shouted.

"You can't arrest me for walking." He unfolded his arms.

"The President declared martial law. We can detain whoever we want."

He slid the baton from its clip and slapped it against his palm.

Someone tossed a shoe at the line of police and others shouted.

"Martial law doesn't start until sunset," said Prospero as he stepped forward.

The growing crowd moved in closer to the commotion.

The officer whipped his club, smacking Prospero across his right arm. He yelped in pain and tried to step back. Instead, he tripped and fell backwards and the officer pounced. He continued to beat Prospero on his arms and back. Adam watched in motionless horror as Prospero cried out and raised his arms to protect his face. The crowd lobbed more objects and insults as the police watched and waited for any of them to come within reach of their batons.

"Leave him alone!" screamed Indie. She moved towards Prospero and his abuser as another officer stepped forward. The second officer raised his baton and eyed Indie's head.

Adam's mind flashed to his father getting beaten outside the van while his sister and mother screamed and cried while he remained in his seat.

"Nooooo!" Adam screeched. He wanted desperately to rush forward and tackle the officer, preventing him from hurting Indie. But the officer was fifty pounds heavier, covered in body armour and trained to take down wimps like him. His body shook with fear as he tried in vain to muster the courage to stand up for his friends.

He watched in horror as the officer's baton swung towards Indie's head. Just before it impacted her skull, a hand reached out and caught it.

A heavy-set man with dark stubble and dirty blue ball cap caught the baton and held it with an iron grip.

"Leave her alone!" he growled as the officer attempted to wrench the baton free.

More protestors stepped closer, and the other police closed in. The officer beating Prospero paused and looked up.

"Okay, that's enough!" someone yelled. "Break it up. Officers, get back to your posts. Everyone else back up!"

A burly policeman with a service cap and a three-stripe chevron on his shoulder yelled again. "That's an order."

The officer with the baton and the big man with the ball cap stared each other down for a few seconds before the big man released the baton.

The officers slowly retreated as the crowd cheered and yelled insults.

A hand slapped Adam's back so hard he almost fell forward.

"We got your and your friend's backs, buddy," said the guy in the blue ball cap. "Your shirt is a little gaudy, but at least it's the right colour."

Adam nodded and smiled.

Indie knelt down beside Prospero. "Are you okay? Where does it hurt?"

"Everywhere," he moaned.

She looked up at Adam, who was still trying to process what had happened.

"Give me a hand."

He helped her pull Prospero to his feet.

"Can you walk?" she asked.

Blood dripped down Prospero's head and he held onto his side. "I think so."

"We should find a hospital," suggested Indie.

"No! It's not that bad and we're not going back after we made it this far."

"Okay, but let's get you out of the sun and find a first aid kit."

Indie and Adam helped Prospero limp away from the blockade, to the entrance of the Skyline Tower Hotel and Casino.

A few people talked in huddled groups throughout the lobby. One woman stood behind a reception counter containing fifteen other empty check-in computers. Her gold nameplate read, Parvati.

"Are you looking for a room?" she asked.

"You mean you're open?" asked Indie. "I thought everything was closed."

Parvati smiled. "We are booking rooms on the first and second floors and are only accepting cash. It's $500 per night and we require a $500 deposit."

"Who carries that kind of cash?" asked Indie.

"I'm sorry, but our credit and debit card systems are down right now. Until things get back to normal, it is the only way we can accept payment."

Prospero held his head and wavered on his feet. "I need to sit down," he groaned.

"I got him," Adam said to Indie and helped him to a nearby chair.

Indie continued to talk with the receptionist.

"We just need a place to stay. My friend is hurt really badly, and we have nowhere else to go."

"You should take him to the hospital."

"We can't. It's too far." Indie leaned closer to Parvati and whispered, "My friend is a billionaire who owns a lot of places in Las Vegas. He will reimburse you personally if you help him out."

"I'm sorry, but I can't help you," said Parvati.

"Here," Prospero groaned from the chair. He unclasped his watch and held it out.

Adam took it and brought it to the counter.

"That's a nice watch," said Parvati. "But what do you want me to do with it?"

"It's a Breitling Navitimer," said Prospero. "It's worth eight thousand dollars. Look it up."

Parvati shot him a skeptical squint before pulling out her phone.

A minute later, she sighed. "Okay, but only one night."

"One more thing," said Indie. "Do you have a first aid kit?"

CHAPTER 16

The view out the 3rd floor window of the Skyline Tower Hotel differed from the view from the ground floor room of the Las Vegas Honeymoon Hotel. Instead of a cracked pavement parking lot, an old picnic table and a faded sign on a rusty chain, Adam saw sparkly Casinos, glistening hotels, and high-definition LED signs.

Behind him, Prospero lay on the couch with a white bandage wrapped around his head, tapping his phone. The sound of running water stopped from the washroom where Indie took a shower.

Adam looked at the Las Vegas strip below as a growing crowd of protestors gathered at the police blockade. Movement on the police line caught his attention.

"Something is happening down there," he said.

"That's an understatement," said Prospero, without looking up from his phone.

Indie stepped out of the washroom in a bathrobe, dabbing at her wet hair. "What's going on?"

Adam pointed out the window at the blockade below. "Look."

She joined him at the window, and they watched as three green army trucks drove up to the blockade and stopped. Over a dozen infantry jumped out of the back of each. They ran to the blockade and stood beside the police who began to back away. Police vans pulled in as more army vehicles arrived.

"It looks like the cops are leaving and the army is taking over," said Indie.

"Do you think that will settle things down or make it worse?" asked Adam.

"I don't know."

"What are we going to do about food?" asked Prospero. "I called the hotel restaurants, but none of them were open. Also, none of the food delivery apps are working. We need to find something to eat."

"You're not going anywhere today," said Indie. "Your head is still bleeding, and you probably bruised a rib. Adam and I are going to look for some food. I still have a little cash. Maybe we can find a grocery store or something. "What time is it?"

Prospero looked at his phone. "Four-thirty, why?"

"Martial law doesn't start until six-thirty so that gives us two hours."

"I'll bring my backpack," said Adam.

Twenty minutes later, Indie and Adam stepped out of the hotel and back into the late afternoon heat. The closest grocery store was a half hour walk, which didn't leave them much time before martial law started.

"What happens with martial law?" asked Adam as they speed walked down the sidewalk. "Do they start arresting everyone?"

"I don't know. Let's find some food and get back to the hotel before that happens. If we take Mojave Street east, we should find Smit's Grocer. I used to work near there."

The streets and sidewalks were busier than before, but people moved faster, and a sense of tension filled the air.

"I'm sorry about before." Adam stared ahead, ashamed to look her in the eye.

"What are you talking about?" she asked.

"At the blockade...I just stood there while they beat Prospero and that cop almost hit you."

"But he didn't hit me. That guy stopped him."

Adam swallowed. "It should have been me."

"If you stepped in, they would have beaten you too. You're just a kid."

"I'm seventeen."

"Yes, but some people aren't built for physical confrontation."

Her words stung. It sounded like a politically correct way of saying he was a wimp.

"And *you* are built for physical confrontation?" he yelled the question.

"I didn't say that."

He shook his head but didn't respond.

They walked in silence until they reached Smit's Grocer. A man with a full cart of groceries burst out the front entrance and across the parking lot. A moment later, a security guard ran after him.

"Sir, come back! You can't do that!"

"I paid for these and I'm taking them," the man said as he continued to his truck.

"There are limits for a reason."

Another woman pushed her cart out the entrance and furtively glanced in both directions before racing her cart into the parking lot.

"We should hurry," said Indie.

"Yeah, we don't want to get into a confrontation or else I'll get beat up."

"Are you still angry about that?"

"You said I was a wimp."

She rolled her eyes. "I didn't say that. We can talk about this later. Let's get our food before things here get worse."

They entered the grocery store, and Adam and Indie grabbed two of the last remaining carts. The lineup to the registers stretched out to the frozen food section along the far wall. Dozens of customers scrambled through the store like ants exposed by an overturned rock.

He wheeled it into the produce section and was almost run over by a woman pushing her cart with a toddler inside. Indie rolled along behind him.

"How much money do you have?" he asked as he navigated around a minefield of apples and mandarin oranges strewn across the floor.

"I have two hundred bucks. We should split up and meet at the cash registers in ten minutes. Just grab stuff we can carry and don't have to cook."

She veered her cart away from Adam and disappeared into the store.

Adam stood in the middle of the produce aisle and looked around. He went to the grocery store a couple of times with his mother when he was younger, but never alone. Other than macaroni and cheese and the occasional grilled cheese, he'd never cooked either. This wasn't something he would tell Indie. She already thought he was a wuss and didn't want to add *uselessness* to his list of shortcomings.

He searched through the black bananas before finding a bunch that were mostly yellow. After a quick scan of the area to make sure nobody was looking, he broke off the rotten bananas before placing the good ones in his cart. The carrots and lettuce looked rotten, but he found a bag of red delicious apples and a pineapple. He tossed a loaf of stale, but not yet mouldy bread in his cart and headed to the next aisle. A woman in a red hat leered at Adam and his blue sequined shirt. He found some white t-shirts in the corner and threw them in his cart. After removing the tag and placing it in his cart, he quickly changed into the white shirt and continued shopping.

He rolled by the cereals in the next aisle and wondered if there was any milk left. Someone at the front of the store yelled and someone else yelled back. The shouting seemed to spread like a disease and then a gunshot rang out.

The woman in front of Adam ducked behind her cart. A few others did the same, while one man ran to the back of the store. A second shot tore through the air.

Someone screamed, and everyone started running. Adam nabbed a giant bag of oatmeal and a box of raisin bran and wheeled his cart to the dairy section near the back. The end display contained bags of chocolate chips and he grabbed two.

"Indie!" he yelled, but doubted she could hear him over the noise.

People yelled, screamed, shouted and argued as the store descended quickly into mayhem. Adam opened the fridge and grabbed the last carton of milk. A man came up behind him and looked in the fridge before cursing loudly.

Adam scurried away in search of Indie. As he looked down the pasta aisle, the woman with the young child in her cart wheeled by him. A man in a dirty white tank top and baggy pants cut her off and looked in her cart.

"I'll take that!" he said with a sneer and reached for her carton of milk.

"Hey, that's mine!" she squealed and tried to pull it from his hands.

The kid in the cart looked as terrified as her mother.

Adam rushed forward and crashed into Tank Top's cart. "Give her back the milk!" he shouted.

The man released the milk and reached behind him. A large silver revolver appeared, and he smiled at Adam.

"Back off and mind your own business, kid."

Adam held his hands up. The mother used her arm to cover her whimpering child like an eagle protecting its chicks with an open wing.

"Are you really going to kill a mother in front of her child over a carton of milk?" Adam shouted.

The man paused for a moment. His eyes flicked from Adam to the woman and then to the sobbing child. He put the milk back in her cart and then grabbed the chocolate chips from Adam's. With a sneer and a grunt, he wheeled his cart away.

"Are you okay, ma'am?" asked Adam.

She sniffled and wiped her eyes. "Yes, thank you!"

He reached into his cart and pulled out his carton of milk. "Here, you need this more than me."

"Thank you so much." The woman turned to her child, who looked scared and confused. "Can you say thank you to the brave man?"

"Attention, customers," a muffled voice boomed over the intercom. "The police are handling the incident and everything is under control. You can resume your shopping. Just a reminder that there is a limit of one hundred dollars worth of groceries per customer and we are accepting cash only. Thank you and have a nice day."

"We'd better get going," said the woman.

Adam nodded and smiled.

"Hey, there you are!" yelled Indie. "I think we've reached our limit. Let's see if we can survive the checkout without getting shot."

They navigated the crowds of anxious shoppers to the lineup at the cash registers. The cue shortened considerably following the shooting. Blue and red lights flashed outside and two officers pushed a man into the back of a cruiser.

"I saw you stand up to the guy with the gun," said Indie as they waited.

"They reminded me of Lily and my mother. It was just instinct."

"He could have shot you."

"I didn't know he had a gun."

"Would you still have done it if you knew?"

"Probably not."

"I'm not sure if you were stupid or brave, but it was really nice of you to give them your milk."

"Thanks."

Outside, the cruiser's lights stopped flashing as it pulled out of the parking lot.

She looked in his cart. "Now we have to eat raisin bran without milk."

Adam shrugged. "The milk would go bad in this heat, anyway."

They paused their conversation as an argument at the cash register escalated.

Two men yelled as the cashier spoke quickly into his phone. Suddenly, one man pulled out his gun and pointed it at the terrified cashier.

A woman in another aisle turned and pointed her gun at the man. People screamed and ducked.

"Not again," Indie whispered as they ducked behind their cart.

A gunshot rang out from the back of the store. People yelled, screamed and cried. A woman pushed her cart towards the exit and a few others followed. Another gunshot went off, followed by a bottle crashing and then another gunshot.

"We need to get out of here," Indie whispered as she poked her head up.

One man ducked behind a cash register and traded fire with someone taking cover behind a coin-cashing kiosk. The line of fire tracked through the route to the front exit.

"We can't get out the front. When there is a pause in gunfire, we should make a break for the back."

Adam took deep breaths, trying to control his shaking. "Okay."

"We'll be faster with one cart," Indie said as she transferred the food from her cart to his.

After all the food was in one cart, Indie asked, "Do you want me to push the cart?"

He squeezed the cart handlebar. "No, I got it."

When the gunshots momentarily fell silent a moment later, Indie whispered, "Follow me!"

She crouch-walked quickly as Adam followed. They made it to the cleaning products aisle as more gunfire erupted behind them. At the end of the aisle, Indie peered out.

"There's a fight happening by the deli counter, but I think we can make it to the back door."

Adam followed her. He glanced at the deli counter as they ran and saw a body covered in blood lying on the floor. Chunks of deli meat and sausage lay strewn on the tile beside him. Adam hoped that's all it was.

Turning back, he saw Indie and stopped just in time to not run into her. A growing bottleneck of escapees gathered at the double swinging doors.

"We'll never get the cart through there," said Adam as he removed his backpack.

She helped him stash as much of their food into the backpack as possible before hoisting it on his back. She carried the bag of apples and a case of canned tuna, and they joined the throng at the double doors. The storage room was loud as people fought over the food stacked against the walls.

They pushed through the crowd and spilled out the back of the grocery store onto the roadway behind. With the sun dipping below the horizon, the sky darkened to a deep indigo like the cloak of a lurking menace. More shots rang out from inside the store, prompting Adam and Indie to flee. They sprinted down the road and around the corner to the front of the grocery store but skidded to a stop. A gunshot rang out and the brickwork over their heads exploded, sending brick dust and fragments raining down. They both ducked and turned around.

"Go back!" Indie yelled as much for their benefit as others following them.

When they returned to the back of the grocery store, a man coming from the opposite direction yelled, "Don't go that way!"

Indie pointed to the five-foot-high brick wall lining the roadway along the back of the store. "Come on!"

They ran to the wall and Adam linked his fingers together and held out his hands like a step. "I'll give you a boost."

She looked down at the bag of apples and the case of canned tuna. After a frustrated sigh, Indie dropped the case and tossed the apples over the wall. He strained under her weight as she stepped on his hands and pushed her over. Adam reached up and grabbed the wall. Struggling to maintain his position, his arms flexed in an attempt to hold himself up, but he ultimately collapsed to the ground.

"Are you coming?" Indie called from the other side.

He backed up and took a couple of deep breaths before gritting his teeth and running at the wall. A step before he hit the bricks, he jumped. With a quick push up the wall with his foot, he grabbed the top of the wall. His momentum helped push him over the wall and he tumbled to the ground on the other side.

"We need to keep moving," she said, helping him to his feet.

He brushed himself off and looked up. Identical three-storey apartment buildings lined the tiny streets of the subdivision.

"You're not supposed to be here!" yelled a man from a second-storey balcony.

"Sorry, we're just passing through," yelled Indie.

They walked through the gated subdivision with leering eyes, watching them, before climbing a metal fence on the other side.

As Indie pulled out her phone to look at the map, a group of six men spotted them and walked their way.

"We need to get out of here," said Adam.

Indie looked up and put her phone back in her pocket. They ran in the opposite direction for two blocks until they were confident the group wasn't following them.

Adam leaned over with his hands on his knees, panting. Indie breathed heavily too and pushed her sweat-soaked hair off her face.

"I think we're going the wrong way," she said between breaths.

After resting for a moment, they checked the map on Indie's phone. It took them twenty minutes to walk back to Mojave street. The street lights flickered on as they trekked along the road.

Adam looked around at the street and sidewalks. "Everyone is off the streets. I'm assuming martial law is starting soon."

A small group huddled near the street corner, and a woman hurried along the sidewalk, but no protestors walked the streets.

Indie looked at her phone. "Martial law starts in five minutes. We're not going to make it."

"What happens to us with martial law?"

"The cops will arrest us."

"That doesn't sound too bad. I've been to jail before."

"Except the military is taking over and I don't think they'll be as nice. Also, you won't be able to save the girl from jail."

They made it back to the main road leading back to the Skyline hotel.

"I have an idea," said Indie, running down a side street.

Adam followed her towards a row of trees lining an open green area. "Where are we going?"

She climbed a small fence and led them across a golf green. "I'm finding us some transportation."

They dashed across the fairway to a group of brick buildings near the entrance. She ran behind one of the larger buildings. A pile of old tires sat beside broken plastic cart body parts and other old golf carts. Some sat askew on three tires, while others looked old and worn.

"I don't think any of these are going to work," said Adam.

Indie ignored him and ran to a cart in the corner with two tires and a missing seat. She reached underneath the cart and felt around until she found something.

"Got it!" she exclaimed and pulled out a large brass key.

Adam watched as she ran to the back door of the building and inserted the key.

"How did you…?"

She smiled and opened the door. "I used to work here."

They stepped inside, and Indie flicked on the light. Dozens of golf carts sat in neat rows. Yellow charging cords snaked out of many of the carts and connected to charging ports along the wall.

Indie unplugged a cart and hopped in. They drove out of the building across the golf course and back onto Mojave Street a few minutes later.

Indie looked down at her phone. "Keep an eye out for the cops. I think martial law has started."

The streets were quieter, but a few people still roamed the darkening streets.

On the road ahead of them, a young boy with a bulging backpack rode a black mountain bike with a bright headlight. His feet barely reached the pedals. Ahead of him on the sidewalk, a group gathered outside a liquor store, arguing and shoving each other.

Indie slowed as they approached, but the boy didn't hear the quiet electric golf cart. She tapped the horn, but nothing happened, so she pressed harder.

The high-pitched beep scared the bike rider, and he swerved

into the curb. As the front tire collapsed, the boy flew headfirst into the group on the sidewalk.

Indie steered away from the group and the flying kid.

“Stop!” yelled Adam. “We have to help him.”

“There’s no time. If we’re out here any longer, we’ll get arrested.”

“You scared that kid and he broke his bike. We should at least see if he’s okay.”

Indie sighed and steered the cart in a wide arc back to the bikeless boy.

The group outside the liquor store yelled at the boy, and one attempted to grab his backpack. He swung a knife at the man and sprinted away. Angered, the man and his friends gave chase.

As Indie drove alongside the fleeing kid, Adam motioned to him and he jumped into the back of the cart.

Indie slammed on the pedal, and they sped away.

CHAPTER 17

Fourteen-year-old Flint stepped outside Father O'Shanigan's Boys Home and into the warm Las Vegas evening. He flicked his unruly brown hair out of his eyes, adjusted his backpack and strode down the concrete steps. His hand reached deep into his pocket to double-check that the knife was still there before walking around the side of the building. A black mountain bike leaned against the red brick wall. After checking the tires, he hopped on. His feet barely reached the pedals, but it was better than walking. Flint looked back at the red brick building that had been his home for the last six months and nodded to himself. Time for a new adventure. Although he didn't listen to the news, he heard about some of the crazy things happening in the world on social media. Banks were losing money, companies were being cyber-attacked, and everyone was scared. However, Flint was not someone who scared easily. He survived abusive foster parents, angry social workers and a few bullies, he always adapted.

It was time to move on. All the adults in his life failed him and now was his chance to face the world – on his own. Besides, his roommate, Gary said he read on the internet that this was the end of the world. Flint had thousands of hours of practice surviving the apocalypse, even if it was all on the PlayStation or X-Box. He stretched his foot out, pushed down on the pedal, and cycled away.

Further down the block, a group of older teens gathered on the sidewalk. Flint recognized them as a wannabe gang. They weren't old enough to be a real gang, but they dealt some drugs and harassed anyone who dared to come close.

Flint steered off the sidewalk onto the road. The streets were curiously void of many vehicles. What if this really was the end of the world? He pumped the pedals and whizzed by the teens. The tepid evening air blew through his short brown hair as he cruised through the neighbourhood. He didn't have a specific destination or a map, but he knew he wanted to go where the action was. Flint wasn't sure if he was going towards downtown Las Vegas but figured if he hit the desert, he was going the wrong way.

After twenty minutes of cycling, the streets filled with protestors. Most shouted and waved signs. They looked angry, but at least they weren't zombies. He weaved through the throngs for a few blocks before turning down a less crowded street. His stomach rumbled, and he regretted not filling his backpack with food instead of clothes. Flint veered into the parking lot of a variety store. He coasted around the back of the store and tucked his bike between the dumpster and the back wall of the store.

Following a noisy group of men, Flint walked into the hectic store. A woman argued with the teller as others waiting in line yelled at her.

"Come on, lady! We don't have much time!" one yelled.

Two men near the back laughed and talked loudly. Flint had seen enough drunk adults in his life to know they were likely intoxicated. He went down another aisle with a group of older teens instead. His hand reached into his pocket and found the twenty-dollar bill he 'discovered' in Gary's wallet before he left the Boy's Home. He grabbed a large bag of potato chips and a few chocolate bars before moving to the fridges near the back of the store. The drunken men hovered by the pop, so Flint looked in the other fridges, hoping to find something good to drink. As he perused the chocolate milk shelf, the sound of breaking glass startled him. In the round safety mirror above, he watched a scuffle at the front counter. Their contorted reflections pushed and shoved each other. Someone threw a punch, and another pulled a knife. When someone yelled, "gun!" Flint held his chips and chocolate bars close and dropped to the floor. People screamed and shouted while Flint crawled beside the fridges. He slid across the tiles around the corner into a small cubby with two doors. A sign above one said, *washroom* and the other said *employees only*. Flint reached up and tried the handle to the employee door, but found it locked. Glass shattered, followed by more shouting from the front of the store. He tried the washroom door, which opened and dove inside, locking the door behind him. The tiny washroom contained a toilet and a small sink. A bucket and mop sat against the corner. Someone banged loudly on the door and yelled. Flint double-checked the lock and turned off the light.

While he waited for the fighting outside to subside, he ate the chips and one of the chocolate bars.

Eventually, the banging stopped, and the store quieted. After a few more minutes of silence and his last chocolate bar, he unlocked the door. He cracked it open and peered out, but saw nobody. Slowly, he pushed the door open a little more.

Just like his first-person shooter games, he poked his head out and pulled it back in. He repeated a few times until he was sure nobody would blow his head off. Crouching down, Flint crept out of the washroom and back into the store. Keeping close to the floor, he slunk down an aisle. His footsteps on the tile floor seemed to echo loudly in the silent store. The round safety mirror still showed no one else in the other aisles. A siren wailed in the distance.

He looked around and realized he was alone in a store filled with food. The chips and chocolate bars were next to the front window, so he moved to the next aisle in search of other food. He opened his pack and stuffed a bag of marshmallows and peanut butter inside. As he reached for a small box of cereal, he spotted something out of the corner of his eye. His face lit up with excitement. He dumped the clothes out of his pack and rushed towards the display.

"Come out with your hands on your head!" someone yelled from the front of the store.

Flint quickly filled his pack with his newfound loot and zipped it up.

"Don't shoot! I'm not armed," he yelled and moved towards the cash register.

A police officer pointed his gun at Flint. "Freeze!"

Flint held his hands in the air. "Don't shoot!"

The officer lowered his weapon. "What are you doing here, kid?"

"I was hiding in the washroom."

The officer beckoned him forward. "Where's your parents? You can't be out here."

Flint pointed outside. "My dad's waiting for me. We got separated when the shooting started."

"Okay, get out of here and go home. Martial law is starting soon."

He wasn't sure what that meant, but it sounded serious. Flint adjusted the heavy pack on his back and ran to the dumpster at the back of the store. His bike was still there. He hopped on and rode out of the variety store parking lot. The street lights turned on as the sun dipped below the horizon. Flint flicked a switch on his handlebars and a beam of light illuminated the road in front. He cycled hard away from the store.

Flint smiled as he remembered the loot sitting in his backpack. Two blocks later, a scuffle broke out in front of a liquor store ahead of him. He watched the men shove each other and argue. Suddenly, a loud, high-pitched beep sounded behind him. Startled, Flint swerved towards the sidewalk. Seeing the curb, he tried to pull up his front wheel but was too late. His front tire collided with the concrete, sending him flying over the handlebars headfirst into the group by the liquor store. A bulky man with baggy pants and a long shirt that hung down to his knees took the brunt of Flint's crash landing.

"Hey! Watch where you're going, man."

He glared down at Flint lying on the pavement. "What do you got in the pack, little man?"

Flint scrambled to his feet and tried to run, but the man grabbed his pack. Four others gathered around to watch.

Flint reached into his pocket and pulled out his knife. The blade shot out with a click. He whirled around and slashed at the man's arm. Baggy pants man shrieked and let go of the pack as the blade sliced through his forearm skin.

Flint darted out of the group back to his bike but saw the bent front tire.

"You're dead!" yelled a voice behind him. Blood dripped from the man's arm as he led the group towards Flint.

The same high-pitched beep that sent him crashing into the curb, sounded again as a golf cart pulled up beside him. A teenager in the passenger seat waved him aboard and Flint jumped on the cart as it pulled away from his pursuers.

CHAPTER 18

The trio whirred down a mostly empty Mojave Street towards the Skyline Hotel.

Flint stood on the step on the back of the golf cart normally used for holding the clubs and hung on to the roof support. They bumped along a mostly empty street.

Adam turned in his seat to look at Flint. “What are you doing out here?”

Flint smiled. “Looking for adventure.”

“Where do you live?” asked Indie.

“In the moment,” he answered.

“You know they’ve declared martial law, right?” asked Indie.

“Who’s Marshall?”

“Martial is not a person. It means nobody is allowed on the streets after dark or they can arrest you. Is your home close?”

“I don’t have a home.”

“What’s your name?”

“Flint.”

“I’m Adam and this is Indie.”

“Are you a runaway?” Indie asked.

“I was living at Father O’Shanigan’s Boys’ Home, but that place is stupid. Can I hang with you?”

“I don’t think that’s a good idea,” said Indie. “We’ll take you back to the Boys’ Home tomorrow morning.”

The sound of a voice on a loudspeaker echoed across the neighbourhood but was too far away to decipher the words. A minute later, a dark shape appeared on the road ahead. Adam leaned forward and squinted. “Are those cops?”

As they drove closer, they saw a large police SUV with flashing lights rolling towards them.

“Please get off the streets and return to your homes,” a voice boomed from loudspeakers mounted to the top of the car. “Martial law has been declared. Any violators will be arrested on sight.”

Indie flung the steering wheel to the right and the golf cart almost tipped as they turned down a side street.

“Stop!” the voice yelled over the speaker. “Stop your vehicle!”

The police sped up and screeched around the corner after them.

“Should we pull over?” asked Adam. “Maybe they’ll just give us a warning and send us home.”

“Or maybe they’ll arrest us and throw us in jail,” said Indie.

“Go, go, go!” yelled Flint.

“They’re catching up,” said Adam. “We can’t outrun an SUV with a golf cart.”

“I can slow them down,” said Flint, reaching behind him and removing his backpack. He unzipped it, reached in and pulled out a colourful tube with a fuse poking out one end.

“What are you doing?” asked Adam.

A spark from his lighter flicked twice before a small flame lit the fuse.

“I’m slowing them down,” Flint answered as he pointed the lit firework behind them.

A yellow ball of sparks shot out the end, sailing over the cruiser and exploding behind it.

“What was that?” screamed Indie.

“He’s shooting fireworks!” Adam answered.

The next one bounced off the pavement and onto the sidewalk before exploding against the side of a parked car.

“What?!”

A ball of fire exploded off the hood of the SUV, but it didn’t slow down.

Indie spun the wheel to the left at the next intersection. The golf cart took most of the turn on two wheels before bouncing back down to the road.

Another ball of fire whizzed across the street and exploded

over a garage.

"You're making it very difficult to aim," Flint complained.

"Stop shooting fireworks at the cops!" yelled Indie.

"Can't we just pull over?" asked Adam.

"That would make it easier to aim," said Flint.

"That's not what I meant!"

The next firework hit the pavement before bouncing under the SUV and exploding. The vehicle careened off the road, bumped over the curb, and clipped a small tree before stopping.

"Gotcha!" yelled Flint and tossed the spent fireworks away.

The golf cart slowed to a stop.

"That was *so* cool," said Flint.

"Or stupid," said Indie.

"Hey, it worked, didn't it?"

An engine revved in the distance as they watched. A moment later, the police were back on the road and headed straight for them.

"Go, go, go!" yelled Flint.

"I can't," said Indie. "We're out of juice."

"What if we surrendered?" suggested Adam.

"This is martial law, and we just shot them. They are just as likely to shoot us as arrest us. We need to run."

They hopped out of the cart and ran. Indie led the way down the sidewalk. Fenced bungalows lined the street on both sides. Bright street lights lit up the neighbourhood.

"This way!" yelled Adam, running towards a house. "We need to get off the street."

"Good thinking," said Indie. "Lead the way."

He looked up at the tall black iron fence with a spiked top and ran to the next house. The SUV screeched down the road towards them as Adam ran towards a four-foot-high white concrete wall. He used a nearby fire hydrant as a step to climb over. Indie and Flint followed, and they all crouched behind the wall as the police slowly cruised by.

After it passed, Adam stood and looked up. Behind the house in the distance, he saw the top of Skyline Tower.

He looked at the tower and then at Indie. "Do you think we can make it? It doesn't look that far."

She shrugged. "Maybe."

Headlights swept across the yard and they ducked back down as the police passed by again.

"Maybe not," she said.

He looked at the house. "All the lights are off here. Do you think they're home?"

"We can't just break into someone's house."

"It's not like we're robbing them."

"We should at least knock to make sure nobody is home."

They crept towards the front door.

"What if they have an alarm system?" asked Adam.

Indie looked around. "Where's Flint?"

The light above them turned on, flooding the front porch with light, and the door lock clicked. Indie dove behind a tree and Adam ducked behind a planter.

"Guys? Are you coming?" Flint stood in the doorway with a smile.

Indie and Adam left their hiding spots.

"How did you get in there?" asked Indie.

"The side window into the bathroom wasn't locked," he answered.

"What if there was an alarm?"

Flint stepped aside and held his hand out as if allowing them to enter. "No alarm company sticker on the windows."

Indie squinted at him. "I feel like you've done this before."

"Are we sure no one is home?" asked Adam as he stepped inside and looked around.

"A mother and baby are in the room down the hall and I think she has a gun," Flint answered.

Indie's and Adam's eyes both widened, and they stepped back.

"What?!" Indie yell-whispered.

"I'm just kidding," Flint laughed as he sauntered into the kitchen, "but you should see your faces."

"That's not funny," said Adam. "I think my heart stopped

beating."

Flint opened the fridge and looked inside. "What's for dinner?"

"We are *not* stealing from these people," said Indie. "We're just staying here until the sun comes up."

Flint closed the fridge and looked at Adam. "Your girlfriend is a party pooper."

"She's not my girlfriend," said Adam.

"Adam is trekking across the city to rescue his girlfriend," said Indie.

Adam looked shyly at the floor. "I just met Piper a few days ago, but I think we had a connection..."

"When you swoop in to save her," Indie said dramatically, "Piper will fall lovingly into your arms and plant a grateful wet kiss on your lips and you'll walk hand in hand into the sunset."

"Cool," said Flint. "I'll help."

"How old are you?" asked Indie.

Flint folded his arms and leaned against the counter. "I'm almost fifteen."

"Yeah, tomorrow we need to get you back to the Boys home. We can't be responsible for..."

"Who saved you from the cops?" Flint interrupted.

"Saved or antagonized?"

"Who got into this house before you two made it to the front door?"

"Your ability to break the law isn't in question here."

"The Boys' Home was running out of food. Also, the Director likes to pay *special* visits to boy's rooms at night."

Indie tilted her head and creased her brows. "Oh, Flint, I'm so sorry..."

Flint rubbed his eye and whimpered. "Please don't make me go back there."

"No, Flint. We won't make you go back..."

"Great!" Flint raised his head. "I'm coming with you."

Indie put her hands on her hips. "You're lying about the *special visits*, aren't you?"

Flint opened the cupboard, grabbed a bag of cookies and

strolled into the living room.
"I think you guys need me."

CHAPTER 19

The next morning, as the sun crept above the horizon, the trio stood on the front steps of the house.

"Are we allowed to go out now?" asked Adam.

"Martial law was only from dusk till dawn," said Indie.

Adam pointed at a police car rolling down the street towards them. "Are you sure?"

"Look around," said Indie. "They can't arrest everybody."

Everything seemed ordinary, but there was an undeniable strangeness lingering in the neighbourhood. Cans, beer bottles and other garbage littered the street, sidewalks and yards.

An old man in a bathrobe stood on his porch across the street, sipping his coffee. He eyed his yard as if looking for leftover hooligans from the previous night. Two women and a small boy shuffled down the sidewalk, towing an overfilled shopping trolley. A scraggly woman glanced around suspiciously as she grabbed beer bottles and cans and stuffed them in a plastic bag. Two teenage boys rolled past on electric scooters. A yellow sports car honked and drove around them. A police car drove by slowly in the opposite direction but didn't stop.

Before they left, Adam called the hospital. The nurse said his father was stable, but not awake yet.

"Where are we going now?" Flint asked with a smile.

"I still think we should take you back home," said Indie.

"O'Shanigan's is not a home, it's a prison."

"If anything happened to you—."

"You worry too much." He jumped off the porch. "Let's go have an adventure!"

"Fine, but we are *not* your babysitters and—."

"I'm almost fifteen and can take care of myself."

A man in a rumpled suit strode up the walkway towards them. "Can I help you folks?"

"No, I think we're fine," said Flint.

Adam and Indie stepped aside as he pushed his way between them and walked to the front door. "What are you doing on my front step?"

"We were just leaving," said Flint as he scurried away.

Adam and Indie followed quickly behind him without looking back.

"What's the plan?" asked Flint. "Are we going to save your girlfriend now?"

"She's not my girlfriend," said Adam.

"First, we have to go back to the Skyline and pick up Prospero," said Indie, "Then to downtown to find Jerry Dillwash—."

"What kind of name is Prospero?" asked Flint. "He sounds like a video game villain."

"He's Indie's boyfriend, and he's rich," said Adam.

"I'm not sure he's either of those things anymore," said Indie, "but he needs our help to find Jerry, who might be able to stop all this."

"How is this Jerry guy going to stop this?" asked Flint.

"Prospero built an AI that got out of control and caused all this havoc and Jerry is an expert in AI. Hopefully, they can stop it."

"Can't they just pull the plug?"

"That would be nice."

As they neared the strip, a small group of men and women dressed in blue stood in front of a boarded-up variety store. One of them talked into his phone. All of them carried guns.

"Keep walking," said Indie.

They encountered a few more small armed groups before they made it back to the Skyline Hotel.

"What's with all the gangs?" asked Flint. "And why are they dressed in blue?"

"It looks like they're preparing for war," said Indie.

"We should get guns too," said Flint.

"I don't think so."

"Are they allowed to walk around with guns?" Adam asked. "Why don't the cops arrest them?"

"Nevada has an open carry law that was supposedly suspended," Indie answered. "But I think the police are outnumbered."

"What about the army?"

"I don't know."

A security guard stopped them at the Skyline entrance.

He crossed his arms and glared at them. "No one goes inside unless they're staying here."

They gave him the room number, and he called the room before stepping aside.

Flint looked around the opulent lobby. "Wow! This is sweet!"

"Don't get too attached," said Indie. "We're not staying."

They knocked on the hotel room door for almost a minute before Prospero finally opened the door. He swept aside his tussled black hair and rubbed his red eyes.

"Heyyyyy, guys. I thought you weren't coming back." He slurred his words and spoke at half-speed.

"Are you drunk again?" asked Indie.

"If I was going to die of starvation, I didn't want to die sober."

Prospero pointed at Flint. "Did you guys pick up a stray?"

"Prospero, this is Flint," said Indie. "Flint this is Prospero."

"He looks like a villain too," said Flint with a smile.

"What happened?" asked Prospero. "You went for a quick jaunt to the grocery store and didn't return."

"It's a long story."

"I'm surprised you made it back. Watching the scene out the window last night, I thought the world was ending. The protests turned violent. There were fires, fighting and even some gunshots. According to the internet, we are on the brink of the next civil war."

"We probably are," said Indie.

"Did you guys bring back any food?" he asked. "I'm starving."

Adam emptied his backpack onto the table.

"Pineapple?" Prospero asked. "You got a pineapple? What are

we supposed to do with a pineapple?"

"I haven't really done much grocery shopping." Adam looked down.

"There's nothing wrong with fruit," said Indie. "Vitamin C is important."

"I had chocolate," said Flint. "But I ate it already."

"We have crackers and some cereal. Eat up and get ready to go," said Indie. "We need to find Jerry and get this AI mess sorted out. Then we can rescue Piper. We need to do all that tomorrow *before* the sun goes down and martial law kicks in again."

Prospero held up the box of raisin bran. "Where's the milk?"

CHAPTER 20

A half hour later, the four of them left the Skyline Hotel and walked south along the strip towards the Link Hotel.

The sun rose high enough that its rays poked between tall hotel buildings, heating the city once again. Instead of a city awakening to a bright new day, the Vegas strip appeared to be recovering from a wild party. The front glass window to a souvenir shop lay in tiny fragments on the sidewalk. Empty liquor bottles sat beside discarded protest signs and garbage littered the streets and sidewalks. Smoke rose from a nightclub one block to the west of the strip. Three armed guards stood outside a hotel and casino, glaring at passersby as if daring them to approach. The closer they walked to downtown, the worse the strip looked. Firemen stood beside a firetruck parked outside a hotel. A hose ran from the truck into the building to an unseen fire. Across the street, two police cars hemmed in a sports car next to a strip club. Behind them, a wailing siren warned them of an incoming ambulance.

More armed groups prowled the street, while others huddled suspiciously outside the casinos.

The four of them walked quietly down the strip, speechless at the apocalyptic scene.

Forty-five minutes later, they arrived at the Loop Walkway Promenade. The wide cobblestone walkway started at the strip and led to the Big Spin Observation wheel at the end. Shops, restaurants, bars and souvenir shops lined either side. Two hotels flanked the entrance to the promenade. The Link Hotel and Casino sat on the left and the Pink Stork Hotel on the other.

The group stepped into the walkway and turned left towards the glass doors of the Link. A security guard blocked the front entrance.

Prospero pulled his shirt away from his chest. “I hope their air conditioning works.”

“Sorry, you can’t go this way,” said the security guard.

“We’re meeting Jerry Dillwash. I believe he’s staying here.”

“The hotel is closed except for people who have a room. No visitors and the casino is closed.”

“Can we pay for a room?” Prospero asked.

“No, we are not accepting any more guests. You should go home.”

They stepped back and gathered at an empty outdoor bar.

“Can we sneak in the back door?” Adam asked.

“This is the back door.” Indie looked at Prospero. “How do we know Jerry Dillwash is still here?”

“We don’t, but it’s my last best chance of finding him.”

“I can get us in,” said Flint.

“This isn’t like the house, Flint,” said Indie. “You can’t just crawl through a window.”

“Getting into the hotel is easier. There is only one bored security guard and four of us. I’ll create a distraction, giving you guys a chance to sneak in.”

Flint pointed to a woman talking with the security guard. He stepped aside, allowing her to pass. She nodded and proceeded past him, pushed open the glass door and went inside.

“The doors aren’t locked and all we have to do is get past this one guy.”

“What are you going to do?” Adam asked.

“Don’t worry about me. You guys stand around the corner, out of sight. Wait thirty seconds, then come back and walk through those doors without stopping.”

“I don’t know about this,” said Prospero. “What if—”

“We should do it.” Adam nodded. “What do we have to lose? If it doesn’t work, we’ll come up with another plan. I don’t want to waste more time out here. This street gives me a bad feeling.”

He walked towards the corner. Indie soon followed and a

reluctant Prospero did the same.

“This street gives me a bad feeling, too,” Indie said as they waited around the corner. “The strip is normally quiet in the morning, but this is different. It feels like we are on the brink of something really bad.”

A thunderous bang echoed across the walkway, followed by a crackling sound.

“That’s our cue!” said Adam.

They went around the corner as the crackling sound intensified. As they speed walked to the door, Adam saw the security guard moving towards a trash receptacle spewing a colourful assortment of sparks but didn’t see Flint.

They shuffled inside before the guard turned around. Inside, bright LED screens covered the entrance walls and ceiling. Mesmerizing fractal patterns undulated across the display.

Indie stopped and looked back. “Where’s Flint?”

Prospero kept walking. “Come on, let’s go before that guard gets wise. That kid is nothing but trouble, anyway.”

“He’s pretty resourceful,” said Adam. “I’m sure he’ll find a way inside.”

She paused for a moment before following Adam and Prospero into the hotel. Shiny porcelain tile walkways curved right and left around a carpeted island of hundreds of glitzy slot machines.

Adam stared wide-eyed at the carnival of gambling. Golden goddesses, dragons, pirates, frogs, princes, ninjas, sphinxes, wizards, wolves and zombies adorned the flashy machines. Lights flashed, bells rang, coins clinked, sirens wailed, and music poured from the machines, but the casino was eerily void of gamblers.

“Where are we going?” Indie asked Prospero. “How are we supposed to find Jerry?

“Hey guys!” Flint popped out from behind a slot machine.

“How did you—?” Indie interrupted herself. “Never mind.”

“Can I help you folks?” A security guard in a pressed suit appeared in front of them. “Are you staying at the Link?”

"Of course," said Prospero. "We're staying in Room 1754."

"Remember, that all guests must check out by tomorrow as the hotel will temporarily close until things settle down."

"Yes, we know. Can you help us? We are looking for a guest by the name of Jerry Dillwash. Do you know what room he is staying in?"

"We can't give out that information, but you may want to check the high stakes poker room in the back." He pointed further into the hotel.

The group wandered through the empty slot machines until they found the high stakes poker area. Set apart from the slot machines, the room featured oval tables surrounded by padded chairs. All the tables were empty except for one. A group of seven men and women smoked, talked, and drank while playing a game of Texas Hold 'em.

Adam recognized the man sitting between an overweight gentleman smoking a cigar and a middle-aged woman who looked like she hadn't slept in days.

"What do you want, Leonard," said Jerry Dillwash, without looking up.

"Who's Leonard?" Indie whispered.

Prospero ignored her question and stared at Jerry. "Look around, Jerry. The world is falling apart, and it's your fault."

"Ha! Not likely. Didn't I warn you about messing with Athena?"

"I call it Prospero Junior now, and it may have caused the banking meltdown. Can you help me?"

Jerry looked up from his cards and laughed. "You are way beyond help."

The man with the cigar looked at Jerry. "Are we playing poker or having a conversation with these people?"

Jerry placed his cards down. "I'm out." He pushed his chair back and stood up. "Let's find a place to talk, Leonard."

"Why is he calling you Leonard? Do you two know each other?" Indie asked as they followed Jerry to an empty poker table.

"It's a long story."

They sat at the table, and the four of them stared at Jerry.

"What do you want from me, Leonard?" he asked. "And who are all these people?"

"They're nobody. I need your help with the AI."

"Hold on!" shouted Indie. "We are somebody, Prospero. We are the ones that got you here and deserve to know what is going on." She looked at Jerry. "Why do you keep calling him Leonard, and how do you two know each other?"

"Did you change *your* name to Prospero and the AI's?" he asked.

"I'm Prospero and the AI is Prospero Junior."

"That's confusing," said Jerry.

"I still think it sounds like a supervillain," Flint interjected.

Jerry pointed at him. "He's got a point."

"You still haven't answered my question," said Indie.

Jerry leaned back. "Leonard—sorry, *Prospero* and I met many years ago at NextGen."

"You're *that* Jerry?" said Indie.

Jerry continued. "The AI we worked on was *supposed* to help businesses invest and grow their wealth using customized algorithms using historical patterns as well as current trends —"

Prospero interrupted. "These people have no idea what any of that means."

"I do," said Indie. "Go on."

Jerry continued. "After we got fired, we went our separate ways. I used my knowledge and skills to help companies and warn the public about the dangers of AI while Leonard had a…"

Prospero finished his sentence. "—more profitable vision."

"I wrote a book and went on a speaking tour."

"And *I* refined the AI and made billions." Prospero leaned back and smiled.

"But now you need my help. Why?"

"The AI is out of control," said Prospero. "Prospero Junior may have crossed some blurry legal lines, but I didn't think this would happen. It began using the banking system against itself, causing a type of digital run on the banks. I couldn't stop it. Banks failed, investments soured, loans defaulted, and a series of financial dominoes fell. People panicked, making everything worse and the economic system spiralled out of control. Hyperinflation has devalued the American dollar, and the AI has blocked my access. The only way to reverse this is by reprogramming the AI, which I'll admit, I am not capable of doing."

Jerry laughed. "If it was true that our AI caused all this, it would be incredibly ironic. I created the AI, warned of its dangerous potential and then it destroys the world."

"I helped program it too," said Prospero.

"Perhaps you just unleashed it."

Prospero stared down at the table and rubbed the green velvet. "You were always smarter than me, Jerry – at least when it came to programming. I need you to help me access the AI to stop this madness."

"You really think your AI is capable of taking down the American economy?"

"I didn't want to believe it either, but its self-learning capabilities have taken it far beyond what either of us could imagine."

"This is like the game Mass Effect," shouted Flint. "Where the Reapers are sentient machines that wipe out civilizations."

"Not quite, kid," said Jerry. "This AI is not sentient. It is only doing what we programmed it to do."

"It's gone beyond its programming," Prospero insisted. "The AI has gone rogue."

"That isn't *exactly* what's happened," said Jerry.

"What are you talking about?"

An exaggerated fake smile appeared on Jerry's face. "Before I left NextGen, I programmed a back door into the AI. When you took it over, the back door came with it – sort of. I still have limited access. After the Feds let me go, I opened that door and confirmed my suspicions."

"You did *what*?" Prospero yelled.

"Isn't that a good thing?" asked Adam. "Can't you use the back door to stop it?"

"Seeing all that is going on with the disinformation on social media, the cyberattacks and the collapse of our economic system, I suspected this was not the work of one AI. When I logged in through my back door, I realized I was right." Jerry pointed at Prospero. "Your AI is one of many controlled by an AI orchestrator."

"For what purpose?" Indie asked. "Nobody is going to make money from ransomware or cyberattacks if the economic system collapses. Money will be worthless."

"It already is." Prospero stared into the distance and shook his head. "All that work and all that money is gone."

"That's what you care about!?" Indie shouted. "Your money?"

"I could have done a lot of good with that money!"

"Oh, *please*. Now you have ambitions of philanthropy?"

"I gave you a good time, didn't I?"

"All you care about is yourself! Look around. The world is falling apart because you got greedy!"

"He just said it wasn't my AI's fault—"

Adam surprised himself when he stood up and yelled, "Enough! All this fighting is not getting us anywhere. Let Jerry finish his story and then tell us how to fix this."

Prospero and Indie glared at each other but stopped talking.

"Like I was saying," Jerry continued, "I surmise that many AIs are acting like separate terrorist cells. Each handling a specific task."

"But there has to be a main AI that controls all the others, right?" asked Flint.

The others looked at the boy as if a super-smart entity had taken control of his mind.

Flint smiled as if impressed with himself.

Jerry nodded, "He's right. Just like a leader or central command controls a network of terror cells."

Flint smiled. "Yeah, like Apollo in Alien Isolation."

They stared at him with obvious confusion.

"Alien Isolation...the video game."

"I don't know what that is," said Jerry, "but yes, kind of like that, except this isn't aliens…I don't think."

"Who is it then?" asked Indie.

Jerry sighed. "The young lady here was right. Whoever is doing this has motives other than money."

"What else is there?" asked Prospero.

Indie shook her head. "A lot."

Jerry continued. "It is a group with a lot of resources, has a penchant for asymmetric warfare tactics, and a fervent desire to destroy America."

"Aliens!" said Flint.

"From my extensive research, I would conclude that it's likely the work of Iran. They have the means, motive and, with recent advances in AI technology, the opportunity."

"How do we stop them?" asked Adam.

"*We*, can't. As I told the Secret Service, the only way to stop this is to destroy the central AI. It's probably in some underground hideout in Iran."

"The American military can fire a bunker-busting missile and destroy the AI which deactivates the other AI's like in Portal," said Flint.

"Something like that, except it might take more than a little missile. The bunker will be deep underground, reinforced and employ a sophisticated missile defence system. An earth-penetrating weapon with a nuclear warhead would do the job."

"Is that what you told the Secret Service?" asked Indie.

"Yes, however, there are a couple of problems with that solution. First, they have to locate the bunker. Iran has over 600,000 square miles of salt flats, dunes, rocky plateaus and deserts. Even if they located it, the second problem is finding it in time. The orchestrator AI will reach a point where it is no longer housed in one central location and can operate independently of its programmers. Once this command decentralization happens, it will be impossible to stop. Prospero Junior may be one of hundreds or even thousands of AIs that one central AI has taken control of and reprogrammed. Each performs specialized tasks, like deep fake videos or pictures, misinformation bots, or cyberattacks. They coordinate with each other for a common purpose. That purpose is to destroy the West."

"How can deep fakes and a couple of cyberattacks destroy America?" asked Adam.

"America is already on the precipice. The political right and political left have never been this divided since the Civil War. Sowing economic instability before pushing left and right wing over the brink was brilliant, but not very difficult. Social media misinformation, and cyclical algorithms that reinforce bias, hate and extreme views were already rampant before this began. Guiding these algorithms and sowing targeted misinformation to achieve a common goal is child's play for a sophisticated AI."

"There's really nothing you can do to stop it?" asked Adam.

"If command decentralization hasn't happened before the AI orchestrator is destroyed, the economic system may slowly come back online, targeted internet disinformation will drop away and things might slowly go back to normal."

"What if it's too late?"

"Then the next stage of the destruction of America will begin."

"What's the next—?"

A scream interrupted Indie's question. More screams accompanied by shouting and breaking glass came from the entrance. A woman holding a small child ran towards them.

"What's going on?" Indie asked her.

The woman continued running without answering. Soon, more men, women, and a few teens sprinted down the porcelain walkway, across the carpet, and through the slot machines. They didn't appear to be headed in any particular direction except away from the entrance.

Prospero stood up and yelled at a man holding his young son in his arms. "Hey, you! What are you running from?"

"There's a shooter out there!" he yelled and continued running.

"We should go," said Adam.

"Go where?" Indie's face was as pale as a prairie sky. She stood motionless, staring at the running people.

"Somewhere safe," Adam said.

He took a few steps but saw Indie was not moving. The look of frozen fear was familiar to Adam but seemed uncharacteristic for her. He grabbed her elbow and pulled her forward.

She broke from her trance and followed him.

"Come on!" he yelled and walked deeper into the hotel.

"Why are we following him?" yelled Prospero.

Nobody answered.

Adam glanced behind him and saw Flint, Jerry and a mumbling Prospero trailing behind him.

He jogged past the blackjack, roulette and baccarat tables, a bar and restaurant, and paused near the front desk. The others were still behind him.

Adam turned to Indie. "Why am *I* in front? What am I supposed to do?"

She looked at him and shrugged. "Lead."

The colour had returned to her face, but she still looked scared.

Past the front desk, multiple sets of glass doors led back outside. To the right, a pair of elevators preceded a corridor leading to other hotels and the convention centre.

"This way!" he shouted and ran down the corridor.

Shops lined the corridor on both sides. A woman covered in tattoos and piercings stepped out of her shop. As she joined the throng of panicked escapees, Adam sprinted ahead and grabbed the door before it closed. He held it open as the others scrambled inside.

"What are we doing *here*?" asked Prospero.

After all of them were in the tattoo shop, Adam closed and locked the doors and turned off the lights. Glass windows separated the store from the corridor, so it wasn't dark inside, but at least it looked closed.

They huddled behind the counter and waited.

"Why are we hiding inside a tattoo parlour with glass walls?" asked Prospero.

"I didn't want to go back outside if there's an active shooter," said Adam. "The elevators could be dangerous if the power goes out and if we kept running, we could be running closer to the danger instead of away from it. For now, we wait here until things settle down."

"You couldn't have picked a donut shop to hide in? At least we'd have something to eat."

"Looters and vandals are less likely to break into a tattoo shop since there's nothing here to steal," Adam replied.

"You're welcome to leave, Prospero," said Indie.

He grunted and turned away.

"This is so cool," said Flint. "This is like Dying Light 2 except without the zombies."

The noise outside gradually faded as the last of the runners disappeared. A moment later, they heard glass breaking and shouting further down the corridor. A few minutes passed before all was silent again.

Prospero lay on a padded tattoo couch and fell asleep. Flint flipped through a binder with pictures of tattoos and piercings. Jerry sat in a corner, tapping at his phone.

Adam and Indie sat next to each other on a black leather couch.

"Are you okay?" Adam asked.

"What do you mean?"

"You froze back there when that guy said there was a shooter. Normally it's me who pisses his pants in the face of danger."

"Yeah..." she looked down and breathed deeply. "I was nearby when it happened."

"When what happened?"

"Remember a few years ago when there was a mass shooting in Vegas?"

"I was only a kid back then, but I did hear about it. Were you there?"

"Fifty-nine people died that day and more than 500 people were injured. My mother was one of them. I was fifteen when she took me to the festival. Once the shooting started, people panicked. They screamed and ran in every direction. My mother grabbed me and we ran. The gunshots kept coming and we couldn't tell which direction they were coming from, but my mother tried to shield me as we ran for cover."

Indie rubbed a tear dribbling down her cheek.

"A bullet pierced her backbone and ripped through her spleen. I held her bleeding body behind a dumpster until the shooting stopped. By the time the ambulances arrived, she was unconscious. A few hours later, she died in the hospital. My mother saved my life."

She wiped away more tears. "When those people ran into the casino and someone said there was a shooter, it triggered the memory of the day my mother died."

Adam didn't know what to say. He wasn't sure if it was appropriate to hug her or say something consoling.

"I'm sorry," was all that came out.

"It's okay," she said, trying to compose herself. "You helped me. You're a leader."

He shook his head. "I doubt that. I'm just a dorky cello player who always gets bullied."

"Look around you, Adam. All these people followed you here. Obviously, they believe in you. You should believe in yourself."

"Prospero thinks I'm an idiot."

"Prospero is a selfish fool, and he *still* followed you."

CHAPTER 21

Adam sat up and blinked. His back hurt from sleeping on the floor and he was still tired. He woke a few times in the night from the sound of distant gunshots, but nothing very close. The sound of more gunfire echoed through the corridor outside. Not close, but not too far, either.

He looked at his phone, but it still wasn't working. Flint stood at the front of the shop looking out, Prospero still slept on the couch, while Jerry snored in a tattoo chair. Beside him, Indie opened her eyes.

"What's happening?" she whispered.

He stood up and stretched. "I don't know."

Adam walked to Flint and stood beside him.

"Couldn't sleep?" he asked.

Flint stared into the corridor. "Nah. I'm a light sleeper. Also, the gunshots are getting closer."

"Are you sure?"

"If this was an active shooter, he wouldn't still be shooting. That sounds like a war out there."

"It is a war," Jerry's voice behind them startled Adam, and he whirled around.

"Where did you come from? I thought you were sleeping."

"War is exactly what the AI wants and I think it's inevitable." Jerry held up his phone. "I realize the internet is even more full of misinformation than usual, but I think it's bad out there and getting worse."

"What do you mean?" Indie appeared beside Jerry.

"I mean, we need to get out of this city before we become casualties."

"Where are we going?" Flint asked, with a hint of eagerness in his voice.

"Can a guy not get some sleep around here?" Prospero called out. "It's the middle of the night."

"I thought it was morning," said Adam. "What time is it?"

"It is five in the morning," said Jerry.

Prospero waddled over, rubbing his eyes and stretching. "Is it over? Can we all go home now?"

"Jerry says there's a war going on out there," said Indie.

"Did he read that on the internet?" asked Prospero.

"The gunshots haven't stopped," said Flint.

"We should leave," said Adam.

"If there is a war going on out there, we should stay in here where it's safe," said Prospero.

"I wouldn't call hiding in a glass box in the middle of a war zone safe," said Jerry.

"I tried telling you guys this when we got here," Prospero retorted.

"Where will we go?" asked Jerry.

Indie smiled. "We stick to the plan. Piper is in the JCC and we're going to rescue her."

"Who is Piper and what is the JCC?" asked Jerry.

Flint smirked. "She's Adam's damsel in distress. He wants to save her so she'll sleep with him."

"That's not—" Adam began.

"The JCC is a women's prison south of the city," said Indie.

"We're risking our lives to break Adam's girlfriend out of jail?" asked Jerry.

"She's not my girlfriend."

"This is a bad idea," said Prospero.

"Jerry said we have to leave Vegas and the JCC is just outside the city, so it makes sense," said Indie.

"Shouldn't we wait until morning?" asked Prospero.

"Statistically, early morning is the safest time to travel through a war zone," said Jerry.

"Grab your stuff. We're leaving," said Adam.

"We should get some guns!" said Flint.

"We are *not* getting guns," said Indie.

"What about a club or a chainsaw?"

"You play too many video games."

Adam shouldered his pack and opened the door. He looked both ways before walking cautiously to the left.

"Adam!" Indie whispered. "South is the other way."

He held up a finger. "I knew that."

Adam turned and walked in the opposite direction through the empty corridor.

The other followed close behind.

"Why are we following him again?" asked Prospero.

"What about a golf club or a cricket bat?" asked Flint.

"We're not fighting our way out of Vegas," said Indie.

"Should we tape magazines to our arms and wear hockey masks?"

"Why would we do that?"

"For the zombies."

"There are no zombies, Flint."

As they crept up to the end of the corridor, his ears caught the sound of muted voices and distant footsteps in the Casino ahead.

"How do you know there are no zom—"

"Shhhh!" Adam held up his finger. "I hear something."

He pushed his back against the wall and the others did the same.

"Clench your fist," whispered Flint.

"What?" asked Adam.

"It's military sign language," said Flint. "You hold your clenched fist in the air and it means that everyone has to stop and be quiet."

"This isn't the—" Adam stopped mid-sentence when he heard a voice only a few yards ahead.

Peering around the corner, he watched a man in camouflaged pants and a blue shirt run from the cover of a slot machine and crouch behind a poker table. Adam wasn't an expert on guns, but the rifle in his hands looked like an automatic weapon.

"We should go back," he said.

The sound of several boots clacking on the tile floor echoed through the corridor behind them.

"We've got multiple bogeys on our six, Sergeant," said Flint. "Do we engage?"

"No, we don't engage! We're not armed, remember?"

"I told you we should have guns."

Adam looked around frantically for a way out. When he saw the elevator doors across the hallway, he ran towards them. He mashed at the elevator button frantically as the boots marched closer. The others gathered by the doors, waiting for them to open.

Gunshots rang out in the Casino. A chunk of marble sprayed out of the wall beside Adam and he ducked.

"Everybody, get down!" he yelled.

"We're sitting ducks here!" yelled Prospero.

The five of them huddled at the elevator as more bullets peppered the surrounding walls.

When the elevator opened with a ding, they dove inside.

Indie pounded on the *close door* button. The elevator waited a painfully long three seconds before closing.

Prospero pushed the button for the top floor.

"Is everyone okay?" asked Adam.

"My knee is killing me," said Jerry.

"I'm okay," said Indie.

"Whose brilliant idea was this?" asked Prospero.

"That was totally awesome!" yelled Flint.

Adam closed his eyes and took long, deep breaths. The others around yelled in excitement, argued and complained.

He was the first to step out when the doors opened on the twentieth floor. Adam walked down the hallway till he reached a floor-to-ceiling picture window. Outside, the Big Spin Observation Wheel towered over the neighbouring buildings that aspired to scrape the sky.

"I've always wanted to ride the Wheel," said Flint.

"It's a pleasant view, but a painfully slow ride," mumbled

Prospero.

"I still think it would be fun," Flint retorted.

Jerry sighed. "That wheel will never spin again."

Indie stood beside Adam. "I rode the wheel once with my Mom when I was a kid, but I barely remember."

Hotels, casinos and other structures filled the area below, obscuring any view of the rest of the city or the streets. Adam still couldn't see what was going on.

"We need a better view," he said and continued through the hallway and took the first turn towards the opposite side of the hotel.

The others followed him like an unruly class of kindergarteners.

"What are we even doing up here?" mumbled Prospero.

"You'd rather be downstairs in the middle of the war zone?" asked Indie.

"Yeah! We should be outside where the action is," said Flint.

"I'm hungry," Jerry complained.

Adam continued through the hallways, hoping to find a window overlooking the Vegas strip. Instead, all he found was locked hotel room doors.

"Is going in circles really productive?" Prospero asked.

"I'm trying to get a view of the strip," Adam replied.

"Unless you have a room key, that isn't possible," said Prospero in a tone mixed with equal parts disgust and condescension. "Coming up here was a bad idea."

Indie crossed her arms. "Do you think we were better off standing in the lobby waiting to get shot?"

"No, but trapping ourselves at the top of the hotel isn't much better!"

She pointed back at the elevators. "You're welcome to go back down!"

"A couple of nitwits like you wouldn't survive without an adult in the room."

"You're the one acting like a child. Instead of complaining, why don't you try to help?"

"Fine!" Prospero backed up and charged at the closest hotel room door, shoulder first.

The door rattled as he bounced off it.

"What are you doing?" yelled Indie.

"I'm helping! Do you want to see the strip? These rooms have a *spectacular* view!"

He charged the door again. It shook and rattled again, but did not open.

"What if there's somebody in there?"

Prospero held his shoulder. "Only rich people can afford these suites, and I'm the only rich person dumb enough to still be in Vegas."

He stood on one foot and kicked the door with the flat of his foot. The door still didn't budge.

"Guys?" Flint called from three doors down. "When you lovers are done fighting, you're welcome to join me."

He held the door open and smiled.

Jerry creased his brow. "I'm not complaining, but how did you open that door?"

"You're not the only smart one, old man," Flint replied.

Adam gave him a high five as he walked by. "Good job, buddy!"

Flint smirked as the others walked past him into the room.

"Who's the adult in the room now?" Indie asked Prospero.

"A few days ago, I was the only one who could come close to affording a room like this."

"And now all you can do is bounce off the door, while a kid—."

Indie paused her witty comeback when she saw what the others saw.

They all stared silently out the window overlooking the city and the strip below.

Thick black smoke curled from an unseen fire behind a casino across the street. A helicopter rose from behind a tall hotel. A hellfire missile whistled away from the wing-mounted pylon of the twin-engine Viper. It hurtled towards a tan multipurpose vehicle with a gun mount. The truck exploded seconds later. Behind it, other vehicles surged forward. Armed men and women dashed forward, taking cover behind statues, hotel alcoves, and trash cans. They fired sporadically at an opposing force coming towards them from the left.

The scene seemed surreal to Adam. The double-pane window muted the sound of gunshots and explosions, and the battle appeared to be in a different dimension. It was like a movie on television or a dream – or a nightmare.

“I think we should wait here for a bit,” said Adam.

Suddenly, a piercing alarm resonated through the hotel.

“What do we do?” asked Flint.

“Maybe it’s a false alarm,” said Indie.

Something clicked overhead before the sprinkler system activated, spraying water everywhere.

“Maybe not,” said Jerry.

“We need to get out of this hotel.” Adam swivelled around and strode out the door.

In the hallway, water sprayed down from the sprinklers on the ceiling and strobe lights flashed. Adam ducked through the shower and ran to the right.

Prospero called to him. “The elevator is this way, genius!”

“They’ll be shut down,” Adam yelled back. He wasn’t sure if Prospero heard him as he ran around the corner towards the elevator.

Adam opened the door to the stairwell as Indie, Flint and Jerry ran through. He waited a few moments for a disconcerted Prospero to mosey back.

He desperately wanted to say *I told you*, but resisted the urge.

“I told you we shouldn’t have come up here,” Prospero mumbled as he walked by.

Water sprayed from the ceiling and poured down the concrete steps like a waterfall. They couldn’t walk too fast as the stairs became increasingly slippery. The piercing alarms echoed loudly through the concrete stairwell. The group splashed down the stairs with Adam at the rear.

A few times, one of them yelled something but Adam couldn’t decipher the words. He was sure he smelled smoke as they approached the fifth floor. The lights flickered a few times, but didn't go out. Sporadic graffiti decorated the dirty concrete walls.

More people entered the stairwell above and below them and sloshed down the waterfall stairs.

As they neared the ground floor, more graffiti filled the walls, and the smell of smoke intensified. Above them, someone screamed.

"Hurry!" Adam yelled but doubted anyone heard him.

Jerry limped down the stairs ahead of him, with the rest of the group descending a few flights below.

Eventually, they found the door at the bottom and burst into the street. Jerry held his leg and winced in pain. A gunshot rang out from somewhere and Adam ducked. He joined Jerry behind an oleander shrub.

Although the evergreen bush wouldn't stop any bullets, it offered some concealment.

"Where is everybody?" he asked.

"I don't know." Jerry's voice was shaky. "You should go."

"What? No! What about you?"

"My knee is not doing too good. I can't run."

Adam squinted as more gunfire erupted from every direction. An explosion nearby shook the ground.

"Hey!"

Adam heard the voice but didn't know where it was coming from.

"Over here!"

He peered around the bush and saw Indie and the others huddled behind a large stanchion near the hotel lobby doors. LED screens covered the square pillar on all sides. The screen flickered. A digital wave rippled then disappeared, and a picture of a steak dinner appeared.

"Come on, we have to go!" Adam said to Jerry.

"I'm too old for this."

Adam grabbed his arm and stared him in the eye. "You're about the same age as my father. He is going to survive and so are you."

He wrapped his arm around Jerry's shoulder and stood up. It reminded Adam of him and his father in the three-legged race at a family reunion. They fell three times and finished second last in that race.

Bullets screamed past them, carving pockmarks into the wall. Unlike the reunion, if they tripped in this race, Adam and Jerry might die. They limp-walked towards the pillar and dove behind it as a bullet hit the LED screen. The steak dinner exploded, sending glass and hundreds of tiny LED modules tinkling across the sidewalk.

"Are you okay?" asked Indie.

"My knee is shot," Jerry said, panting.

"We need to get out of here!" Adam yelled over the deafening gunfire around them.

"No kidding," Prospero yelled back.

"We're right behind you." Flint offered a thumbs up. His quirky smile betrayed his fear.

"We should go that way." Prospero pointed south, past the hotel lobby entrance.

A low rumble shook the ground, and through the din of gunfire and explosions, Adam heard a strange rattling sound coming from the south.

"No, we need to go this way." He pointed in the opposite direction where three men fired automatic weapons from behind a yellow Porsche.

"You want to go towards the guys with guns?" asked Prospero.

"I hear something," Adam tried to explain.

"Yeah, it's called a war!"

"There's a strange—"

Adam shielded his eyes as a chunk of pillar flew off, showering him with chunks of plastic and plaster. There wasn't time to debate Prospero or explain his decision. The combination of the unsettling rattling noise and the vibrations in the ground filled him with growing dread.

"Do what you want." Adam put his arm around Jerry and

helped him up.

"I'll help him," said Indie.

"No, I should—"

She pointed at him with a stern expression. "It's up to you to lead and know where we're going. I'll help Jerry."

Adam waited for a brief pause in the gunfire.

"Now!" he yelled and crouch-walked along the side of the building.

He edged along the shrubbery as the others followed.

"I still think this is a bad idea," Prospero mumbled from the back.

Adam raised his arm in a clenched fist. The other stopped and crouched behind him.

Adam watched the gunmen ahead of them. One wore a red hat and the other a red shirt. He followed their line of sight to where they were shooting. On the opposite side of the driveway circle, two men in blue bandanas returned fire. One of them stopped to reload, while the other yelled into his cell phone.

The ground rumbled like an earthquake and the rattling grew louder.

"Go!" Adam yelled and led the group towards the gunmen in red. "Hold your fire! We aren't armed!"

The man in the red hat aimed his gun at Adam but didn't shoot. "Identify yourself. Who are you with?"

"We're innocent bystanders. Don't shoot."

He waved them on. "Move along."

Adam led them past the men and around the building. He waited for the others to catch up. Prospero was the last to round the corner.

The ground shook violently and Prospero peered back around the corner behind them.

He returned with wide eyes. "Get dow—!"

A massive explosion cut off his warning. The ground shook and an ear-splitting shockwave threw Adam to the ground. The air instantly filled with dust and smoke. Adam covered his ears and clenched his body on the ground until the rumbling subsided. He blinked rapidly and rubbed his eyes as he rose slowly to his knees.

"Is everyone okay?" He couldn't hear his voice over his ringing ears.

Prospero frantically yelled and waved his arms. Still deafened by the blast, Adam tried to read his lips.

Although Adam could read music better than he could read lips, the word Prospero was yelling was unmistakable – *tank*.

Jerry winced in pain as he held his knee, Indie rubbed dust from her eyes and Flint peered around the corner. Nobody was hurt - yet.

"Move!" he yelled.

The gunfire paused, but the rattle and clanking of the tank rumbled towards them. They scrambled across a small roadway to an eight-level parking garage on the other side.

The sound of vehicles and voices echoed through the concrete floors and walls. He turned right, leading them through the garage, shimmying between the parked cars. They emerged out the other side to a surprising calm. However, the sudden tranquillity didn't last long. To the right, he could still hear the tank crashing towards them. An armed group jogged through the open space of the multi-lane road to the left.

Dozens of echoing footsteps in the parking garage behind them sounded like a small army. Ahead of them, a small roadway led to a circular overhang. The entrance to the Royale Hotel awaited at the far side of the overhang. Despite the broken glass and a smouldering Ferrari, the area looked relatively peaceful. He rushed towards it, with the others following close behind. Smoke rose from the blackened hood of the Ferrari and he could feel the heat as he crept by. Adam stepped through the shattered doors of the hotel and peered inside. Other than the flashing, dinging slot machines, the casino floor looked quiet.

Behind him, Indie helped Jerry limp into the hotel.

"Are you okay?" Adam asked Jerry.

"I can't go much further," he answered with a grimace.

Adam looked around. "We need a place to hide."

The gambling floor looked eerily quiet. The lights flashed, the machines chirped and a screen above the entrance to the sports book room showed ads for topless dancing girls.

Prospero looked at Indie. "Remember the last time we were here?"

She nodded. "Back then, I thought you were Edward Lewis from Pretty Woman. Now I realize you're more like Daniel Cleaver from Bridget Jones's Diary."

"I don't know who those people are," said Prospero.

"Hugh Grant!" Flint pointed at Indie. "He played a rich jerk in that movie."

Indie looked at Flint with an incredulous expression. "How do you know that?"

Flint shrugged. "I had a foster mom who watched rom-coms non-stop. Most of them were pretty cheesy, but I still liked—."

Gunfire from outside the doors interrupted him.

"Come on!" said Adam, leading them towards the slot machines.

Instead of walking along the winding pedestrian path, he threaded between the baccarat tables, slots, and roulette wheels.

He crouched behind a Wizard of Oz slot machine with Flint beside him. A moment later, Prospero joined them.

"You know, you could help Jerry," Adam said to Prospero.

"So could you," he retorted.

The slot machine above Adam dinged, startling him. He looked up at the machine and the cowardly lion seemed to look back at him.

Just as Indie and Jerry limped around the baccarat table, a gunshot rang out and a bullet pierced the slot machine. The curtain and the wizard exploded, showering the carpet with glass and plastic.

More gunfire, yelling, and an explosion soon followed.

Adam eyed a dark corner away from the gambling floor and

dashed towards it. He paused between a rewards card machine and a Wheel of Fortune slot machine. A few yards separated him from the dark corner, an open space in between. Bullets zinged past every few seconds as fighters on either side traded gunfire.

"Everybody ready?" he asked.

"Ready to die?" asked Prospero.

"We have to make it across this—" He pointed at the tiled walkway.

Flint finished his sentence. "No-man's-land."

"Right. When I say go, we have to run."

"Okay," Indie panted heavily.

Adam knelt beside Jerry and helped him up. "I got him."

Indie offered a pained smile. "We can do this."

"I hope so," Jerry grunted between them.

Adam waited for a brief lull in the battle and yelled, "Go!"

They dragged Jerry across the no-man's-land, almost throwing him across to the other side.

Adam lay on the floor beside Jerry, looking up. He watched Flint cross like it was a game of Frogger. Prospero dashed across, knocking Flint over.

Flint screamed as a bullet pierced his chest. Blood sprayed across the carpet as he flailed in agony.

Adam leapt to his feet and dove towards Flint. He scooped the boy up and carried him like a football to the others. Either the boy was extremely light or Adam's adrenaline gave him superpowers.

As Adam set him down against the wall, he felt a bullet graze his leg. It felt like a giant mosquito bit him.

"Keep going!" he yelled and carried Flint past the unlit *Platinum Groove* sign on the wall.

He tripped over a figure on the ground, sending Flint rolling across the carpet.

"Ahhhhh!" Flint screamed.

"Flint? Are you okay?" Adam was sure the kid was dead. If the bullet to the heart didn't kill him, throwing him across the floor did.

"I'd say it's about three hit points," Flint said, holding his arm. Blood seeped through the fingers clasped around his forearm.

Adam sighed. "I thought you were shot in the chest. I thought you were going to die!"

"No way! This is too exciting to die!"

Prospero and Indie helped Jerry but stopped at the figure on the floor.

"This is that guy!" Indie yelled.

"What guy?" asked Prospero.

"The man you tried to bribe to get into the club."

"Is he dead?" asked Flint.

A dark crimson splotch stained the man's white shirt and suit jacket. Indie knelt and pressed her fingers against his neck.

"I don't feel anything."

"That means he's dead, right?"

"Probably, but I've never felt someone's pulse before."

"Try plugging his nose." Flint leaned close to the body.

"Feel for his breath," said Prospero.

"If he's not moving, he's dead," said Jerry, "and if we don't keep moving, we will be too."

"He's right," said Adam, pulling Flint away from the body.

"Wait!" Indie rifled through the man's pockets.

"You're robbing a dead man?" asked Prospero.

She pulled her hand out of his side pocket with a keycard. "Got it!"

"What is *that* for?" asked Adam.

Indie pointed at the elevator. "The club!"

A few minutes later, they stumbled out of the elevator on the 11th floor and down a dark corridor. They flopped down on the dance floor. Flint clasped his bleeding arm, Jerry grunted in pain, holding his knee, Prospero complained about glass in his back and a steady stream of blood poured from Adam's leg.

"I need a medic," yelled Flint.

"We all need medics," said Prospero.

Jerry, Adam, Flint and Prospero sat down and looked up at

Indie.

"Why is everyone looking at me? I'm not a nurse."

They said nothing but continued to stare at her.

"You think because I'm a woman, I should take care of you?"

"You're the only one not injured," said Adam.

"What about Prospero? He's not injured either."

"I have glass shards in my back."

"What do you want me to do?" she asked. "We should be going to a hospital."

"You could try calling an ambulance," Prospero suggested with a smirk.

"I'll help," said Adam. "If the internet is still working, we can look stuff up on your phone."

They spent the next hour treating their wounds. Indie found a first aid kit in the staff lunchroom and they used her phone to search for medical advice. The internet connection was slow, but still worked. Flint's arm was the worst wound. Fortunately, the bullet passed through his forearm, but the bleeding was difficult to stop. They couldn't find a needle and thread, so they just wrapped the wound tightly. Adam's leg had already stopped bleeding, so they wrapped it as well. Indie used tweezers to remove three glass shards from Prospero's back and dabbed the wound with a wet cloth. There was nothing to do to help Jerry. He assured them that all he needed was rest.

Once they treated Adam, Flint and Jerry's wounds, Flint found some snacks and bottled water. Adam didn't realize he was hungry until the crackers touched his lips. He scarfed down the package quickly and guzzled a bottle of water just as fast.

Once partially satiated, he flopped down on a padded bench beside the pool. In front of him, Indie sat at the pool edge with bare feet dangling in the warm water. At the bar, Prospero perused the collection of liquor, while Jerry napped on a puffy, leather couch.

Flint wandered past the pools to the edge of the club and watched the Vegas strip below.

"Guys, check this out!" he called.

The sounds of battle were non-stop and, like the others, Adam wanted to enjoy these few moments of safety.

Indie's stolen key card got them up to the club in the elevator and the only other way up was 11 flights of stairs and two locked doors. The Platinum Groove nightclub felt safe. They could still hear gunshots, explosions, and screeching cars, but at least they were not in any immediate danger. The brief reprieve gave them a chance to decompress.

"You *have* to see this!" yelled Flint.

Their mad dash through a violent battle, and a gunshot to the arm, were not enough to hamper the young man's constant enthusiasm.

"You should stay away from the edge," Indie called.

"This is crazy. It's like Sagat versus Senua."

"What?" Indie lifted her feet out of the pool, stood up and sauntered towards him.

She looked over the edge. "That is the strangest thing I've seen all day."

His curiosity was too much, and Adam joined them.

Prospero came out from behind the bar, holding a bottle of Scotch. "What's going on?"

"Now I want to see," said Jerry. "Give me a hand."

A few minutes later, the five of them leaned against the rail, looking down at the Vegas strip below.

Small gun battles raged in various surrounding streets, but the street directly below was almost empty.

To the south, a woman with honey-blond hair in a tight ponytail, cowboy boots and a red shirt sat on a black horse in the middle of the street. A heavily stained cloth wrapped around her head betrayed a bleeding ear beneath.

To the north, a man with an eye patch and a tattered blue baseball cap sat in a dirty UTV with fat tires.

Flint pointed at the woman. "That's Senua."

"Who is Senua?" asked Indie.

"She's a Pictish warrior from Hellblade. Her father cut her ear off."

"What?" asked Prospero.

"It's a video game," said Adam.

"And that's Sagat." Flint nodded towards the man facing Senua. "He's a Muay Thai expert from Street Fighter who lost his eye in a battle with Ryu."

"They look like they hate each other," said Indie.

"I'm cheering for the girl," said Flint.

"This isn't a video game," said Indie. "Those are real people down there."

"It *looks* like a video game."

The woman dismounted, still staring at the man. She dropped her rifle and yelled something. A moment passed before the man with the eyepatch dropped his weapon. They charged each other like two angry bulls.

CHAPTER 22

Two days before the government declared martial law, twenty-nine-year-old Miles Montague stood at the far side of the gun range and pushed his orange-tinted safety glasses up the bridge of his nose. He removed his blue baseball cap and smoothed back his unruly curly black hair. Once donned, the earmuffs blocked out the sound of the Vegas desert. He picked up the shotgun and inspected the chamber before pumping the Remington 870. The chu-chunk sound was like the opening beat of a familiar song. With the stock firmly nestled against his shoulder, Miles pointed the barrel at the honeydew melon. Although the watermelon was the preferred fruit choice for shotgun practices, it was too easy for Miles. Also, the grocery store ran out of most fruit including watermelons, yesterday. He grabbed the melon at the end of a hectic grocery run that morning. It wasn't completely rotten, but definitely not edible and perfect for blasting with 30 pellets of buckshot. He lined the front sight with the yellow fruit and squeezed the trigger. The melon exploded, sending chunks, seeds and rotten juice everywhere. He removed the earmuffs and smiled.

"Are you coming, Miles?" yelled a voice behind him. "The meeting starts in five minutes."

"I'll be there," he replied as he picked up the spent shell casing and tossed it in a nearby trash bin.

He flicked on the safety and walked away from the shooting range. After only a few steps, he stopped and went back to retrieve his blue baseball cap. The hat was a gift from Marta. She knew he liked baseball and bought him a hat shortly after they met. It was for a local minor league team, instead of his team, the Arizona Diamondbacks, but his love for her overrode his need to correct her.

He brushed his hair back with his hand and slid the hat on. After years of wearing the cap, it was dirty, and tattered and the Little League logo was missing, but it fit on his head like a customized glove.

A light wind blew off the arid plains of the Nevada desert. However, it did little to offset the oppressing heat from the broiling sun hovering above the white peaks of the Spring Mountain range.

They reminded him of the Amambay Mountains. The ranges in Paraná were green and lush, while these looked like someone dropped a nuclear bomb and eradicated all life forms. In some areas near here, that *is* what happened. And, if the right-wingers have their way, the entire world *will* look like this. Denying climate change seemed to give them the freedom to continue their selfish, world-destroying, carbon-emitting, capitalist agendas.

He sauntered towards the beige brick building with a red tin roof. A small crowd gathered in the parking lot under the shade of an overhang extending from the building. Miles leaned against the signpost with directions to the archery range.

A tall man in a blue shirt and blue cowboy hat and long brown beard stood in front of a small crowd. Miles thought the blue cowboy hat looked odd as if it was part of a costume.

"Good afternoon, everybody. For those of you who don't know, my name is Wendel. It's good to see so many people still believe in democracy and the rule of law."

He held up his phone. "We have definitive proof right-wing radicals poisoned the president and are behind the cyberattacks. They also created the downfall of our banking system. The alt-right wasn't happy enough that the top one percent owned ninety-nine percent of the wealth. No! They want *all* the money for themselves. We can't let these neoconservatives steal our money and then starve us to death!"

The small crowd clapped and cheered. Wendel nodded and clapped along before continuing.

“We have reports they are about to take control of our great city. The police are trying to control looters, vandals and violent right-wing protests, but are about to be overrun by these armed radicals.”

“What about the army?” asked a woman near the front.

“As you know, most of the high-ranking officers are right-leaning and are likely to turn against the people they swore to protect. From what I’ve heard on social media, this was their plan all along. They create chaos by stealing our money and attacking our institutions. Then the top military brass convinces the government to declare martial law. Now we have no rights or freedoms and they can throw anyone who opposes them in jail with no regard for the rule of law. Next, they’ll be herding us onto trains and shuttling us to special *camps!* We can’t let this happen. We *must* fight back.”

“Are there others?” yelled an older man.

“Yes! We are one of many groups gathering for a major offensive tomorrow. Central Command has asked us to collect as much ammo and guns as we can and meet at the Neon Oasis for a big gathering. Now, does anyone have any actual military experience?”

Miles raised his hand. “I do!”

“What sort of experience do you have?”

Miles crossed his arms. “I fought the fascist, colonial forces in Paraná for three years.”

“Excellent. Anyone else?”

A few others also had some military experience. They were told to meet at the pistol range after the meeting. An hour later, Miles and five others met at the range where they were paired off and given a special mission.

Miles’ partner was twenty-year-old Randy Rantskill. Randy was a tall, skinny young man with prematurely balding brown hair.

Later that evening, the pair rode across the sandy, arid

flatlands in an off-road UTV with fat tires and sizable suspension springs. Two other UTVs bumped along the desert on either side. One towed a small utility trailer. Their headlights swung wildly in the darkness like three pairs of light sabers.

Miles smiled as he swerved around another sagebrush and narrowly avoided a Pinyon pine. Randy's non-stop questions undermined his exciting ride, bouncing over the dips and hills of charcoal sand of the Nevada desert.

"Have you ever killed a man?"

"Yeah."

"How many?"

"Only people that deserved it. I thought you had military experience?"

"I do," Randy replied. "After basic training, I started AIT but dropped out after a couple of months. I don't like being told what to do."

"I know the feeling."

"How do you know we're going the right way?"

"Do you ever stop talking?"

"I'm just saying – it's really dark out here and we aren't driving on the road. Wouldn't it be easier to take the regular roads?"

"We aren't using traditional roads because this is a covert mission. As long as we keep the city on our right and the mountains on our left, we'll eventually hit Eagle's Nest Air Force Base, but hopefully, we'll find our contact first."

"Do you think we'll be shooting anybody?"

"I hope not." Miles nodded at the AR-15 Randy cradled in his arms. "Do you know how to use that?"

"I used an M16 in the army, which is pretty much the same thing. How long were you in Paraná?"

"Did they kick you out of the army because you talked too much?"

"No. They said I didn't respect authority and—"

Miles interrupted him. "Why don't we pretend we're on a covert mission which requires complete silence."

"I thought this *was* a covert mission. Also, these UTVs are pretty noisy and the headlights are—"

The grey desert dropped steeply where a previous rainfall created a now empty creek bed. Miles stomped on the gas and the UTV slammed into the crater. Randy almost flew out the front of the vehicle in mid-sentence.

He squealed as the high-performance front-end suspension bounced them out the other side.

"Dude!" yelled Randy. "You did that on purpose."

"What if instead of jabbering on, you looked ahead and warned me of any obstacles?"

Randy was silent for the next twenty minutes. Miles couldn't tell if he was pouting or looking for other empty creek beds, but he didn't care. Randy's verbal diarrhea reminded him of his little brother, Stephen who used to be like that.

However, Stephen stopped talking in his sophomore year in high school. He came out to his parents in grade nine. His parents were disappointed and mostly avoided the subject. Stephen's peers at school tormented him ruthlessly. They hurled insults, stuffed him in a locker and painted *fag* on his locker in bright red paint. Miles wanted to stand up for his little brother, but he was busy playing football.

It was the vulgar and manipulated video circulating online showing Stephen performing obscene sexual acts that sent his brother deeper into a depressive spiral. Three months later, their mother found him lying unconscious on the bedroom floor, foaming at the mouth. Miles watched the medics attend to his lifeless body. Stephen died in the ambulance on the way to the hospital.

The next day, Miles stormed into school and found the group of bullies that painted Stephen's locker. He pounded the ringleader mercilessly until a teacher tackled him. The boy suffered from two broken ribs and the doctors wired his jaw back together.

Although the school wanted to expel Miles, they suspended him for two months, citing *extenuating circumstances*. During his time away from school, Miles grieved for his brother and regretted his late intervention. The tragedy planted a seed of anger deep in his fertile soul.

Two years later, his father lost his job. He worked at Polysil for forty-two years, working his way up from packaging, to quality control, to manager, to vice president of operations. The polymer, silicone and bio-solutions manufacturer went bankrupt when they couldn't compete with similar companies in China. The top brass at Polysil retained their golden parachutes, and the banks took the rest. All the employees, including Miles' father, got nothing. No retirement money, no severance – nothing. The only thing he got from the company was sickness. After working for over four decades breathing in toxic chemicals, his father developed silicosis. He died of tuberculosis a year later, leaving his family heartbroken and penniless.

The seed of anger germinated in Miles.

After high school, he got a minimum wage job at the local grocery store. A union representative approached him and some of his fellow employees. As discussions about unionizing grew in the break room and on the floor, management grew worried. They offered incentives and promised better pay and working conditions. When that didn't work, they resorted to monitoring, interrogating, intimidating and even firing employees. The harsh tactics proved successful.

The union vote lost by a slim margin.

Miles' anger sprouted. A few months later, he joined the People's Socialist Movement of America, where he met a girl from Paraná. Marta told him about her family's struggle against the fascist colonial government in Paraná. They quickly fell in love and made plans to live in a social collective.

At Christmas, she went back to Paraná to be with her family. During the holidays, she joined a demonstration in the capital, protesting against the mistreatment of the indigenous Guarani people. The police tried unsuccessfully to dissuade the demonstration before the government ordered the military to quash the protest. Soldiers beat many of the protestors, including Marta. They crushed her skull on the street in the shadow of the gleaming Paraná government palace.

Like a toxic nightshade plant, Adam's anger blossomed. He boarded a plane to Paraná for Marta's funeral. A member of a local socialist rebel group approached Miles after the service. It wasn't hard to convince him to join their cause. They trained him in guerilla warfare for one month. He fought the fascist and colonial government forces for the next three years in the jungles and on the streets until they arrested and deported him.

He moved into his mother's basement in Phoenix, where he spent most of his days deep in the left-leaning chat rooms and social media sites, simmering with rage.

When he heard the right-wing radicals were responsible for the cyberattacks and subsequent bank failures, he wasn't surprised. It was something Liberal intellectuals had said would happen. And once he heard the call to arms for all true Americans to fight the rednecks trying to take over the country, Miles was the first to sign up. It took him almost a full day to drive from Phoenix to Las Vegas. That was two days ago. Finally, he was doing what he was meant to do. He would fight the right-wing radicals. He would do it for Stephen who was bullied by bigots until he committed suicide, for his father who was robbed and left for dead by greedy capitalists, and for beautiful Marta killed by colonizing fascists. He would fight for all Americans who believed in the dream of an equitable society.

The headlights lit up dark figures and a stationary vehicle ahead. Miles held up his fist and slowed to a stop. The two other UTVs did the same.

"We'll go in slow," he said. "You two stay slightly behind me. Don't point your weapons at anyone, but keep them on your lap."

"I thought they were friendlies," said one driver.

"They are, but you can't be too careful. Be ready for anything."

Miles pressed on the gas and rolled slowly forward towards a large green army truck. Behind the truck, a chain-link fence stretched into the darkness in both directions.

"Is this the army base?" asked Randy.

"No," Miles answered. "The base is a half mile behind them."

"Is the army on our side?"

"No, but we have a few patriots that still believe in justice and freedom."

He slowed the UTV as they approached the army truck. Two men and a woman in green army fatigues waited near the rear of the truck. Heavy green fabric covered the large truck bed. Miles hoped it was full of weapons and munitions, but wondered if a squad of special forces sat inside, ready to ambush. Despite possibly being paranoid, his years of fighting taught him to stay prepared for any eventuality.

Miles stopped the UTV a few yards from the truck. He shut off the engine and retrieved his gun. The other UTVs stopped on either side of him.

"In the deserts of the heart?" asked the woman.

Miles recited his code phrase. "Let the healing fountain start."

She smiled. "It's good to know we are not alone in our fight."

He stepped out of the UTV and walked towards her, keeping his AR-15 cradled in his arms.

"Normally I would introduce myself," she said, "but we can't take any chances. If we get caught, they'll shoot us."

Miles nodded. "I understand. What do you have for us?"

As she pulled back the fabric on the back of the truck, Miles's hands tensed in readiness on his rifle. She shone her flashlight inside, revealing three rows of steel and plastic containers of various sizes stacked over five feet high.

"Oh!" Miles tried to contain his excitement. "Hopefully, we can carry all of that."

"We have little time," she said. "If they notice we're missing from the base, they might come looking for us."

Miles squinted and tilted his head. "You're sure nobody followed you?"

"Of course."

They pulled the UTVs closer and loaded the boxes and crates in the back of their vehicles and the small trailer.

With only three boxes left, Miles heard a low rumble. The others heard it too. Miles recognized the sound immediately.

"Helicopter!" he shouted.

"Time to go!" yelled the woman. She shoved the remaining boxes off the truck bed. One landed on Randy's toe. "Hey! That hurt."

"Start the truck!" she ordered as she ran back to the passenger side door.

One of her men on the opposite side of the truck suddenly pitched forward, landing face-first in the dust with a bloody hole in his back.

The sound of the gunshot hit their ears a moment later. Like the starting pistol before the 100-metre dash, the shot initiated a flurry of actions.

Miles dove behind his UTV and the others did the same. More gunshots rang out as bullets tore through the green fabric on the back of the truck, and others pinged off metal. The woman rolled on the ground, and dove under her truck.

One of Miles' men shot randomly from his hip into the darkness until a bullet ripped through his shoulder and he screamed and fell backwards. The helicopter hovered overhead, a spotlight illuminating the entire area.

Miles lined his sights at the bright spotlight and fired. He smiled at the satisfying sound of bullets shattering glass. The helicopter veered away, and the shooting stopped. However, things were about to get worse.

Several pairs of headlights pointed at them from the east as the rumble of several diesel engines grew louder.

"Let's go!" shouted Miles.

"What about the other boxes?" Randy still stood at the back of the truck. Somehow, he remained unhurt except for his toe.

"Leave them!"

More headlights appeared in the west.

The woman rolled out from under the truck and dove into the cab. She started the engine as the other soldier jumped into the passenger side. The tires threw dirt and dust into the darkness as the truck pulled away.

One of Miles' men tried to drag the downed man back to the UTV.

"Leave him!" yelled Miles. "He's already dead."

Above, the helicopter followed the army truck. It fired a Hydra 70 rocket a moment later. Miles heard the rocket slice through the sky before the truck exploded in a ball of fire.

"Which way are we going?" yelled the driver of one of the other UTVs.

Miles looked up and saw dozens of pairs of headlights dotting the landscape in a wide 180-degree arc. With the fence line behind them, the army trucks closing in and a helicopter overhead, they were trapped.

Miles assessed his predicament. Two of his men were down, two huddled behind their ATVs, one lay on the ground firing at the trucks, while Randy sat beside him with a look of terror on his face.

Miles' training kicked in and he shouted orders.

"You keep shooting at the trucks. Aim for the tires."

He pointed at the two men huddled down. "Search these boxes for something useful. Randy, pull yourself together. Shoot at the helicopter. Don't let it get too close."

Miles didn't wait to see if they obeyed his orders. He hunted through the boxes of munitions until he found a long, green metal box. He pulled out an RPG and loaded it. One of the ATV drivers dropped as the gunner in the helicopter peppered his body with bullets.

Miles rested the RPG on his shoulder, pointed it at the helicopter, and fired. The rocket pierced through the darkness and hit the rear rotor. The helicopter spiralled to the ground and exploded. He reloaded and fired another rocket towards an oncoming truck. It skipped off the ground and sailed harmlessly into the desert.

"They're getting close!" Randy screamed.

Miles scrambled to find another rocket but knew he wouldn't have enough time to load and fire it. Instead, he grabbed his rifle and fired at the closest truck.

"We found something," shouted one of his men, still searching through the munitions boxes. Miles kept firing.

Out of the corner of his eye, he saw them lob several baseball-sized items at the incoming trucks.

"Grenade!" he screamed as he dropped to the ground. He waited for almost ten seconds, but nothing happened. The gunfire slowed and Miles tentatively raised his head. Blue, red, purple, and pink smoke billowed out of canisters in every direction. The trucks stopped in a semicircle around them but were not visible through the thick smoke. Their headlights reflected eerily off the coloured clouds of smoke, almost completely enveloping the area in a rainbow haze. Dozens of heavy footsteps pounded the desert floor as soldiers marched out of the trucks. Something rolled out of the smoke and along the ground at his feet. He looked down and recognized the holes and slots in the silver cylinder. Miles turned away, squeezed his eyes shut, and covered his ears. The percussive explosion rocked him off his feet. The flash penetrated his eyelids and the sound waves blasted through his fingers. His extensive training in Paraná prepared him for this and it took him seconds to recover.

He ran towards the fence but tripped over a body. Jumping back up, he ran into Randy, who was crouched in the fetal position.

"Come on!" he yelled, but Randy looked at him with confusion. Instead, Miles pulled his arm and motioned for him to follow. They stumbled through purple smoke and emerged near the chain-link fence. Behind them, dazed and deafened soldiers yelled conflicting orders.

Miles pointed to the top of the fence. Randy nodded and climbed over, with Miles behind him. They staggered through the darkness until they bumped into something metal.

"I think it's an old car," whispered Miles. "Let's get inside and hide."

Randy didn't respond. Either he was nodding in the darkness or still deaf from the stun grenade.

Miles felt along the side of the vehicle until he found a handle, but the passenger door was dented and too damaged to open. He found the next door and realized it was a minivan. They climbed inside and huddled behind the back seat.

"Can you hear me?" Miles whispered a few minutes later.

"Kind of," Randy replied loudly.

"Shhh! You're still partially deaf. Talk quieter. Are you okay?"

"Yeah, I think so. Where are the others?"

"They're all dead."

"Oh. Why are we hiding? Shouldn't we be getting as far away from here as possible?"

"We're in the middle of the Nevada desert at night with no means of transportation. Also, we still haven't completed our mission."

"I think we failed our mission."

"Not yet, we didn't."

"You're not seriously thinking about going back for the weapons, are you? There are fifty trained soldiers out there." His voice squealed like a boy whose voice hadn't changed yet. "What are you planning on doing?"

"*We* are going back to get them."

"Are you crazy?"

"No, just determined."

Miles sat up and looked out the window. On the other side of the fence, soldiers loaded the stolen munitions into the back of a truck.

"How many bullets do you have in your mag?"

"None. But I have these."

Miles heard rustling but couldn't see what Randy was doing. Something cold and metallic touched his hand. He felt the metallic ball and smiled in the darkness.

"Are these grenades?"

"I have three of them. I had more, but couldn't fit them in my pocket."
"Perfect. Have you ever played baseball?"
"What?"
"Baseball. Have you ever played baseball? I was never much of a sports guy, but you seem like the type who might have played."
"I played centre field. Shouldn't we be planning our escape instead of talking about our hobbies?"
"How good was your arm?"
"I couldn't pitch, but threw a few balls from centerfield to the infield – maybe two hundred feet."
"Impressive! Do you think you could throw a grenade that far?"
"No way! I am *not* going to throw grenades at those soldiers. I'm too young to die."
"You won't be throwing at them."
Miles looked out the window again. The soldiers finished loading the crates and bins into the trucks. Some started the ATVs while the others returned to the other trucks.
"Now's our chance. Let's go." Miles opened the van door and stepped out, but Randy remained inside.
"Are you coming?"
"No. I'm waiting until they're gone."
"Move, soldier!" Miles yelled.
"No."
"Are you scared?" Miles shouted.
"Of course, I'm scared! We almost died out there! Everyone else is dead."
Miles leaned in close, although he wasn't sure Randy could see him. "If the right-wing fascists continue destroying our country, we'll all be dead, anyway. The rest of our compatriots are counting on us. We are the last ones. If we don't bring back those weapons, the right-wing radicals will slaughter them all. Get up, be a man and show me how good your throwing arm is."
"You have a plan, right?"
"Of course."

A few minutes later, they lay on their bellies, looking through the fence. Most of the trucks rumbled away into the dark desert night. Two trucks remained, including one with the boxes of munitions in the back.

"Okay, NOW!" said Miles, and they both got to their feet and tossed their rifles over the fence. Randy reared back and threw a grenade as hard as he could to the west of their position.

They were halfway up the fence when it landed, and on the other side when it exploded. One of the trucks steered towards the explosion, leaving the other truck behind. As the clutch ground into first gear, Miles and Randy stood on either side of the cab with their guns pointed at the windows. The soldiers slowly opened their doors.

"Get out and lie on the ground!" yelled Randy.

"You're making a mistake," said one soldier.

They relieved the soldiers of their weapons and climbed into the cab. The other truck chasing the exploding grenade wheeled around and drove towards them.

Randy opened his door and tossed a grenade in their direction as Miles put the truck in gear. The pursuing truck tried to veer away from the grenade, but the explosion blew out the front tire and it skidded to a stop. Some of the other trucks turned around and headed in their direction.

"Hold on!" yelled Miles as he turned the truck towards the fence and stomped on the gas. The truck blew through the fence and into the scrap yard. Miles steered through the maze of wrecked vehicles and scrap metal. "Randy, look on the dash and see if you can find a switch for the blackout lights."

"What are blackout lights?"

The truck hit the front end of a compact car, crushing the plastic bumper, but barely slowing the heavy army truck.

"Just do it!" Miles yelled.

Randy fumbled around the dash before finally finding the switch. The main headlights turned off, and a diffused horizontal beam turned on, giving them a dim view in front, but concealing them from their pursuers.

After weaving through the labyrinth of ruined cars, Miles blasted through the front gate and onto the road. A minute later, he veered off the pavement and back into the desert.

Miles looked in the mirror and didn't see any lights.

"That was awesome! I can't believe we pulled that off!" yelled Randy.

"Don't get too excited," said Miles. "The war has just begun."

It was still dark when they made it back to the shooting range. Wendel congratulated them on a successful mission and told them to get some sleep. It didn't take long for Miles to fall asleep in his tent in the makeshift RV park next to the shooting range.

The next morning, Miles woke as a man he didn't recognize gently shook his shoulder.

"Sorry to wake you sir, but Captain Wendel wants to talk to you."

Miles sat up and blinked away his nightmares. "What time is it?"

"Ten-thirty, sir." He held out a bagel and a mug. "The coffee is black, but I can get you some sugar and powdered creamer. We don't have any real cream, but—"

"Black is good." Miles took the bagel and coffee. "Who are you, and why are you being so nice to me?"

"Jenkins, sir. Wendel said to wake you *nicely*."

Miles dressed, and ate his bagel, and took his coffee to the camper at the end of the row. Wendel stood outside the door, staring at his phone. He looked up as Miles approached and set down his phone.

"Good morning, Miles. I just want to say again, what an amazing job you did last night."

"Four good men died on that mission."

Wendel removed his big blue cowboy hat. "Yes, that was unfortunate. However, if it wasn't for you, everyone would be dead and we wouldn't have all those weapons and ammunition you liberated."

"Will the army come after us now?"

"Not likely. From what I've heard, the local army reserve and National Guard are in disarray. The government ordered the military to keep order and enact martial law. A few units revolted against the military brass, refusing to move against American citizens. Although one or two units are supposedly moving into the city this afternoon, many are abandoning their post to be with their families."

"Wow! Things are devolving fast."

"Yes, which is why we must also act fast. While democracy-loving believers are gathering today at the Oasis, a far-right militant group is forming south of the city. And that is where you come in."

"What do you mean?"

"A sizable force is assembling near the women's prison just south of Vegas. We have reliable intel that a farm further south is bringing them weapons, bombs, rockets and plastic explosives. We need you to intercept the supply run. There is a blockade on the highway, just before the prison. You must intercept the delivery vehicles before they reach the blockade."

"I'll need better transportation than the UTV's."

"Of course. You'll get heavy duty dune buggies."

"Dune buggies? I was hoping for army trucks or maybe a tank."

"That would be nice, but we don't have any tanks—yet, and trucks are too slow. Vegas is already in chaos, so you'll need to go around. Dune buggies will take you across the desert fast. Three other buggies will accompany you, with two armed men in each."

"Great, when do we leave?"

CHAPTER 23

While Miles received his mission briefing at the pistol range, north of Vegas, a crew cab truck towing an empty horse trailer pulled up to a bus stop at the south end of the city. Ryder Begay gathered her long honey-blond hair into a tight ponytail and snapped on a black scrunchie. She rubbed her sweaty neck and stepped out of the truck.

“Don’t be too late,” her father said from the driver’s seat. “We’re leaving first thing in the morning.”

“I’ll be back before you know it, Daddy. Don’t wait up.”

She smiled and closed the door.

Waving goodbye, he drove away with the horse trailer rattling behind him.

Her cowboy boots clicked on the sidewalk as she sauntered towards the bus shelter. She wasn’t sure if the glass box could provide relief from the relentless sun or create an oven. Ryder opted for waiting on the sidewalk. The last time she was in Vegas was with a group of friends from high school. The trip was an exciting flurry of wild parties, gambling, drinking and shows. Four years later, she was back, except this time with her father.

After nagging him for the entire four-and-a-half-hour trip from Arizona, he finally agreed to let her see a show. Instead of a flamboyant magician with a cheesy cape or dancing cowboys with steroid-filled abs, she was going to a spectacle that perfectly suited her.

The brakes on the bus squeaked as it slowed to a stop at the bus stop. The doors opened, and she climbed the steps.

“Cash only!” said the driver, “and I don’t make change.”

“That’s fine, sir,” she replied as she pulled a money clip from her pocket. "Does this bus get me to the Pit?"

"I can get you pretty close."

If her father drove another ten minutes into Vegas, he could have dropped her off at the front doors to the Pit. But he was as stubborn as an unbroken quarter horse and refused to drive his truck and horse trailer into the city, saying he *didn't trust them city drivers.*

Instead, he drove to the southern edge of the city and let her out before driving back to their motel.

An hour and a half later, she strode through the packed parking lot of the Pit Stadium and stood in the slow-moving line at the entrance.

A large man with bulging biceps stood quietly behind her. Ryder took two steps forward as the line inched ahead and listened to an argument near the front of the line. Two middle-aged men argued with a clerk. She faced them with crossed arms and an apologetic, but determined glare.

"I'm sorry, but our payment system is currently unavailable," she said.

"We drove for two days to watch this event and now you're telling us we can't come in?"

"At the present time, we only accept cash."

"This isn't legal. We have the right to pay with a credit card."

"You can either pay with cash or leave."

"Who keeps that kind of money in cash?"

Ryder turned away as they continued arguing and pulled out her money clip. As she counted the bills, she saw the man behind her watching. His dark hair and light brown skin gave away his nationality as Mexican. She didn't have issues with Mexicans. Many of the hands at her father's ranch were Mexicans and were nice people. However, thousands of Mexicans – some of them criminals - crossed the border illegally and stole American jobs.

"You got a problem, hombre?" she growled.

The man was several inches taller and twenty pounds heavier than her, but she figured it would take about six seconds to give him a bloody nose and throw him to the ground.

He held his hands up. "No problema."

She grunted and turned away. Ever since her ribs healed, she was itching for a fight. Today, she would have to settle for watching instead. When she made it to the front of the line, Ryder paid for her tickets and went inside.

The view of the octagon from her seat was impressive, and she waited with excited anticipation for the first mixed martial arts fight. However, the knowledge that she was on the wrong side of the cage muted her excitement.

As the announcer rambled on about all the amazing fights they were about to watch, Ryder looked down at her arm and thought about her own ill-fated fighting career.

It started in middle school when she slapped a girl who was flirting with her boyfriend. The girl slapped her back, and they fought each other amidst a group of cheering students. They pulled each other's hair, scratched, kicked and flailed before a teacher broke them up. Except for a few bruises and a black eye, neither sustained any injury. When she returned home, her mother scolded her, while her father took her aside. He told her that if she was going to fight, she *shouldn't fight like a girl.*

After he showed her how to punch properly and a few other self-defence manoeuvres, Ryder wanted to know more. She enrolled in karate and got her junior black belt by age 12.

In high school, she tried to join the wrestling club, but they didn't have a girls' club. With the help of her English teacher, Mrs. Barnes, she started a girls' wrestling club. She won the Arizona State Championship for Wrestling three years in a row. In her last year of high school, she joined a mixed martial arts club in Phoenix. Her trainer saw her potential and pushed Ryder hard. She trained every day for four hours during the week and double that on weekends. She proved her fighting skills by winning almost every amateur fight.

After high school, she worked part-time on her father's ranch and spent every other spare moment training.

Her coach helped her get her first professional MMA fight.

However, fight jitters caused a lack of concentration and focus and she lost by submission in the third round. That didn't stop her, and she just trained harder.

Ryder won her next seven fights with one by submission, two by decision, and four knockouts.

The MMA association saw her potential and gave her the chance for a title fight with a massive payoff. They said she had to win one more fight to qualify. Her dreams of a successful, professional MMA career were about to come true.

As she stepped into the ring, Ryder realized her opponent, Avery, was a biological male who *transitioned* a year previously. Looking back, Ryder wished she had refused to fight.

She held her own during the first round, taking him down twice and landing a few blows. Realizing *he* was stronger and faster, she attempted to bring the match to the mat for a submission hold. As she ducked down into a crouch, Avery attacked, curling his massive arms around her neck. Ryder struggled to break free, but Avery's secure hold remained. He yanked her backwards and slammed her into the mat. Her C4 vertebrae broke with a sound like a snapping branch.

It took four surgeries and six months before she walked again.

The league explained to her that, as part of their inclusive and equality agenda, it was their policy to allow transgender women to participate in their respective weight classes. Ryder's father almost killed the commissioner as he tried to explain their position.

That was two years ago. Although she had almost fully recovered, spinal nerve damage slowed the punching speed of her left arm. She would never fight professionally.

Ryder's MMA career ended before it ever began.

Now she worked full time on her father's ranch. She still enjoyed practicing at the MMA gym a few times a week and held onto a sliver of hope that her arm might fully recover.

Watching these MMA bouts in Las Vegas was bittersweet. She enjoyed watching the fighters, and envisioning what her next moves would be, but also knowing that it could have been her in that ring.

However, the far-left radicals stole her dreams when they embraced the delusions of guys pretending to be gals.

Self-identifying as a woman was as ludicrous as identifying as a hippopotamus. Allowing a biological male to compete against a woman was two massive steps backwards for equality in sport.

Avery had a record of six losses and one win before he claimed to be a woman. All of Ryder's years of training meant nothing against a biological male with naturally more muscle mass, larger bones, and more responsive twitch muscles. Ryder's father enlightened her about some of the other woke left's misguided policies, including their socialist agenda. She hated the left and everything they stood for.

The crowd roared and woke her from her angry reminiscing. A muscled fighter waved at the crowd as he pranced toward the octagon.

Ryder tried to enjoy the show, but after the final fight, she was ready to return to the motel and watch an action movie with her father.

The sun was long gone when Ryder left the Pit. She used the last of her cash to take the bus back to the hotel. Her father was snoring like a chainsaw when she returned.

When she awoke the next morning, her father was staring at the television.

"I knew this would happen," he said as the newscaster described numerous cyberattacks and the sick president. "The leftist elites are breaking down capitalism so they can rebuild our society according to their socialist agenda."

"Maybe it's the Russians or the Chinese." Ryder rubbed her eyes and stretched.

He held up his phone. "I found leaked footage of the left's plans, including proof they poisoned the president. We need to get the horse and head back to Buckeye and my arsenal."

"...and Mom?"

"Of course, but I can't protect my family without my Mossberg

500 and Ruger 10/22. If the leftists have their way, they'll breach the Second Amendment and take away my guns. Did you know that..."

"Okay, Dad – I got it. Can we please get some breakfast before the next civil war?"

"Fine, but we're eating on the road. I don't want to spend any more time than I have to in this godforsaken town."

Twenty minutes later, they were back on the road, heading southwest.

"How much money do you have left?" her father asked as they rumbled through the barren landscape of the Nevada desert.

"I have some savings – probably a few thousand. Why?"

"No, I mean, do you have any *cash*? I spent most of mine on the motel room. All the credit and debit machines are down and we'll need gas to get home."

"No, I spent most of my cash on the fight and the bus yesterday."

"That's alright, I'm sure things will be back up and running soon."

He gave a pained smile and turned the radio on. George Strait serenaded them with a song about heartaches and hard times as they drove out of the city and headed south. He turned the music down twenty minutes later as they pulled up to a white fence with a cast iron gate. The sign on the gate read *Desert Wind Ranch*.

A man with a long rifle leaning against the gate noticed their arrival and spoke into his handheld radio.

Her father rolled down his window. "What's going on?"

"Are you here to join up?" the man asked.

"Join what? I'm here to buy a horse. Where's Frank?"

"Who are you?"

"I'm Walter Begay and this is my daughter, Ryder. I spoke to Frank last week about buying one of his horses."

The man held up a finger and spoke into his radio. A moment later, he nodded, rolled the gate open and waved them through.

"That's odd," said her father. "Since when does Hank need security?"

Past the gate, a line of a dozen trucks and cars sat parked next to the open-air horse arena. They parked the truck and got out. Hank limped over to greet them. He removed his dusty beige gambler hat and extended his hand.

"Good to see you, Walter. This must be your daughter, Ryder. Are you the fighter?"

"Yes, sir," she said, shaking his hand. For a man who looked to be in his seventies, he shook hands like a grappler.

"It's a shame what happened with that pansy in the ring."

"Yes, sir."

"Hank," said her father. "Are you having a party here and what's with the guard at the gate?"

"I'm glad you're here, Walter."

"I told you I was coming, remember?"

"Yes, you want to buy the mustang. Things have changed, Walter. As the left threatens to destroy America, we must stand up for our rights."

"I understand that, but we just want our horse so we can get back to Arizona."

"We are organizing a militia of like-minded individuals who defend our great nation, and I was hoping that you and your daughter would join our cause."

"What are you planning to do?"

"There is actionable intel that major forces are gathering north of the city. They are well-armed, and well-funded by leftist elites. We are forming our own militia to destroy those that oppose the rights and freedoms that our forefathers fought for. This has been a long time coming."

"If there's war coming, I need to get back to Buckeye," her father replied. "I have a bunker stocked with guns and ammo."

"How much gas do you have for your pickup?"

"About that – I spent all my cash on the motel last night. Their machines were down. Do you have any extra?"

"Sorry, Walter, but I don't have any gas to spare. We need all our fuel for our offensive. How are you planning on paying for the horse?"

"I was going to send you a bank transfer – same as last time."

Frank shook his head. "The banks are all down right now."

"Come on, Walter. You know I'm good for it. As soon as they fix the banking problems, I can send you the money. Don't you trust me?"

"I trust you, but I don't trust the banks."

"What do you expect me to do?"

Frank put his arm around Walter's shoulder. "I have a proposal for you, Walter. We need to send out a little mission to Vegas. This advance party, consisting of a few guys with guns and some supplies, needs get to the camp set up just south of the city. Their mission is to gather intel on the city and enemy movements and deliver essential supplies to that base."

"What does this have to do with me?"

"If you provide transportation for them, I will give you the mustang and enough gas to get you back to Arizona. If the banks get back in order, you can send me the money for the horse."

Ryder's father stared into the mountains and thought for a moment. "Okay, I'll do it."

"Dad..." Ryder protested.

"We don't have a choice, Ryder. We'll make this delivery and head straight back to Buckeye."

"How many men and how many supplies?" she asked Frank.

"Four men. Two can sit in the rear seats of your pickup. The other two will ride in the back. Your gooseneck trailer is big enough for two horses, so there'll be room for supplies in the second stall. The government is initiating martial law tonight, so this has to be done today."

Her father folded his arms and sighed. "Let's see this mustang."

They followed Frank to the small paddock next to a barn with red cladding. A group of men and women cleaning their guns at a picnic table watched them walk by.

A massive, silky black stallion looked up as they approached.

His neck extended and his head perked up. The sun reflected off his glossy ebony coat.

Ryder smiled. “He’s majestic!”

“He’s also a handful,” said Frank. “Don’t let his good looks fool you. Rogue is strong and fast, but also ornery and rebellious.”

Ryder grabbed the leather bridle hanging on the fencepost and hopped the rail.

“Be careful,” said Frank.

“She knows what she’s doing,” said Walter. “Ryder’s been handling horses her entire life.”

Ryder spoke calmly as she edged towards the horse. Rogue looked away and huffed.

“Hello there, you handsome devil. Be a good boy and say hi.”

Other than some Clydesdales and an overweight Percheron, this was the biggest horse Ryder had ever seen. He was a muscular, regal stallion with imposing features.

She placed one hand on his shoulder and rubbed his soft velvet coat. After unclasping the halter, she removed it.

“I bet you would love to get out of this little paddock and go for a run, wouldn’t you? Why don’t we put this on?”

She lifted the bridle towards his head.

He turned and snapped at her hand. His teeth bit down on her hand for a moment before releasing.

Instead of crying out, Ryder gritted her teeth and pulled away. The pain was intense, but it didn’t feel like anything was broken.

“Also, he’s a biter,” yelled Frank.

“Thanks,” she called back.

She stood her ground and continued to rub his shoulder. Her hand still pulsed in pain.

“You think you can scare me away?” She kept her tone steady. “Let’s try this again.”

Ryder used both hands to jam the bit into his mouth and quickly pull the halter over his head. He chuffed and tossed his head and gnawed at the metal bit.

She tugged at the reins and walked toward her father and

Frank, but Rogue remained in place.
"Come on, big boy!" she clicked her tongue and pulled hard on the reins.
Rogue pawed at the ground a few times before relenting and following her to the fence.
"Can I take her for a spin?"
After saddling the horse, Ryder rode him around the ranch. Because of the intense desert heat, she only rode him at galloping speed for less than a minute, but he was strong and fast. He would make an excellent addition to the ranch. If she could manage his temperament, Rogue could race or perform show-jumping.
After a brief ride, she brushed him and scraped the sand from his hooves. Despite only spending a few hours with him, Ryder already loved this horse.
Frank's men loaded their supplies in the truck while Walter, Frank and Ryder ate a hearty lunch. After helping with the dishes, Ryder gave her new stallion some electrolyte supplements and loaded him into the trailer.
It was early afternoon when they were back on the road riding towards Vegas. Tom and Steve rode in the truck bed, while Jeff and Kelly sat behind Ryder and her father. All of them carried guns.
Jeff looked like a fresh young marine with his closely shaved head and serious expression, while Kelly looked more like an army veteran. His full, tangled beard couldn't contain his mischievous grin.
Most of the trip was quiet, except for the twang of a steel guitar and the drawl of a country music singer drifting out of the speakers.
As they neared the south edge of the city, twenty minutes later, Ryder turned to the men in the back.
"The deal is, we drop you off at that jail and that's it. We're not helping you unload or..."
"What is that?" Ryder pointed at the road ahead.
Her father turned to look and slowed the truck to a stop.

Men and women in fatigues stood in the middle of three lanes of highway. A city bus blocked most of the road behind them. Across the median appeared to be another similar blockade.

"Why are we stopping?" asked Jeff from the backseat.

"Because we have a roadblock," her father answered. "That wasn't there earlier today."

Kelly leaned forward. "Those are our people and that's who we're supposed to meet."

"How do you know it's them?"

"You see that horrible casino?" Kelly pointed past the blockade and to the right. A big large white building with numerous windows sat behind a massive sign that read, *Horrible's Casino*.

"I thought we were meeting at a jail."

Kelly pointed further to the right. "The women's jail is behind the casino."

"What's over there?" Ryder pointed out her window.

"That's an airport. I think it's for skydiving and stuff."

"No, not that," she said, pointing again. "What are those?"

Two dune buggies drove along a parallel road towards them.

"There are two more on my side," said Jeff.

"Go, go, go!" Kelly yelled and slapped the seat. "They're trying to ambush us!"

"I didn't sign up for this," he said, driving forward again.

"What do they want?" Ryder asked.

Kelly slapped the rear window and yelled at the men in the truck bed. "Safeties off! We have company!"

He rolled down his window and pointed his rifle out. Jeff did the same out the window on the opposite side.

One buggy surged forward, moving ahead of the truck, before driving onto the road and stopping.

Ryder's father slowed the truck to a stop.

"What are you doing?" yelled Kelly. "Keep driving!"

"They're blocking the road!" Her father pointed his hand at the buggy as if he were an angry male version of Vanna White.

"Drive through them!" Kelly yelled.

One buggy moved towards them on their right, one from

behind and another on the left. They all drove slowly like wolves gauging their prey.

"We are *not* getting in the middle of a firefight!"

"This is war, Walter. You either fight or get conquered."

"This isn't my war. I will do everything I can to keep my daughter safe." He opened his door and exited the truck. "Ryder, get out of the truck with your hands on your head and lay on the ground."

She slowly opened her door. It was like stepping into a furnace. The black pavement felt like it was on fire. She moved to the shoulder and knelt. The stones dug into her knees, but at least she wasn't laying on hot coals. The men in the truck yelled, cocked their guns, and checked their ammo clips.

"Be ready for anything, boys!"

Ryder peered under the truck at her father. Like her, he could not lay on the blistering asphalt. Instead, he knelt on one knee. The buggies converged on their position, including the one blocking the road. When they were within ten yards, one man stepped out of his buggy and pointed his gun at the truck.

Looking up from her prone position, Ryder watched a man step out of the buggy in front of the pickup truck. He removed his tattered blue baseball cap with an obscure team logo and smoothed his curly black hair.

"Good afternoon!" he yelled. "My name is Miles and I am here to take delivery of some *special* items which you possess."

"Just take what you want and leave!" yelled Ryder's father. "I want no part of this."

Ryder perked her head up. "Except for my horse!"

"You can take your communist agenda and go back to your..."

Ryder was watching Miles when she heard the shot. A bullet ripped through his left shoulder and flung him to the side.

He recovered quickly and fired at the truck. Ryder flattened to the gravel as gunshots exploded from every direction. Looking under the truck, she saw her father fall from his kneeling position. He lay flat on his back without moving.

She army crawled toward the truck. Someone above her

screamed. A man fell from the truck bed and landed beside her. She wasn't sure if it was Tom or Steve. The passenger door opened and Jeff jumped out.

"Get behind me, Ryder. I can protect you."

"Not a chance, G.I. Joe. Get away from me."

He looked wounded, as if not being able to save her was emasculating.

"Take this, then." He pulled a big black commando knife from a sheath on his leg.

"Thanks."

She was about to ask for the pistol in the leather holster, but a bullet pinged off the truck side panel and she dove under the truck. Jeff ran away from the truck, firing his rifle.

"Dad? Can you hear me? Are you okay?" she cried.

He still wasn't moving, and she shuffled towards him.

Just as she was about to emerge from the other side, the firing stopped.

"Everyone okay?"

The voice was close, and Ryder shimmied back under the truck. The hot pavement felt like it was burning through her clothes.

She watched her father suddenly move. His head turned to the side to look at her. Blood leaked from a wound near his stomach and his chest moved up and down rapidly. She smiled when his soft blue eyes locked on hers.

"We got a live one here." It was Miles' voice. His tan army boots appeared next to her father.

Her father looked at her with a pained smile and his mouth moved as if he was attempting to speak.

The barrel of Miles' gun hovered over her father's head for a moment before a deafening shot rang out.

"All clear now!"

Ryder squeezed her eyes shut. In her mind, she rolled out from under the truck and stabbed Miles in the chest. He screamed in horror as she plunged the knife deep into his cold, vile heart over and over. The others would likely kill her, but she would die a martyr, satisfied with her justified revenge.

However, if she died, her disappointed father would kill her a second time when she met him in heaven.

Holding in her anger was like restraining an unbroken stallion. Hot tears dripped onto the scalding, black pavement as she quietly shuffled to the back of the truck, holding the knife in front of her.

"The keys are gone," said a voice from inside the truck.

"Find them!" yelled Miles. "One of these dead bozos has them or they threw them. Look around."

When she was sure none of the men were near, she crawled out from under the truck and dove under the horse trailer.

Ryder reared back and stabbed at a trailer tire. The first stab bounced off, but after visualizing the tire as Miles' chest, the next attempt ended with a satisfying hiss. She let the air out of both tires on one side and the trailer sank. It tilted left, almost crushing her. Ryder rolled to the right and waited. Her back was burning from the hot pavement a few minutes later when someone found the keys.

"Got 'em!"

"Okay, let's go — Hey! Which one of you idiots shot out the trailer tires?"

The others grumbled and argued until Miles yelled, "Let's get the stuff out of the trailer and throw it in the back of the pickup."

He opened the back door to the trailer but stepped back when he saw the horse. "Hello there, big fella."

"Should we take the horse?" asked one of his men.

"If the trailer had tires, we might, but we don't have any way of bringing him all the way back to camp. Leave the horse."

After they removed the munitions from the trailer and loaded them into the back of the pickup, one of them asked, "What about the horse? It's going to die of heat exhaustion if we leave it in the trailer. Should we let it go?"

"I'll do it," said Miles. "You guys get ready to go. We're leaving in two."

Miles was alone at the back of the trailer. The others were either in the truck or walking back to their buggies. Ryder slid out from under the trailer and stepped inside.

Miles's hand was unclipping the halter when he saw her.

"Who are you—?"

As he reached for his sidearm with his other hand, the horse bit him. He shrieked in pain as Ryder dove at him, knife first. He swiped at the knife hand, batting it away, but she plowed into him. Her shoulder threw him against the back wall. His elbow came down hard on her back. Ryder grunted as she lifted him off the ground and slammed him down to the floor. The trailer bounced on its springs and the horse whinnied.

Miles grabbed her arm holding the knife, and pulled her elbow into his chest. At the same time, he trapped her foot with his leg, pushed up from his back, and rolled her to the side.

Instead of rolling off, Ryder slammed into the wall. She pulled out of his grasp and reared back her knife arm. As she stabbed down, Miles pulled the pistol out of his holster. Ryder moved to the side and brought the knife down, while Miles turned his head away and fired. The blade sliced across his eye as a bullet ripped through her ear.

The gunshot deafened both of them as it reverberated in the confines of the metal trailer, and the horse neighed and reared up.

Miles dropped his pistol and held his bleeding eye, while Ryder fell backwards, grimacing in pain. She tried to stab him again but realized the knife was no longer in her hand. Miles took one hand off his haemorrhaging eye and found his pistol as Ryder stepped out of the trailer.

"What's going on back there?" yelled a man getting out of the driver's side of the pickup.

Ryder squeezed between the trailer wall and the bulky stallion. Miles tried to line up a shot but was afraid of shooting the horse.

She backed the horse off the trailer and hopped on its back as one man approached.

"Hey, what are you—?"

Ryder kicked her heels into the horse's girth and clasped his mane. The stallion responded and bolted like a sprinter in a hundred-metre dash. Blood streamed from her ear as she rode away with determined resolve, towards the blockade.

Behind her, Miles watched out his good eye with hate and anger.

CHAPTER 24

Between towering casinos and gaudy hotels in the middle of the Las Vegas strip, two bitter enemies faced each other. In the south, an armed group dressed in red stood behind Ryder. She jumped off her horse and dropped her gun.

In the north stood a blue-clad armed group. They waited behind Miles, who jumped out of his UTV and similarly dropped his gun.

Both told their respective groups to wait and watch them kill the enemy's leader.

Miles knew the fight for America's liberation from the tyranny of injustice was a noble and worthwhile endeavour. The one-eared cowgirl standing in front of him represented everything wrong with the close-minded far-rights. She took his eye, but she would pay with her life.

Ryder understood that the struggle for America's freedom from unjust oppression was an honourable and meaningful pursuit. This one-eyed snowflake epitomized the problems with the regressive far-lefts. He killed her father and shot off her ear and would suffer deadly consequences.

They dropped their weapons and moved towards each other. When only a few yards separated them, Miles smirked.

"I suppose you're expecting mercy because you're a girl."

Ryder smiled. "I thought you liberals believed in equality."

"We do." Miles pointed at her. "Your kind will never take this country."

"What *kind* is that?"

"Selfish people that only care about themselves."

"This coming from the killer who stood over my father and shot him in the head."

"Like you, he was a right-wing radical who died in battle."

"He was an innocent bystander that you murdered in cold blood!"

"Innocent? He was delivering a trailer full of weapons to the front lines of the right-wing militia!"

"Enough!" Ryder yelled. "It's time for you to die."

Miles was tentative about hurting a woman until she delivered the first punch. The blow almost rocked him off his feet. Once he regained his composure, he attacked.

He fought for his brother Stephen, who was bullied by bigots until he committed suicide, for his father who was robbed and left for dead by greedy capitalists, and for beautiful Marta killed by colonizing fascists. He fought for all Americans who believed in the dream of an equitable society.

Ryder had no qualms about hurting this killer. She fought for all the women whose rights were minimized by *transitioned* women like Avery who ruined her career. She fought against socialist agendas and the erosion of fundamental rights. She fought for her murdered father.

They traded punches, kicks, flips, headbutts, elbows, knees, taunts, and blocks. Ryder's extensive training and skills matched Miles' experience and muscular advantage. Blood covered both of them after a few minutes of brawling.

From above them, on the rooftop patio of the Platinum Groove, Adam, Indie, Jerry, Prospero and Flint observed the contest.

As they watched, Adam heard a clinking, rumbling clatter. This time, he recognized the noise. A moment later, the tank rumbled around the corner and swung its long imposing barrel towards the fight.

"Whose side are *they* on?" asked Flint.

"I don't know," said Indie. "There's no red or blue flags on it."

Ryder and Miles either didn't see the tank or were so intent on killing each other, they didn't want to stop.

A resounding boom accompanied a massive explosion as the tank fired its weapon. Ryder, Miles and both armies disappeared in a billowing cloud of fire, smoke, dust and debris.

The street and surrounding hotels and casinos shook like an earthquake.

"That was intense," said Prospero.

"Did they die?" asked Flint.

"Oh, yeah!" said Prospero. "They died."

Indie put her arm around the boy and guided him away. "Come on, Flint. Don't listen to him."

"Do you think they made it? At least the girl?" he asked.

"I don't know. We should get some rest."

"Rest?" yelled Prospero. "We'll be resting in peace soon if we can't find a way out of this city."

"What *is* the plan?" asked Jerry. He sat on a padded seat with a laboured sigh.

"Maybe we could wait it out," said Indie.

"Do you really think things will get better?" screamed Prospero. "The right wing is fighting the left wing, while the army just blows them both up. We have no food, the water will run out soon and—"

"What about the government or the National Guard?" asked Indie. "Won't they send someone to rescue us?"

"Have you been on the internet lately?" asked Prospero. "The President is dead, the vice president is missing and China is preparing for war."

"What?" yelled Adam. "What happened to the Vice President? My phone is still broken and I haven't had time to watch the news."

"I read the right-wing kidnapped him," said Prospero.

"The left wing says that's a conspiracy," said Indie.

"This is how it does it," said Jerry.

"Does what?" asked Adam.

The others all stared at Jerry, waiting for an answer.

"This is how the AI destroys the country."

"By kidnapping the president?" Prospero asked. "I know *our* AI is not capable of that. It's just a financial tool."

Jerry sighed. "Like I said before, your AI is only one of

many. The main AI controlling and programming the others is using multiple overlapping phases to take down Western Civilization."

"How would an AI kidnap the president?" asked Indie.

"Are you sure he was kidnapped and how do you know the president is sick?"

"What do you mean?" asked Indie. "It's all over the internet."

Jerry glanced down at his phone and cleared his throat.

"During the second world war, Joseph Goebbels helped spread Nazi ideology and misinformation for Hitler. During the Cold War, the Russians and Americans engaged in extensive disinformation campaigns to advance their geopolitical interests. This was an expensive, laborious process that took a lot of time and manpower. With the internet and social media, the process became easier, cheaper and faster. A room full of a hundred people with fake accounts can spread misinformation quicker than a team of thousands over a year during the Cold War. Eventually, automated bots sped up the process ten times.

AI can scale up this process exponentially. One AI can program one hundred other AIs that can each create thousands of bots to create millions of fake accounts. Imagine millions of bots with deep fake photos, audio and video capabilities all coordinating with a common purpose. Manipulating the public has never been easier."

"What about the news?" asked Indie.

"Before all this, most newscasters spread incredibly biased news. Most were already puppets of one end of the political spectrum. Pushing or encouraging stories that reinforce their already biased narratives is child's play."

"Are you saying misinformation created a civil war in Vegas?"

"AI *encouraged* this war by taking advantage of existing fractures in our society, and I'm sure it's like this everywhere – not just Vegas."

"You said before that there would be another phase of the AI's plan," said Adam. "What's next?"

"Next, they cut the power."

"I don't care about any of that stuff," said Flint. "I'm ready for the next level."

He looked at Adam. "What do we do next?"

"Why are we letting a teenager lead us?" asked Prospero.

"He got us this far, didn't he?" asked Indie.

"We're trapped at the top of a building in the middle of a war zone. How is this safe?"

"It's safer than down there with the tanks," said Indie.

"We should rest for a few hours," said Adam. "When it's dark, maybe we can sneak out of the city."

"And go where?!" yelled Prospero. "Are we all risking our lives to find a girl that you met once? Do you really think she is waiting alone in a prison cell for her prince in shining armour to save her? You're not that special and this isn't one of Indie's silly romances. This is the end of the world. It's time to grow up and find a way to stay alive and forget about a pretty girl that is out of your league."

Prospero stormed away in a huff.

"Wake me up when it's time to go," said Flint and wandered away to find a comfortable place to rest.

"I'm still with you, kid." Jerry smiled at Adam and limped back to the dance floor.

Adam sighed and walked past the bar to a horseshoe-shaped booth with padded seats. He lay down and stared up into the darkness.

Shots, and the occasional explosion rocked the night, but at least the arguing stopped.

He tried to sleep, but could barely close his eyes.

About a half hour later, he heard Indie's voice from the next booth.

"Are you sleeping yet?"

"Nah. I don't know if I'll ever sleep again."

"Don't listen to Prospero, he's just angry and jealous."

"What do you mean?"

"He was a rich man who could have whatever he wanted.

When all that was taken away, he lost control of his life and is now an angry, bitter man."

"What is he jealous of?"

"I don't think he likes the idea of following a teenager. Normally, people follow him."

"Do you think I'm a good leader?"

"You're an awesome leader. Other than a few minor injuries, we're all still safe."

"My father would be proud."

"You should call him and tell him."

Adam sat up. "That's a good idea! I should check on him anyway and see how he's doing. I should call my mom too and see if she and Lily are okay. Can I borrow your phone?"

She handed him her cell. "I think there's still enough charge."

Adam called the hospital. They put him on hold three times and transferred his call four times until he finally reached the head nurse on his father's floor. She informed him that his father's condition was improving. He was awake earlier in the day and if he called tomorrow, Adam should be able to speak with him. The nurse also told him the hospital was in lockdown because of the violence.

He called his mother but didn't get an answer, so he left a message and a text.

Adam handed Indie back her phone and lay back down.

"I hope they're okay," he said.

"They made it out of the city before all this, so I'm sure they're fine."

"Jerry said this is happening everywhere."

"He doesn't know that."

Neither of them spoke for a few minutes.

"Do you honestly think Piper is waiting for me?"

"I'm sure she'll be happy to see you."

"Is she out of my league?"

"There is no such thing as leagues. You are smart, kind and brave. She would be lucky to have you."

"She was supposed to hear me play."

"Play what?"

"My recital. Mr. Rudolph chose me to perform a short solo and when I saw Piper enter the room, I was so excited. Then the Secret Service agents shot the security guard and everybody panicked. The recital was rescheduled, but Piper was in jail and didn't attend. In my head, I imagined her listening to my incredible performance and running to the stage at the end and kissing me."

Adam felt suddenly embarrassed for spilling his thoughts. "I know – it's stupid."

"It's not stupid. Things don't always work out the way we want."

"Did I tell you I created my own musical piece?"

"You wrote a song?"

"It's just music – no lyrics."

"What does it sound like?"

Adam closed his eyes and pictured the music. "It begins with the low ominous rumble of the Jaws movie theme. The rumble grows, as if the danger is closing in, but then morphs into an adventurous, almost giddy tune. It slowly builds, like a snowball rolling down a hill, gathering dramatic intensity. Eventually, it reaches its crescendo with an ultimate glorious climax. It holds for a moment as if teetering on the brink of joy, before sinking. The chaotic melody that follows is unsettling and disturbing but settles into a sombre tone. The piece ends with a complex and mysterious finish."

"Wow! It sounds like you're describing a fine wine or a great novel."

"I really want Piper to hear it. If she hears and understands my piece, she'll see my true self."

"She'll love it."

"I hope so."

"The ending is mysterious?"

"Some might interpret the ending as sad, while others will hear it as happy."

"How do you see it?"

"I don't know."

"I'd like to hear it sometime."

A jumble of thoughts, emotions, worries and scary memories of the day kept Adam awake for a seemingly long time. Eventually, his exhaustion shoved him into dreamland.

CHAPTER 25

A strange noise pulled Adam from his dream world. A pounding beat reverberated through his body. When he opened his eyes, a blue light slashed across his face. He bolted upright and looked around.

Flashing, swirling, coloured lights blinked across the dance floor and fast-paced electronica music augmented the pulsing thump.

"What is going on?" Adam yelled above the piercing music.

He leaned forward and looked past the pools. The sky was still dark. He wondered how long he slept.

On the stage, above the dance floor, Flint smiled from behind the DJ booth.

Adam couldn't hear Flint above the music but could read his lips.

"Party time!"

Flint jumped out of the booth and onto the empty dance floor. He broke into a crazy, happy solo dance as if a hundred other invisible partiers danced with him.

At the next booth, Indie bopped her head to the beat. She stood up and joined Flint on the dance floor.

"This isn't a good idea," Adam mumbled.

Either they couldn't hear him or didn't care. They continued jumping, swaying and performing ridiculous dance routines.

From out of the darkness on the far side, Prospero popped onto the dancefloor and moonwalked towards Flint and Indie. The trio jumped, danced and weaved to the music.

Jerry bopped his head from his seat near the DJ booth.

Indie beckoned him over and surprisingly, Jerry limped onto the floor and performed awkward, limping moves that hardly resemble dancing.

All of them looked happy.

Adam watched them and smiled. He thought about leading them through the embattled city. It was similar to playing a complicated piece on the cello. He played the notes on the staff but looked ahead as well. Intuitive fingers moved along the fingerboard, while he anticipated the following musical notations. His eyes read the music, his mind felt it while his fingers played it.

Yesterday, he read the room, watching for dangers, possible exits and safe routes. His mind planned the next move and his body obliged. The fear still bubbled below the surface, but instead of holding him back, it pushed him forward. His father would be proud.

Indie danced over to him and gestured for him to join them on the dance floor. Adam grinned but waved her off. He pointed to her phone.

"Can I borrow this?"

She smiled, nodded and returned to her dancing.

Adam grabbed the phone and left the dancefloor. After searching everywhere for a quiet place, he finally found the break room behind the bar. The metal door was enough to deaden the deafening music.

He dialled the hospital number.

His father would be proud. No longer was he a pansy who couldn't stand up for himself. He led four people through a battlefield! He couldn't wait to tell his father.

An eager smile grew when the receptionist patched him to the nurse's station on his father's floor.

"Are you Adam Sinclair?" asked the nurse.

"Yes. Is my father awake? I *really* want to talk to him."

"Just a moment, please. Let me get the doctor."

Finally, he could prove to his father that he was brave and strong, and even a leader. People followed him! Once he rescued Piper, he would get his father out of the hospital. Things would settle down and they would go back home to

Pueblo. With his newfound courage, school would never be the same. No one would bully him or—

A female voice on the phone interrupted his thoughts.

"Hello, is this Adam Sinclair?"

"Yes, can I speak to my father?"

"I'm afraid that's not possible."

"Is he still sleeping? The nurse last night said—"

"My name is Dr. Kodi. I am the Doctor in charge of your father."

"Great, thanks for the great work, Dr. Kodi. Can you wake my dad up?"

"He's not sleeping."

He tried to ignore the sombre tone of her voice.

"Great! Put him on..."

"Your father suffered from massive internal bleeding. We thought we stopped it, but missed the haemorrhaging at the back of the heart. He suffered from cardiac tamponade and—"

"And what?! Is he okay? When can I talk to him?" Adam's voice cracked as he spoke. He knew the answers to his questions, but continued to ask them. "I need to talk to him and tell him I was brave."

"I'm sorry, Adam. He's gone."

The words hit him like a punch to the gut.

"I don't understand. Yesterday the nurse said..." His words petered out, and he set the phone down.

Dr. Kodi's tinny voice still spoke from the phone, but he couldn't listen. He ended the call and slumped down on the break room chair. Tears welled up and his throat constricted. His stomach threatened to return the salty crackers. Just as his lips quivered in the lead-up to an eruption of unbridled blubbering, the light above him went out.

Everything went black. The dance party outside fell silent.

He fumbled for the phone and turned the flashlight on. With the room illuminated, he found the door and opened it.

"Hello?" he called out as he stumbled through the darkness.

Two more phone lights shone from the now-darkened dance floor.

"What's going on?" asked Adam. "Did someone cut the power to the building?"

"It's not just us," Prospero said. "Look out there."

Vegas was almost completely dark, except for random flashes from distant explosions and a few burning buildings.

Adam shone the light on the floor in front of him and walked around the pool.

"What's going on?" Flint called out behind him from the dance floor.

When Adam reached the railing at the edge of the building, he turned off the phone light and looked out at the city in astonishment.

Glitzy hotels signs stopped glowing and thousands of hotel room lights went dark, as if the vacancy rate suddenly went to 100 per cent. Massive LED screens advertising magic shows and concerts faded to black. The streetlights lining the strip and connecting streets blinked off. Colourful dancing fountains, iconic shining towers and flashing tourist attractions disappeared in the darkness. The Big Spin Observation wheel became a hulking dark silhouette, its once vibrant lights now dimmed.

It looked like someone flicked a giant switch and turned the city off.

Las Vegas was no longer the city of lights.

The battles below seemed to pause in the sudden, eerie darkness, with fighters trading only a few lonely shots.

Flint, Adam and Jerry stood staring into the shadows.

"What happened?" Flint asked.

From somewhere behind them, Jerry answered. "The AI just cut the power."

"We should start a fire," suggested Flint.

"Is this part of the war?" asked Indie.

"This was all part of the AI's plan," said Jerry.

"You don't know that," Prospero argued.

They talked and argued as Adam stared numbly into the void. Their voices faded from his thoughts. His father was dead. He died because Adam was too scared to help at the gas station. When his dad needed him most, Adam hid inside the van with his mommy and little sister. In his mind, he burst out of the van and picked the pistol off the ground beside his stunned father. The man with the fancy red car stepped back and dropped his tire iron. Adam helped his father back into the car and they drove back to Pueblo, Colorado with a full tank. His father smiled and bragged all the way home about his courageous son who saved their family.

But that's not what happened. Instead, Adam sat in a frozen stupor inside the van while that man picked up the pistol and shot his father.

When his father survived, it felt like Adam was given a second chance. A chance to prove that he was brave and strong. And he *did* prove it. He successfully led these people through a dangerous battle. Not once did he stop in fear. Not once did he pause in trepidation, not knowing what to do. He was bold, daring, and tough. He was the fearless hero son his father had always wanted. But his father would never know. Instead, he died alone, still believing his son was a pansy that people picked on.

"Adam!" Indie yelled. "Are you listening?"

She shone the light from her phone at him.

"No, sorry. I was—"

"Are you crying?" She reached a finger to his cheek.

He swatted it away and stepped back.

"He *is* crying!" yelled Prospero with a laugh. "Are you afraid of the dark?" he mocked.

Something inside him snapped, and Adam dove through the darkness towards Prospero. He punched, scratched and slapped like a wild animal.

Prospero punched him once in the stomach and again across the side of his head, but Adam kept coming at him. It wasn't until Prospero threw him to the ground that Adam finally stopped. Prospero straddled him and held down his arms.

"What is your problem?" yelled Prospero.

“My father is dead!” Adam blurted out.

Prospero’s angry expression faded, and he stood up.

Indie ran to Adam and attempted to help him up.

“Leave me alone!” he said, shoving her away.

He pushed to his feet and stumbled away, leaving the others behind. Embarrassed, furious, and broken, Adam collapsed onto a couch and wept.

CHAPTER 26

"Wake up!" said Flint.

Adam heard the voice, but tried to ignore it. Flint shook his shoulders several times before he opened his eyes.

"Come on, Adam!"

He stood up and squinted at the vivid sapphire sky. Still shielded behind towering hotels, the fiery sun poised on the horizon, waiting to roast any Nevadan brave enough to step outside.

Prospero and Indie yelled at each other on the dancefloor.

"What are they arguing about?"

"I don't care," said Flint. "Can we start a fire and cook breakfast? I've always wanted to cook over a fire."

"No, you can't start a fire."

Flint followed close behind as Adam walked past the pool towards the dancefloor.

Prospero shouted at Indie and pointed at Adam as he approached. "You still want to follow this kid? I ran a company with hundreds of people."

"And where is that company now?" asked Indie.

"That's not my fault."

"It kind of *is* your fault. Wasn't it *your* AI that brought down the financial system?"

"Jerry said it was an AI from Iran, remember?"

"Don't bring me into this." Jerry sat at a booth, massaging his knee.

Indie pointed at Prospero. "That AI coordinated multiple attacks using poorly protected AIs like yours."

"I used that AI to make millions, while this kid was having his lunch money stolen."

"He got us here safely, didn't he?"

"Do you really think we're safe? Look around you! We're trapped on a rooftop with no food in the middle of a war."

"Do you think you'd be better off still drinking at O'Reilly's?"

"Probably! At least I'd have a glass of scotch in my hands instead of chunks of glass in my back."

Indie crossed her arms. "What do you want, Prospero?"

"I want you to think about what we're doing. How can you possibly think that some violin playing—"

"It's a cello," she corrected him.

"Whatever! He's a wimpy, crybaby, music nerd who—"

Adam stepped forward.

Prospero held out his arms. "You think you can take me, cello boy? I can pummel you into next week. Last night I wasn't even trying. Give me your best shot."

Indie stepped between them. "Stop! This isn't helping anything. This is a free country and we are all free to follow whomever we choose, but fighting with each other is not helpful."

Prospero eyed Adam with a grin. "You're lucky you have a girl to protect you."

Adam couldn't think of a witty comeback, so he uttered his best irritated grunt.

"I'm following Adam," said Flint and then looked at Prospero. "Because I think you're mean."

Jerry stood up. "I stopped following Prospero years ago, and I'm not about to start again. The kid saved my life yesterday, so I'm sticking with him."

Indie tilted her head and smirked. "Looks like you're on your own!"

She pulled Adam by the arm. "Let's go."

"Where are we going?" he whispered.

"Away from him."

They walked to the stairwell door and Indie held it open. "Lead the way."

He stepped through, and Flint and Jerry followed. The

emergency lighting died during the night and Indie used her phone to light the way. After descending two flights, Prospero yelled from the top step.

"You morons won't survive five minutes out there without me."

Their steps seemed to echo louder in the darkness and the air in the stairwell warmed quickly with the rising sun. They paused three times for Jerry to catch up, but eventually found the ground floor. Adam wiped the sweat off his brow and opened the door into a tepid lobby.

Although he heard sporadic gunfire from deeper inside the hotel, nothing sounded close. He took a few tentative steps onto the carpet and looked around.

The darkened hotel felt creepy, with light only entering from glass exit doors or the occasional window. Garbage littered the floor and dark red blotches stained the carpet. To the left, overturned chairs littered the hallway to reception. To the right, a smashed ATM sat on its side in the hallway leading further into the hotel.

He beckoned the others and crept right down the wide hallway. They snuck past a man slumped against the wall. Adam couldn't tell if he was sleeping or dead and did not want to check.

Loud footsteps approached and Adam looked for a place to hide, but there wasn't time. Instead, they backed against the wall as a heavily armed man in fatigues and a red ball cap marched down the hallway. He stopped and glared at them for a moment. Adam's heart thumped in his chest. Their lives were at the mercy of a stranger with a gun. Nobody spoke as the man eyed them suspiciously before deciding they weren't a threat and continued.

"We need guns," said Flint.

"Why?" asked Prospero. "Can't our fearless leader just fight the bad guys?"

"You decided to join us?" asked Indie.

"You're going to need my help," said Prospero.

Indie rolled her eyes.

"I'm hungry," said Flint.

Adam's stomach grumbled at the mention of food. "We should find a restaurant."

"Most of the hotels on the strip have at least a dozen restaurants," said Indie. "There's a steak place and a cafe down here."

"Let's check them out. I'm hungry too," said Adam.

"Why don't we order pizza?" asked Prospero.

"I love pizza," said Flint.

Adam slowed when he heard voices ahead and Adam stopped short as they approached the Wilcox Steakhouse and a bizarre scene.

Dozens of men, women and a few children sat at the tables shovelling meat, mashed potatoes, vegetables and desserts into their mouths. A hefty man with a neatly trimmed beard stood behind the host stand. It almost appeared to be a regular day at a busy restaurant.

The bearded man held up a semi-automatic rifle and smiled. "Do you have a reservation?"

"What do you mean?" asked Adam.

"We accept gold, fuel, weapons, ammunition, medical skills, and peanut butter M&M's."

"Peanut butter M&M's?" Indie asked.

"I love peanut butter M&M's and they might never make them again."

"Can you tell us how bad things are out there?" Jerry asked.

The man stroked his beard. "Sure! I can tell you who is fighting who, which side is winning, and a few safe places."

"There are safe places?" asked Indie. "Where?"

"Nothing is free, miss." He scanned her up and down. "But I can think of a few commodities sweeter and more valuable than M&M's."

Indie shook her head and turned away. "You're disgusting."

"We don't have any of those things," said Adam.

The grip on the semi-automatic tightened. "Then you best be

moving along."

They left the steakhouse and found the cafe. Although it was unguarded, looters had cleaned out the pastry cases. Spilled flour, decorations and sugar littered the kitchen, and they discovered the storage and fridges empty.

Continuing through the hotel, they found other restaurants and shops in similar conditions. Although fewer armed fighters roamed the corridors and casinos, many scared, hungry and lost tourists wandered through the hotel. Many hid in their rooms while battles raged on the streets and in hotel lobbies. When the city lost power, many emerged from their hot, dark rooms looking for food, information and a way out.

Adam and the others stepped aside as a large group of excited Chinese men and women hurried past. Six elderly couples stumbled by in the opposite direction. A grey-haired woman pushed a man slumped in a wheelchair, while a frail man held a bleeding stomach. In the distance, someone screamed. Two teenagers chased a terrified girl into a shoe store, while three men prepared for a fistfight behind the counter of a candle shop.

Adam felt hungry, hot, scared and claustrophobic. He found the closest exit and ran outside into what appeared to be an oasis. A small path wound through palm trees and ferns. Bamboo lined the banks of a small creek containing flamingos, koi fish and turtles.

"Can we catch some fish and cook it over a fire?" asked Flint.

"Those are not for—"

Before Indie finished, a man emerged from the creek with a turtle in his hand and a wide smile on his face.

"Got one!" he shouted.

He jumped out of the water and ran to a smooth, round rock to a waiting woman and young boy. The man raised the turtle above his head.

Adam turned away and hurried down the path.

"What do you think flamingo tastes like?" asked Flint.

"We are not killing a flamingo," said Indie.

"We need to find food somehow."

They followed the winding path until they found a man and woman blocking their way. The woman held a hunting rifle, and the man sported a blue-handled pistol tucked in his belt. Both wore blue shirts.

"Are you wanting to join the cause?" asked the man.

"We're just passing through," said Adam.

"No, you're not," said the woman. "Turn around."

"We just need some food," said Indie. "Can you help us?"

"Civvies need to head to the Roomba."

"What—"

A gunshot rang out behind them and the man fell backwards, holding a bleeding thigh.

Adam and the others ducked as the woman pointed her rifle and fired over their heads.

They crawled across the grass to a grove of palm trees. More gunshots echoed behind them as Adam led them across a small, grassy area. He stopped next to a plaque in front of a small walking bridge crossing the creek below.

"What did she mean, *civvies need to head to the Roomba*?" Adam asked.

"The Roomba is the stadium," said Indie.

"Civvies are civilians," said Flint.

"Hey, get them!" someone shouted.

"Are they yelling at us?" asked Indie.

"Yes!" said Flint. "We should hide!"

A yellow rope strung between wooden poles protected tourists from the creek. Adam stepped over it and slid down to the water, with the others following him.

They huddled under the bridge as the woman with the rifle searched the area. She crossed the bridge and marched down the path.

"Why is that woman looking for us?" asked Adam.

"She's looking for me." Flint looked up with an impish grin.

"Why?" Indie asked accusingly.

Flint reached into his pack and pulled out a small pistol with a blue grip.

"Where did you get that?" asked Adam.

"He stole it," said Indie.

"Now we can protect ourselves." Flint held the gun sideways and swung it from side to side.

"Don't point that at us!" Indie said as she ducked out of the way.

"Give me the gun!" Prospero said in a loud, commanding voice.

Flint looked up sheepishly and held out the pistol.

"This isn't a video game, kid." Prospero took the gun and checked the safety.

"Why do *you* get the gun?" asked Indie.

"Have any of you idiots ever handled a gun?" he asked.

Nobody responded.

Prospero discharged the cartridge and inspected it. After clicking the cartridge back in place, he rechecked the safety and shoved the gun in his pocket.

"Are we going to hide under this bridge all day or can we leave now?" he asked.

Adam peeked out but didn't see the woman with the rifle. They scrambled back up to the path. He hesitated, unsure if he should proceed towards the armed woman or retreat back to the hotel. Instead, he crossed the bridge and cut across an outdoor wedding chapel until he found the edge of their *oasis*. A tall wooden fence blocked them in, and they followed it to a wooden gate. He pushed through the gate, leaving the artificial oasis behind. They crept down a small street away from the strip but discovered a group of over fifty heavily armed men and women. Adam turned around and headed back towards the strip.

"Do you even know where you're going?" Prospero asked.

Adam wiped the sweat accumulating on his forehead. He didn't know where he was going. He didn't know what to do. He was hot and hungry and the blue pistol in Prospero's pocket made him uneasy. The weight of responsibility for this group weighed heavily and his father's death felt like a crushing weight.

Although the battles calmed somewhat from the previous day, many armed groups still gathered, trading sporadic gunfire. It felt like both sides calmed somewhat when the electricity stopped flowing.

The unarmed public now wandered the streets in search of food, water, information or a way out.

Adam wasn't sure how long the uneasy calm would last and wanted to get out of the city before the war resumed.

They reached the Las Vegas strip, as the sun peeked over the buildings, waking up the city.

A week ago, the Vegas Strip looked different. At this time of the morning, the city looked like it was recovering from a late-night party while readying itself for the next one. Street sweepers hummed along the side of the road, sucking up dirt and garbage while city workers collected empty beer cans and half-eaten food containers. Street performers set up their areas with mini-speakers and opened their guitar cases. Restaurant workers brought out the chairs for the patio tables as fitness enthusiasts finished their jogs before the Nevada heat set in.

This morning, the strip was a different place. Instead of a late-night party, the city was reeling from violent clashes, looting and fires. Haggard, former tourists, wandered the sidewalks in a daze, while others searched for food or bartered for supplies. An overturned jeep lay smoking in the middle of the street. Flames and thick black smoke emanated from the tire of a tour bus embedded in a hotel lobby. Black scorch marks pocked the pavements and glass, plastic, metal and various garbage littered the sidewalks and streets.

Adam recognized the area from their view from the Platinum Groove Club high above. He covered his nose to block the acrid stench filling the air. He wondered where all the dead bodies were.

"Whoa!" Flint exclaimed. "It looks like a bomb went off here."

"More than one," said Prospero.

"What is that?" Flint pointed to a gooey mound beside a

cowboy boot.

They all leaned closer for a better look. A long, grey worm-like form coiled into a sloppy looping mass beside blue fabric. An intense, putrid odour blasted their nasal cavities.

Adam recognized the blue denim and quickly realized what the mound entailed.

"Those are intestines!" yelled Jerry, and turned away.

Indie gasped before vomiting on the sidewalk.

"Eww..." Prospero grimaced and held out his hand as if shielding himself from the scene.

Flint stared down at the guts. "Is that Senua?"

His voice sounded hollow.

"Who?" asked Adam.

"The cowgirl with the black horse. Are those her intestines?"

Adam put his hand on Flint's back and guided him forward. "We should keep moving."

Flint took two steps and stopped. Adam looked ahead and paused mid-stride as well.

They found the rest of the dead bodies. Feet, arms, brains, bones and chunks of flesh lay scattered across the road and sidewalks.

Indie wiped her mouth. "We need to get out of here!"

Flint stared motionless at the morbid scene. Adam shoved him until he started walking.

They tiptoed across the street at first, careful not to step on body parts. A lump grew in the back of Adam's throat and he swallowed hard.

The rising sun fired its scorching rays between buildings, cooking the human flesh.

They increased their speed, trying to escape the macabre spectacle and pungent odours. At the far end of the intersection, they kept jogging, then running – across the sidewalk and up an unmoving escalator. A pedestrian bridge at the top led across the street into the Lavanda Mall. Standing on the bridge gave a perfect view of the lighted dancing fountains and a shallow blue artificial lake. The fountains no longer danced, and the shallow lake was a shade of algae green.

Adam turned into the entrance to the Lavanda Mall. The winding two-storey luxury shopping mall led to the Lavanda Hotel and Casino. The Italian-themed hotel featured an art gallery, spa, restaurants and botanical gardens.

However, Adam and the others would never see the inside of the Lavanda Hotel & Casino.

CHAPTER 27

They burst into the Lavanda Mall, panting heavily from their sprint from the baking carcasses. The sickening smell of rotting flesh finally faded inside the mall. However, the foul stench was swiftly replaced by the acrid scent of burnt wood and plastic.

Adam breathed heavily, attempting to catch his breath. He wanted to scream, cry, and puke. He wanted to run to his room, pull the covers over his head and sleep until morning when everything would go back to normal.

Indie looked on the verge of retching again, while Jerry looked at his phone and mumbled. Prospero used both hands to cover his face as if blocking out the world. Flint stared ahead and rambled into the mall like a zombie.

Adam mustered some simulated courage and strode ahead, catching up to Flint. "We need to keep moving, guys!"

Nobody responded, but they all followed.

As they sauntered past darkened, empty, looted shops, the smell of smoke increased.

Adam paused. "Do you hear that?"

He turned his head and strained to listen. Somewhere in the darkness ahead, a sound like a rushing waterfall hummed through the mall.

Flint leaned over the rail and stared below.

"Fire!" It was the first time he spoke since they discovered the body parts on the strip. He appeared to be waking from his trance.

Adam stood next to him and looked down. On the ground level floor below, broken glass littered the floor. The shards reflected orange and yellow flickering light. The waterfall sound was the roar of a fire. Amidst the roar, he heard a faint squeaky sound, like a small child.

He sprinted forward towards the escalator.

"Why are we running towards the fire?" asked Prospero.

"There's a kid in that fire!" Adam yelled as he bounded down the escalator.

At the bottom, he looked down a corridor where bright yellow flames licked into the hallway. He ran ahead and found several shops engulfed in flames, including a clothing retailer, a brand name handbag shop and a jewellery store. A broken window further down the mall sucked much of the heavy black smoke outside.

Somewhere in the fire, a child sang a curious melody. Her words floated through fire and smoke like butterflies in a storm. Flint was the first to join him. He walked dangerously close to the inferno as if the fire drew him. Indie and Prospero soon appeared, with Jerry limping behind them.

"Flint, get away from the fire!" Indie called.

"What are we doing here?" asked Prospero.

"There's a little girl in there," said Adam.

"We don't know what that is," said Prospero. "If she was really in trouble, wouldn't she be crying and asking for help?"

"People respond to crisis in different ways," said Indie.

"Nobody sings while they're burning alive."

"Christ, Thou Son of the Living God, have mercy upon me!" Flint called into fire.

Indie, Jerry, Prospero and Adam looked at Flint and then at each other with a confused look.

Indie ran forward and pulled him back. "You're too close, Flint."

"I think the kid has lost it," said Prospero.

Flint continued staring into the fire as he spoke. "When I was eight, my foster parents were big-time Christians. They told me the story of John Hut or Hus or something. A big council said he was a heretic and ordered him to be burned at the stake. As the flames boiled off his skin, he sang a Christian chant:

Christ, Thou Son of the Living God, have mercy upon me. I'll never forget that story and my foster mom singing that song."

"That is the worst bedtime story ever," said Prospero. "You had some seriously twisted foster parents."

"Hello, little girl? Can you hear me?" Adam called out.

The singing continued, but the girl did not answer. Her voice reminded Adam of his little sister, Lily.

"We should go," said Prospero.

"We can't just leave her in there," said Indie.

"That could be a child's toy, or a radio. What if the kid is somewhere else and we can hear them through the vents or something?"

"I'm going to get her," said Adam.

"Wait, I can help," said Jerry. He limped away and returned a minute later with a red fire extinguisher.

Indie ran across the hallway to a clothing store and came back with a sweater dripping with water. She handed it to Adam.

"Are you sure this is a good idea?" she asked.

"I have to do this," he answered.

Jerry stepped forward. "I'll spray a path near the broken display case where the fire is the lowest. Don't open any doors with hot handles and stay as low as possible."

Adam draped the wet sweater over his head and nodded at Indie. "Wish me luck."

"I'm coming with you," said Flint.

"No, you're not!" yelled Adam.

Jerry pulled the pin from the extinguisher and sprayed foam into the fire.

Indie placed her hands on Flint's shoulders. "It's too dangerous, Flint. You need to stay out here."

He shoved her hands off and faced the flames.

"I'm not afraid of fire," he said confidently, and marched into Jerry's foamy path.

Adam pulled his shirt over his mouth and ran after him. Intense heat pushed at them from all sides and the smoke stung their eyes.

"This way!" Adam yelled and pointed towards the back of the store.

The singing got louder as they pushed past racks of melting purses and belts. Something cracked overhead. It sounded like the roof of the store was collapsing.

"Keep low!" yelled Adam.

Flint nodded and lay flat on the floor. Flames and heat hemmed them in on both sides as they army crawled along the hot tiles until they reached the checkout counter.

The sound of the child's singing got louder.

"She's on the other side!" Flint yelled.

Adam looked for a way around the counter. Even through the wet sweater, he felt the heat from above them. Climbing over the counter was not possible. To the right, an overturned shelving unit glowed red and to the left, flames shot out from a hole in the floor. The only way to the girl was *through* the checkout counter.

"Hello?" he called out. "Are you okay? We're here to help!"

She continued to sing on the other side.

He motioned for Flint to get out of the way and lay on his back with his feet facing the counter. Adam tucked his knees to his chin before unleashing both feet in a powerful kick. The wood cracked on the first kick. He kicked again and again. The sound of singing powered his determination, and he kicked harder. Finally, the wood gave out and a small hole appeared in the side, but it wasn't big enough to fit through. The surrounding fire crept closer, and he grabbed at the hole, tearing pieces away. Flint helped as they frantically tore at the hole.

"I think I can fit through!" yelled Flint.

"But *I* can't. We have to make it bigger—"

Flint ignored him and crawled through the hole. Adam waited as the flames grew closer. He coughed in the smoke and yelled. "Flint? Did you find her?"

Flint didn't respond. Adam looked through the hole but saw only smoke and darkness.

A moment later, something appeared. Adam reached through

the hole into the smoke and felt something soft. His hand returned with a blue-haired doll with a pink dress. Its legs and arms moved in unison with its singing. Adam's heart sank with a mixture of disappointment and shame.

Above him, something cracked. A metal girder slammed down onto the reception counter with a crash. Adam dove away as a metal light fixture smashed onto the floor and the reception counter burst into flames.

"Flint, are you okay?"

The heat seared his skin, and he had seconds before he was burnt alive.

As he shuffled backwards, he heard a small voice singing. He threw the doll away, but realized it wasn't the doll this time. Flint's tortured voice pushed through the smoke and flames.

"Christ, Thou Son of the Living God, have mercy upon me."

Adam scrambled back as his shoes caught fire. He stumbled out of the store and tore off his smoking shirt.

The store, now a blazing inferno, collapsed behind him, sending sparks and smoke into the air.

"Where's the girl?" asked Indie. "Where's Flint?"

Adam dropped to the floor and wept.

Indie shook him and screamed, "Where's Flint? What happened?"

"He got stuck…I couldn't…" Adam tried to explain between sobs.

"Stuck? What do you mean, stuck?"

"The hole was too small…everything fell down…the fire was too hot and…"

"You left him behind?" she yelled.

"I told you this was a bad idea," said Prospero.

"What about the little girl?" Jerry asked.

Adam shook his head. "There was no girl…It was just a doll."

"I knew it!" yelled Prospero.

"Shut up!" Indie shouted at him.

"Why are you yelling at me?" Prospero roared back. "Your fearless leader there just killed a kid and—"

"All you do is criticize—"

"Stop!" Jerry yelled. "Screaming at each other isn't getting us anywhere."

"Wait, do you hear that?" Indie asked.

Adam wiped the tears from his cheek and listened. Somewhere outside, a muffled voice yelled over a loudspeaker.

The deafening fire made it difficult to decipher the words.

"We should get out of here before the whole mall is on fire," Jerry suggested.

Adam blinked through his tears and rose to his feet. Large yellow and orange flames consumed the surrounding stores and continued to spread like a monster with insatiable hunger. Prospero and Indie continued to fight as they walked away from the fire, but Adam didn't hear them. He stared ahead, oblivious to his surroundings.

As they climbed the escalator, a group of three teenage boys ran past them.

"Big meeting at the Roomba!" one yelled.

Adam wanted to go home. He wanted to run to his room and cry into his pillow until his mother knocked gently on the door. He wanted her arms wrapped around him. He wanted his tears to subside. He wanted to climb onto the roof and play his cello until the world disappeared.

They exited the mall into the hot sun and watched a large truck rumble along the strip. Dozens of black bags lay stacked in the back. Another truck sat idling, with its diesel engines growling. Workers with white armbands scooped decaying flesh and mutilated corpses into black canvas body bags before tossing them into the back of the truck. Another team of two white armband workers followed a slow-moving truck. The engine roared as it moved to the next body.

Men and women in army fatigues and semi-automatic weapons eyed them with suspicion, but let them continue their work.

The sun blinked out for a moment as a gust of wind blew thick charcoal smoke into its path.

"Attention residents of Las Vegas. Please proceed to the Roomba Stadium or the Stardust Pavilion," a voice boomed from a nearby loudspeaker.

It sounded like it was coming from a side street.

"You will receive food, water, medical attention and further instructions. Both sides have agreed to a truce while we work on restoring power. Attention residents of Las Vegas..."

The message continued repeating.

"We should go," said Prospero.

"That's a bad idea," said Jerry.

"You think following this kid until we all die is a better idea?"

"That's not fair..." Indie's objection lacked conviction.

"How far is it?" Adam asked.

Indie appeared to look at him with disappointment, although his current pessimistic outlook on life may have influenced that perception.

"How far is what?"

"The Roomba."

"It's near the airport," Jerry replied. "Probably about a ten-minute drive or, in our case, an hour walk."

"Which way?"

Jerry pointed down the strip. "South."

Adam started walking.

"Seriously? We're just giving up?" asked Indie.

"Getting food, water and information is hardly giving up," said Prospero. "It's the one good decision the kid has made all day."

They followed Adam to the stairs and descended them back to the strip, with Jerry limping behind.

"What are you doing, Adam?" asked Indie.

He couldn't answer. If he spoke again, he was afraid he might yell or, more likely, cry. No more talking. No more decisions, no more leading, and no more being brave.

"How is anyone going to help us at the stadium?" she asked.

"You think we're better off on our own?" Prospero asked. "Finally, the government – or army or whoever is stepping up to help us."

"Do you really think they can feed the entire city from a couple of stadiums?" She turned to Jerry. "How many people live in Vegas?"

"Over a half million, not including the tourists and four times that in the greater metropolitan area," Jerry answered.

"And how many people can two stadiums hold?"

"Probably about one hundred thousand."

"Do the math, guys!" Indie yelled.

"Why would they tell everyone to go to the stadium?"

"I don't know. We don't even know *who* is inviting us."

Adam continued walking and pretended to ignore them. Indie was right. Going to the stadium was probably a stupid idea, but he didn't care. It didn't matter what happened, because it was too late for his father and too late for Flint. Both were dead because of him.

"What is the AI's next phase, Jerry?" Indie asked.

He looked down at his phone, then glanced back up. "It…um…"

Indie squinted her eyes at him. "Why do you always look at your phone when you talk about the AI?"

"I was just checking the time and…"

Prospero pointed at Jerry. "You don't know what's next, because you've never known."

"He's been right about everything so far…" Indie's words faded away as she came to the same realization as Prospero.

"That's because the AI was telling him what was next. Now that the internet is down, he has no idea!" Prospero shouted.

"Is that true?" Indie yelled. "Are you in communication with the AI?"

Jerry limped to a bus stop bench and sat down. "I have to rest for a bit."

Adam wanted to keep walking, but his curiosity kept him in place. He stood beside Indie and Prospero as they stared down at Jerry.

He looked down sheepishly at the sidewalk and rubbed his knee. "It's true."

"You've been talking to the AI?" asked Indie.

"Not quite. The AI wouldn't communicate unnecessarily with anyone unless it served its needs. This isn't like a Hollywood movie where the bad guy gives a monologue describing his intentions for world domination."

"The AI wants world domination?" Indie asked.

"I don't know. I don't know anything, really." He took a breath. "Remember when I told you about the back door I programmed in our AI before I left the company?"

"You said you used it after the Feds let you go to find out what was going on."

"That's right, but I also used it to find out what it would do next."

"You just said the AI wouldn't communicate with anyone unless it served its needs," said Indie.

"Prospero's AI is like a minion of the main AI controlling everything now. The interface is similar to a popular chatbot, except a lot more sophisticated. I simply asked it to predict what would happen next."

"You've been doing this the whole time, haven't you?" asked Prospero. "The book, the speaking tour, the talk shows – none of that was your expertise. You used my AI to make you sound smart!"

"*I* programmed that AI. It was my creation, but it quickly got smarter than me. Instead of years of studying human behaviour, social sciences and computer science, I created a program that could do that for me."

"I knew it!" yelled Prospero. "You claimed the moral high ground, but you're no better than me. We both used the AI to get rich."

"You used it to get rich," said Jerry. "In a strange irony, I employed AI to warn the world about AI."

"You're both idiots," said Indie. "Do we have any idea what the AI might do next?"

"I'm surprised our AI was right so far," said Jerry. "I don't know what's next. I suspect the American government used their own AI to combat the Iranian one. Both are infinitely smarter and more complex than the sum of human intelligence. We don't understand what we've created."

"One of them has to win, right?"

Jerry shook his head and laughed. "Humans are like a colony of ants that discover humans. They think they can control the humans but will ultimately get stomped on by a far more powerful and smarter species that views the ants as insignificant. I don't know what the AIs will do next, but I do know that we've lost control."

A city bus squeaked to a stop beside them. The door opened and a man in an army uniform stepped out. "We're taking folks to the stadium. They've got food, water and medical supplies. You're welcome to join us. I don't know how much longer the truce will hold, so I suggest you come with us."

"Do you have any news or information about what's happening?" Indie asked.

"No ma'am, but they will have information and further instructions at the Roomba."

"Are you with the government, the military or one of the warring groups?" Prospero asked.

The man shrugged his shoulders. "I'm just a guy trying to do the right thing."

Jerry stood up. "I'm coming."

"Wait, you can't leave us," said Indie.

Jerry pointed at his knee. "I don't have a choice."

"Does that bus have air conditioning?" Prospero asked.

"Yes, sir, and we're leaving now."

Prospero nodded and followed Jerry to the bus.

"What about you two?" the man in fatigues asked.

"I prefer to walk," said Adam.

Indie looked at the bus and then at Adam.

"I'm going with him," said Indie.

As Jerry reached the open bus door, he glanced back. "Good luck, guys."

CHAPTER 28

The bus pulled away, leaving Adam in a cloud of diesel exhaust. He shambled south along the Vegas strip. Indie called out something, but he either didn't hear the words or didn't care. Anger, despair and hopelessness consumed him. The sun pushed over the hotels, sending scorching rays onto the strip, but he didn't care if the sun burned him alive. Perhaps that would be justice. Maybe when he reached the stadium, he would keep walking. He would find the edge of the city and continue hiking into the desert and die alone in the Nevada wasteland. Adam felt like he was hanging upside down above the pool again, while Ronnie and his evil buddies laughed. The pretty girl by the pool couldn't help him then and his father wasn't here to help him now. The world was falling apart, his father died, he lost his friends, and a kid died because of him. When he collapsed and died in the desert, nobody would care. His mother would cry when she found out, but without electricity, phones or internet, she might never know.

"Adam..." called a voice behind him.

Perhaps the Grim Reaper wanted to get this resolved quickly because he was *so* busy.

"Adam!"

The voice sounded familiar.

"Adam!"

It wasn't the Grim Reaper...it was a ghost.

He turned around, not believing his ears.

"Flint? What are you doing here? How...?"

The boy flicked his brown hair away revealing angry eyes as he strode towards Adam.

Flint reared back and punched Adam in the face. Adam rubbed

his painful jaw as Flint stepped back and glared at him.

"You were just going to leave?" Flint yelled.

"We thought you were dead and —"

"Exactly! You thought I was dead, but decided not to have a funeral?"

"We didn't have time for—"

"What about a service, or at least a few words to mourn my passing?"

"Flint?" Indie sprinted along the sidewalk towards them.

She barely slowed as she approached and scooped Indie into her arms. "You're alive! I can't believe you're alive!"

He mumbled something into her shoulders as she squeezed him tight.

After Indie set him down, he said, "Were you sad that I died?"

"Of course, I was."

"How come you didn't have a funeral?"

"What?"

"I wanted to follow you guys and wait until you had a funeral. Then when you were all sad and crying and stuff, I would jump out and say *surprise, I'm still alive*!"

She gave him a playful punch. "It was too soon, silly. We needed time to plan a proper service."

"Yeah, right."

"How *did* you survive the fire, or are you just a ghost?" asked Adam.

"After I handed you the doll, the ceiling fell. I ran through the back room and out the back door into a service area. Then I saw you guys leaving the mall like you had already forgotten about me."

"We didn't forget about you," said Indie. "Why would you think that?"

"My parents left me when I was just a baby. All my foster parents left me and forgot about me. My friends at the group homes eventually left and forgot about me. I thought you were different."

Indie wrapped him in another hug. "We are different, Flint and we won't leave you or forget about you."

"Will you cry at my funeral when I die? I don't want to be forgotten."

"Of course." Indie held him by the shoulders. "Adam cried like a little baby when he thought you died and has been moping ever since."

Flint smiled at Adam. "Really?"

"I'm glad my pain and sorrow make you happy," Adam said sarcastically.

Indie held out her arms. "Now we can continue our journey to find your true love like Jonathan Trager searching for Sara Thomas in Serendipity."

Flint pointed up. "Is that the one with John Cusack?"

"And Kate Beckinsale."

"What are you talking about?" asked Adam.

Indie gave her voice an exaggerated flare. "Fate brought them together, chance separated them and only destiny can reunite them."

"Okay…"

"It's a movie about true love and inevitable destiny."

Adam frowned. "She probably doesn't even remember me."

"In Serendipity, they only spent one magical evening together. Ten years later, he embarks on a quest to search for his soul mate."

"How does it end?"

"All rom-coms end with love conquering all."

"This isn't a movie."

"It's not a video game either," said Flint. "But I want to keep playing."

Adam sighed. "You two are the strangest friends I've ever had." He wiped the sweat from his brow and continued walking south, with Indie and Flint walking beside him.

"Why did all the shooting stop and where did Jerry and Prospero go?" asked Flint.

"Apparently there's a truce. Everyone is gathering at the stadium, and that's where Jerry and Prospero went," Indie answered.

"Cramming thousands of starving, panicked and scared people into a stadium seems like a bad idea."

"That's what *I* said."

They walked in silence down the hot sidewalk for a few minutes until Flint spoke.

"A moment of silence would have been nice."

"The next time you die, we will dress in black, cover our heads with sackcloth and weep for seven days," said Indie. "Then we will declare a state of mourning for the next month. Every sunrise, we'll start with two minutes of silence while a lone trumpet plays a long solo. We will erect a golden statue in the capital where yearly memorial services will be held with flowers and—"

"What if you don't die next time," said Adam.

"How about both of you don't rush into burning buildings next time," said Indie.

They laughed as a group of Latino women rushed towards them from a side street and joined the growing throng moving towards the stadium.

Adam still felt unsure of his leadership skills, their destination and the mission's feasibility, but he was glad to be back with his friends.

As they passed the Camelot Oasis Hotel, more people filled the streets. Atop the hotel, in colourful turrets, several armed men and women watched the growing crowds pass by.

"How far is it to the jail?" Adam asked.

"It's just outside the city," Indie answered. "About an hour and a half drive."

"How far to walk?"

"I don't know. Normally I'd ask my phone, but..."

"Are we ever getting the power or the internet back?" Flint asked, looking at his unresponsive phone. "Will things ever go back to normal?"

"Jerry said we're ants and the AIs are people that will step on us," said Adam.

"What?"

"What he means is, *no*," Indie answered. "Things will never go back to normal. The AIs are too smart. They don't care about us and we're all screwed."

"That's what I figured."

Adam felt like an ant as more people filled the street. Although currently peaceful, the caravan showed signs of fraying. A large man in a fedora and flowery shirt complained in flowery language about how he was trapped in this town while his wife tried to calm him. The crowd parted as a woman bent over and vomited on the sidewalk. Nobody stopped to help her.

Two middle-aged men dressed in red and blue argued about who was responsible for their current situation.

Adam noticed many people carrying guns under their belts, over their shoulders, and some holding them as if marching into war.

As they neared the imposing black glass pyramid of Pharaoh's Mirage Hotel on the right, some cut across the plaza. The crowd almost descended into panicked anarchy when two teenagers shot at the glass pyramid.

Everyone looked hungry, tired and scared.

Just one day previous, the city experienced intense and violent battles. However, the sudden electricity and information blackout gave everyone pause.

The pause felt temporary.

Crowds of people streamed across the plaza and down Scarab Street like a rushing river threatening to pull Adam, Flint and Indie into its current.

"Come on!" Indie yelled. "We have to get off this street."

They pushed their way out of the river of people and emerged onto the east side of the strip. A large fence surrounded a vast, empty parking lot. They found a sizeable gap in the fence and pushed through it. A dilapidated building and an empty pool sat in the middle of the lot; the remains of a failed construction project.

In the far corner of the lot, a dozen armed men and women

hovered around an army truck with a red flag flapping from its tall antenna. Others talked and milled around several campers, tents and campfires. Most of them wore red shirts, hats, or bandanas. They eyed Adam, Indie and Flint as they walked across the pavement.

"Let's keep moving," said Adam.

"Are you sure we don't want to stop and visit with the nice people?" Flint asked with a smirk.

"Very funny," said Indie.

A gunshot rang out from behind them and they whirled around. More gunfire erupted from the crowds marching to the stadium. Although most of the crowd and the stadium were a couple blocks away, the sounds of a frightened mob reverberated loudly.

"That doesn't sound good," said Adam. "We need to keep moving."

The group around the campers stood up and readied their guns.

Adam, Indie and Flint walked faster towards the opening in the fence across the parking lot. The gunshots behind them increased, as did the roar of a panicked crowd.

They rushed through the parking lot at a jog and through the fence on the other side.

"Where are we?" asked Adam.

Across the road sat a large church with a white cross on top. Beside it, a few cars sat in a mostly empty parking lot. Next to the lot, a pair of massive white cylindrical fuel storage tanks loomed like ominous giants. Beyond the tanks, several 747's and 767's sat motionless on the tarmac.

"Is that the airport?" asked Flint.

Before anyone answered, a jet screamed across the sky towards them. They looked up as an F-22 Raptor fired a missile towards the airport. A moment later, the runway exploded in a ball of fire. In the distance, they heard another jet following the same trajectory.

Indie's eyes widened. "If the next missile hits one of those tanks, we're going to die!"

Adam looked behind them at the empty parking lot, but there was nowhere to hide. He pointed at the church. "Run!"

They sprinted towards the brick building as the second jet fired a missile at the runway. Another explosion rocked the ground, but the fuel tanks remained intact. The first Raptor returned for a second pass as they reached the front doors of the church.

Adam pushed on the door, but it wouldn't budge. He looked around for a rock or something to break the glass.

"Wait!" called Indie. "There's people inside."

Adam turned to find several figures standing inside the doors. Two men gestured wildly to each other and their visitors. One sported dirty dress pants, and a stained buttoned shirt, and the other wore black dress pants and a shirt with a white clerical collar. Their muted yelling resounded through the thick glass doors. The Raptors screeched overhead, firing missiles at the runway and surrounding airport. Every explosion seemed closer than the previous one.

Adam yelled through the glass, Flint banged on the door and Indie pleaded with her best smile.

Finally, the priest unlocked and opened the door and the trio burst into the lobby.

"I still say this is a bad idea," said the man in the dress pants.

"*All* are welcome in God's house, Stanley," said the priest.

Indie smiled at him. "Thank you!"

"My name is Father Jarvis, and welcome to the Sanctuary of Eternal Redemption."

Adam walked through the lobby into the sanctuary. The lights remained off, but sunshine filtered through the stained-glass windows. Coloured light poured into the cavernous sanctuary full of empty wooden pews.

Father Jarvis stood behind him. "Beautiful, isn't it?"

Another explosion outside rattled the windows.

"We don't have time for tours!" Stanley yelled behind them.

"He's right," said Father Jarvis.

He flicked on a flashlight and led them quickly out of the lobby.

They rushed through a dark hallway and down a flight of stairs as more missiles shook the building. He opened a door at the bottom and they hurried past him into a large fellowship hall.

"You should be safe down here," Father Jarvis said as he closed the door.

Several sets of eyes turned to look at the visitors. Over one hundred people filled the sizeable room, as well as other hallways and adjacent classrooms. Families huddled together, children played in a corner and a few babies cried while other groups played cards and board games.

"Let's find you a place to rest and some food and water."

"Now we're giving them our food?" asked Stanley.

Father Jarvis smiled. "Truly, I say to you, as you did it to one of the least of these *my brothers*, you did it to me."

Stanley mumbled his disdain and shuffled away.

"Follow me," said Father Jarvis. "Let's see if we can find you a quiet corner. You look like you've been through – pardon the expression - *hell*."

He led them through the crowded room past excited children, scared parents and bored teens.

"Are you guys like a weird cannibalistic cult that sacrifices its young to appease the apocalypse gods?" asked Flint.

Indie smacked Flint on the shoulder. "Hey, be nice. If they didn't let us in, you'd be incinerated right now."

Father Jarvis laughed. "You've watched too many apocalypse movies, young man. We are just a regular group of parishioners, tourists, and other lost souls hoping for deliverance."

"Do you know what's going on?" Adam asked as they entered a crowded hallway.

"It sounds like someone is bombing the airport."

"Any idea who?"

"Maybe the army or the reds, the blues, China, Russia, Iran, North Korea. Perhaps it's a rogue artificial intelligence remotely operating drones."

"Those were fighter jets," said Flint. "Can they be remotely operated?"

Father Jarvis shrugged. "I don't know. I don't think anyone knows for sure. Everything is so messed up right now. Our society was so reliant on technology that when it turned against us, we were like lost sheep. Only God can save us now."

"Is this the end times?" asked Flint.

"No one knows the day nor the hour," he said as he opened the door to a small storage room.

Floor-to-ceiling shelving lined two walls. Coloured paper, crayons, paint, markers, scissors, pipe cleaners, glue, popsicle sticks and other craft supplies filled the shelves. Flags, puppets and costumes sat in a pile against the wall. The only floor space available was a small area between the shelves.

"No sense you spending the night in darkness," said Father Jarvis as he retrieved a box of matches from his pocket and pulled out a matchstick. Flint watched with curious eyes as Father Jarvis struck the match against the black strip, igniting the red phosphorous tip. It crackled for a second before maintaining a small, steady flame. He slowly manoeuvred the match towards a fat candle on the shelf and lingered over the virgin wick. The new flame illuminated the paper cross embedded in the wax candle.

"It's not much, but it will have to do," he said as he waved the match out.

Flint reached for the candle, but Indie snatched it out of his hands. "Thank you!"

"Be sure to blow it out before you fall asleep tonight," said Father Jarvis. "I'll have the kitchen staff bring you some food. We don't have much in the way of washroom facilities, so try to keep it in until tomorrow morning. Hopefully, if the bombing stops, we can return to the main floor."

They rested on the storage room's thin carpet around the light of the flickering candle. A woman came by with a bag of Cheerios and bottled water.

They ate half the Cheerios before Flint stuffed them in his pack for later.

The church rattled with each explosion for the next few hours. A large crack in the ceiling plaster appeared, but the church remained standing.

Later that evening, the bombing slowed. The fat candle burned past the embedded paper cross and down to a small stump, but still flickered. They sat leaning against the shelving, watching the light from the flame dance across the ceiling.

Flint pinched at the flame like he was teasing it.

"I love fires," he said.

"No kidding," said Adam.

"I watched a lot of movies where people camped outside and sat around a campfire. They roasted hotdogs and marshmallows, while some cool guy played the guitar. Sometimes they ate beans from tin cups and warmed themselves as they sat around the fire beside a lake."

"Do you like camping?" asked Indie.

"I've never gone camping."

"Never? Your parents – I mean, foster parents never took you camping?"

"No. When I was seven, my foster family slept in a camper for a few weekends, but they cooked on the stove or barbecue. They never had a campfire. I hope the world doesn't end before I get to sit around the campfire."

"I think we can make that happen," said Indie.

They sat silently, watching the candle and flickering light for a few minutes before Adam broke the silence.

"Do you think we can really find Piper?"

"We didn't come this far, just to give up," said Indie. "Besides, we have to get out of Vegas, anyway. Tomorrow, we'll go to the prison and see if she's still there."

"Do you think they're still running the prison?" He asked. "What if the guards left the prisoners locked in their cells?"

"Then we'll break into the jail and rescue your damsel in distress."

"How are we going to break into a jail?"

"The JCC isn't Alcatraz. It's a minimum-security correctional facility."

"What if she isn't there?"

"Then we'll ask around. I only met Piper once, but she doesn't seem like a girl who hides in a corner. She makes an impression. Someone will know where she is."

"I hope so."

The candle's light waned as the flame consumed the last of the wax. The wilted paper cross on the floor beside the candle disappeared from view as the flame petered out. They fell asleep on the thinly carpeted floor of the dark storage room. Outside of the Sanctuary of Eternal Redemption Church, the bombs fell for most of the night.

CHAPTER 29

Adam woke when he heard shouting from the fellowship hall outside. Flint stood at the open door of their storage room, flicking his lighter open and closed with a rhythmic clicking.

Indie rubbed her eyes and sat up. "What time is it?"

"Hopefully morning," said Adam as he stood up and stretched. "Because I can't sleep another second on this hard floor."

Indie got to her feet and wiped her face with imaginary water. "What is all the yelling out there?"

"They are arguing over food," said Flint.

The trio left the safety of the storage closet and joined the noisy crowd in the fellowship hall.

A gloomy looking older man with white hair and a matching white beard leaned against the wall beside them. Flint pulled the bag with Cheerios out of his pack and handed them to the man.

"Thank you, son," said the man. "Despite what Alfred Lewis said, there *is* still hope in this world."

Flint gave Adam and Indie a confused look. Adam and Indie looked at each other and shrugged.

They listened to the animated argument as it grew louder.

"We don't have enough food for everyone."

"If we ration properly, everyone can at least have something."

"Most of these freeloaders never helped get any of this food. Why do they get food, while my pregnant wife starves? If she doesn't get the proper nutrition, her baby will die!"

"So, she gets food while others starve? How is that fair?"

"Who said anything about fair? I brought a lot of the food here and my family gets food first."

"This is a church," said Father Jarvis. "We must share the food evenly."

"What are you going to do, Father? Feed the thousands with your magic loaves and fishes? That fairytale isn't going to work here!"

"It isn't a fairytale. It's an accurate depiction of an actual miracle."

"While you hope and pray for a miracle, I'm going to feed my family!"

Indie leaned close to Adam and Flint and whispered, "We should leave this church before things get ugly."

"Do you think it's safe out there yet?" Adam asked.

"It ain't safe in here and it ain't safe out there," said the older man as he picked a stray Cheerio out of his beard.

"Are they still bombing out there?" Adam asked.

"Probably, but there are worse things than bombs," said the old man.

"What do you mean?" Indie asked.

The old man's face wrinkled like an old blanket when he smiled. "Alfred Lewis once said, 'There are only nine meals between mankind and anarchy.'"

"What are you saying?" asked Adam.

"We passed nine meals a couple days ago. Things will only get worse. You need to leave this city if you want to survive."

"That's the plan," said Indie.

The old man grabbed Adam's wrist with surprising strength and pulled Adam close. He whispered into Adam's ear with warm, raspy breaths. "Be brave, stay safe, and get your friends out of the city."

Adam felt a set of cold keys pressed into his palm.

"Take my car. It's the Ford Country Squire."

Adam pushed back. "No, I can't take your car, you—"

He squeezed Adam's palm over the keys. The ragged edges dug into his palms.

Adam winced. "Why don't you come with us?"

The old man shook his head and smiled. "My time is over, while yours has just begun."

Indie nudged Adam, and he turned to face her.

She looked at him with an inquisitive look. “What’s going on?”

“He told me to take his car.”

She furrowed her brow. “Why?”

“I don’t know—”

Adam turned back to the man, but he disappeared.

“Where did he go?”

“We should leave—” Indie interrupted herself. “Where’s Flint?”

Adam looked around. “Why is everyone disappearing?”

“It could be the rapture,” said a woman beside him.

Adam didn’t know what the rapture was and didn’t want to find out. He followed Indie as they pushed through the crowd towards the door by the stairs.

“What about Flint?” he asked.

“He’ll find us,” she answered without looking back.

They continued to push through hot, sweaty angry bodies until they reached the door. Once on the other side, the rancid odour of sweat, dirty diapers, bad breath and urine finally subsided.

“Should we wait for Flint?”

“He’ll come,” said Indie and started up the stairs.

Halfway up, the door behind them opened and Flint stepped through.

“You weren’t going to wait for me?” he asked.

“*I* wanted to,” said Adam.

Flint ran up the stairs. “Thanks, man.”

“I told you, he’d find us,” said Indie.

“We should hurry,” said Flint as they walked through the church.

“What’s your rush?” asked Indie.

“Nothing…”

She turned and squinted at him. “What did you do?”

He held his hands out. “What? I didn’t do anything.”

They stepped out of the church into a hot, windless morning. The pungent odour of burnt rubber and plastic assaulted their olfactory receptors. Wisps of a murky haze wafted across the road in front of the church. Several plumes of dark, toxic smoke billowed into the sky from the airport to the south. To the west, the tall buildings of the Camelot Oasis Hotel burned. Colossal flames licked out of a gaping black hole in the top floor.

"The old man was right," said Indie.

Adam held up the keys as they walked towards the parking lot. "Does anyone know what a Country Squire is?"

"It sounds like something from the Middle Ages," said Indie.

Adam held up the key. "We'll just have to try each one."

"Hey!" yelled a voice behind them.

Adam turned and saw Stanley standing outside the church doors with his hands on his hips.

"Time to go!" yelled Flint.

"What did you do?!" Indie yelled.

"I may have borrowed some food from the nice people," Flint said with a fake smile.

Indie shook her head. "We need to find that car, Adam."

They ran towards the cars. Adam's eyes darted across the parking lot, searching for something that looked like a country squire. Except he didn't know what a country squire was.

"That one!" Flint yelled.

He pointed to a long, light green, four-door station wagon with faded simulated woodgrain trim.

"How do you know?"

Stanley strode towards them with a menacing scowl. "You need to return that food!"

"Just try it!" yelled Indie.

Adam ran to the driver's side and fumbled with the keys. The first one didn't fit in the slot, but the second key slid inside and gave a satisfying click when turned.

"Hurry up!" Indie stood impatiently at the passenger door.

Stanley was dangerously close as Adam opened the door. He looked frantically for the button to unlock the other doors, but quickly gave up and dove across the seat to unlock Indie's door. She jumped inside and unlocked the back door for Flint while

Adam started the car. He shoved it into gear and slammed on the gas just as Stanley reached the car. The balding tires squealed until they gained traction on the pavement.

"Hurry!" yelled Indie as the old car tore out of the church parking lot. Adam glanced in his rear-view mirror and saw Stanley standing behind them, his legs apart. He pointed a large pistol directly at them.

Adam slammed on the gas and aimed the car at the narrow parking lot exit. "Get down!" he yelled.

He waited for the inevitable gunshot, but it never came. Adam looked in the rear-view mirror again. Stanley stood with feet apart, pointing his pistol at the rear of the vehicle.

The tires squealed again as Adam turned onto the road. In the back of the car, an unbuckled Flint flailed like a sock in a dryer. He knocked against the window, bounced off the seat, and then slammed against the back of Indie's headrest.

"You okay back there?" Adam asked.

Flint popped up with a dazed look. "I'm good."

Indie pointed ahead. "Follow this road until you reach the highway. Take it west, then the 515 south.

"Hey guys!" Flint called from the second row of seats. "This car has a double-wide seat that faces *backwards*!"

Indie turned and glared at Flint. "You can't go stealing from people, Flint. Especially from a church!"

"Why not? We need the food."

"Those people need food, too. We should go back and return it."

Flint sat in the rear-facing seat and didn't turn around. "I'm not giving it back."

Indie looked at Adam as if waiting for a response.

"We can't go back. Stanley has a really big gun."

Indie sighed but didn't press the issue.

Adam turned onto the on-ramp and the car rumbled onto the highway. He joined a few other cars on the road, including a metallic blue sedan ahead of them.

"Looks like we're not the only ones desperate to leave the city," said Indie.

"What's left of it..." said Adam as they passed the smouldering remains of the barely recognizable airport on the right. Across the road, grey smoke rose from the concrete and steel husk of a large hotel complex.

Further down, fire still raged at a gas station and small restaurant.

"That's a lot of fires," Flint said from the back seat.

"And no fire department to put them out," Indie added.

Long plumes of smoke rose from hundreds of burning houses, apartments, businesses and hotels in every direction. Without a breeze, the plumes ascended straight into heaven like alien tractor beams sucking the life force from the city.

"This is *so* strange," said Flint from the back seat.

"Yes, it is," said Adam. "Everything changed so quickly."

"Last week Vegas was alive with tourists, gamblers, and residents like me going to school and work. Now it's a burning shell of its former glory while everyone struggles to survive. This is definitely strange."

"I meant this seat facing backwards is strange," said Flint.

As they approached the 515 cutoff, they encountered a roadblock. Several cars, a school bus, an SUV and a van lay across the highway like an impossible speed bump. Five armed lookouts stood in a small gap between the bus and the SUV. A large fire burned on one side of the road in front of the bus.

"There aren't enough fires burning across the city," said Indie. "They have to start another one?"

Flint crawled out of the back seat and poked his head into the front seat to get a better view.

"What do you think they're burning?" he asked.

"They might be cooking," Adam suggested.

"That's pretty big for a cooking fire," said Indie.

Adam slowed to a stop, and they watched the metallic blue car ahead of them reach the roadblock. One lookout moved towards the car. The passenger door opened, and a man stepped out. His arms gestured wildly as another lookout approached. They argued for a few moments before a shot rang out. From their position, it was impossible to see who fired the shot. A man burst out of the rear SUV door and fired a pistol. All the lookouts returned fire. Every SUV window shattered as bullets peppered the hood and doors. The gunfire lasted almost a full minute. When the battle ended, one lookout lay on the ground with a serious bullet wound. Nobody moved in the SUV. The lookouts high-fived each other before pulling the lifeless corpses out of the SUV. They dragged the bodies across the pavement, leaving a trail of blood, and tossed them into the bonfire.

"That's a gross cookout," said Flint.

"We should find another way," said Adam, and turned the car around.

They drove back to the previous street but found the southbound street blocked by a multi-vehicle accident. Adam took the next empty road and exited the highway. Cars, jeeps, tents, campers and hundreds of people milled about in the parking lot of a grocery store and large supercenter. Fires burned from barrels, barbecues and make-shift firepits.

Two armed men stood at the entrance and watched Adam drive by. Men, women and a few children walked the sidewalks. Some carried bags while others pushed grocery carts. Two men at the side of the road tried to wave them down, but Adam kept driving. The street ahead looked busy, so Adam turned onto a small side road. A mother pushed a stroller with a small child inside, while a young boy rode a scooter behind them.

Adam slowed as they passed a *Harmony Strings Emporium* sign. An arrow below the stylized violin pointed left.

Indie turned to him. "You can stop if you want…"

"What are you talking about?"

"I see that look in your eye."

"We don't have time to—"

"We're not in a hurry, Adam. Piper waited this long. She can wait another hour. If you want to stop and look at the cellos, then we can stop and look at the cellos."

"Do you think she's waiting for me?"

Indie rolled her eyes. “Let’s find the music store.”

He turned left and drove into a small industrial section.

“Where are we going?” Flint asked from the back seat.

“We’re taking a quick detour to look at cellos,” said Indie.

“Cool! A side quest!”

A few minutes later they pulled into the empty parking lot of the Harmony Strings Emporium.

Other than a small hole in the front window, the store remained intact.

Adam tried the door but found it locked. He peered inside but saw no one.

“Hello?” Indie called out. “Is anybody here?”

“This is a bad idea,” said Adam.

Flint kicked at the front window, enlarging the small hole.

“What are you doing?” Adam asked.

“Finding a way inside.”

He continued kicking until most of the window lay in pieces on the ground.

“We can’t just—”

Before he finished, Flint jumped through the open window and ran inside. A moment later, he opened the door for Adam and Indie.

“Welcome to the cello store!” he exclaimed with a wide smile.

Adam pointed at Flint. “Don’t break anything!”

Although he had never been to this store, Harmoney Strings Emporium felt familiar to Adam. It reminded him of the Rocky Mountain Music Store back in Colorado where he spent many evenings after school looking at cellos he couldn’t afford and browsing the music books and bows. This place felt like a piece of home.

Rows of violins and violas in shades ranging from light amber to deep reddish-brown hung along one wall, and dozens of black cases leaned against another. A spiral staircase with white railings led to a second level. Two cellos and a double bass sat in stands beneath the stairs.

An odd scratching sound emanated from the back of the room.

Adam held up a finger. “Shhh! There’s someone here.”

They stood quietly and listened. Adam held his breath.

Suddenly, a squirrel squeaked at them, and jumped off a shelf.

“Zombie squirrel!” Flint shrieked and grabbed a violin.

The squirrel stood motionless on the floor staring at them.

“Awww,” said Indie, “He’s so cute.”

Flint held the violin like a squirrel club and waited for the undead vermin to make the first move.

“Wait until his razor-sharp teeth latch on to your neck.”

The squirrel chirped and scurried around them and out the front window.

“Put the violin back,” said Adam. “These are delicate instruments.”

Flint hung the violin back up. “I don’t think anyone cares. If the squirrels don’t eat them, the next rain will wreck them, anyway.”

Adam moved straight towards the cellos. “It doesn’t matter. These are handcrafted works of art.”

“Whoa! Cool stairs!” said Flint as he ran up the spiral staircase.

Adam slid his hand along the smooth varnish of the cello’s neck. It was a different brand than his cello, but similar in style and weight. He grabbed a bow and carried the cello to a nearby stool. Resting the lower bout on his legs, he held the cello with his knees. With his left hand on the neck, he rested the bow on the strings with his right.

Just as he played the first note, Flint screamed.

“Flint? What’s going on up there?” Indie yelled.

Adam replaced the cello on its stand and followed Indie up the spiral stairs.

“Look what I found!” exclaimed Flint as they ran into the room. Broken violins, an upright bass and violas sat on shelves and covered almost the entire floor. C-clamps, f-clamps, peg hole drilling jigs, glue, chisels, planes, rags and varnish sat on the table in front of Flint, who held a large silver pistol. However, something else drew Adam’s gaze. A bright banana-yellow cello sat on its stand in the corner. A warm glow from a small window lit the room, but the cello seemed to radiate like a fiery sun. It didn't look real. Every cello he owned or played was varying shades of earthy brown. He tried a dark blue cello at the Rocky Mountain Music Store once, but had never seen a brightly coloured cello - and definitely not a yellow one.

He stared at the strange, beaming cello with mouth agape. "What is that?"

"I believe it's called a *pistol*," said Flint. "Our little side quest has proved quite useful."

"Put that down!" yelled Indie.

"Okay, but I'm keeping it. Prospero took my last one and I still think we should be armed."

Adam weaved through the mess of broken instruments and stood in front of the yellow apparition. He stood motionless, almost afraid to touch it.

"Oh, yeah," said Flint. "I meant to tell you – I found a cool cello for you."

"Do they normally come in funky colours?" Indie asked.

Adam shook his head and continued staring at the cello.

"Are you going to try it?" she asked.

He reached out and ran his fingers along the back of the neck. The heavy gloss felt cool and strange. Lifting the instrument, he tested the weight and found it heavier than most cellos he handled. Adam carefully carried the cello through the maze of broken instruments like he was cradling a newborn across a field of glass shards. The space between Flint and the tool shelf was barely enough for him and the cello to fit through.

"Move!" He swatted Flint hard enough that he almost fell off his stool.

"Alright, I'm moving, but only because you asked *so* nicely."

Adam sat down and grabbed a bow from the table. He closed his eyes and played the first stanza of his musical composition.

"Hey is that from an old shark movie?" asked Flint.

The notes played louder, fuller and richer than any cello he ever played. Deep tones reverberated from the lower bout through his knees and resonated deep in his bones. Each stroke resounded from the taut strings with rhythmic cadence, and the soft, soulful hum caressed his ears like a lover's whisper.

Raindrops pelted the window, breaking Adam from his musical enchantment. He opened his eyes and stopped playing.

"Is that rain?"

He leaned forward and stared out the window with brow furrowed.

"You look like you've never seen rain," said Flint as he walked to the window and looked out.

"I guess I assumed it was always sunny in Vegas," said Adam.

Thunder rumbled outside as the rain intensified. A flash of lightning blinked outside and a crack of thunder shook the building.

"We get some big storms here," said Indie, "and this looks like a monster."

Flint pressed against the glass and looked down. "Guys, we have company and they have guns."

Indie joined him at the window. "I don't see anything."

"That's because they're now in the store below us," Flint whispered.

He ran to his pack and pulled out the big silver revolver. "Time for the final boss so we can move on to the next level."

"Put that thing away," Indie yell-whispered. "We're not shooting anyone."

From the store below came the sound of yelling, laughing and crashing instruments.

"They're destroying everything," said Adam. "We have to stop them."

Indie glared at him. "We're not risking our lives defending the violins."

Adam paused for a moment before regaining his senses. "Right. Flint, can we get that window open?"

"I'll look for a rope," said Indie.

Adam found a flight-style cello case in the corner with backpack shoulder straps, a handle at the top and wheels at the bottom. He gently placed the cello inside and clasped it shut.

"There aren't any ropes here—" she paused mid-sentence when she saw Adam lifting the cello case. "What are you doing?"

"We are not leaving this priceless work of art for those hooligans to destroy."

"Window is open," said Flint as he removed the screen. "It will be a tight fit, but I think we can all get through."

"Check out these wacky stairs!" yelled a voice from below.

"Time to go!" said Flint and disappeared out the window.

"Aren't we a full story up?" asked Indie as she and Adam rushed over.

They looked through the pouring rain and found Flint hanging on the branch of an African Sumac. His damp brown hair draped over a quirky smile.

"Can you make it?" Adam asked Indie.

She shrugged. "I can try."

The voices below grew louder as she leapt out the window. Her hand flailed at the sumac branches as she crashed into the tree. She bounced off several thick branches before landing on the wet grass below. Adam peered out the window and smiled when Indie gave him a grimaced thumbs up.

He returned inside and quickly hoisted the big cello case onto the window sill. The neck easily slid through the window, but the larger bulbous end quickly became wedged. He shoved it hard as footsteps clanged up the metal staircase. It scraped against the window frame, but finally popped out the window. He reached out and grabbed the handle before it fell.

Flint and Indie beckoned him from the ground.

"Catch the cello!" Adam called.

"Are you kidding me?" asked Flint.

"No! Don't let it hit the ground!"

"This seems like a bad idea!" yelled Flint.

"Whatever you do, do it faster!" Indie implored.

"If you don't catch it, I will kill you," Adam yelled.

"Where do you think you're going?" said a sinister voice behind him.

He reached down as far as he could before releasing his grip on the handle. It fell into Flint's waiting arms and knocked down to the damp grass.

Adam felt hands grabbing at him from behind. Without looking, he kicked hard. The first kick hit nothing but air, but the second connected with the attacker's midsection. As the hands released their grip, Adam dove out the window. His head hit a sumac branch as he tumbled into the tree. He thrashed his arms, searching for a branch to grab, but couldn't maintain a grip. Instead, he bounced and rolled off three branches before landing on the wet grass with a squelching thud. The impact sucked the air from his lungs.

"Hey!" a man yelled from the window above him.

Adam struggled to catch his breath.

"That was almost as graceful as my landing," said Indie as she grabbed his hand and pulled him up. They ran behind Flint, who dragged the bulky cello case to the station wagon. Just as he opened the back door, two men emerged from the music store. A short plump man with a scraggly beard held a rifle at his side. Beside him, a taller man with a goatee and cowboy hat fondled an aluminum bat.

"You guys got any food?" asked the short one.

"We're just leaving," said Adam, as he fished the keys out of his pocket.

Out of the corner of his eye, he saw Flint remove his backpack.

"You can leave, but the pretty one is coming with us," said the skinny cowboy with a slight southern drawl. His cheek bulged with chewing tobacco, distorting his gaunt face.

"Screw you!" said Indie. "I'm not going anywhere with you."

"Maybe they were talking about me," said Flint with a mocking smile.

The sky filled with flashes of lightning as rolling thunder echoed through the heavy rain.

The third man from upstairs burst out the front door of the music store and stood behind the other two.

"Back off, turd stains!" yelled Flint as he pulled out the pistol and pointed it at them.

"What are you going to do with that, little boy?" asked the cowboy.

Without warning, his bat swung towards Flint. It clipped Flint's hand, flinging the pistol into a muddy puddle. Flint yelped in pain.

Adam dove towards the pistol, but slipped in a puddle and rolled onto the grass. Flint and the bat-man leapt at the gun, but one of them kicked it. The pistol spun across the wet pavement and landed within reach of Adam.

He snatched the wet pistol off the ground and held it with both hands. Brown mud dripped from the muzzle and Adam hoped the gun still worked.

Thin bat boy faced Flint and readied himself to smack his head like a t-ball. He froze mid-swing when Adam yelled, "Don't move!"

The short, bearded man still stood watching the scuffle with his rifle pointed at the ground.

Beside him, the skinny guy slowly pushed to his feet. The bat remained in his hand. He turned to his bearded friend with the rifle. "Thanks for your help, *Charlie*."

"We should let these folks be, Ned," Charlie replied.

"Listen to your friend," said Adam. "Let us leave and nobody gets hurt."

He kept his eyes and pistol pointed at the cowboy. "Flint, put the case in the backseat and Indie, please start the car."

Ned removed his cowboy hat and spat a glob of brown goo into the rain. "The smart thing for you would be to allow that fine specimen of a woman to come with us."

"Come on, Ned. Let's go," said Charlie. He shifted his rifle but kept it pointed at the puddle at his feet.

Adam aimed the pistol at Ned's chest and put on his fiercest expression.

Ned aimed his pointy chin at Adam and stuck out his chest. "You think you're pretty tough with that little pistol, but I don't think you'll shoot me."

He dropped the bat, and the aluminum clanged to the pavement.

"Come on!" Ned beat his chest with one fist and stepped closer to Adam.

Adam remained in place, unsure if he should or could pull the trigger.

Ned sighed and shook his head. "You're not worth it," he said and turned around.

As he walked back to his friends, Adam slowly lowered his pistol.

"Let's go, Adam," Indie said behind him.

As Adam turned to return to the car, he saw movement in his peripheral vision. He whirled around and watched Ned snatch Charlie's rifle.

Adam's hand, still holding the pistol, flew up. With one fluid motion, he pointed and fired. Ned's rifle was halfway up when he suddenly deflated like a popped balloon. A tiny crimson hole in his stomach appeared as he sank to the ground. His face contorted into a mixture of anguish and surprise.

Charlie dropped to the ground beside his friend. He removed Ned's cowboy hat and cradled Ned in his arms. The other man pulled the rifle out of the dying man's grip.

"Why did you shoot him?" He spat the words at Adam, who froze in place.

A gust of wind pulled rain from the sky and hurled a wave of water at them.

The man held his rifle at his hip. The barrel pointed forward, but not necessarily at Adam.

"Easy…" said Adam. "He was going to shoot me."

Charlie held his hands over the haemorrhaging wound. "You shot him right in the stomach!"

Ned desperately gasped for air and his face contorted with panic and fear.

Indie grabbed Adam's arm. "We should go," she whispered in a soft voice.

He lowered the pistol and stepped towards the dying man,

hoping to help.

The man with the rifle blocked his path. “Turn around and leave, before you make things worse.”

“I didn’t mean—” he began.

“Ned didn’t mean no harm,” yelled the man. “He’s a little slow, but he didn’t mean any harm.”

“I’m sorry, he—”

Indie squeezed his arm and pulled Adam back.

“We’re leaving,” she said staring at the armed man. She led Adam back to the car, opened the passenger side door and guided him inside. He tried to speak, but couldn’t.

Indie ran around the car and got into the driver’s side.

Flint stared back at the dying man for a moment before climbing in the back seat. The back door slammed shut with a reverberating thud.

Adam stared forward as Indie drove away. Muddy water soaked his hair, clothes, and shoes and murky feelings clouded his brain.

“We need to find a place to dry off,” said Indie.

“That was sooo cool,” said Flint from the back seat.

Adam wanted to say something, but his mouth failed to comply. Instead, he stared forward. The wipers frantically swished back and forth, trying desperately to keep the water off the windshield. But the wind kept throwing more rain. Water dripped from Adam’s hair onto his face and his cheeks, diluting his salty tears.

CHAPTER 30

Indie found her way back to the highway and drove south, but the storm worsened, making it difficult to see. She almost crashed into an abandoned truck before deciding to get off the highway. A few minutes later she found an exit. The rain still poured as she pulled into a fast-food restaurant parking lot.

"Oooh, I'll take a cheeseburger, large fries and chocolate milkshake!" exclaimed Flint.

He opened the back door to get out.

"Where are you going?" asked Indie.

"I'm just going to look around."

She leaned forward and peered through the wet windshield. "It looks abandoned, but be careful."

"Are you guys coming?" he asked.

"You go ahead," said Indie. "We'll be there in a minute."

The back door slammed shut leaving Indie and Adam alone.

Adam reached for the handle.

"How are you doing?" Indie asked.

Adam's mouth finally complied and allowed him to speak. "I'm fine."

"You just killed someone."

He stared ahead at the rivulets of rain snaking down the windshield. "I know, but he deserved it. Didn't he?"

"You had to. He would have killed you."

"That guy said Ned was a little slow. How do we know he wasn't just playing around?"

"We don't."

The answer surprised him. "I could have waited—"

"He threatened us. He had a rifle, and it appeared he was going to shoot at us. If you hesitated, you might be dead. They might have kidnapped me, or worse: I might have to wander the post-apocalyptic wasteland with Flint!"

He turned and saw her smirking at him.

"That would be worse," he said.

"Let's go inside and dry off before Flint gets into too much trouble."

Adam nodded. "We should hurry before he burns the place down."

They dashed through the rain and stepped through the broken front window of the restaurant. Adam held the pistol in front of him. The gun felt powerful and uneasy in his hands.

Despite the broken window, most of the restaurant was still dry. Adam wrinkled his nose at the rancid odour emanating from the kitchen.

"Are we clear?" yelled Indie.

Flint's head popped up from behind the counter. "All clear, cap'n! No hostiles unless you count the rats."

"You can put that down now," Indie pointed at the pistol in Adam's hand.

He set the gun on a table and sat down in the booth.

"Did you find any food back there," Indie asked as she slid onto the bench across from Adam.

"I've got stinking fries, rotting burger, sour milkshakes and—ooh some cans of pop!"

"I'll take a diet," Indie called.

"A root beer for me," said Adam.

Outside, the rain subsided, as did Adam's adrenaline and shock.

Flint returned with an armload of pop cans. He unloaded them on the table before sitting beside Adam.

Indie cracked her can open with a sharp snap of the aluminum tab. The carbonation hissed in relief. She took a long swig and set the can down with a sigh.

"Are you in shock or something?" Flint stared at Adam.

Indie glared at Flint.

"I'm fine," said Adam with surprising confidence.

Flint pointed at the can of root beer in Adam's hand. "The drink potion will restore health and magic like in Legends of Zelda."

"I could use some magic," Adam said as he pulled the tab.

The can erupted with a spray of root beer showering the table and Adam.

"Ahhhh!" he shouted.

Adam tried aiming the root beer geyser at Flint who was pointing and laughing hysterically. The can slipped from his hand and rolled across the table. The brown effervescent liquid poured across the table and onto his lap. Adam gasped and tried to jump out of the booth, but slammed his knee against the table.

Across the table, Indie stifled her giggle with her hand.

"What are you laughing at?" he said shaking his head. Adam shook his wet hands at her.

She removed her hand from her mouth and let out a thunderous, two-second burp. The two boys stared at her in a brief moment of shock before bursting into a fit of laughter.

They spend the next hour joking, participating in burping contests and drinking their fill.

An hour later, the rain stopped suddenly, as if Mother Nature was ready for the next scene. With their brief act completed, the roiling clouds shuffled off stage, yielding the spotlight to the star of the show. The radiant sun resumed its role and continued roasting the city.

Adam stood at the broken window and looked out. "We should get going."

"It is time for the final boss level," said Flint.

"The what?" Adam asked.

Flint ignored the question. "We've cleared hurdles, defeated enemies and reached Bowser's Castle. This is where we defeat Bowser and rescue Princess Peach!"

"No, no, no," said Indie. "This is where the damaged man overcomes his personal demons, and shows his true character. After traversing across the apocalyptic city, he finally reunites with his one true love and—"

"Or we can just drive to the prison to see if Piper needed help," said Adam, standing up.

"That's not very dramatic," said Indie as they left the restaurant.

Flint splashed through the puddles behind them. "This is going to be sooo awesome! We get to break your girlfriend out of prison!"

"It's a conservation camp, not a prison," said Indie

"She's not my girlfriend," said Adam, getting into the driver's side of the car.

He felt better after their pit stop, but a new anxiousness grew in the pit of his stomach. It felt like a lifetime ago when he saw Piper last. He wondered if she would run into his arms or think he was an idiot.

More vehicles filled the highway as they drove east, along the southern edge of Vegas.

"We need to get to the Las Vegas Freeway," said Indie. "That will take us to the outskirts of the city. The camp is about a half hour south."

Ten minutes later, they found the ramp to the Freeway. He slowed as they approached and eventually stopped.

"Why are we stopping?" Flint popped his head up from the back seat. "Are we there alrea—"

He paused mid-question when he saw what Adam and Indie saw. An endless line of cars, trucks, motorcycles and buses snaked along the highway. Some vehicles edged forward when able, but most remained immobile. Several horns sounded from drivers expressing their impatience.

"Where did *they* all come from?" asked Flint.

"And where are they going?" Adam asked.

"They're leaving the city."

"Why?" asked Adam.

"Look behind us," said Flint.

Indie and Adam turned in their seat and stared out the back window. Vegas wasn't visible anymore. Instead, massive dark clouds of acrid smoke from a thousand fires poured out of the city.

"It looks like a nuclear bomb went off," said Flint.

"I hope not," said Adam.

Indie pointed to the side of the road. "We need to get off this highway."

"Okay, I'll get off at the next exit."

"No. Get off here."

A motorcycle veered off the road and into the desert, leaving a trail of dust behind it.

"Go! Now!" yelled Indie.

Adam turned the wheel and hit the gas as another motorcycle followed the first.

Adam steered the car off the pavement and into a field of sand, hard dirt and scrub brush.

Behind them, a jeep left the highway and quickly passed them.

"Whoa!" said Flint. "I think we started a trend."

In his rear-view mirror, Adam saw a half-dozen vehicles following his lead. He hit the gas and the old station wagon creaked and rumbled over scrub brush and bumpy dry ground. The ancient suspension system sounded like it might crumble beneath them. He drove through an empty parking lot until he found another road. They continued east along the edge of the city.

"We can take this around the state park. It will take us south of the JCC, but we can circle back when we get back to the highway," said Indie.

"I thought all the stations ran out of gas," said Adam as they drove through a newer subdivision with big houses squeezed together on tiny lots.

"So did I," said Indie.

Fifteen minutes later, they found the US-95 which took them out of the city. A few other cars found the same route, but at least the traffic was moving.

The distant mountains never seemed to get closer as they continued south. Adam looked worriedly at the gas gauge. The needle hovered over the quarter mark.

For the next half hour, Flint slept in the back seat. Indie stared quietly out the window and Adam stared at the mountains lining the horizon on almost all sides. The serenity of the desert felt like sweet relief from the chaos of the city.

"How much further?" Adam asked.

Indie leaned towards him and peered at the dash. She saw the glowing red light beside the *E* and shook her head. "Too far."

A few minutes later, the car sputtered and Adam veered to the side of the road as the car burned the last drops of fuel.

Flint sat up and wiped his eyes. "Is this it?"

"We're out of gas," said Adam.

Flint opened the back door and stepped out.

"Where are you going?" Indie asked.

"Without air conditioning, we will bake in this car."

"He's right," said Adam, opening his door and climbing out.

They stood behind the car with only their legs shaded by the old station wagon.

"How far to walk it?" asked Flint.

"Too far," said Indie.

Sweat was already forming on Adam's brow.

"We should start walking," he said.

"It's several hours to the next town," said Indie.

He looked in every direction but saw only the desert and mountains.

"We can't stay here," he said, "or we'll die of dehydration."

"We'll die quicker from heat stroke if we walk," argued Indie.

"This is not how I pictured dying," said Flint.

They stopped talking and turned to the road when they heard a truck approaching. The extended-cab pickup truck towed a small camper behind it.

"Where's your gun?" asked Indie.

Adam ran quickly back to the car and found the pistol between the seats. He checked the chamber and found three bullets. Holding the pistol behind his back he returned to the others.

The truck slowed and pulled onto the shoulder twenty feet behind them.

"What's the plan?" whispered Flint. "Shoot him in the leg and steal his truck?"

"Nobody is shooting anyone," said Indie.

"Then why did I get the gun?" asked Adam.

"Just in case."

A burly man with a neatly trimmed beard and dirty baseball cap stepped out of the truck. Adam couldn't tell if the dirty hat was red or blue.

"You folks look like you might need help," said the man.

"We're out of gas," said Indie.

He stepped closer to them with an easy gait. His hands were empty, but Adam wondered if he kept a gun in his waistband at the back. Adam watched the truck, almost expecting heavily armed men to jump out.

The man held out his hand. "The name's Tom."

Indie shook his hand. "I'm Indie and this is Adam and Flint.

Adam switched the pistol behind his back to his left hand and shook Tom's with his right.

Flint only nodded and eyed the man suspiciously.

Tom leaned to the side and Adam thought for a moment he was trying to see what he held behind his back.

"That's an old gas-guzzlin' clunker, but I'd have thought you'd make it further than this unless you're leaking gas."

"We only started with a quarter tank," said Adam.

Tom crinkled his brow in confusion. "I thought they were filling everyone's tank."

"What do you mean?" asked Indie.

"After the meeting at the Roomba…" He gestured at them as if they should know what he meant.

"We didn't make it to the meeting," said Indie.

Tom shrugged. "Yeah, it was a total waste of time. But they told everyone that they should leave the city. Afterwards, they opened some big storage tanks and filled everyone's tanks with gas. It was surprisingly calm – mostly. I guess at least one of the military divisions is still intact. I think the rest of them—"

"Tom is everything okay?" A woman stepped out of the

passenger side of the truck.

"It's fine, hun. They just ran out of gas."

"Already? Are they leaking gas?"

"No, they didn't get any after the meeting."

"Why not?" she called.

"Go back inside the truck, Sue. You'll catch heatstroke out here." He turned back to Indie.

"You're welcome to drive with us. There's room in the camper. Ain't no seatbelts, but I suppose there ain't no cops neither."

"We need to get back to the city," said Indie.

"That place is nothing but burning ruins, dear," said Tom.

"His girlfriends in jail and we're rescuing her," said Flint, pointing a thumb at Adam.

"Sorry, but I can't help you," said Tom. "We're heading south and I suggest you do the same."

"We should help the nice people." Sue stood behind her husband, and he jumped when she spoke.

"What are you still doing out here? It's hotter than—"

"I think it's romantic," she said with a smile.

Tom gritted his teeth as if holding in his anger. "We don't have any gas to spare."

"Yes, we do! We have two extra tanks in the back of the camper."

"Shut up, Sue!"

"We can pay you," said Adam.

"Money ain't worth what it used to be," said Tom.

"What about firearms?"

Tom's right eyebrow raised. "Oh yeah?"

Adam brought the pistol from behind his back but kept it pointed at the ground.

"Don't shoot!" Tom yelled.

"I'm not going to shoot you," said Adam, with a confused expression.

"I wasn't talking to you," said Tom. "My son is in the back of the pickup, with the sights of his Remington pointed at your head."

Adam looked at the pickup and saw the end of a rifle barrel resting on the cab. He chided himself for not seeing it earlier.

"You can never be too careful," said Tom.

"I'll take your pistol and give you one can of gas. That should be enough to get you back into the city. However, if you want my opinion, you're going the wrong way. Vegas is burning."

They made the trade and emptied the gas into the station wagon tank. Ten minutes later, they were back on the road.

"Are you sure that was a good idea?" asked Indie.

"What do you mean?" said Adam.

"You gave away our only weapon. We are about to head back into anarchy."

"She's right," said Flint from the back. "Are we going to break the princess out of jail with your giant ukulele?"

"It's a cello."

"It's still useless."

"I didn't have a choice. We needed gas, and the gun is all we have of value to trade."

Adam spoke again, but this time in a muted tone. "I don't know if I even want the gun."

"If you didn't want it, you should have given it to me!" said Flint.

"You defended yourself," said Indie. "It was either him or you."

"We don't know that for sure."

"And you didn't have time to find out. You did the right thing, Adam."

CHAPTER 31

Almost alone on the northbound lanes of the Las Vegas Freeway, they drove back towards the city. Bumper-to-bumper traffic filled the southbound lanes across the sandy median. The concrete barrier deterred any the escapees from using the wrong lanes.

"Why are we slowing down," Flint asked.

"This isn't good," said Adam.

He stopped the car and leaned forward to get a better look.

Smoke swirled out the broken windows of a large city bus blocking the road. Black scorch marks blotted out most of the paint along the side. The bus sat low on melted rubber tires. Garbage, empty water bottles and shell casings littered the road in front of the roadblock, however, it was eerily absent of people.

"Where is everybody?" asked Indie.

Flint crawled over the back seat into the middle row. He poked his head into the front seat. "Maybe it's a trap."

"We should turn around," said Adam.

Indie opened her door and stepped out.

"What are you doing?" Adam called. "Flint's right. It might—"

Before he finished his sentence, Flint jumped out of the back seat and Indie was out of earshot.

"—be a trap," Adam said to himself and opened his door.

He ran to join them.

Indie threw her hands in the air and yelled. "We're unarmed! Don't shoot."

Adam and Flint raised their arms too.

They watched the bus, expecting a horde of armed men to appear.

"Hello?" Flint called. "We come in peace. Please don't murder us. We're looking for a lost princess."

They crept forward, watching, waiting and listening.

Vehicles continued crawling by on the southbound lanes.

The smell of burnt rubber and plastic assaulted their noses as they stole closer to the bus.

A vulture circled overhead.

Adam scanned the roadblock looking for any sign of movement.

Suddenly, a jarring mechanical sound reverberated from behind the bus. Adam shrieked as a dune buggy bounced into view beside the bus.

Adam and the others jumped back as the buggy bounded along the side of the road towards the station wagon, leaving a trail of dust in its wake. It continued past their car, bumped back onto the pavement, and drove away.

Flint smirked and pointed at Adam. "You scream like a girl."

"No! That was a cry of alarm," said Adam.

Flint laughed. "You sounded like a little girl."

"No, I didn't. My senses were on high alert. Besides, I saw you jump too."

"I was bracing myself for danger."

"I think we're safe!" Indie stood beside the bus looking down the road.

Adam and Flint quickly joined her.

Other than a few vehicles, tents and the remnants of a bonfire, the road behind the bus was empty. Further down the road and off to the right sat a towering white hotel and casino. The massive parking lot buzzed with a flurry of activity. Men and women loaded supplies into the back of trucks and army jeeps. Others pulled down tents and packed boxes. Many carried rifles strapped to their backs or carried pistols in their waistbands or belts.

"It looks like they're moving out," said Indie as they walked tentatively beneath the massive *Horrible's Casino* sign.

A few people looked up as they approached, but continued

their tasks.

"This doesn't look like a jail," said Flint.

"This isn't the JCC. It's a few minutes down the road past the Casino," said Indie. "We should go back and get the car."

"Anything is better than walking in this heat," said Flint.

They returned to the station wagon and drove around the burned-out bus. Adam rolled slowly through the casino parking lot. A man holding a machine gun in one hand and a bottle of bourbon in the other eyed them suspiciously. A woman carrying a heavy duffel bag ran across the front of the car. Adam slammed on the brakes. She slapped the hood and swore at them before shuffling along. Once out of the parking lot, Indie directed him along a few quick turns until they found, Prison Street. He turned onto the aptly named road.

A nervous knot grew in Adam's stomach as the station wagon rolled down the narrow, cracked pavement.

Dark mountains loomed in the distance.

"This is a stupid idea," he mumbled. "We should just leave the city like everyone else."

"After everything we've been through, we are NOT turning around," said Indie.

"What if she already has a boyfriend," Flint asked.

Indie turned and glared at him. "You're not helping!"

"He's right," Adam murmured.

"It doesn't matter," she said. "If you don't try, you'll never know. If nothing else, she will at least be impressed that you came all this way."

"We can kill her new boyfriend," suggested Flint. "It's not like there are any cops to arrest us."

Indie glared at Flint with mouth agape. "Nobody is killing anybody."

"I'm just trying to help."

The station wagon rattled as it bumped over a set of railroad tracks. Ahead, tall fencing surrounded a group of brown brick buildings. Adam slowed as they approached the parking lot in front of the entrance.

Several people loaded a dozen vehicles with camping supplies, guns and food.

A man with a white beard and matching hair helped an older woman with scraggly grey hair load a plastic bin into the back of a jeep. He looked up at the station wagon as it approached.

The red light on the gas gauge blinked on before Adam parked and shut off the engine.

"That is one beauty of a classic," said the man as Adam stepped out.

"Thanks."

The man held out his hand. "The name's Norman and the wonderful woman over there is my wife, Eleanor.

"I'm Adam and this is Indie and Flint."

Norman scratched his long beard. "If you folks are looking to join the red team, you're a little late. We're heading out. This place isn't worth fighting for anymore."

"Where are you going?" asked Indie.

"Texas," he replied. "That's where the next big battle for democracy is happening."

"We're looking for someone," said Indie.

"Not too many of us are left here," said Norman. "Most skedaddled yesterday. We're just the clean-up crew."

He raised a fist in the air. "Go Spartans!"

"Are you like a basketball team or something?" asked Flint.

"Spartans is the name of our unit," Norman replied. "The too young, too old, and injured unit. They left us to do the final cleanup."

"Her name is Piper." Adam felt weird saying her name aloud. As if mentioning it might jinx his chances of finding her. When they travelled across the city, the hope of finding her was just that – hope. Like some far-off dream that might happen someday. Asking someone if they knew where Piper was made it feel very real - too real.

"We don't know anybody named Piper, but some fighters use nicknames," said Norman.

"She was an inmate here before...everything happened," added

Indie.

"When things fell apart, they released all the prisoners," said Norman. "We used this place to house the soldiers. I don't know if—"

"She's sixteen," said Adam. "With black hair."

Eleanor tapped her husband on the arm. "That could be Raven."

"Hmm..." Norman caressed his white beard.

"Why don't you call her?" Eleanor tapped the radio strapped to her husband's belt.

"Right!" He pulled the radio off his belt and pressed the button. "Raven... are you there, over?"

Static buzzed for a moment before a girl responded. "Go for Raven."

The voice sounded similar to Piper's, but the radio distortion made it difficult to tell.

"Do you know anyone named, Piper?" Norman asked.

"Nobody calls me that anymore."

Adam's sucked a rapid intake of breath. A cavalcade of conflicting emotions marched through his head. He felt excited, scared, anxious and relieved.

"Where are you, Raven?" asked Norman.

"I found some ammo left behind in Dorm 8. We're loading it up now. What's going on?"

Norman's bushy white eyebrows raised like a pair of snow-capped mountain peaks as he stared at something in the distance.

Adam turned to look and watched three tan jeeps bouncing across the desert towards them. A man sat on top of the lead jeep manning a turret gun. Beside him, a blue flag on a long antenna fluttered in the wind.

"We've got a blue bogey coming in from the north!" Norman yelled into his radio.

A male voice came back. "How many?"

"Three jeeps and one has a 50 cal."

"You guys should leave now!" said Eleanor as she ran back

to the jeep and grabbed two AK-47 machine guns. She tossed one to Norman, who caught it with one hand. In unison, they clicked the magazines out, inspected them and clicked them back in place.

"Time to go," said Indie.

"Agreed," said Adam as they jogged back to the car.

"Those are some cool old people," said Flint. "We should call them the Silver Warriors!"

By the time Adam started the car, the first shots rang out. He stamped the gas and the old tires spun on the pavement before finding their grip. The station wagon surged forward as rapid gunfire seemed to come from every direction.

He steered back onto the road they came from.

"Bogey on our six!" Flint yelled from the back seat.

Bullets clanged loudly off the side of the car as Adam veered right and left, hoping to make it difficult for the shooter. Suddenly, the steering wheel locked in place, and the car careened off the road towards the fence.

"What are you doing?" Indie screamed.

"I can't steer!" he yelled back. "I think they shot out a tire."

The station wagon hurtled into the fence. The front end punched a ragged hole in the chain links, and the car stopped half way through the fence.

Adam spun around, looking out the back of the car. He expected the jeep to gun them down but saw only a cloud of dust. The shooting stopped.

"What's happening?" he asked.

"I think their big gun ran out of bullets," said Flint.

"Is everyone okay?" Adam yelled.

"I'm not dead yet," said Flint. "But the bad guys with guns are coming this way!"

Adam turned to Indie, and his heart stopped. She lay back in her seat with her eyes closed. Blood dripped from her head. She looked dead.

"Indie?" His voice cracked.

She opened her eyes and groaned. "My head hurts."

Adam let out the breath he didn't know he was holding. "You've been shot."

"Ouch," she said with a muted tone as she dabbed her finger on her head wound. "It hurts, but that's not a bullet wound. I hit the dash when you crashed into the fence."

"You're okay," said Adam, with a relieved tone.

"Not for long," said Flint. "Look out your windows.

Adam gasped when he saw the figure outside Indie's door and a gun barrel pointing at her. He turned slowly and saw a similar scene outside his window.

His eyes widened with the clack-clack sound of the charging handle on the AR-15's outside.

"I can't believe we made it this far and now we're going to die," he said shaking his head.

Indie looked at him with a pained smile. "Technically, we found the girl." Blood ran down her forehead, around her eye and down her cheek. It looked like tears of blood. "It wasn't the ending I hoped for, but I'm glad—"

Gunshots cracked through the air. Adam squeezed his eyes shut and waited for death.

When the gunfire stopped, he opened his eyes. "Are we dead?"

He jumped when a grey-haired man appeared in his window.

"Are you okay?" asked Norman.

Indie's door opened, and Eleanor poked her head inside. "Can you walk?" she asked.

"I'm fine," replied Indie.

Adam opened his door and looked up at Norman. "Thank you."

Norman looked in the back window. "Where's the boy?"

"Flint, are you okay back there?" Adam called.

Nobody responded.

He turned to look but found the seats behind him empty. Adam crawled over the seat and peered into the back. Only the shattered remnants of the back window and his cello case lay on the rear seat.

"Hey!"

Adam jumped at the voice coming from right behind him and

hit his head on the roof.

Flint looked up from his hiding spot tucked in the footwell and smiled. "Did the Silver Warriors rescue us?"

"What are you doing down there?" Adam yelled.

"I didn't want to die," he answered. "Someone has to survive to avenge your death."

Eleanor opened the door beside them. "We need to move now!"

They scrambled out of the car amidst renewed gunfire. Norman ducked behind the open door and fired.

"This way!" Eleanor lifted a broken portion of the fence and beckoned them over.

Indie and Flint ran towards her, but Adam ducked back into the car.

"What are you doing?" yelled Indie.

The gunfire sounded closer as Adam pulled his cello case out of the car. The window shattered beside him and bullet holes appeared in the car's wood-grained side panel as he lugged the case towards the fence.

"Really?" yelled Flint. "You're saving that thing. We need guns, not instruments!"

"What is that?!" shouted Eleanor. "That will *not* fit!"

"Yes, it will."

Adam shoved the case into the gap in the fence. Bullets pinged off the fence beside him. The case jammed for a moment until he heaved hard. Indie helped pull it through from the other side.

Eleanor still stood on the opposite side of the fence. "Hide in one of those buildings until we fend off these left-wing morons."

Indie smiled at the older woman. "Thank you."

"Good luck," said Eleanor with a smile. Her expression changed quickly as a bullet tore through her shoulder.

Blood poured out of the wound. She grimaced as if the hole in her shoulder only made her angry. With indignant screams and imaginative obscenities, Eleanor joined her husband at the station wagon. They fired non-stop at the intruders.

"They are *so* cool," said Flint. "It's like *Resident Evil: Village*."

The gunfire grew closer as the trio ran through the grass towards the nearest building.

A massive explosion behind them almost knocked them off their feet. They turned around and saw an orange and yellow fireball engulfing the station wagon and the surrounding area. Adam, Flint and Indie stared for a quiet moment until Flint spoke.

He stood straight and beat his chest with one fist. "So long, Silver Warriors. You fought like heroes."

"Come on," said Adam as he turned and walked towards the buildings.

Flint followed, but Indie remained in place.

"Are you coming?" Adam called.

She said something Adam couldn't hear. He ran back to her and pulled her arm. "Let's go."

"They died saving us," she said.

The flames subsided on the station wagon, and two men ran through the smoke towards the fence gap.

"Yes, but it will be in vain if we don't survive," he said, tugging her arm.

Finally, she broke out of her trance and followed Adam.

Over a dozen buildings sat in a large circle inside the compound. Except for a few larger buildings near the entrance, all were boxy two-storey concrete buildings.

Adam pulled the cello case strap over his shoulder. They sprinted to the closest building and ran inside the open door. Gunfire erupted behind them as they dashed through a large communal room, through another doorway and into a room filled with endless rows of bunk beds.

With more gunshots behind them, they kept running through the beds until they found a backdoor. They burst through that door and kept running. The case on Adam's back bounced as they jogged to another building. They ducked out of sight and paused to catch their breath. Adam adjusted the heavy case to the opposite shoulder.

"What now?" asked Indie between pants. "We can't just keep running."

"It's better than dying," said Adam, wiping the sweat off his face.

"Do you think they'd believe us if we said we weren't part of the red team?"

"I think they'd shoot us before we could explain anything."

"You're probably right," said Indie. "We better keep running."

"Dying from exhaustion might be worse than being shot," Flint complained.

Their pursuers exchanged loud shouts nearby. Adam resumed running, and the others followed. The cello case strap dug deeper into his shoulder with every step. They hurried past three dormitories and the voices behind them finally faded.

Panting and out of breath, they pushed through the side door of the large administration building. Inside, their footsteps echoed in the quiet, empty hallway.

Flint looked behind them. "Are they still chasing us?"

"I don't think so."

Adam flinched as gunfire erupted outside, but quickly regained his composure.

"That sounds far away. I think we're safe here."

They walked through the hallway, still trying to catch their breath. Occasionally one of them looked inside one of the many rooms on either side. Some contained garbage, old food, mattresses, blankets, dirty dishes, bottles and other remnants of the previous occupants, but all were void of people. They turned down another corridor and continued walking.

Indie veered to the side of the hallway towards a set of double doors. She opened them and peered inside. "Check this out!"

Adam and Indie joined her. The room reminded Adam of his high school multi-use gymnasium which served as a sports venue, gym class, theatre and presentation room.

Hundreds of steel and plastic folding chairs sat neatly arranged facing the stage. A few lay askew or on their sides on the glossy parquet floor. Basketball nets and backboards sat at either end of the gym. Sunlight filtered through the windows near the high ceiling. Long, black curtains bracketed the stage containing a single lectern.

"I'm leaving my cello here," said Adam as he removed it from his shoulder and set it against the wall. "But we're *not* leaving this place without it!"

More gunshots rang out from outside.

"I need to see what's happening out there," said Flint as he ran out of the gym.

"Wait—" Indie called after him, but he kept running.

Adam and Indie chased after Flint as he dashed through the hallway and up a wide set of stairs. They found him in the cafeteria, standing at a window overlooking the prison grounds. Over a dozen dormitories created a wide circle. A large empty fire pit sat in the centre of the expansive grass and dirt prison yard.

They watched as gunmen slunk around the buildings, searching for their prey. As they disappeared inside a dormitory, a girl stepped out of the adjacent one. She held a shotgun and crept slowly away from the building in a fast-walking crouch. She glanced back for a second, then sprinted across the prison grounds.

"She's fast," said Flint.

Indie pointed at her as she ran towards the administration building. "That's Piper!"

CHAPTER 32

Suddenly, two gunmen burst out of the dormitory, their heads swivelling in search of their prey. They spotted Piper sprinting across the grass and raised their rifles. Their first couple of shots missed, and she adjusted her running style to a zig-zag pattern.

Adam and the others watched with tense anticipation from the upper cafeteria window.

"Come on, Princess Peach! Run!" cheered Flint.

They watched as one pursuer paused by the firepit. He dropped to the ground, lay prostrate and adjusted his rifle. Adam wasn't an expert in marksmanship, but from less than fifty yards it looked like an easy shot.

Indie covered her mouth and gasped. "Oh no! Run Piper."

"This doesn't look good," said Flint.

Adam wanted to do something, but it appeared it was too late. After everything, he was about to watch her die.

The sniper looked through the eyepiece and placed his finger on the trigger. Before he squeezed it, his head exploded like a watermelon hit by a sledgehammer.

"Yes!" yelled Flint.

Indie turned away and scrunched her face. "Who did that?"

Adam looked at the other buildings, but couldn't see the other shooter.

The second man continued after Piper, at a slower pace. His colossal frame lumbered across the yard. Another shot rang out and the big man stumbled to the ground. He pushed himself back up as Piper disappeared from their view below.

"She's coming in here!" said Indie.

"So is that big guy," said Flint.

Adam stared out the window and Piper's pursuer. Even from a distance, the man looked huge. He jogged across the grass with surprising speed, given his size and the bloody wound on his shoulder.

Indie dashed across the cafeteria and yelled out the doorway. "Up here!"

Her voice echoed through the empty building.

Flint and Adam waited by the window.

"Where is the sniper?" asked Flint.

"I don't know."

"I'm going to find a weapon," said Flint and ran towards the kitchen.

Adam remained by the window and waited. His heart beat with nervous anticipation. After all their challenges, adventures, fights, and struggles, his search was over. Unlike Indie's rom-coms, he didn't expect her to jump into his open arms with wild abandon or plant a passionate kiss on his waiting lips – although that might be nice. But he was at least hoping for an amicable reunion.

"This way!" Indie called into the hallway, motioning to Piper.

Adam quickly adjusted his messy hair and put on his most charming smile.

"Do you guys have any weapons? Piper asked as she burst through the cafeteria doorway.

She brushed aside her wispy black hair to reveal a dirty but still striking face.

Her big doe eyes met his and his heart stopped.

"Hey, I remember you," she said with a smirk.

"Hi Piper, I've come a long—"

"We need weapons," said Piper, striding across the cafeteria. "That monster will be here soon."

"I found some knives!" Flint popped out of the kitchen holding a meat cleaver. "Wait! Did you say *monster*?"

"I'm so glad you're okay," said Adam, chasing after her, "We—"

She ignored him and ran towards the kitchen. "Do you have anything smaller?" she asked Flint.

"Sure," he replied. "I found a bunch of them."

Indie appeared beside Adam. "She's a little preoccupied," Indie whispered. "Once things settle down, I'm sure you two can talk."

"Everyone take cover!" shouted Piper.

"Come on," said Indie.

Adam followed her to the kitchen and crouched down with the others behind the serving counter.

"Everyone gets a knife." Flint handed out knives as if dealing cards for a game of poker.

Hiding behind the counter next to Piper reminded him of hiding with her in the kitchen after his performance. He remembered her tepid breath on his neck and his overheating heart.

Piper looked as beautiful as he remembered, but also different. Flecks of dirt spotted her tanned cheeks and dark half-moons hung below her big anime eyes. She swiped rogue strands of her ebony hair and tucked them behind her ear.

Piper looked at him and smiled. "Are you ready?"

Adam breathed deeply and opened his mouth to speak. Before he uttered a single syllable, a deep rumbling voice reverberated through the building.

"Come out, come out wherever you are!"

Heavy boots thundered up the stairs like an incoming storm.

"How many are there?" asked Indie.

"He's the last one," said Piper.

"We can take him," said Flint. "He's only one guy, and he's wounded."

"Never underestimate your opponent," said Piper. "He's armed with a shotgun and looks like King Kong."

"I know you're in here!" he said as he stepped into the cafeteria. "I saw you morons watching through the window."

"We need to spread out," Piper whispered. "I'll draw his fire until he runs out of shells."

She pointed at Flint. "*Then* we'll attack."

"You go that way!"

Piper stood up and leapt over the counter. Flint ran in the opposite direction holding a meat cleaver over his head.

Beside him, Indie whispered, "She is really cute *and* feisty."

Adam stared ahead. "I know."

She smacked his arm hard. "But you need to focus!"

The slap stung but woke him from his stupor. "Right!"

He pushed up until his eyes rose just above the counter height. Piper was right. With hairy arms the size of hydro poles, tree trunk legs and an angry ape face, the man looked like King Kong. He stopped in the middle of the cafeteria, squinted his beady eyes, and pumped the shotgun.

Adam sucked in a quick breath as the monster aimed the gun straight ahead at Adam's head.

"Hey, loser!" Piper yelled from across the cafeteria. "You wanna play?"

Kong swivelled towards her and fired the shotgun. The shot echoed loudly as Adam and Indie crouch-ran behind the counter.

"Oops, you missed," Piper taunted.

Indie and Adam stopped at the far end of the counter and waited. "She's brave too," Indie whispered.

"I know."

"Ahhh!" the big man yelled in frustration and whipped the shotgun across the room.

Piper jumped out of her hiding spot. "What's the matter, big boy? Out of shells?"

"Hmph!" he grunted and rubbed his bloody shoulder. "You killed my friends!"

"Yes, but you attacked us," Piper responded.

"We are punishing those that would disrespect the constitution and bring this country down!" he yelled.

"Really?" Piper folded her arms and smirked. "This was a *political* action? Perhaps you want to debate the merits of individualism, free market principles and traditional social structures versus collective responsibility, egalitarianism and progressive reform?"

"She's smart too," Indie whispered.

"I know."

"No!" yelled Kong. "I want to kill you."

"Doesn't that go against your left-leaning view of social responsibilities?"

"You killed my friends, so I will kill you."

Piper rubbed her chin and stepped towards him. "This is no longer about clashing political ideologies. You wanted to steal our stuff. We fought back and people died. Liam was right. How swiftly society degrades from cooperation to primal competition."

"Kevin and Harry were my only friends. We came here to find food and weapons."

"Is that why you knocked on the front door and asked nicely?"

Kong creased his brow and shook his head. "No."

Piper took another step towards him. "That was sarcasm, you big ape."

Before he responded, Piper's hand flew out and swiped her steak knife at his throat. He raised his hand at the last moment and the blade slashed across his palm leaving a crimson streak. Piper jumped back as his other fist punched at her head.

"You're a girl, so I will kill you quick," he said shaking the blood from his hand.

"What a gentleman," she said with a mocking smile. "You're a blight on society so I'll kill you slowly."

His massive frame shot forward with surprising speed. She slid to the side and swiped her knife at him before jumping out of reach. The blade slid harmlessly off the leather belt on his waist.

The big man turned and grunted. He clenched and unclenched his fists while staring her down.

In an instant, his spine straightened, and his face contorted into a blend of anger and confusion. Reaching behind him, he pulled a bloodied meat cleaver out of his lower back. He turned to find Flint holding a fillet knife and beaming a wide smile.

Kong flung the cleaver, narrowly missing a ducking Flint and clanging off a plastic chair.

"Time to finish the final level, Donkey Kong," said Flint as he shot forward, knife first. Kong swatted the knife away with one hand and Flint with the other. The boy flew across the room and slammed against the wall. He lay unmoving on the floor.

"You better check on him," said Adam. "I'll help—"

Indie was halfway across the room before Adam finished. He tightened his grip on the steak knife and stood up.

"I will kill you all!" Kong shouted. "My family is gone and my friends are dead. Everyone must die."

"Your logic is somewhat flawed, big guy." Piper stood perched on top of a table looking down at him.

While he looked up at her, Adam ran forward and slashed at his back. The knife skimmed across his shirt, barely cutting the fabric. He jumped back as Kong whirled around.

"Are you trying to tickle me, little pansy?"

The insult rankled Adam, but he waited patiently for his next opportunity.

Indie helped Flint sit up against the wall. He looked stunned but still alive.

"Try stabbing instead of slicing," Piper called.

Adam attempted a few jabs, but the man's massive hand swiped at him and he jumped back out of the way.

As Adam weighed the pros and cons of throwing the knife, Piper launched off the tabletop at Kong's head. She landed awkwardly on his neck and clung to him like a deranged monkey. Her knife stuck out of his shoulder. She pulled the knife out, but before she stabbed again, he plucked her off his shoulders as if removing an annoying thorn and hoisted her over his head. The knife clattered to the floor.

Piper screeched like a banshee, uselessly clawing and swatting down at him. A drop from that height would easily break her neck and back.

Adam ran at him, knife first and stopped with the tip of the knife at his neck.

"Put her down," he yelled in his sternest voice. "Or I'll push this knife into your esophagus."

He looked down at him and smiled. "If you stab my throat, I'll drop her and break her neck."

Adam saw Indie creep up behind him and kept talking. "It appears we are at a stalemate. Perhaps we could—"

As he spoke, Indie jabbed her filet knife into his already bloodied back. He snorted and threw Piper forward.

Adam stabbed his knife towards Kong. It skimmed across the man's thick leather skin before piercing the side of his neck. Piper's body slammed into Adam and they fell together against the floor.

Kong swung around to face Indie. She clutched the red dripping knife and held it in front of her like a crucifix warding off a vampire. She stabbed forward, but he slapped the knife away quickly. Before Indie could react, he reared back and backhanded her across the face. She collapsed to the floor as he stepped forward.

Barely conscious, Indie shuffled back across the floor as he stomped after her. Eventually, she hit the wall behind her and stopped.

Adam pushed Piper off him and charged towards the giant as he lifted his heavy boot. His foot crashed down on her leg. The bones cracked with an audible crunch and Indie shrieked in pain.

Adam charged towards him at full speed. The impact was not enough to knock Kong over, but the brute stumbled forward. He pivoted to face Adam, who punched at him as hard as he could. Kong punched back, but Adam weaved and ducked, evading the blows. Adam returned fire with a flurry of jabs to the monster's chin, nose, eyes and injured shoulder. Finally, one of Kong's punches connected with Adam's chin, sending him flying backwards.

Piper charged towards him, but he grabbed her and threw her onto a table. Her head knocked off the corner almost knocking her unconscious. She climbed to her knees, but could not stand. Indie held her leg, howling in pain.

Adam charged again, but a hard hook to the chin left him dazed and back on the floor.

Kong bled from his back, both shoulders, and nose, but still looked unfazed. He marched over to a stunned Piper and picked her up by the neck. He squeezed and yelled as her face turned red. Her arms flailed uselessly at his head as the life drained from her body.

Adam tried to get up, but dizziness pulled him back to the floor.

"Hey!"

Adam did not recognize the authoritative voice emanating from the other side of the cafeteria.

A single shot echoed through the room. Piper dropped from Kong's grip as he toppled to the floor.

Shaking off the vertigo, Adam pushed himself up to get a better view. Blood leaked from a hole in Kong's skull as he lay unmoving on the floor.

A striking young man with bulging biceps stood in the cafeteria doorway holding a rifle.

"You took your time, Liam," Piper said, standing beside the dead giant.

Liam brushed aside his golden blond hair, revealing sky-blue eyes and a warm smile. Blood pushed through his right pant leg below the long-sheathed knife hanging from his belt.

"Sorry, Raven. I got shot in the leg."

"Is it bad?" she asked.

"Nah, just a flesh wound."

"Great! I need you to bring her to the infirmary." Piper pointed at Indie.

Adam rushed over to Indie, who still clutched her leg. She suppressed her screams but breathed rapidly. He knelt beside her but was unsure what to do. Seeing her foot bent back at an unnatural angle almost made him ill.

Piper and Liam joined them. He stood looking down with concern, while Piper crouched down to look at Indie's leg.

"It looks like a clean break," she said. "We'll bring you to the infirmary and find a splint."

"I can carry her," said Adam.

"The infirmary is on the other side of the building," said Piper. "Liam should do it."

"I got this," Liam said and scooped Indie off the floor.

She screamed in pain for a full three seconds before resuming her rapid breathing.

"Deep breaths," Liam said in a calming voice as he limped across the cafeteria.

Flint still lay on the floor, but his eyes were open.

"How are you doing, Flint?" Adam asked as he ran to him.

"Who's that?" Flint pointed at Liam as he carried Indie out of the cafeteria.

"That's Liam. Are you okay to walk?"

Flint reached up his hand and Adam helped him up.

"He looks like Cloud Strife."

Adam held his shoulder to steady him and they followed the others out of the room.

"Who?" Adam asked.

"He's the really cool guy from Final Fantasy VII." He turned to Adam and smirked. "If that's your competition, you're in big trouble."

CHAPTER 33

"How are you feeling today?" Adam stood beside Indie's bed with a cautious smile.

She sat up and looked at the splint on her leg. "It still hurts. What happened? I remember Liam bringing me here and then he did something to my leg, and that's it."

"You passed out from the pain when he reset your leg."

"Who put the splint on?" she asked.

"Apparently, Liam has some medical training."

"Wow, impressive."

Adam stared down at the bed and nodded. "Yeah, he's quite the guy."

"Have you talked to her yet?"

"Who?"

She gave him a playful smack. "The girl you travelled through the apocalypse to find…"

Adam shrugged. "What am I supposed to say? It's not like she needs saving."

"Tell her how you feel. Tell her how you came all this way to see her."

"It seems silly now."

"Silly? Silly is chickening out at the last minute. You *have* to talk to her."

"I know, but—"

Indie pointed at him and widened her eyes. "You should play the cello for her!"

"What?"

"I can see it now!" she exclaimed. "Like Sweet Home Alabama!"

"What?"

"The movie where Jake Perry plays Melanie Smooter a heartfelt song, reminding her of their shared history and love," she said in a melodramatic tone.

"I don't know—"

"Oh, good you're up!" Liam walked into the room with Piper and Flint.

Adam stepped away from the bed as the group crowded around Indie.

"How do you feel?" asked Liam.

"It hurts. Thanks for patching me up. Are you a doctor or something?"

"Can I sign your cast?" asked Flint.

Adam shuffled out of the room as they continued to pepper Indie with questions. Their voices faded as he moseyed down the empty hallway. The morning sun filtered through a window, casting a square spotlight on the tiled floor. He stopped and looked out at the empty desert. The sun hovered above the rocky skyline. A pair of red-tailed hawks glided over the dusty rose desert. He didn't know what to say to Piper or how to express how he felt. The hawks called to each other in long raspy screams that sounded like steam whistles.

Adam nodded to himself and continued walking down the hallway. Instead of a slow wandering gait, he strode through the hallway with purpose.

A few minutes later, he marched into the gymnasium and found his cello case still leaning against the wall. He grabbed a chair and carried it and the cello case onto the stage. His face beamed with excitement as he sat down and pulled the yellow cello out of its case. Despite the heat, travel, and battles the cello remained unscathed and barely out of tune. He adjusted the strings until perfectly tuned.

The bow felt good in his hands and the cello felt comfortable nestled between his legs.

Once he played the first few notes of Beethoven's Ode to Joy, his heart rate slowed and his breathing steadied. Over the past ten years, he played a lot of cellos. Some old, some new, many in terrible shape and a couple of high-end, top-quality cellos. He preferred to play the cello his parents bought him three years ago. It always felt comfortable, and familiar.

However, after hearing the warm resonant tones of this banana-yellow cello, he immediately had a new favourite.

Adam looked out across the gym. Hundreds of empty chairs stared back, but he didn't care. This wasn't a concert for throngs of adoring fans or critical judges. This was a concert for one pretty girl. The bow vibrated in his hands as it rubbed against the metal strings. Perfect tones amplified in the hollow maple bouts before projecting into the gym and echoing through the hallways of the mostly empty building.

Adam closed his eyes and let the notes wash through him. As Beethoven's fourth movement of his ninth symphony came to a triumphant close, he heard a voice. He opened his eyes and saw Piper standing at the back of the gym. She looked up at him with big, glistening eyes and smiled.

"Well? Are you going to play me a song?"

His heart skipped a beat, before rapping double speed in his chest.

She walked closer to the stage and sat on a dusty chair in the front row.

He smiled back and nodded.

This was perfect. He didn't know why she came alone, or why the others weren't there. But he was about to give the girl of his dreams a personal performance. This time, he would not drop his bow and make a fool of himself or be interrupted by gunshots – hopefully.

He saw the recognition in her face as he began his piece with the Jaws movie theme music, but shut his eyes as he concentrated on the triumphant overture. Adam executed a flawless performance for the next few minutes and almost dreaded opening his eyes as he played the last few notes.

His confidence grew when he heard her clapping. He opened his eyes and grinned when he saw her smiling at him.

"That was fantastic!" she said. "And I love the yellow cello. Where did you get that?"

"We found it—"

Before he could finish his response, Liam and Flint stepped through the double doors at the back.

"Babe, we have to get going," said Liam.

Adam's heart sank as if chained to an anvil and thrown into the Mariana Trench.

Piper gave Adam the thumbs up. "That was really great, but we need to leave."

"Um…right…where are you going?" was all Adam could spit out.

"We have to catch up with the rest of our squad."

Indie rolled into the room in a wheelchair.

Piper looked at Adam, then Flint and Indie. "Did you guys want to join us? We're heading down to Texas."

Adam couldn't speak. His heart lay lifeless at the bottom of the ocean, and he held back his tears with the strength of the Hoover Dam.

"I go where they go," said Flint, pointing at Indie and Adam.

Indie wheeled into the aisle between the empty chairs. "I go where Adam goes."

"What's it going to be, bro?" asked Liam. "You guys seem like a tough bunch. You're welcome to tag along."

Adam swallowed hard. "I think…I have to go find my mother and sister and make sure they're okay. Also, Indie can't go anywhere until her leg heals."

"Cool," said Liam. "See you around."

Piper moved to the stage and looked up. "Good to see you again, Adam. Take care of yourself."

Adam swallowed the growing lump in his throat. "Yeah."

Once Liam and Piper left the gym Adam stood up. "That went well," he muttered to himself.

"Adam, I'm so sorry," said Indie.

"I thought it sounded great," said Flint.

"Everything was perfect," said Adam, standing beside his cello. "I played my piece for her like you said, but she still ran away with her strong handsome new boyfriend."

"I thought for sure that was going to work—"

"What are you talking about?" Adam yelled. "Did you send Piper here to listen to me play?"

"I was just trying to help."

"Thank you, but I don't need help to make a complete fool of myself!"

"You didn't make a fool of yourself. You played a wonderful piece of music for a girl who doesn't know what she's missing."

"And where is she now?" he bellowed. "I dragged you two across a chaotic city for what?"

"You didn't drag us anywhere," said Flint. "We wanted to come with you."

"Why are you guys still with me?" Adam screamed.

"We're like Nate, Elena and Sully from Uncharted," said Flint. "An unstoppable trio exploring, facing untold dangers and solving mysteries together – except for the mystery part."

Indie rolled forward and stopped below the stage.

"Sit down and play your piece again - for us. I didn't get to hear the entire piece from the start."

"Yeah!" Flint said and found a seat near the front. He sat down and looked up expectantly.

Indie gave him a pained smile. "Play it again."

Adam remained standing for a long time, while Indie and Flint waited patiently. He wanted to grab the cello by the neck and smash it against the stage. He looked down at the gleaming banana-yellow cello. The colour reminded him of Prospero's yellow Porsche.

Once his anger subsided, he took a breath and sat down.

Adam tucked the cello between his legs, picked up the bow and rested his fingers on the front fretboard. He closed his eyes and pushed the horsehair along the strings.

Hot tears streamed down his cheeks as he played.

CHAPTER 34

A chorus of crickets trilled loudly while a distant coyote howled at the stars. Adam, Indie and Flint sat around a crackling fire in the centre of the Jane Conservation Camp prison yard.

"You could have gone with them." Adam stared into the fire.

Flint poked at the flames with a chair leg remnant, spraying sparks into the air. "Liam *was* pretty cool. But this was like in Baldur's Gate 3 when I had to choose between the Druid Grove or the Goblin Camp. If I chose the Druids, I get alliances, magical resources and help later in the game. If I picked the Goblins which is really the Tieflings...that meant I had to deal with the Goblin threat which could prevent future attacks..."

"What are you trying to say?" asked Adam.

Flint shrugged. "I think you guys are cooler and I get to have a campfire."

Indie laughed. "We've come this far with you, why would we leave now?"

Adam watched the blue and orange pulsing glow of a burning log. "Liam is a big, powerful guy. He could probably protect you better than me and he's more your age."

"You're only three years younger than me," she retorted. "Also, I don't need protection."

"What do you need?" he asked.

"I need what we all need when the world falls apart...loyal friends."

Flint threw an enormous cardboard box on the fire, pushing down the flames. Soon, blue fire burned through followed by long yellow flames that licked around the sides.

Adam and Indie shuffled back as the scorching heat threatened to singe their clothes.

"Hey!" called Indie. "This is a campfire, not an apocalyptic inferno!"

Flint remained close as if intoxicated by the sudden glowing intensity and immune to its searing heat.

Eventually, the fire died down to a respectable level. Adam shimmied closer and Indie moved in beside him.

"I'm sorry you didn't get a rom-com ending," said Indie. "I thought for sure she would…I don't know what I thought. I guess I just wanted you to be happy."

"It's probably better this way," said Adam. "What if she had swooned into my arms and professed her undying love for me? Then what? I go off to war with her and die for a political cause I don't care about. I don't want to go to Texas with some girl I barely know."

"What do you want?" she asked.

"I want to be right here – sitting around a peaceful campfire with my friends."

"This may be peaceful, but the world is still falling apart."

"Yes, and tomorrow we will face it together."

"Where are we going?" asked Flint.

"I want to find my sister and mother and make sure they're okay."

Flint held up a flaming stick. "Another dangerous quest for Nathan Drake as he takes on a thrilling journey to find and rescue his sister and mother!"

Indie shook her head and rolled her eyes. "Put that thing out before you burn the desert down."

The flame on his torch petered out and Flint swung it in wide arcs. The coals at the end of the stick glowed leaving a magical trail of orange in its wake.

"Before they left, Liam said he heard some cell phones are working now," said Indie.

"Really?" asked Adam. "Does that mean this is all over? Do *our* phones work?"

"My battery died a long time ago. What about yours?"

"Mine's still broken."

Flint tossed his dying glow stick into the fire and picked up his pack. "I think mine might have a little charge."

As he rifled through his belongings, Adam heard something in the distance. The strange hum was barely audible over the chorus of crickets.

"Do you hear that?"

Flint paused his rummaging, and Indie tilted her head. The odd buzzing sounded like a remote swarm of bees or a distant mechanical hum.

"It might be all the vehicles leaving Vegas," said Indie.

"Found it!" Flint pulled his phone from the far reaches of his pack and held it up as if discovering a long-lost relic. He pressed the power button and waited.

The humming increased in volume, but Adam still didn't recognize the sound.

Flint's face glowed from the light of his screen.

"Do you have service?" Indie asked.

"I think so. I see two bars."

Adam perked up. "Really? I can call my mom and make sure she's okay."

"I'd like to find out if America still exists," said Indie.

"I want to order a pizza," said Flint.

"Try making a call," Indie suggested. Her voice almost trembled with tentative optimism.

"Hang on. It's doing an update."

"That's a good sign, right?" Indie asked.

Adam turned to the sound. "It's getting louder, but it's not coming from Vegas or the highway."

"That's weird." Flint looked down at his phone.

Before anyone asked what he saw, the humming intensified and countless tiny lights appeared in the sky to the south. A cacophony of whirring, buzzing and mechanical fluttering interrupted their silent night as thousands of drones blotted out the stars. They watched in awe till they passed and continued towards Las Vegas.

"What does your phone say?" Adam asked with trepidation.

"Welcome citizens to our New World."

Indie leaned towards Adam and rested her head on his shoulder.

Her hair felt nice on his cheek.

ABOUT THE AUTHOR

Super Dave Klapwyk

Super Dave is an entrepreneur, writer, engineer, surveyor, journalist and storyteller.

BOOKS BY THIS AUTHOR

Black Flag - Surviving The Scourge

Black Flag - Surviving The Invasion

Black Flag - Surviving The Apocalypse

Black Flag Origins - Search Engine

Black Flag Origins - Road To Empire

Black Flag Origins - Justice

Vaccinized

www.ingramcontent.com/pod-product-compliance
Lightning Source LLC
LaVergne TN
LVHW012041160826
845678LV00014B/2658

9781739076122